DOORWAYS TO THE DEADEYE

ERIC J. GUIGNARD

JOURNALSTONE
YOUR LINK TO ARTIST TALENT

JournalStone books may be ordered through booksellers or by contacting:
JournalStone
www.JournalStone.com

The views expressed in this work are solely those of the author and do not necessarily reflect the views of the publisher, and the publisher hereby disclaims any responsibility for them.

ISBN: 978-1-947654-97-6 (sc)
ISBN: 978-1-947654-98-3 (ebook)

JournalStone rev. date: July 26, 2019

Library of Congress Control Number: 2019941530

Printed in the United States of America

Cover Design and Layout: Mikio Murakami
Interior Layout: Lori Michelle
Edited by Scarlett R. Algee
Proofread by Sean Leonard

DEDICATION:

For my younger brother, Jeffrey Guignard,
who supported me unconditionally in everything I did,
and passed away too young while I wrote this book.
May his memory and adventures live on in all else that awaits us.

ADVANCE PRAISE FOR
DOORWAYS TO THE DEADEYE

"Eric J. Guignard's *Doorways to the Deadeye* isn't just a magnificent, magical, mystical epic; it's really a long, hard look into the heart of the myth of America. With this, his first novel, Eric has crafted an extraordinary tale that will haunt readers long after they finish it."

—Six-time Bram Stoker Award ®-winning author Lisa Morton

"Rich, strange, and wonderful, as if Stephen King and Ray Bradbury were sitting together weaving a tale over a camp fire. So good I didn't want it to end."

—Michael Marshall Smith, *New York Times* bestselling author of *Spares*, *The Anomaly*, and *The Straw Men* trilogy

"Concerned with everything horror should be concerned about—history, poverty, language, loneliness, the liminal spaces between places where people vanish and stories flourish—*Doorways to the Deadeye* is a hundred old-school railroad tales reconfigured by Eric J. Guignard into something new, strange, haunting, and haunted. This is a ride worth hopping, and it will take you somewhere you really haven't been."

—Glen Hirshberg, Shirley Jackson and International Horror Guild Award-winning author of the *Motherless Children* trilogy

DOORWAYS TO THE DEADEYE

A Partial Roadmap to Hobo Symbols

 Road

 Railroad

Catch Train Here

 Do Not Enter

OK to Enter

 Went This Way (Followed By Name and Date, e.g. Jo Bob, Fall '34)

Go This Way

Don't Go This Way!

Turn Right

Turn Left

 This Way, But Fast!

Go Around

Here (This is It)

 Here (Place)

 OK to Sleep Here

Medical Help Here

 Talk Religion For Food Here

Mean Dog Here

Man

4 Men, etc.

Woman

Loose Woman

Armed Man

Rich Man

People (Use same marks as Men or Women)

 Rich People (e.g.)

 Poor People

 People Will Yell at You

 People Will Beat You

 Nice People

 Tell Hard Luck For Food

 Fake Illness For Food

 Safe Camp

 Hold Your Tongue

 Bread (or Food) Here

 Work Available

 Police Alert

 Police Inactive

 Jail or Prison

 Alcohol Town

 No Alcohol Town

 Athanasia

LUKE THACKER, 1955

THE TRAIN RIDE going to Charleston had always been one of Luke's favorites. The thick green pines and Carolina sweetbay would begin to loosen up and he could catch some faraway views of the Ashley River turning one way and the Cooper River turning the other, both bound for the harbor, the same as himself. Sometimes he would think it a race and urge the boxcar to roll a bit faster, but most often he just sat inside the empty freighter's open door, letting his legs hang in the air and his shoes bob along, tapping out the song beat of serenity.

Today, there wasn't any preference at all; slow or fast didn't matter, but that he'd reach his destination. Though Luke had been to Charleston often enough, this particular visit had been a long time coming. His steel carriage had been carrying him toward it across a great time and a great distance, for there he had business to attend. Being a man of no financial means, of course, this particular business had nothing to do with occupation or enterprise; Luke was searching for someone, and that person was soon to be found.

He imagined how this showdown would play out, and he thought back with tinges of anger and shades of despair on their prior encounters, and that got him remembering a lot of other things, how the train tracks of life were always extending, crossing, changing direction in strange ways, until they arrived at the end of the line in a faraway stationhouse.

A voice came from the deep shadows lolling at the back of the boxcar, breaking his thoughts.

"I never cared much for the rails," the voice said. "Too much racket. A man can't carry on a decent conversation without shouting."

"I didn't hear you get on," Luke replied, barely looking back.

"My point exactly."

Luke nodded and took another look at the twinkling waves of the faraway Atlantic Ocean. Charleston was near. He swung his legs up onto the car and stood in a loose-kneed sway, letting the motion of the clattering train ride up his legs the way a sailor moves on a ship's deck in heavy swell. The car's interior was a world of darkness, bisected by a single swatch of light passing in from the open door.

Luke briefly considered that the open door was the only access inside, and he'd been sitting at it for a long time. But there were other ways to get on a train. They both knew it. And the other man had somewhat of a reputation for being able to break into—as well as out of—resistant spots, a reputation that persevered even after his days had come to a messy end.

"Been a long time, Johnny," Luke said.

"Even now, time is fleeting," the voice replied. There was a rustle, and something metal clicked. "But I still get around, and you wouldn't believe the things I hear. Everywhere I travel, tramps claim a Crossbuck Luke sighting, or they talk up one of your campfire hearsays. Some name you've built."

Luke smiled, aware of what that meant to him emotionally as well as consequentially.

A red glow materialized from the back shadows: the tip of a cigarette.

"I know what you're here for," the voice continued. "And I came to watch you kill Smith McCain."

DANIEL GREENBERG, 2019

My name is Daniel J. Greenberg, and it's taken over three decades to start writing about Crossbuck Luke Thacker and the other dubious characters that flourished in the stories King Shaw told me long ago.

Of course, King was just one of many lost souls I met in 1985 in soup kitchens and shelters and alleys so dark they caused the shadows to invert, their gloom shining like slashes of ebony light. I was reporting on inner-city poverty then, and its effects on mental illness. I was even nominated a finalist in 1987 for the Pulitzer Prize in Explanatory Journalism for my series of reports detailing the plight of children and veterans living on the street. President Reagan called me "a spotlight in the darkness of epidemic homelessness." I would have won the award, too, but Leon Dash beat me that year with his examination of teenage pregnancy, which had reached a record high for the twentieth century. Parents were more concerned their chaste daughters were being sexually influenced by the media than worrying about the forgotten society that survived on handouts and hope.

Another reason I didn't write about Luke and King was because in the 1980s, I was invincible. I practically glowed with health. I ran five miles a day, had a grad degree in journalism from Columbia University, and squirreled away more money in bank accounts than I would ever spend. The tales King Shaw told me were of death and ghosts and fairy tales. They were fun to hear—and he was one hell of a storyteller—but they weren't verifiably "true." I reported on the facts and the lives of the living, not the campfire yarns toasting to people's reminiscence from half a century prior.

But King got one fact right: people change. Our perceptions and values are fluid things; they flow strange ways in our young years, and even stranger ways in our old.

By no means am I old geriatrically, but I'm old in the regard that my days are running low. I've been battling cancer of the prostate and losing that fight, round by agonizing round. The disease just reached stage four, which means it's spread to other organs, and I've only got a few months left to walk the sunshine and tell people about what really matters now in life.

I've been thinking about King and Luke lately, and the funny thing is that the stories I once disregarded as fiction suddenly somehow seem possible. The people, the events . . . The more I think on them, the more they solidify, like painting a picture and gradually working in the details. Maybe what's in your mind doesn't always translate the way you expect onto canvas, but it's a process you keep at until you're satisfied you've done the best you can. I started writing the stories down and they've somehow gotten stronger in my memory than they have any right to be, as if they've been feeding and growing while I wasn't paying attention.

King told me that Luke Thacker was a legend, and that those who carried the legend with them became a part of it.

Over thirty years later, I believe him.

King Shaw was the last man who knew Crossbuck Luke in the flesh, and I may well be the last man living who knew King. There's a nice synchronicity in that. If someone were to ask King about Luke's life, he might have spat a comet of chew at the sidewalk and started out with something like this: "Luke's life began on the rails and ended on the rails."

King might then have looked at his own crippled legs and shook his head, and asked if you had a bottle of Jim Beam to share, to warm the words up. But whether you had a bottle or not wasn't essential; you were in for some blue-ribbon adventures.

The stories a person tells are lives in themselves. Even if you've heard the same old tale from the same old man, it's told a little differently each time. Maybe a gal's dress was blue as the sea or maybe it was her eyes. Maybe she wore a blouse with a button popped off, so with a quick glimpse you could catch a view of heaven. Like lives, some stories are short and some are long; some are dull and some fill you with wonder. In the end, how much of what King said was truth or lie or dream or lore doesn't really matter.

As it happened, I shared that bottle of Jim Beam with him over the course of four days before he died. In return, he shared the following narrative . . .

LUKE THACKER, 1929

Lucas Mathilda Thacker never knew his father, but his mother was an entertainer, a prancing wild mink in rouge and loose stockings. She travelled from city to city, dancing and drinking and pulling grafts on old men who still believed in genteel love. Each time her true character was discovered, she simply absconded for the next town of fools with little Luke in tow. She actually bore Luke on a train, screaming as his hard head popped from between her legs somewhere between Dallas and New Orleans. The squealing of wheels on steel track was the first sound Luke heard, even before his mother's cooing voice. And when Luke thought of who his father might be, he imagined he was conceived on a train, the rocking of a slow-moving carriage matching the cadence of two people rolling together in a sleeping berth. *Creak, creak, creak*, until the boiler blew and the whole thing settled to a stop for the night.

His mother finally found true love or, rather, a wealthy paramour, and settled in Savannah, trying to balance an illusion of respectable folk life against the backdrop of gin and self-indulgence. Unfortunately her departure from landloping wasn't to be enjoyed; a year after the vows were consummated, the good Lord called upon Luke's mother, requesting she join his troupe in the great dancehall in the sky. Luke was only eight when she obliged. He kissed her gravestone and said he loved her, but he didn't feel much loss in his heart.

Luke's stepfather beat him afterward, regularly and thoroughly, as much a therapy to cope with the loss of his bride as it was a sense of injustice; just looking at the strange ebony-haired child was a daily reminder of her premature death. So Luke ran away, living amongst Savannah's forgotten alleys, a new crumb dropped beneath the stained cushion of the city. Naturally he felt lost and unwanted, restless and resentful. A few miserable years passed until Luke decided no place could be worse than his current environs, and he set out to build calluses on his feet.

He caught the open door of a freight car headed up to Little Rock and then eastward to Nashville, then to Wichita, then to Boise. Luke quickly learned that the times he was most happy were when he was moving, feeling the rocking beneath him back-and-forth like an iron cradle, and listening to the *chug-a-chug* sound of wheels moving, soothing as a lullaby.

Luke was young when he left, though he looked and acted older than the years accorded him. He was tall and gangly with skin that paled to milk in the winter and tanned to honey in the summer, much like a wild animal shedding its fur annually to molt stronger coats. Dark eyes set close together, peering over a long nose like a predator wolf's, though his disposition was considerably more passive, closer to that of a curious dog, sniffing where he pleased and meaning no intentional harm. This particular wolfish aspect of his face, however, saved him from unfortunate confrontations more than he could realize. Having an aggressive, knowing appearance caused potential assailants to wonder if he were as easy a mark as the next lonely kid who might wander along.

This wasn't to say Luke hadn't encountered his due share of hard troubles. Being pubescent and alone frequently met with viciousness and trickery. Each year on the rails, he'd been beaten, cut, hustled, reviled, burned, robbed, and generally ostracized.

Once, he'd even been raped. Luke tried to bury that particular memory, but occasionally, when least expected, it'd pop up in his thoughts just long enough to remind him of his easy vulnerabilities.

. . . He'd only been thirteen years old when that incident occurred. Luke had hopped a boxcar in Effingham, Missouri, and found another 'bo already nestled inside. The man was dapper and spruce, as much as hobos can be—meaning his clothes didn't have holes in them, and he'd shaved that week—and he introduced himself as Natty Nash. Nash was gregarious and shared a bag of peanuts with Luke, and when he suggested they ride together a spell, Luke agreed. Back then, Luke was of the opinion two travelling 'bos were safer than one. Nash said they should bed down on solid land, so they left the train and found an old manger that was so dusty even the spiders were sneezing. Nash cuddled up close and his hand squeezed Luke where no one 'cept himself had ever squeezed before. Luke recoiled, but Nash didn't let go. His other hand showed a razor knife.

"They also call me *Naughty* Nash," he said, and forced Luke to the ground. Natty Nash was mean then, and when he finished he set to Luke as a punching bag.

Soon as Nash was done and run off, Luke searched out the local constable and reported the attack, broken-toothed and bleeding from his defiled orifice. The constable just replied with a smirk that Luke probably deserved whatever had happened and, more n' likely, probably enjoyed it. Luke slunk away, catching the Alton line to St. Louis, vowing never again to beg police for recompense and, secondly, never again to suffer such a violation.

In future faces of turmoil, he retreated if opportunity allowed, but fought back savagely when necessary. Such were the cruelties of life that convinced Luke the world was largely an inhospitable berth, and taught him to always be wary, and suggested his affairs might eternally remain as cold and dreary as the soiled long johns he wore all year through.

But Luke also found endless satisfactions.

Besides the happiness he gained in the act of travelling itself, Luke discovered great pleasure in learning new things. While his mother had been alive, Luke had attended school just long enough to develop an eagerness for knowledge that extended to any and all matters. He wanted to know why one flower bloomed red and another purple. He asked bees how their tiny wings made such a whopping sound; questioned mountains why they grew so large; queried spiders why they had eight legs, when less could do just fine. Luke wondered at life and death, and who came before him, and who would follow. He sought to understand the worth of man, the differences or, more often, the similarities of character, and what drove him and so many others to roam without aim, pushing personal frontiers solely to see what lay on the other side.

In this way Luke spent his days staring and wondering at his surrounds, sitting in the rolling boxcars of America, and he gained his education in travelling trains, and he forged his occupation in jumping them. He grew up quick, and he worked where he went, and society called him a hobo, and he tended to agree. He carried what little he owned in a torn rucksack on his back. His shoes never lacked holes. His only friends were other 'bos, and young Luke got to know most of them with some degree of fondness.

THE HOBO CODE, 1931

"Got big plans today, Luke?"

The question came from Hazel. The old man had a long cigarette clamped hard between brown teeth, and his words had a way of flowing around it in thin, unbroken streams. "New laws to write, pretty gals to dine, movers and shakers to hobnob alongside?"

"Naw, figure I might take a day off from all that high livin'," Luke said, luxuriously stretching out his long limbs. Even while lying on the damp floorboards of the shuddering boxcar, he felt comfortable while the train was moving.

"That's good, son. Everyone needs time to relax once in awhile. Even God took vacation that seventh day."

"Yup. Maybe tomorrow, I'll get back to reshaping this ol' world."

The woman, Po' Chili, threw a radish at Luke that fell short. She chucked another that went far. "You can start by reshaping these roots. Slice 'em up, and I'll make a soup."

"No rest for the weary, eh, son?" Hazel said.

"You too," Po' Chili added. "Start a fire. Breakfast ain't gonna make itself."

Po' Chili had mottled skin, colored in some areas and pale in others, and if you squinted your eyes you could have imagined her as an old

Dalmatian dog. Her eyes were bloodshot and her jowls hung like an old dog's, too, but Luke didn't believe she was a step past thirty years. Folks on the rails lived hard lives, and their bodies showed for it. Chili was bulky in the torso and lanky in the limbs, with kinky hair that knotted at regular intervals, as if she once tried to make pretty braids out of it but had given up halfway through. She was sweet enough once you got to know her, and plenty tenacious. Luke thought that in different circumstances she would have been a fine teacher or mother. As it was, the only mothering she did now was for Hazel.

"Must be nice, bein' Queen Boss of everyone," Luke said to her. He tried to make his voice sound flinty and cool, like Hazel's, but it still came out reedy, not yet through with the odd ways of puberty.

Po' Chili threw another radish, this one whopping him between the eyes. He picked it up and took a bite. "Tastes kinda bitter."

"It's a radish. Ain't known for being sweet."

"This one's worse than usual."

"Came from that farm back in Norville."

"Norville?" Luke muttered. "They was using bat turds for mulch. Don't do much for the appetite."

"Fertilizer is fertilizer. Helps the crops grow and we eat it. 'Less you'd rather go hungry. That can be arranged."

"I'll eat radish." Luke pulled out a small pocket knife with a nicked, dull edge and began to peel.

"If food or no food are the options, I think I'll take the former as well," Hazel cut in.

Po' Chili snorted. "Thought as much."

If Po' Chili was no older than thirty, Hazel wasn't a day younger than sixty. He was short and stubby as a tree stump and walked like he was takin' a squat. He'd been drinking whiskey for so long he said he'd first tasted it on his mother's teat. It caused him to look deathly ill; Hazel had a jaundiced tone to his skin, and the whites of his eyes had turned amber, as if his liver and kidneys had closed up shop long ago. But he was smart, and he could still hop cars with the best of them, and Luke had seen Hazel knock a man out that was twice as big as him with one quick uppercut to the jaw. Maybe by now it was the whiskey that gave Hazel his strength to keep going, like some witch's potion laced with the elixir of life.

The three of them ate their breakfast of radish and soup with tree bark in it, and Hazel drank from his bottle and smoked another cigarette, and the train engine whistled a long toot that scared birds into flight. They were travelling to Portage, Michigan, on the hopes of picking blueberries on a farm, to earn a few more coins, to survive a few more days.

"Fine day out, fine day indeed," Hazel admitted to the blue sky showing through the freight car's open door. "Think I might make the most of it."

The train lumbered along, and the trio turned to point out landmarks of civilization flashing through the forest: a leaning billboard, a gaunt telephone pole, the gray roof of a country church.

Each surface was marked with strange, half-hidden symbols written by other passing hobos, and Hazel explained them to Luke. He didn't have to explain much, as Luke had been riding the rails three years by now, which seemed like thirty, and long enough to understand the basics of the Hobo Code. Hazel, however, knew more, so Luke listened intently to what the older man said, soaking up new interpretations and intoning his own deeper reasoning.

Rail riders lived their lives by the guide of these symbols.

They passed a small covered bridge that arched over twin turtle-green creeks. Scratched across the bridge's side in large black lines was a series of emblems, likely drawn from coal.

"Damn it," Hazel said. "Damn it in a bag."

"Wha's the matter?" Po' Chili asked.

"Did you see that? Harvesting's off in Portage. The road's ruined with 'bos. Too many, they're getting turned away."

She scrunched up her face. "How d'you figure?"

"Did *you* see it?" Hazel asked Luke.

"Most of it, I think," Luke replied. "The arrow, the direction we're going, intersected a circle, so that meant not to go this way. If the arrow would have just been next to the circle, without crossing it, that would have meant to continue."

"That's right. What else?"

"There was a shovel with three diagonal lines over it, so it meant 'no work.'"

"Close. It said there *was* work, but now it's filled. If the shovel would've had an 'X' over it, that would have signified there was never any work available to 'bos in the first place."

"Okay. Then there was a triangle surrounded by a circle, and that's what told you there were too many others trampin' up there, and nothing to be gained."

"Good boy, you're learnin'."

And Luke *was* learning. The Hobo Code was a written language as essential and all-encompassing as any scripture, and Luke watched and studied and believed all that was related to it. The symbols were becoming part of the country, a dialect marked in everything from mud to whitewash to ink to hog's blood, drafted on any surface to communicate amongst the nation of transients. It recited the rules of itinerant living, handing out directions, suggestions, warnings, and even sordid hobo gossip.

Though, like advice, not everyone took it on face value.

"Who's to trust anything writ by some unseen bum?" Po' Chili asked. Hazel and Luke looked intently for more signs to indicate where to travel next, while she waved it off. "Seems to me, anyone could have marked that to keep us away from Portage, cause less competition for himself."

"No, pretty girl," Hazel said. "That would be contrary to the Code. Hobos must work together. If someone wrote information that was untrue, it'd be like lying to ourselves."

"And that don't happen already? What are you thinkin' each time you take a swig?"

He ignored the swipe. "It's faith, you either believe in the Code or you don't. Can't pick some parts to trust and not others. If it says don't go to Portage, it's speaking truth. I've been following the Code a long time, and it's not steered me wrong."

"Humph. And look at the good life it's brought you."

"Those who claim a good life wouldn't pay much attention to the Code. They don't even see it."

"Or maybe they do the opposite of what it says."

Hazel sighed. "It's enough to get by. I'm not dead, I'm not doing bad as others. We find work when we need it. Find food before we starve, shelter before we freeze. It's how I found you." He nuzzled his head against her neck.

"Well, now I know that Code is loaded." But she smiled and squeezed into him.

"How'd you learn the Code first off?" Luke asked. "Someone teach you, or you just figured it?"

The older 'bo leaned back and clamped on his cigarette, and a bit of smoke drifted up, and a bit of ash sauntered down. The boxcar was muggy and stank of rot and piss, and Hazel's cigarettes were welcome as perfume, covering up the sickly odors that all worn-down boxcars seemed to emanate.

"Little of both," he replied. "The Code's always been here, just that it takes time and trust to recognize. Ever notice when you hear a word you thought you never heard before, suddenly you hear that word everywhere you go? The symbols are the same. Once you realize what it is you're looking at, you see them all over."

Luke nodded his understanding. Some of the symbols were obvious enough: a smiling, happy face meant things were good at that spot, a frowning face meant things were bad, while a zigzag line for the mouth meant it was hostile.

But the meanings of other symbols had no reference to implied associations at all; you either knew what the mark meant or you didn't. A top hat to the left of a triangle signified wealthy people were around. A diamond shape with a single line running downward and to the left meant that it was okay to pass, but to hold your tongue. Hobos understood these characters, while regular stiffs scratched their heads.

"What now?" Po' Chili asked.

Hazel didn't speak, just shook his head, reading more complicated signs on tree trunks and trestles as the freighter grumbled along.

A giant advertising board sprung out from the passing landscape. On one side, thirsty travelers were invited to drink Coca-Cola at Gunther's Drug Store, and on the other side, hungry travelers were invited to eat Campbell's Soup at Mom's Diner. Faint hobo marks were painted in each corner. Hazel made a strangled sound, like something leapt down his throat and wasn't willing to come back up.

A patch of bright forest came after that, reflecting midmorning sunlight. Luke saw the others' faces awash with angelic glow, like how heaven-bound souls were depicted in old religious paintings. But there was something else besides the bright light that affected Hazel's face, because his eyes began to twitch and some water was filling them, and that also reminded Luke of the misery those heaven-bound souls always seemed to be enduring.

"We got to get off," Hazel said quietly.

Luke and Po' Chili didn't argue, just prepared to jump out. They brought themselves to the edge of the boxcar's doorway and set their legs out first like sitting in a chair, waiting for a piece of ground to come along that was mostly free from trees or stones.

The train wasn't moving fast, only about twenty miles an hour, up a slight incline. It was a long, heavy train, weighed down by filled tankers, overflowing grainers, and crammed hoppers. It was an easy jump off.

Hazel and Po' Chili landed like they were walking. But when Luke hit the earth, a treacherous root snatched at his ankle, and he stumbled and rolled from the momentum. A boot came off and his shirt tore, and his pockets emptied into the scree. Hazel just stared off in the distance, while Po' Chili came over to help Luke up.

"What came over him?" Luke asked.

Po' Chili shrugged and answered without giving an answer. "Seen something."

Hazel started motioning to a grove of trees, his fingers dancing upward as if writing a question on the air.

"I don't always agree, but he believes in it, gets all worked up," she said. "He don't worry about the things that worry me, sayin' the Code'll take care of everything. But when the Code don't do it, what happens?" Po' Chili pointed a hitchhiker's thumb to herself. "Me. I get it done. That Code is the same nonsense as reading fortunes in the palm of your hand, you ask me. We make our own luck, control our own lives, though I won't claim much discipline over mine. Should never've left home when I did."

Hazel stopped gesturing. His splayed fingers turned limp, giving up, and he turned to Luke and Po' Chili.

"I missed my chance," Hazel said to them. "Missed it long ago." His yellowed eyes flicked to Luke, boring into him. "My future's not long to last, but you've got a ways yet, son."

Hazel walked away, into the woods, stomping on infant flowers along his way.

"He'll come back," Po' Chili said. "Always does, just don't ask when."

Luke took a deep breath, then let it out slow. He didn't feel like standing there doing nothing. An apprehension took hold—an urgency—to get back on the train and travel, anywhere, it didn't matter, so long as he was moving.

He fidgeted. Po' Chili crossed her arms.

She said, "You need to go, be my guest."

Luke felt embarrassed at the sudden, desperate need to simply flee, as if the solitary act of lingering in her company had turned unbearable.

"You and him are a lot alike," she continued. "Can't nest anywhere long. Always on the move, searching for something you don't know about."

Luke thought a moment before answering. "Just doesn't seem natural to stay in one place. We're not trees, you know. We don't bear roots."

The train had long since vanished, but the tracks still sang: *Come to us, roll away, the journey here's so fine. You don't know what you're missing farther down the line.*

"We all need some sort of roots," she replied. "If you don't grow a few early on, you'll like to wither up from all that blowing back and forth."

"I'll know what I'm looking for when I find it."

"That it, *hm?*"

"It's all I've got."

"I suppose you see a sign right now that's telling you to keep going."

Luke smiled. Behind Po' Chili stood a battered wood signpost that read: NO TRESPASSING. Freshly painted over it was a circle extending a line of three arrows, one after the other. The hobo mark incited her very words: *Keep Going.*

Po' Chili said, "You ever writ one of those symbols for other 'bos to read?"

Luke laughed once and rubbed the pimples on his chin. "No, I just follow 'em. Guess I'm more busy thinking of where I'll be going next, how to find food or work. Don't consider much to compose something for those coming after me."

"You and every other tramp on the rails."

"Sounds pretty selfish, now you bring it up."

She asked, "You ever seen anyone else write a symbol?"

Luke thought on it. He'd been around so many other hobos, in camps, on trains, reading the symbols, discussing them, following them. It made sense he must have been there while someone drew out their wisdom of the road. But try as he might, Luke couldn't remember a single instance. "Can't recall any."

"I been with Hazel a long time," she said. "I been with other 'bos before him, groups, tramp jungles, whole towns of drifters. Ain't a one of them ever wrote one of those damn marks as far as I can tell."

"Funny . . . " Luke said. He wasn't sure where Po' Chili was going with this.

"What I want to know is," she said, her voice flat and hard as Texas prairie, "who's leaving all these notes for us? How is it everyone else knows where we're going, what we need, and when? Who is it that's always one step ahead of us, dropping bread crumbs that are perfectly timed, just relevant for us, the moment we see them?"

Luke didn't have an answer.

"Who's talking to us?" Po' Chili asked. "Who's talking to all the tramps following this Code?"

She didn't say any more on the subject, but it caused Luke to wonder.

Hazel still hadn't returned, and Luke guessed it'd be awhile before he came back. He wanted to say good-bye to the old man after they'd travelled together the past couple weeks, but he also didn't want to linger around for God's ages. The sudden urgency to take leave grew stronger.

The jointed tracks picked up their tune: *Hurry now, move along, the day won't last much more. Night is right, same as light, keep looking for the door.*

Luke was lucky when it came time to needing trains. Some 'bos waited days for engines that never arrived. When Luke needed one, *sensed* he needed one, it wasn't long until a locomotive happened to come steaming his way.

And one came his way that very moment, as if answering a call. It was an older Great Northern engine with a crimson roof and broad brass rods at the wheels that looked tarnished and stained from long use. The coal car was blue-gray and leaning a bit to one side with each *chug* or *lug,* like a limping man trying to walk in a hurry.

"I guess this is you, then," Po' Chili said.

"Guess so," Luke replied. "Give my regards to Hazel. He's right, y'know. I've got a ways yet."

"As do we all."

"I'll see you another day," Luke said. "A sign told me."

The train chugged by, and Luke jumped on, and he was gone, though he would see Po' Chili again, just as the sign foretold.

From there Luke crossed the country back and forth, slowly discerning its mysteries the way one stumbles upon the secrets of a new home. He thought often of Po' Chili's simple question as to who left the messages he obeyed, and wondered, also, as to what greater knowledge he might someday receive from them. Luke couldn't read and write in words very well, the way most others could, but he got to know that language of hobo pictures better than anyone else, even Hazel, and all that occurred before the day he suspected was his sixteenth birthday.

LUKE AND JOHN, 1934

Three years later, Luke rode a westbound Pensy line on a day so hot he could fry a tomato on a rock.

The train rolled by dusty farms, tall windmills, seas of corn, and then a pale billboard declaring Van Wert, Ohio. Luke noted them all, not by what they represented commercially as attributes of engineering, domestication, or divisions of property, but by what they *communicated*. The hobo language was spreading, drawn on any surface that could act as a canvas.

For a while the train ran adjacent to a long fence that kept cattle off the tracks. Every fifty yards, a slab of wood indicated whose property it was, and on one slab was a hastily-painted double-sided arrow with quills on each end. This puzzled Luke, as usually the arrow mark was one-sided and accompanied by a name or a town, giving directions where to go. This double-sided arrow didn't make sense, as it indicated opposite directions and, instead of a name, was accompanied only by a big yellow question mark.

A half mile later came a buttermilk-hued field with a derrick's framework jutting from its midst. A couple of men in bowed hats walked around it with hammers and saws, acting busy. The derrick looked to be new construction, but painted on its scaffolding was a large symbol in wind-worn paint: the number eight laid on its side, another mark Luke wasn't sure what to make of.

For years he'd followed the signs as means to an end, providing ways to subsistence, shelter, and protection, but still he'd not figured their origins, ever since Po' Chili had asked: *Who's talking to us?*

And that brought up even more questions, because he'd been noticing changes appearing in the language, messages that were somehow showing up personalized just to him . . .

How else could Luke explain when he'd passed through Grand Forks last year and saw a stick figure sign for "Bad Man" outlined under the eave of a junkyard shack? Usually that advice meant to get oneself the opposite direction, but the next symbol read as "Come Inside." Luke had cautiously crept to it, keeping in mind every fast escape should the need arise. There was a hole for a window cut into the aluminum sheet wall, and a towel used for its curtain had fallen away. He'd peered inside. A mattress with springs popping from its seams occupied most of the litter-strewn floor, and occupying that mattress was a man he'd immediately recognized. It had taken six weeks to heal physically from his run-in with Naughty Nash, but the scars on his soul were eternal.

Normally, Luke would have taken the path of retreat, better to avoid danger. But he'd felt a charge; the signs had *directed* him there like he was being led, and if he followed them, he'd be safe.

In his pocket had been the small knife with a nicked, dull edge. He'd entered the shanty, its tin door squealing terribly, but Nash never stirred. An empty bottle of gin lying beside the mattress accounted for the man's oblivion. Luke had drawn the knife and proceeded upon his own bit of *naughtiness.* When he'd left the shack bloodied, the signs under the eave were vanished.

The memory dissolved, and the Pensy train kept on, passing next an old barn with sun-bleached sides sinking into itself like a rotting gourd. A blue symbol was painted on the barn: a pair of curved lines angled over a dot. Luke knew that symbol well—*okay to sleep here.*

The barn's slat roof was so full of holes it could have been used as a sieve, and its walls looked rotted and wet, like a roadkill carcass. Yet against all reason, Luke knew that if he needed to bed down for the night, that place would be okay.

And while thinking of that sign and its message, a strange thing happened—

A fleeting thought shot through his mind as quick and bright as a comet. It was the kind of thought that if you don't latch onto immediately would be gone over the far horizon and never encountered again. Be it luck or instinct or providence, Luke reached out and caught that comet. It burned his mind with a fever of ideas and curious possibilities, and even then he still felt the thought begin to steal away.

It had to do with the hobo signs spreading over the roads of America.

Part of this thought was to the origins of a language, and part considered its perpetuity. Why did most people simply not *see* those signs the way he and other transients did? And why did he, who attended the Hobo Code no more than any other tramp, seem to understand a greater significance than other rail riders?

Something was coming, something he would need to do . . .

The old barn and its blue symbol receded behind like a hazy dream and, with it, the strength of his comet-thought. Luke tried to grasp the dimming thought's intent, this message that had reached out to him across a multiverse, and found it a fleeting task. He remembered the sign he'd previously passed, that dripping-white number eight, laid on its side . . .

With a jolt, another thought rocketed by that he fought to catch, and he comprehended the sign was referencing something universal, something existential. That sideways eight referenced the concept of *infinity*.

And a quarter mile before that had been the double-sided arrow with quills on each end, followed by a question mark. *As if open-ended . . . There's a choice about something. It's asking, which way am I gonna go?*

Luke's mind went reeling, trying to make sense of something greater, like pondering the hints of a coded message. Which, it seemed to him, was all of this hobo language, scattered across the shuttered windows and gray doors and tattered billboards of the nation. It was a great puzzle for him to assemble.

A long shriek of the engine's whistle brought him back from reverie. The train belched and muttered, rumbling along, and Luke watched outside as the golden fields and thin fences tried to keep up. Ahead, a listing water tower began to take form, growing above the turn of land like a fast-blooming tree.

The tower's corrugated tank rose higher than the train, with a chute to unload into the engine's tender, all elevated by a trestle of brown wood stiles. Though not as precarious as the barn he'd passed, the whole thing looked decrepit enough to topple over if someone pushed it hard enough. Its shingle cone roof sank in like the hollow of a sick man's cheek, and the metal cistern was pockmarked with shotgun pellets and rust. Painted on it in broad swathes was another 'bo image: a simple blue door that appeared to hang slightly open from its frame.

It was another symbol Luke had never seen before, and he sensed it was an additional piece of the hobo puzzle.

A new comet-thought rocketed through his mind, bright and flashing: *he needed to get off.* There was an urgency that vanished as quick as it came, and he could easily have considered it a daydream as flitting as the heartbeat of a spittlebug.

But no, there was something around him, something that was touching his mind this moment, and he had to act: either he must pursue the meaning of the symbols now, or the sudden comet-thoughts would rocket away forever.

That painted symbol of an open door was an invitation, telling him to enter.

The train must have been doing fifty miles an hour, enough of a speed that a man could easily break both his legs and every knot in his spine by going out the wrong way. A 'bo generally climbed on or off a train when it was slow, or decelerating to enter or depart cities, or if going around the curve of a track. But the land out here was straight as a bristle, and the train didn't show indication of slowing anytime soon.

He brought himself and his small canvas rucksack to the edge of the boxcar's doorway and sat, legs hanging out, as he always did when readying to jump. The rushing wind blew hard, trying to pull him out on its own terms. Luke grabbed the car's metal frame with splayed fingers and squeezed tight.

Oh, Lord, this is gonna hurt.

He shifted his center of balance and moved his hips so that he teetered on the doorway's thin metal lip. With a grunt and a plea, he swung out and pushed back from his arms and went airborne, free as a falling rock. Luke's guts flew up in his mouth and he flapped his arms like a baby bird trying to fly, and then he hit the earth and bounced.

He turned his body, trying to roll with the momentum. Fortunately, the field dirt wasn't packed hard. It wasn't soft either, but there was enough give that it didn't feel like he ricocheted along a brick wall. His shin smashed a stone, and his hands tore through a bush of thorns, but other than that, after a couple of spirals and twists, he landed all right in a patch of goldenrod.

Luke groaned when he stood. He'd ended up about a hundred yards past the water tower. Between there and here, his rucksack had come undone during flight, and the trappings of his life lay scattered to the earth. He limped around collecting most of it, then made his way back to the tower.

The water tower looked even more ramshackle up close than it had from the train, its exposed frame worn out by the elements, and the trestle fractured and loose. Luke peered up to the metal tank high above and examined the image of the painted blue doorway.

If the symbol meant to enter at some location, Luke couldn't guess where. There was nothing else in the area besides the tower, railroad tracks, and miles of yellow-green meadow. Off in one distance was the blur of rising crops, and in the other distance was a swarm of shooflies darting around witchgrass. Luke examined the structure again, looking for an unseen doorway. If he squinted and thought broad enough, any of the wood trestle's four sides could resemble a tall entrance. The spindly legs and crossbeams simulated a door's frame, but walking under the water tower and out the other side was a lesson in idiocy if he expected to be someplace different than where he'd started.

An eagle screeched from the distance, echoes spreading across the vast blue sky. Luke kicked at gray weeds blossoming from the oak risers. Sweat formed on his temples, and he moseyed in a slow circle around the tower, looking for any other hobo signs. His leg throbbed, and something stung his cheek. A big-eyed lizard white as chalk skittered by.

Had those comet-thoughts been real?

Luke started to think those years of lonely wandering were finally taking a toll on his mind. Fact was, there were plenty more days he'd shared company with birds and rats rather than another person, and there were more days than that he'd starved rather than eaten. How much could the brain take before it just tossed itself off the cliff of reason and began inventing methods of escape from this lost existence?

"Aw, hell," Luke said to himself. He was going to be stuck here a while and would probably have to hotfoot it out at dusk, following the tracks to another train. For now the sun tried cooking him, and the only shade was under the tower.

The painted blue door appeared to hang slightly open from its frame, and Luke couldn't help but wonder: *What piece of the puzzle is this?*

He walked under the symbol, through the trestle. Beneath the metal cistern the air was cool, crowded by too many shadows, as if all the darkness from the meadow gathered here for shelter. Abandoned cobwebs hung like curtains, and he pulled them aside. A blue happy face was painted on the inside of one of the tower's legs.

What did it mean under here? *Okay to stay, or okay to pass?*

Luke walked past the symbol, through the opening opposite of which he'd entered, and found himself outside the rear of the tower. Nothing had changed. The fields were still yellow-green, the sun still hot, and another big-eyed lizard ran by, kicking pebbles at him. The rail line crossed it all, connecting one horizon to the other.

A man walked toward him, and Luke almost tripped over his own legs in surprise.

The man wasn't far away, and Luke couldn't fathom how he'd appeared there, as if the blue sky had just hawked him out. Then Luke saw a glitzy black car behind him. That answered the question of how the man arrived, but Luke next wondered where the car came from. It wasn't there a moment ago.

The man was dressed like a New York politician, pinstriped suit that swished languidly with each movement and wingtip shoes polished so bright it looked like he walked on mirrors. All Luke could think was, *He must be sweatin' buckets under that suit.* But when the man got up close, there wasn't a hint of flush on his skin.

"Afternoon," the man said.

"Afternoon, sir," Luke replied, shuffling his feet. His gaze went to the ground, and he tried to blend into the surroundings the way he did when a cop or railroad dick approached.

"You call my father 'sir,'" the man said. "My name is John, though friends call me Johnny. Maybe we'll be friends."

Luke looked up. John had a handsome face, oiled russet hair, and a thin mustache. His chin was dimpled as a puckered ass. A cigarette hung from one side of his mouth, glowing red embers aligned to that dimple. He seemed familiar in some way, though Luke couldn't place him. Most men Luke met were poor as the day they were born. No one he knew owned wingtip shoes or a car. "Everyone calls me Luke, whether they're a friend or not."

"Well, Luke, I got a question for you, and I don't want you thinking I'm driving on a flat."

"Okay."

"You dead?"

Luke startled. He immediately thought of that fast-moving train he'd just leapt from. Could he really have landed from that without serious injury? He imagined himself lying to the side of the tracks in a puddle of organs and broken bones, his ghost carrying on as if it were still alive.

He leaned on his injured leg and felt the pained swelling over his shin. Dead people didn't feel pain . . . did they? Luke shook his head. "Not yet, I don't think."

The man ran one finger across his pencil-thin mustache in contemplation. "I need a driver. You looking for work?"

"I don't know how to drive."

"Easy as plum pie. Push your foot down to move forward and spin your arms in the direction you want to go."

"Why'd you ask if I was dead?"

John's face scrunched up, and his eyes lost the confidence in them that made him appear so familiar. The glow of his cigarette dimmed.

"It's the damndest thing, but folks don't seem to notice me much anymore. They respond if I talk to them, but their reactions are impersonal, like it's force of habit to acknowledge me, and then afterward they sort of drift away forgetting I'd been there. Used to be, people saw me and they either got away quick or they wanted to shake my hand. Now I'm surrounded by a world of sleepwalkers."

"That *is* the damndest, 'cause I see you just fine."

"Thus my question if you were dead."

Luke scratched his head.

"I'll put it this way," John said. "I've seen a couple people around that I know shouldn't be strolling the streets with a whistle on their lips. It's only them who acknowledge me, though so far they've declined to share company. They're still living in the same means I heard about them, too."

Luke continued scratching his head. John went on.

"Annie Oakley. I just saw her outside Cincinnati, still dressed in rawhide fringe, shooting out coins from people's fingers without them knowing. I met her before, when I was a boy, and I wouldn't mistake her. She looks like how I remember, too, young and strong. She died sick and broke last decade."

"You may not be driving on a flat, but the air sure seems a bit low."

John laughed at that, and the confidence returned to his face. His dark eyes twinkled like turning a light off and on.

"There've been others. I saw Abe Lincoln the other day, and there's no mistaking that mug. He was standing on a street corner in Peoria, proselytizing, and him winking slyly at me the whole time like we were sharing an inside joke. Every person that walked by stopped and listened. When he was done, he moved on, and the crowd turned to each other, wondering why they were grouped up facing an empty soapbox."

"Uh-huh."

"I've got my theories but, regardless, I should know something's strange. I'm one of them. Dead. I was shot in the back by a G-man, yet here I am, talking to you."

"You don't say?" Luke took a step backward, thinking maybe it'd be best if the next train would come barreling along right that moment to whisk him away.

"Hell, boy, it was all over the newspapers. Don't you read?"

"Not much."

"I'm John Dillinger, and everyone says I died last month."

DANIEL INTERVIEWS KING, 1985: DAY ONE

I sat with King Shaw outside a small Mexican eatery. I'd ordered enough food to feed us both for a week, but King barely picked at some tortilla chips while he told me about Luke meeting John.

I normally make it a point not to interrupt people I'm interviewing. Once you get them talking, they're like a smooth-running car. But, like all engines, it takes a bit to hit that 60 MPH mark. If you cut someone off in the midst of speaking, they have to start over, turning on the ignition, putting the transmission in gear, and slowly accelerating to resume their pace. Nobody wants to stop and start, stop and start.

But King was beginning to lose me. I cleared my throat and said, "So the ghost of John Dillinger asked Luke to work for him?"

"That's right," King replied, shrugging his shoulders. "Luke agreed, too, though his employment wasn't for long. Course, at the time Luke didn't believe that was a dead Dillinger or anything, just figured the man was on the wrong side of common sense. Luke was a young buck and didn't know nothing that someone else would pay a quarter for. Most tramps, that left thieving or scrounging off the land. A person in a fancy suit offers you a job, you take it, regardless of his mental state."

"All right . . . " I said, drawing out the words as I flipped back through the scrawled pages of my notebook. "But you also said before, that in 1959 Luke was en route to kill someone named Smith McCain, when a 'Johnny' mysteriously appeared on the train with him. I assume this was also Dillinger?"

"Thought that was obvious."

"Just making sure."

King smiled. It was a rusty action, seeing his hard, dry lips rise along ancient laugh lines. He leaned across the table, as far as the confines of his wheelchair would allow, and I swore I could smell the cancer that was eating away his insides. "I expect you're making the same face right now that Luke made when John told him he was dead."

"Disbelief is a shared human condition."

"Sure, but the nice thing about a story is that you don't have to believe every bit. All you got to do is believe *in* it, and pass it along to someone else."

I liked that sentiment, and underlined it in my notes.

King kept on. "See, Luke and John became good friends over the years. They had a lot in common, both being that kind of rambler who don't cast anchor long at any shore. More than that, though, they were searchers, looking for something and always gettin' in trouble because of it.

"Personally, I never cared much for John. People say the man's arrogance was for show, but I'm telling you that even when an audience wasn't around, his self-opinion was theatrical."

"Oh," I said and nodded big. "You've met Dillinger, too?"

"Too many times, man. Like I said, him and Luke became good friends. And since me and Luke were good friends also, that placed me in John's circle of company.

"By the way, you ever hear that after John died, people said his pecker was a foot long and hard as the mortician's table he laid on? He wasn't that much of a ladies' man in real life; it's just the way his legend turned, due to how the sheet hung in the undertaker's photo. But now women across the country still fantasize about him, and his hubris grows. Way my luck is, if people speak about me afterward, they'll say I was impotent or something. Anyway, that's how he and Luke differed the most. Luke was humble as a nun on Sunday."

I chuckled at that. "All right, so what happened next after Luke met John Dillinger?"

LUKE AND JOHN, 1934, CONTINUED

In the late night hours that were to fall, and seemed to stretch longer than ever, Luke Thacker found himself remembering two things that struck him as peculiar that afternoon with Johnny. The entire day was rather far-fetched, like wispy flashes of a heatstroke, but two things—rather *normal* things—stood out most, perhaps those things that seemed within the limits of his mind to comprehend.

The first was that he found it easy to drive.

"Some people are born naturals when it comes to operating mechanics," John said. "Everyone has secret intuitions or competence in a talent that others haven't got. I think yours is for driving."

Luke would remember that for a long time.

The glitzy black car he'd first seen parked behind John Dillinger was a Model A Ford, and it wasn't as glitzy up close as it appeared from a distance. There was a pair of bullet holes in the driver's door, a cracked headlamp, and a bloodstain on the passenger seat.

Luke looked at the smear of crimson, then at John.

"It ain't mine," John said, and Luke wondered if the gangster was referring to the blood or the car itself.

John started the car once, explaining the clutch and gears to Luke, then turned it off. Luke got into the driver's seat and tossed his rucksack in the back, then copied all John did exactly. At his command, the four-cylinder engine revved loud and alert. He saw it in his mind, a part of him that was suddenly unlocked, that he never knew had been locked in the first place. John didn't instruct him any further, and Luke drove by divination, handling the vehicle as an extension of himself. He skipped across each of its three speeds and the car, in turn, skipped across the fields, jostling northbound between bumps and ruts, shrubs and stones.

Ten minutes later, Luke turned onto a dirt road so narrow he could have shaved with it. A flat wood sign pointed backward to Ohio and forward to Indiana. Luke said, "Well, I'm driving. Where're we going?"

"Just keep at it. Should be crossing Monroeville Road pretty soon."

"Where's that lead?"

"Monroeville."

"Oh."

John's cigarette burned low, the red glow threatening to fry his lips. He flicked it out the window. "There's a little bank there I've got business with. I'm going to rob it."

Luke stalled the car. "What? I'm not a bank robber! I've never stole more than a turnip from a field."

"You're not going to rob a bank, I am. You're just my getaway driver. I'm John Dillinger. I can't drive myself away from the bank that I rob. That's just uncouth."

"But I'll be accessory."

"Naw, all you do is wait outside with the engine running. Everyone knows that don't count as accessory."

There was a lot about the world's ways that Luke didn't yet know, but John's assertion didn't quite feel trustworthy. Luke made a face at him that expressed as much.

John continued. "Hey, you're riding with a ghost. Don't you think you've got other things to worry about?"

"I never said I believed that. You seem as real as me."

John ignored him. "Plus, while you're driving away I can hop on the running board and wave at everyone with their bags of money in my hand. Showmanship, my young apprentice, showmanship."

Luke turned the ignition back on and drove, contemplating John's logic. John lit another cigarette. He offered one, a Chesterfield unfiltered, but Luke shook his head "no." They smelled awful, like burnt cat hair.

"Listen, Johnny, I'll drive you up to that bank, but maybe I'll just walk away while you're inside."

"Suit yourself, but something tells me you'll stick around. Funny thing is, I just happened to be passing by, thinking I needed a driver, when I saw you come flying out of that train like a ball of spit and gristle. I watched you out there the whole time, but I bet you didn't see me until you walked through the doorway."

This caused Luke great concern, as the strange truth of what John said was as plain as him driving a car like he'd been doing so all his life.

"The world's a mysterious place," John continued, "and more mysterious, you keep searching it. You're a searcher, same as me. I can tell. And that doorway you found . . . I seen it and knew right off there was something special happening. The whole tower sort of glowed funny once you came near, like it had its own sunrise."

Luke was quiet, just driving. All John had said was a lot to take in, and it made his head hurt to contemplate too hard.

"By the way," John added, "if we're going to be working together, as your employer and friend, I have a request to make."

"Lemme guess, you want to heist an old lady next?"

"I've done worse, but this request's not as nefarious as that. You need to clean up. A man's judged by the company he keeps, and it smells like you and baths have got a running feud."

Luke felt himself flush. "Suppose I don't notice things like that after a while."

"You sleep in haystacks or something?"

"When I'm lucky enough to find them."

"Sorry. But when you're with John Dillinger, you've got to look like you own the city. I'll take care of you."

Soon they were on Monroeville Road, headed for the town, and box-shaped buildings broke free from the distance, rising like ripe crops. They stopped at the first one, a Texaco gas station, to fill up the Ford.

And that was the second thing Luke remembered as being so peculiar that day: John had been right. *People didn't seem to notice him.*

John Dillinger—the nation's most famous criminal, FBI's public enemy number one, and, not least of all, a man supposedly one month dead—pushed his way between two fat old men jawin' over the price of barley. The men stepped back from the jostle without breaking pace in their conversation. Once John passed, they moved back into the same places they'd previously stood. John had shoved between them on his way to the station's outhouse.

"Even dead, a man's still got to do his business," he commented. "In the meantime, see if you can figure out the gas pump."

Luke figured out the pump just fine and filled the tank, wondering how he was supposed to pay. The last time he'd had money was a buffalo head nickel found in a ditch outside Topeka, and Topeka had been a long time distant.

"Pardon, sirs, what's the damage for a tankful?" he called out to the men.

But the fat men didn't give him notice. Luke called again, and found himself talking as if to the air. Like Johnny, he seemed to be overlooked. Even while baking from the summer heat, Luke shivered, deciding he really was riding with a ghost and that, most likely, he was some sort of ghost himself.

"I don't understand," Luke said when John returned. "When most folks see me, they spit and tell me to not stop walkin'."

"Put yourself in my shoes," John said, then paused. "Funny, the expression would be true: you'd be in real *dead man's shoes*." He elbowed Luke hard in the ribs at his quip, and Luke grunted and hunched over. "Anyway, I've been living this way for a month, but it ain't all bad. Watch this, kid."

John returned to the fat men. One was bald and pale, like a peeled onion, and the other brown and lumpy as a potato. "Say, fellas, you know where I might come across some extra dough? My pockets have been a tad depleted these days."

The two men did a slow double-take, like trying to focus on a buzzing fly that inches closer, 'til it lands on your nose and you're cross-eyed. One moment there'd been no one but themselves, and the next John had their attention.

"Times been tough out here, friend," Onion answered him. "I'm lucky if I make a dollar a day, the traffic that passes through."

"What say you give me today's dollar, then?" John asked. He pulled a small handgun out from under his suit jacket.

Luke hadn't known he'd been carrying it, but he chided himself. *What else would John Dillinger carry? A picnic basket?*

Onion's eyes got big, and he looked like he might cry. "No need for that, mister. Here, take it. I don't want no trouble." The man's chunky fingers reached into his trousers and pulled out two dollar bills.

"Just today's dollar is all I want," John said. "You can keep yesterday's. I don't want you going broke."

John took one bill, then pointed his gun at Potato. "You got a dollar too?"

"I don't, sir. Only about fifty cents to my name, I tell ya." He pulled out his pockets in a jerking motion and a pair of quarters fell out, bouncing on the ground.

"Never mind," John said. "I don't like carrying coins. Too noisy."

"My God," Onion said suddenly. "You're John Dillinger."

"That's right. Tell folks I'm still around. Have a good day, gents, and I hope business picks up for you."

John walked back to the Ford and took his time getting comfortable in the passenger seat. Meanwhile, the two men resumed talking about barley, right where they'd left off.

"How'd you do that?" Luke asked, driving them away.

"Didn't do nothing. People just seem to forget I was standing in front of them."

"Oh." Luke thought for a minute. The Texaco station shrank behind them in the rearview. "But what happens later when that man realizes he's a dollar shy? Won't that trigger his memory?"

"Hasn't occurred that I know of. Don't we lose things all the time we had in hand only moments prior? Don't we just curse a bit, then forget about it and move on with life? Who's to know if someone else hasn't come along and snatched away that loose sock or lucky button or last bottle of booze while we blinked? Maybe there really is a reprobate to blame when your umbrella vanishes on a rainy day, or a piano accidentally drops on your head.

"Maybe someone else will follow after me and place a different dollar in that man's pocket to balance things out. Or maybe that man will never remember he had two dollars in the first place. Maybe he never did."

And that got Luke wondering a whole lot of things about his own life.

John kept on. "All I'm saying is in this past month, I've learned the world isn't as one-layered as I used to believe. Last week, I took a woman to bed and gave her the night of her life. She got up in the morning and didn't say 'hi' or 'bye.' Just ate breakfast alone, then went out the door. Even her cat didn't catch wind of me 'til I batted it on the ear. Then it ran and turned, looking back, wondering what it was running from. As long as I'm engaging someone, I got their full attention. After that, I'm no more than the thought of wind on a still day."

John must have known the question was coming, and he waited for Luke to address it.

"But why am I different? I see you just fine, and I remember you, even when you were away in the privy."

"Truth is, I don't know what you are, kid. Like I said earlier, I seen that tower sort of glow when you came near, then once you went through, you and I were on equal footing."

"Well, I'm pretty sure I'm still living, even if I never believed in anyone cavorting with ghosts before."

"Yeah, I don't think you belong here, though that doesn't mean you have to leave. Stay and have some fun."

They barreled down Monroeville Road, and Luke wondered where his sensibility went. "I'm having a parade already, driving you on a crime spree."

"See, I thought you'd stick around. What harm does it cause if no one can see you?"

Ahead, something large lay in the middle of the road, blocking it. Luke braked and thought of an old joke: *What's black and white and red all over? A chopped-up skunk.*

Instead of a skunk, this was a cow, though its black and white hide was plenty red. The cow was convulsing, dying. No, dying wasn't quite the right word for it . . . Luke stared and realized the cow was *vanishing*, though its disappearance seemed as painful as if it were set on fire.

The animal lay on its side, crying and struggling to get legs under it in an endeavor that was plainly futile. Half of its body was gone . . . not in the sense of having been cut out, but that it simply wasn't there, the way a vanishing shadow is no longer there. The cow's torso opened up, so Luke could see exposed ribs, a pile of guts, and then nothing. The insides faded to wind.

Hovering around the cow, at the edges separating its existence and non, swarmed a small flurry of bright red shapes. Each was formless, undulating blobs no larger than a melted button, but together they surrounded the dying animal in a seamless tide, eating away. The cow—where the cow had been—seemed to leave an imprint in the air, a hole in the surface of reality, like burning an outline through a piece of paper. Flakes of the cow did, in fact, seem to float off like ash, then those too were consumed by the red blobs.

No more than half a minute passed for the cow to evanesce. Then it, with a final *moo*, and the blobs were gone. The blacktop road shimmered in the sun and everything looked normal, pre-cow.

"What . . . was that . . . ?" Luke whispered.

"Damned if I know," John answered quietly. "Seen it happen a couple dozen times now. Whatever it is, gives me the willies. Seems no reason what it happens to, when, or why—animals, buildings, people—those red blobs just show up, devour it, then are gone. It's like everything's got a personal scythe hanging overhead, waiting to fall."

Luke stared at the road, questioning what he saw, questioning everything occurring to him that day.

"Hell, what do I know? I'm just a bank robber," John said and pounded on the dash with a flat hand. "Speaking of which, let's go!"

Luke obliged, grimacing, and drove through the spot the cow had recently occupied.

They turned onto Main Street of Monroeville, Indiana. It looked like every other mid-American town affected by economic hardships, trying hard to maintain a crumbling façade of good fortune. But cracks abounded, showing the grim melancholy underneath. People walked by in clothes that were dull as desert grass, worn-out fashions from decades prior. Most of the buildings were unpainted, just the color of their underlying structure, bleached cement or raw timber or gray stone. Even the buildings that were painted bright hues were still bland as old tea.

"There it is," John said. They pulled alongside a square red structure that was all brick, all business, and the only adornment was its brass-plated name: *First Citizens State Bank*. "Don't worry about parking lawfully, just get me close to the door."

Luke asked, "Why're you doing this? If you really are dead, I can think of a lot better things to do than stick-ups. I mean, what's the point?"

"Well," John said as he stepped from the car and ground the stub of his cigarette under foot, "I just don't know any different, like I'm *meant* to do this. But if I figure out otherwise, I'll be sure to let you know. In the meantime, keep the engine running, for I'll be back directly."

John pulled the handgun from under his suit jacket just as a policeman came walking along, whistling on a merry stroll. Luke tensed, ready to flee. He was terrified of police, having been on the wrong end of their batons more times than he could count. The officer and John crossed paths, and the officer didn't blink at John or at Luke, parked halfway on the sidewalk.

John went inside the bank, and Luke heard a woman scream, then a gunshot, then another scream—this one a man's—then John came running out holding a bulging canvas bag.

"Get us gone!" he shouted, and Luke drove them away, as fast as the gas pedal could lick the floor. John rode outside, standing on the running board, waving at citizens on the street with a bag of their bank's money in hand, just like he'd wanted.

John hollered and shot his pistol in the air as they sped down Main Street past the dusty shops and cafés. Slow-moving pedestrians looked up suddenly as the car tore past, then, just as suddenly, looked back to what they'd been doing: reading a paper, drinking coffee, or scrutinizing shiny appliances in store windows.

Ahead, three men stood evenly spaced across the street, facing the oncoming Ford. From a distance, they appeared more shadow than substance. Luke slowed, not sure what to do. John stopped hollering. The middle man held a long rifle in one hand and his other hand raised, palm out, in the gesture to stop.

Luke braked about thirty feet before them, but kept the engine running. He started to think John had been full of crap, and he'd just been bamboozled into believing he was invisible.

My-oh-my, who's gullible today? he thought. The three men clearly saw them.

"You just robbed that bank," the middle man on the street declared astutely.

"Huh, nope, wasn't us," John replied in a big voice. "Two other fellas looking like us drove off the other direction."

The man with the rifle wasn't having it. He was dressed the same as the other two, looking like Old West gunslingers. Each of them wore spurred boots and flat-topped cowboy hats slung low, and they flaunted mustaches so thick the whiskers seemed to pull down their faces. The man said, "And you're John Dillinger, already a wanted felon. I think we bring you in, there's a tidy reward coming our way."

John didn't like the sound of that, and he climbed inside the car quick. Luke eyed him slow. "I thought you told me nobody could see you."

"I never said that," John answered, offended. "I said people didn't *notice* me. Guess I got someone's attention now."

"Haunt or no haunt, you're still a rapscallion," one of the other men shouted in indignation.

"Hush now, Virgil, I'll do the talking," the middle man scolded. "You just blast 'em if they move funny."

John closed one eye in thought. He said to himself, "Virgil . . . " Then he called out to the men, "Who is it I'd be surrendering myself to, exactly?"

"Marshals of the federal court, serving the United States Department of Justice. I'm Wyatt Earp and these are my brothers, Morgan and Virgil Earp."

"I'll be goddamned," John said. "You're a little out of your jurisdiction, ain't you? I thought you kept affairs around Tombstone."

"The thing about us," Wyatt replied, "is that we like to travel. And sure, we're big news in Arizona territory, but citizens want some law to protect them in other places too."

"You ain't nothing but robbers yourselves," John said.

"These badges say otherwise."

"Hell," John said, turning to Luke. "I think they're serious."

"You don't say."

John leaned back out the window, pistol tucked inside the door. "How about you just let us pass, and I'll be sure to say thank you on the other side?"

"How about you raise your hands or we shoot out each one of your teeth for target practice?"

"Consider this my notice of resignation as your driver," Luke told John.

"Don't give up yet. No one ever said cowboys were bright," John replied. He raised his pistol and shot at the brother on the right, Morgan, who snapped backward, then fell to a knee.

"Hog's puck," Wyatt cursed, and he and Virgil fired their rifles. A pair of holes blew through the windshield, and the remaining glass split into a spider web of cracks.

John shot again, and all the Earp brothers returned fire at the car, even Morgan kneeling on the ground, bleeding.

It took all Luke's effort to not throw up his arms and hide in the niche underneath the steering wheel. He'd been shot at before, but those shots were generally by good ol' boys as warnings to stay away from moonshine stills or as a means of their entertainment, rather than attempts to actually kill him.

"Was that supposed to be a plan?" he asked.

"Just drive!" John shouted.

Luke stomped the gas pedal, and the car barreled forward with a scream. Ricocheting bullets pinged off the fender and grille, and sparks darted from the corners of his eyes like shooting stars. Something in the engine broke, and a burst of steam sprung from under the hood. The rest of the windshield fell to pieces and flying glass cut up Luke's face. John groaned, a patch of red blooming on his shoulder. The wound didn't stop him from shooting more, and he blew off Virgil's hat.

"Damn. The man's too short."

More rounds slapped the car. Luke drove forward and Wyatt was directly ahead, the marshal's face growing large in front of the rushing Ford. Luke looked straight into his eyes, staring him down in a game of chicken, praying the marshal would just sidestep and they wouldn't find out what it felt like for man and machine to collide head-on.

Wyatt didn't move, except to keep shooting. He was unblinking, those peepers cold and hard as iced-over daggers, and they cut through Luke, ordering him—by sheer force of will—to veer away.

At the last, Luke complied. He couldn't do it, couldn't run over another man, even if said man was already dead and firing at him. Luke pulled hard to the right, and the auto lifted precariously on two side wheels with a lurch, about to roll off the road. John Dillinger slid against the door frame and his pistol went flying through the air like a dead bird.

But John didn't complain. Between the last time Luke had looked at him and now, another bullet had come along and hit him square in the head so that he slouched and bounced with the car, as unprotesting as a scarecrow lit on fire.

The Ford almost tipped, but Luke again felt that natural command he had over it, like when he first got behind the wheel. He willed it back onto all fours, the same as Wyatt had willed him to veer in the first place; they both had some control over things that Luke couldn't explain.

He sped around Wyatt. The rear windshield exploded and bullets pinged off the car. A tire blew out and the Ford begin to spin, but Luke took it all as an extension of himself and didn't worry; he steered it back in a straight line, going faster than the leaking engine should have been capable, faster than a car had ever driven. The bag of bank's money had either come undone or was shot through, and bills with different faces on them soared high through the air. The Earp brothers receded in the distance.

Luke drove fast and didn't stop for a long time. The road narrowed and twice another car came from the other direction, sharing the single lane, but each time the other vehicle pulled over nonchalantly as if taking a detour, then got back on the road once Luke had passed. Luke guessed they didn't even realize they were doing it.

"Pull over," John said.

Luke startled. "I thought you were dead."

"I *am* dead. I don't want to die again."

Luke pulled far into a tall field of pillaring cornstalks, leaving tire tracks like the wake from a boat. The car died. He felt his adrenaline ebbing, his heart slowing, and with it his control of the Ford. The car sagged into the dirt, seeming to give up and fall apart at the bolt seams.

"Where are we?" John asked.

"Don't know." Luke turned to the gangster and could see part of his skull through the bullet hole. John's head gushed a fountain, painting his face red. Both men trembled, but for different reasons. Luke added, "I've got to get you help."

"I'll be all right."

"You look bled as a skinned hog."

John spat red. "I'm gonna get those bastards."

"You've got other things to worry about."

"They ruined my getaway. What'll people think? John Dillinger can't handle himself?"

Luke gaped, not trusting his sanity any longer. He touched John's arm to make sure he wasn't imagining the conversation.

John continued, "Suppose I'll be right as a fiddle, once I rest. It's my legacy that's wounded."

"Your what?"

"My legacy, my legend. Don't you get it yet? I'm not a ghost, I'm a memory. That's the thing keeping me around. Annie Oakley as a crack shot, Lincoln giving speeches, the Earps as vigilantes, me stealing. Folks ain't gonna root for me if I can't rob a simple hayseed bank without getting shot up."

Luke was about to tell him to kick a rock and see if any sense was hiding underneath, but then he questioned who he was speaking with. A dead John Dillinger . . . a man who *said* he was a dead John Dillinger, with a bullet hole in his skull.

Even after all he'd been through, Luke still found it hard to believe everything occurring that day. He didn't even know that Dillinger had actually died, aside from John's claim. All Luke had wanted was a job. And now, the Earp brothers? Maybe those men were just regular marshals. He'd never seen a federal marshal before; it could be that cowboy hats and spurs were part of the uniform. He didn't know how else to respond to John, or his own questions, but to state the obvious.

"You don't know what you're saying, you're in shock. A man don't normally survive a bullet in the noggin like that. Even if you're a ghost, or memory, or whatever, I think you're gonna die."

"Maybe. Eventually. Getting shot sure feels like the real thing. Hurts worse than a pecker full of syphilis."

"Can I do anything for you?"

"Yeah, just leave. You lost my gun."

Luke drew back, like deep-down John was blaming him for all their troubles. "I—I did as you said."

"I know, kid. Don't mean to get salty with you. It's just that I do my best thinking alone."

"What am I supposed to do? I'm not dead, I'm nobody famous. I don't belong here."

John rubbed away blood that seeped into his left eye, but more took its place. "My advice is maybe you should find your way back to that water tower you came from."

Luke nodded. It made more sense than anything else. He pushed the driver's door and it slowly creaked open. Fragments of tinkling glass showered down. He pulled out his rucksack from behind the driver's seat.

"One other piece of advice," John said before taking a deep, rattling breath. "Don't ever go to the movies with a woman in a red dress."

So Luke left John Dillinger in the shot-up Ford, hidden in the corn stalks and leaking blood like a faucet that won't turn off all the way. He made his way back to the road and walked it, wondering what to do if the Earp brothers showed up again, and then wondering how it came to be that he should have such a concern.

He'd driven from Monroeville in a panic and, by now, had no idea where the water tower was, or even where the nearest train track ran through. If he could find the right line, he'd just follow it back until he saw the tower.

A small boy came walking along with a fishing pole over his shoulder. Luke didn't know if the boy was alive or dead, living on in someone's memory. He asked, "Say, you know where the railroad is around here?"

The boy didn't answer, just kept walking.

Luke ran in front of him and stopped, the way he'd seen John face the two men at the Texaco station. "Say, howdy, you from around here?"

The boy sidestepped him with a skip and kicked at a rusted can. Luke grabbed his shoulder, forcing the boy to halt, but then he only brushed at Luke like shooing away a fly. The boy still didn't acknowledge him.

Luke thought, *I don't have any bearing at all on people.*

LUKE AND HARRIET, 1934

Luke continued walking that lonely road until the following day. People might not have seen him, but the sun was more perceptive. It cooked him, so the back of his neck burned red as John's head after a bullet gave him that second mouth.

Luke entered a small town called Devine that looked like the little sister of Monroeville, being dull and poor, but smaller. He helped himself to some steamed carrots and cornbread and a cup of coffee from a corner diner that once might have been a saloon. Luke didn't care to take someone else's food, but he cared even less for starving, and not being able to beg or barter for victuals placed him at an even greater disadvantage than usual.

Luke looked for hobo signs, but didn't find many; Devine was far from the rails and highways, not a normal throughway for itinerants, and maybe that was the reason. Maybe there just wasn't much to say in Devine, Indiana, although he did discern some of the usual symbols: a stick figure in a skirt capped by a halo, where a woman was nice, or two hanging fangs beneath a pair of curved lines, where an attack dog was mean. He didn't pay them any attention, as neither batted a lash nor a whisker to his existence.

He searched for a map but couldn't find one, even inside the mayor's office. Cars drove on the only road, heading north or south, and Luke guessed he'd probably been walking the wrong direction all along. He was lost, and getting more scared of never finding escape from this destitute purgatory. Once, he heard a horse galloping through town and imagined one of the Earp brothers scouting for him. He hid behind the counter of a tobacco shop, cringing at the feet of its proprietor.

Upon coming out of the shop, he turned a corner and ran so suddenly into a woman who could see him that she scared him as much as he apparently frightened her.

"Stay away!" she shrieked. She was an old, old woman, with skin wrinkled like a dry sponge. Her eyes were too big for her face and covered with a thin gray film, as if looking at him through a mist.

Whether the woman was a specter like John and the Earps, or was merely able to behold those in this nether-realm, he couldn't say. She hissed and slunk back and made the mark of a cross between an upraised finger from each hand.

Luke obliged. He desperately wanted to speak with another person, but he didn't want to antagonize anyone, not knowing what risky mojo they might possess.

A flatbed truck loaded with timber came along, and Luke jumped on the back, letting it convey him down the road until it pulled up to a lemon-yellow sawmill. Nailed over the front was a regular sign that read *Hap's* and, aside it, a secret sign in chalk symbols that described *Bad Man with Gun*. Luke didn't think it would matter much in his current condition, but he'd been trusting the signs for too long to take any chances about more "bad men."

He decided to keep moving when he heard a sound that was half sobbing, half moaning, coming from a side entrance to the mill. Luke left the truck and crept slow to its door, then looked through a crack he made by pushing the door slightly open.

"Help me," a man's voice whispered. "Help me."

Luke pushed the door open farther, not sure what he was seeing, and not believing what he saw. A man—if it could be called that—lay on the pine floor, writhing like he was on fire. Only half of him was visible, the other half nothing but an outline in air. Red blobs swarmed the man, just as Luke had seen occur to the cow.

The man turned his head to Luke, and the left side of his face melted away. Straps of flesh crossed a disappearing skull, and his hairline began to recede, as if he was slowly being scalped. But his eyes were still intact, and they widened. "You can see me."

"I wish I couldn't," Luke replied. "I—I'm sorry."

"Tell people . . . my name is Hap . . . " the man said. Before he could say anything else, his tongue dissolved like the long ash off a smoked cigar. His ears went too, as did the rest of him in one final convulsion. Where he'd been was something that Luke could define only as "nothingness," a dark fog showing behind the man's imprint, like looking through a hole punched through a piece of paper and seeing only black.

Then the hole filled in. The pine floor was normal as could be, the red blobs dissipated into the air, and the man was gone as if he'd never existed.

"The hell with this place," Luke said to the room, turned, and ran.

He ran and ran, away, down the road toward a dipping sun. The cornfields had long ago vanished, taken over by steadily-thickening groves of pine and hickory and other hardwoods. Luke kept rushing 'til his breath gave out and hot stitches shot up his side. He was thirsty and tired and scared, and he walked into the forest to lie beneath its cool shade. The split trunk of a dying birch provided enough incline to form a decent headboard, and he propped himself against it with the rucksack under the small of his back and lay there a long time, trying not to think of the vanishing man.

I can drive a car, Luke remembered. *Johnny showed me that I can drive a car*. Tomorrow, walking would take second fiddle to vehiculating. He'd told Dillinger he'd never stolen more than a turnip from a field. That protest sure wouldn't hold true any longer.

The sun fell down and the moon came up, and its round light was soft and white, like how Luke used to imagine ghosts *should* be. It was possible that spirits now were just as material as himself and, if that were true, he may even have previously come in contact with them without knowing it, may even had been steered to do things he otherwise might not have done, travelled directions he otherwise might not have gone. But that was a quick jaunt to delirium, considering what else *could have been* due to some unknowable force, and Luke had to make peace with current circumstances, as bewildering as they were.

He was just one lost soul in a lost generation, sinking further down the cracks of society, alone and unmissed, though inexplicably even more mislaid and disregarded than usual. Ants passed over him, and he wondered if they knew he was there, or if he was just a rise in their path. He brushed them off, then wondered further how they'd understand the cause of their displacement.

Weariness set in, and Luke steeled himself for a long, sleepless night.

"Psst," came a muffled voice from the darkness.

"Who's there?" Luke said.

"Don't shout or they'll hear you."

Luke was quiet a moment, listening. He didn't perceive anything a normal forest wouldn't produce. "You see me?"

"I wouldn't be talking if I couldn't see you." For a moment it was quiet again, then, "Don't stand. Crawl to your right, about fifteen feet. Careful of the thorns."

Luke hesitated, then obeyed. He heard a whistle coming from his left, sounding more human than bird.

"I'd crawl quicker, I was you. They're coming."

He did, shoving through plants that poked and tried to snag him with twiggy fingers. A crack of darkness opened, then expanded in front of him, hiding from the light of the moon. A thin brown hand reached from it and took Luke's wrist. He almost shrieked, but the same voice that had been leading him said, "In here."

Luke crawled in, and the ground suddenly gave way and he fell, sucking in his breath. He hit bottom three feet later.

"Shh," the voice said, and closed the trapdoor. In the moment before it sealed, a single lunar beam provided a glimpse of an old woman wearing a kerchief.

Moments later, other voices drifted overhead.

"I can smell him."

"You're smelling yourself."

"Har-de-har. You're funny as a cow turd on a boot."

"And you're perfumed like one. He probably got a whiff and scared off."

"Hush, you two. Y'all are 'bout as dumb as a box of air. Why don't you hire a circus to announce our coming?"

"Hell, this search is wearin' thin quick. I don't think he's worth it."

"I do. I took a bullet in the gut."

"We don't even know who he is."

"More the reason to find out. If he's an *animate*—"

Luke's heart thudded so hard he thought it might be mistaken for a herd of stampeding cattle. But the voices faded and passed, and he remained underground for what seemed half a lifetime.

The trapdoor lifted slightly, and the old woman put her head out, listening. The other half of life seemed to follow until she said, "Okay, let's come up."

They crawled outside and stood. The moon hadn't changed position much since last Luke saw it.

"The Earps are after you," she said.

"I gathered."

"They're not the only ones. There're a couple bounty hunters and an Injun tracker also in pursuit." A pause, then in afterthought she said, "And a Methodist circuit rider."

"Why?"

"To minister to your sins, most likely."

"I mean generally speaking," Luke asked, "why are all those people after *me*?"

"For different reasons. It's what they do," she said, nodding to herself. "They want you as another conquest, an added notch in their belts."

"Cause of the bank robbery?"

"These ones do. Some folks take that business seriously."

"All I did was drive a car . . . I thought it wasn't even accessory."

The old woman shook her head slightly. "Even Washington chopped down a cherry tree, but you have to know when wrong is wrong."

Luke slumped, admitting she was right.

The woman was dark-skinned and stooped-over, dressed in a rough gown that gave her the shape of a short barrel. Her face was all frown, more carved than expressed, with a countenance so stern it seemed ready to rake the devil over his own coals any day ending in "y." She looked like the sort of grandmother he'd imagine sitting in an heirloom rocker, lecturing young children on their manners and eating habits. Yet here she was in the middle of a forest, after midnight, aiding a stranger.

And somehow, she seemed to be holding back.

Luke asked, "What if I hadn't driven the car?"

The old woman let out a hoarse chuckle. "The car and bank don't really matter, young man. They're just lures for different fish." She eyed him, and one brow rose while the other sank. "You don't belong in these parts, so that already makes you some kind of bait."

"Sounds like I've been dealt a rigged hand."

She nodded. "Every decision has its effects, for good *and* ill. Whatever choice you make will be noticed by someone, for different reasons. Where we are, no one changes, and people act on the image that's accorded them. One man's remembered as a killer and another's remembered as a hero. Like I said, it's what they do. It's what *we* do."

"And what is it *you* do?" Luke asked.

"I help people find their way."

Luke puzzled over that.

"Maybe you've heard of me? Those who know, call me Harriet Tubman. Those who don't, call me something else."

He remembered John's revelation about legends continuing to live. Luke hadn't given it much credence at the time, but now that assertion seemed to be growing feet.

"Follow me," she said. "I've got a path."

"Where to?"

"Your destination."

"How do you know where I'm going?"

"You want to return home, don't you?"

Luke nodded yes.

"Well, then, onward," she said. "We're on the railroad."

"We are?" Luke looked around. Even obscured by the night, he couldn't figure how tracks were making their way through the thick foliage.

"This line doesn't use steel or coal, but it helps folks pass through the land a little quicker than you might imagine, not to mention its value in seclusion," she said. "We call it the Underground Railroad. Out here, only a few of us are privy to its access points. You enter it and don't know the routes, you're liable to get lost inside for a long, long time."

Crickets chirped and owls hooted, and not far off a wolf howled, followed by another. Harriet licked a thin finger to the wind, then turned slowly in most of a circle, closed her eyes, opened them, and said, "There."

She led him to a thicket of trees grown so close together that their branches formed a wall solid as brick. She followed the wall, tracing her finger along its spired boughs and woven limbs, and a faint blue spark of electricity followed at her touch.

"It helps with the conductivity," she said. "Licking your finger."

Harriet worked her way along her own path, slipping through invisible hollows in the arboreal barrier, knocking on a knobby oak here or a crooked pine there, until she stopped inside a gloomy rift. A bit more of that blue electricity snapped at her finger. It reminded Luke of the sparks that flared when a train's steel wheels braked hard on the rails.

"Here it is," she said.

Luke followed her inside and the sounds he'd heard before entering the wall of trees became muffled, now just whispers of the crickets, the owls, the wolves, as if he went into another room and everything else was locked out on the other side. Even the moon appeared more distant. It hung in the same place but was dimmed, seen through a shroud.

They continued through the tree corridor, each shape and shadow appearing like a pattern, repeating itself impossibly every few steps. If they weren't walking in a straight line, Luke would have sworn they were going in a very small circle. Then again, didn't everyone who walked in circles think they were moving in a straight line?

"Mrs. Tubman," Luke asked quietly, "where are we?"

"Just Harriet is fine," she replied. As they trod on, she ran her finger along the trees and, wherever she touched, a fading blue electric line was left behind like a lazy, trailing bolt of lightning. Occasionally she'd pause and lick again at her finger. "And answering where we are, depends. If you were looking for an X on the map, I'd say we were outside Greencastle, Indiana. I suppose, though, you're wondering where you are that you can talk to me and others you've only heard about in history books, but not anyone alive."

"That indeed."

"What's your name, young man?"

Luke flushed, embarrassed that she'd introduced herself and he hadn't returned the courtesy. She had, after all, saved him from a bullet in the head like John or, he considered, something much worse that he couldn't yet discern. "Luke Thacker."

"Luke Thacker," she said, "you ever wonder about Heaven and Hell or whatever else may occur once you head six feet under?"

"Sure, sometimes. I guess we all do."

"I wonder about it often, more and more." Her voice fell softly with each word she spoke. "And I question why I'm here and better folks ain't, and what comes after this, and what happens to the rest of them."

She looked back to Luke and, even through the gloom, he saw her face. It had a scholarly conviction to it, the way he'd imagine a teacher might appear, ready to unravel the mysteries of writing or arithmetic; but there was also a sad resignation, as if she bore the cross of the world and her knees were beginning to ache.

"We're in the *deadeye*. The state of collective memory."

Luke didn't say anything, didn't have to. She seemed to know his brain was scratching itself. She let him contemplate, then continued.

"Some of the more learned minds here have pondered this, and I've got my own say: Life is wholly connected, just not in ways you understand. We're all related, regardless who you believe we came from. Be it Adam and Eve or fish with feet, we're cousins. This great cycle of life winds through each thing, which means we're pretty much the same."

Harriet spoke while she walked. Luke nodded along, processing what she explained, satisfied he was—so far—able to keep up. Fact was, Luke was accustomed to hearing all sorts of nutty philosophies, accusations, and even bald-faced lies, as one who spent life among populations who drank more whiskey than water, or suffered illness of the mind that spun claims of persecution or out-of-world ordeals. He knew from experience never to interrupt, with disbelief or disinterest, someone in the throes of rationalizing their existence; everyone had their own religion.

Then again, if she was to be believed, this *was* Harriet Tubman, and he supposed Harriet Tubman wasn't sunk to the same low class of his generally-kept company. She went on.

"What life is, how it ties together, is just one great entity. Our lives are the parts of another life. And that's where you are, in part of another life. We call this place, this state of deadeye, *Athanasia*."

"I'm inside another life?" Luke repeated dumbly. "You're saying Athanasia is, what . . . a thing, a brain?"

"Not quite. What I said about the state of collective memory, we figure it as a shared consciousness, which is how we're all connected. Everything passes through here a time, but that amount of time is different for each. Maybe a few seconds, maybe a few centuries. Maybe longer than you and I can comprehend."

The whole affair sounded utterly asinine, which caused Luke to flush more at what he said next. His voice came out in a low, stilted tone, as if someone else had forced the doubting words across his tongue. For even after all she'd said, all Dillinger had said, all his experiences since the water tower, Luke still couldn't entirely grasp whom, or what, he spoke with. "Um, John Dillinger said the same thing, that he wasn't a ghost but a memory. So all of you are just . . . recollections?"

"Now you're gettin' it. We can mingle with the living, but we're insubstantial, just this wispy trace of our old selves."

Luke nodded more out of reflex than affirmation.

"But more important," Harriet continued, "is that here, the greater an impact you left on the memory of those alive, the stronger you are."

"Oh. So it's only, what, famous people kept around?"

"Honey, it's a cutthroat world. Not everyone can be remembered a long, long time. Some folks done big things in their days, but they're forgotten right off. Other folks, it seems unfair they've gotten popular over the years. If you want to be kept in mind, you've got to keep giving people something to remember you by."

Luke looked down at his feet, watching them move one after the other, following this old woman. There was strange comfort in studying the rhythm of his own steady ambulation, as humdrum as that was. But it was something he was familiar with, something he knew well, the act of walking. And that was exactly opposite of the notions Harriet put forth.

She seemed to understand. "It's a lot to take in, but you'll figure it out with time. If you want to, that is."

Luke pursed his lips and thought a moment, and he was again struck by the repeating patterns the trees made around him, like the stenciled motif of a quilt. There was so much more he did—yet did not—want to know, and finally he said, "I've seen some horrible things. A cow, a man, eaten up by . . . something. Red dots in the air, and they vanish when they're done devouring, and the world seems, I don't know, somehow *changed*."

"The world *is* changed, Luke Thacker, and every moment it's changing more. It's changed by what's forgotten, by what no longer matters. What you seen are the *pox*, the regulators around here. When something ain't got enough sway to be cared about any longer, the pox come along and pluck it from our consciousness. They digest it."

Luke grimaced. "Sounds like a disease, pox. Can they be stopped?"

"You ever heard of an amoeba?"

"Not likely."

"Amoebas are these tiny blobs, shapeless and smaller'n you can see. They're in our bodies, in nature, everywhere. They carry out the process of decomposition, which here is eating the unmemorable." She cleared her throat and nodded. "It sounds atrocious, and it is, and it's a process that ain't stopped for nothing nor nobody.

"Just like waiting to die while you're alive, the pox is our fate here in Athanasia. All we can do is put it off each day, and make the most with the time we're allotted."

Luke realized he had his arms wrapped around himself, squeezing tighter, so his breaths came harder. He tried to relax. "And then what? What happens after you're *eaten* by those things? After you've already died once before?"

"I don't know. No one knows, 'til it happens to them. Maybe you end up in another memory world, maybe you're gone forever. Maybe God finally takes you in. Maybe you're reborn. A thousand maybes and not a single surety. But ain't that all of life?"

Luke didn't have anything else to say, and found himself struck dumb in silence.

Harriet stopped, licked her finger again, rustled around a few trees, then pushed up a limb. "We're here."

She stepped through, and he followed. Outside the tree wall was an orange field, made all the more orange by the rising sun. A railroad track ran parallel to the woodland, raised on gravel ballast about twenty feet away. Opposite the track, sitting in that orange field, stood a small abandoned shed, roofed by uneven planks set at a single pitch. The building looked built for storage, and once might have been filled with coal or firewood. Now it was wide open as a parking lot. The door had fallen off its frame, and Luke could see the sky shining through the shed's rotted back side.

Painted on the roof was the same blue symbol of an open doorway he'd seen on the water tower.

"Just head on through," Harriet said. "I know this ain't where you came in, but it'll get you back where you belong. You'll be somewhere around Kansas City."

"Kansas City?" Luke repeated. "That's over four hundred miles from where we started."

"I told you the railroad helps folks pass across quicker than you might imagine."

He stammered.

"Just go with it," she said.

"Thank you."

Her frown didn't budge, but Luke thought she was smiling. "You get stuck here again, just ask for me. Everyone knows Harriet Tubman."

He thanked her again and began to walk away, following the tracks to the shed. She called after him.

"And Luke Thacker, you ever need to return, just look for this." She traced her finger through the air like drawing on a chalkboard, leaving upon its ethereal surface a shimmering light blue trail. The afterglow shone bright for only a moment before vanishing, but it was enough. He recognized that symbol he'd seen, painted on the derrick before he'd reached the water tower: *a numeral eight, laid on its side*. "The mark of infinity," Harriet said. "The sign of Athanasia."

She turned and slid back into the forest, returning to her own railroad.

LUKE AND ZEKE, 1934

Luke walked inside the shed and looked through the rotted opening in the back wall, not noticing anything to be changed. As with the water tower, there was the symbol of a blue happy face, this one painted over the wall's hole. He turned and went back the way he'd come, just to make sure it compared the same. *Yup*. From within the shed, looking out one way and then the other, each showed the world was turning, and whether he was a regular part of it or not apparently made no difference.

Luke took the matter on faith and exited through the back side. It wasn't long before he heard the distant whistle of a train a-comin'.

At least there was that; his feet would get some relief.

He waited in a shallow ravine full of pink gravel, out of sight, until the train began roaring past, bucking and snorting and rocking side-to-side like a wild iron stallion. The boiler's billowing smoke was its panting breath, and the whistle its shrill whinny. The engine, then a tanker, then a couple dozen carriages and flatbeds stacked with murdered logs. Luke preferred going as far back into the train's procession as he could, though of course there was always the risk that if he let too many cars pass by, the remaining ones would be locked up tight, and he'd be left with nothing but a wish and a long walk.

He tightened the torn rucksack over his back and started running alongside the rails. The Southern Pacific logo passed him again and again, its letters a white smear through the air. Already the train was slowing, as it came to a bend around hills before shooting out across a high bridge. Luke was sprinting now, and the next boxcar that sidled alongside had a door that was partway open, as if it'd been waiting for him. He grabbed a ladder rung with one hand and jumped into the air. This was the tricky part; he had to catch the rung with his other hand too, otherwise he'd go flying in the breeze like a flag on a windy day.

Luke caught hold and climbed up, swinging his legs onto the bottom rung. He reached over and pushed the sliding freight door farther open along its track, then climbed inside. There was always a moment of fear when he entered a car. One never knew who—or *what*—was already in occupancy. There were more times than he liked to remember of coming upon territorial 'bos who didn't want some hayseed boy sharing the same air as them or, worse, men who smiled at him like a grinning wolf facing a fat lamb, then stuck a knife under his chin and stole whatever he carried, before sending him flying back out the door with a boot print on his ass.

Today there was only one man already inside the car, though he was sized as three.

Luke squatted inside the doorframe a moment, getting his legs accustomed to the train's sways, getting a sense for the giant man. Luke nodded to him and spoke flat. "Howdy, 'bo."

The man didn't reply, just farted and re-pillowed a folded bandana under his head.

All transients shared the same greeting, letting one know he counted himself among their number. At the lack of response, Luke felt a gloom surround him, wondering if Harriet hadn't set him free at all. Did the man know he was there, or was Luke still moving through Athanasia? Normally he preferred being overlooked, but facing the prospect of that forever set his skin to crawling.

Luke repeated, "Said howdy, 'bo."

Still nothing. The giant man's skin was a shade darker than coal, and his hulking body strained the stitches of a patchwork suit that looked older than its wearer. Most 'bos tended to situate themselves against a boxcar's farthest wall for protection from others and also out of railroad dicks' eyesight if the door suddenly rolled open while they were asleep. This man lay dead center in the car, as if he owned it and was allowing the train the luxury of carting him around.

The man's eyes flicked up, but Luke couldn't tell if the 'bo was looking at him or through him and out the door. Luke changed his mind, deciding he'd rather not be noticed.

Luke moved cautiously from the door, keeping plenty of room between them. There were some crumpled newspapers and loose straw that smelled like they were used to soak up urine and dead stinkbugs.

He sat down and unslung his rucksack and tried to get comfortable. The wood floor creaked and the wind sang his name up through its cracks and empty bolt holes. Luke felt satisfied when back on trains, a certain peace the way he imagined city folks felt after working in the factory and coming home to sit on a favorite couch with their wife and a herd of children. He'd just have to find another way to escape Athanasia—

"You didn't close the door," the man said, startling Luke. He sounded irritated, like he was looking for someone to take out a misery on.

Least that settled where he was. "Door was already open 'fore I got on."

"You opened it more. I had it open the way I like it."

Luke wished he hadn't even started conversation by telling the man "howdy." He got up and fixed the door so it was partway open like how he first saw it. He kept the man in sight while he walked past. By the time he'd returned to his spot, the man had sat up.

"What's your name, boy?"

"Luke."

"Like the Bible?"

"Sorta. Not the New-Gospel-Luke you're thinking, but short for Lucas." He paused for an awkward silence, then felt obligated to continue. "My momma thought Lucas was a biblical name, though there's not much holy reference to it."

"It don't matter. You ain't no Lucas or Luke from a Bible. Bible names are powerful people, leaders, prophets. A real Luke or Lucas would know manners enough to close a door when he comes in."

Luke didn't reply, sensing more and more the man was just looking for a quarrel, a reason to pummel some sap's face because life had slighted him with current circumstances.

Sometimes, Luke thought, *it's better just to stay silent and let a man talk himself down from a crisis.* Anything he said could be construed as an insult, even if he remarked that a warthog sure had warts.

"How old are you?" the man asked.

"Older'n I look."

The man nodded that answer was good enough, then sat there silently, staring off into space. Ten minutes later Luke began to relax, and the train's peace returned. Abruptly the man picked up their conversation, and the peace shot away like a spooked hare.

"My name's Zeke, in case you were 'bout to ask."

Luke hadn't been. "Nice to meet you."

"I've got a biblical name, too," Zeke said. Then he whispered conspiratorially behind a raised hand. "It's really Ezekiel."

Zeke's chin was stubbled with black whiskers thick as a patch of burrs, and he rubbed at it in thought. "Why do parents give their kids Bible names?" He sounded genuinely perplexed. "It don't do you any favors. It ain't a free ride into heaven. They're just character names like in a picture book."

"I suppose my momma thought it'd be a nice sentiment."

"It don't make sense!" Zeke shouted.

Luke startled, scared again that the giant was just looking for a reason to turn on him. He couldn't figure out where Zeke was going with this conversation, but soon enough the man lost interest and pulled at a splinter in the floor, contemplating something fascinating in its existence that Luke couldn't perceive.

Luke wished he were in a different boxcar and clasped his rucksack tight against him.

Zeke saw the sack, and his rough face turned excited, like a child wanting to know what's inside a brightly wrapped candy box. "What you got in there?"

"Not much. Extra shirt, a piece of soap, a belt—"

"What kind of belt?"

"Just one dried from elk hide. It doesn't fit me anymore, but my momma gave it to me on my sixth birthday. I don't have much else of her but memories."

"Elk, huh? Let's fry it up. I've got a bit of Tabasco sauce a bald woman traded me for a rock. I told her the rock was magic and would grow her hair back." Zeke laughed, a short series of grunts like the dying engine of a flatbed truck.

"Fry up my belt?"

"Your ears built backward, boy? What else we got to eat in here 'sides your skinny ass?"

Luke frightened at that and scooted backward, like a crab in reverse. He didn't know what that statement meant, nor was he of mind to ask clarification. Zeke's crazy tone was enough to warn him to get away.

"Meat is meat," Zeke added, eyes narrowing.

The elk or his ass? Luke's muscles clenched tight. He wasn't a quarter the size of the other man, but a rush of thoughts clamored through his mind, inventorying what he could use as a weapon: his small pocket knife;

a piece of broken green glass lying on the floor; his teeth; his fingers, driven into Zeke's eyes. He'd have to move quick, one strike and leap out the car door faster than a greased hen. If Zeke caught him, there was no telling what grief he might endure.

"What's the matter with you?" Zeke asked. His lip curled up. "I offer you my 'basco sauce and you want to keep that belt all to yourself?"

"I'm not eating my belt."

Zeke's voice roared like a gale wind. "What are you, fucking royalty? Then why don't you go home to the goddamn Ritz!"

Luke's heart thudded louder than the clattering steel wheels beneath him. His muscles clenched tighter, so much he began to shake. He pulled the dull, nicked knife from his pocket, holding it extended from his fist like a small bayonet.

"You know how hard it is to get good 'basco sauce?" Zeke asked. "And you, sitting there with a piece of elk. I haven't eaten anything but grass for four days. Grass and sauce."

Zeke was silent for half a minute. When he spoke again his voice fell quiet like a grizzly bear that growls from a far distance, warning it could charge at any moment. "I oughta whup your ass, just 'cause I can."

Luke slid as far back as possible, until he felt the car's cold metal wall at his back, and even then kept trying to push farther, hoping the wall would somehow open up and he'd fall out safe on the other side.

Zeke kicked a pile of muddy straw with an enormous boot. Luke had seen moose that weren't as large as that footwear. "And maybe I will," Zeke continued. "Then just *take* what I want. Who'd stop me? You?"

Zeke laughed again, the dying truck sound. "You know what else I could take? A new life. That rucksack, your extra shirt, a piece of soap . . . maybe that'd let me live at the goddamn Ritz too, I'll pretend I'm you."

"Stay away," Luke said. He slid sideways along the metal wall, but then hit another. He was in the corner.

"I could," Zeke said. "But I wouldn't."

Zeke slumped at that, and all the disdain and gruff sloughed off, as if a wind had come along and blown the leaves of discontent off his branches. He muttered, then looked away, then sighed and kicked at the straw again, but only because there was nothing else for him to do. Zeke's thick legs were splayed in front of him and he bent over them, running ragged fingers across the floor as if looking for another splinter to contemplate.

He squinted, and his tone returned to the distant grizzly bear just so Luke wouldn't mistake any clemency as goodwill. "I *could* if I wanted . . . "

Luke sensed he might be able to relax, but his body wouldn't comply. His muscles were still tight and trembling. Zeke's emotions were muddier than a river of dung, and Luke couldn't gauge which way that current might turn.

As if to affirm his indecision, Zeke roared again. "Shit, kid. All I want is something to eat." He fumbled through his pockets and pulled out a smooth gray rock. "You believe in magic? I'll trade you this for that elk!"

Luke gulped. "Listen, I got a few soda crackers you can have. It's not much, but I ate some already this morning."

Zeke's face melted. "Soda crackers? Honest to Moses?"

"Sure. I'm not really that hungry." Luke *was* hungry, but if a few crackers could get him free, that was a toll he'd pay any day.

"I ain't tasted soda crackers since . . . " Zeke scrunched up his face in thought. "Since Amarillo." He rolled over to his hands and knees like a puppy about to spring. "I was just a tot in Amarillo, y'know."

A clattering bang sounded, and the train shook and began to slow.

"Shitfire," Zeke muttered. "It's too soon for Topeka."

Steel wheels squealed in a leisurely yawn, drawn-out and weary. Zeke crept to the part-open door and peered outside. From the far corner, Luke saw the sky had turned an ugly crosscurrent of gray and brown, and dust hung in the air as if blooming off the stalks of witchgrass and woolly sedge.

A city rose in the distance, but it appeared the train had stopped short. There sounded distant shouts and then a gunshot.

"It's a raid," Zeke muttered softly. "The bulls are lookin' for riders."

He glanced back at Luke, still clutching his rucksack. "Better run like an Injun, boy. The S.P. bulls out here got a mean streak wider than the Mississippi."

Zeke slid the door all the way open, ready to leap.

But it was too late. A railroad bull was already standing on the other side, pistol in one hand and a blackjack in the other. He wore the regular clothes of a workman—dirty trousers and a frayed shirt—but with an old army jacket pulled over it. The man's face looked cruel, wrinkled from malice and scarred by lifelong displeasure.

"Get the fuck outta there," he bellowed.

Zeke climbed down immediately, head hung low and shoulders slumped like a whipped hound. Was the complacency forced, overly resigned for show? Or maybe that was the real Zeke, hid under a veneer, all cracked and peeling.

"Please, sir. I didn't mean nothing by it," Zeke said. He shuffled his feet, leaning from one side to the other, and looked down at the ground as if it were the most interesting thing he'd ever seen. "I never rode a train before. Just this once, to find work."

"You too," the bull said, seeing Luke. "Line up."

Luke scrambled out and landed next to Zeke.

"What's that in your hand? A nail?" the bull asked.

All three of them looked. Luke forgot he'd been clenching the little knife. He opened his fingers and it fell to the dirt.

A voice called out. "How many you got down there, Thomas?"

"Just two," the bull replied.

The dust thinned enough to see more bulls near the front of the train and a handful of other 'bos. The brakeman was there also, dressed in indigo and white pinstripes. "This is railroad property," he shouted down the line. His voice was high-pitched and raspy.

Another bull walked past, dragging by the feet a skinny man with hair as long and white as a sheet of snow. Luke couldn't tell if the dragged man was drunk or dead or just beat up.

On each side of the jointed track sloped a couple feet of packed earth and gravel. Beyond that, prairie land stretched to each horizon, filled with grass that was taller than most men, all of it in different shades of yellow. The land seemed to tilt slightly, the grass swaying to one side under a creaking wind.

One of the 'bos broke from the group and ran suddenly into the prairie grass. His head bobbed, then he ducked down and vanished.

"Stop!" a front-end bull shouted, firing a gunshot in the air.

A half-dozen more 'bos turned and ran the other way into the tall grass. The front-end bulls cursed and chased them, veering off in different directions. Five tramps were left behind, huddled and shrugging their shoulders like a brood of hens. The brakeman apparently didn't like the odds of standing alone in the open against them. He hot-footed it back into the engine and slammed the compartment door shut. The tramps glanced down the rail toward Zeke and Luke and the bull with them, then dispersed into the open land, looking for shelter from the dust, most likely to just wait for the next slow-moving train to come along.

"Got any money?" Thomas the bull asked Zeke and Luke.

"No, sir, not one red cent," Zeke said.

Luke just shook his head.

"This is for riding our train," Thomas said, and the blackjack whistled through the air in a short arc, cracking the side of Zeke's head. He groaned and fell to one knee.

Thomas kicked him in the ribs with a cowboy boot so pointed at the toe it could have been used as a pool cue. "Now get the fuck gone."

"Yes, sir," Zeke said. He stood and fast-walked away into the prairie without looking back.

Thomas then swung the blackjack against Luke, and Luke felt his head twist in a circle. He sank to the dirt while a rainbow of flashes burst all around. Another gunshot cracked from far away, and its sound echoed inside his skull.

"You're a purty thing, ain't you?" Thomas said and licked his lips with a dry tongue. "Maybe you can *earn* your ride."

Thomas looked around and saw there was no one else, then holstered the pistol to one side of his belt and the blackjack to the other.

"Back inside." Thomas hauled Luke up by the rear of his collar and shoved him toward the boxcar. Luke's rucksack lay spilled aside the tracks. "Them others gonna be gone a few minutes, I suppose. That's all the time I need."

"Lemme go," Luke said without much conviction. He knew a man with a gun was a man who could do as he pleased.

Thomas replied by boxing him in the back of the head. "Move."

The open boxcar loomed before him, and its interior had somehow turned darker than when Luke was inside only moments earlier. Luke dragged his steps, feeling for an opportunity to feint to the side and bolt.

"I said move!" Thomas struck him from behind again, harder this time, and Luke was knocked forward. His forehead slammed against the steel carriage, and he ricocheted back and fell, everything turning fuzzy the way it did after he'd drunk too much hooch.

He looked up to Thomas and saw a black shape rise behind, seeming to unfurl like a billowing wraith. Luke's vision focused, and the wraith was Zeke with his arms stretched high. Zeke brought his fist down on the top of Thomas's head, as if he were hammering upon the top of a railroad spike. That was the sound it made, too, just a dull *whack* and a ringing echo. The bull made a kind of chewing-snoring noise and his eyes spun in different directions like pennies rolling down a drain. Zeke hit him again, and Thomas the bull was done. He crumpled to the dirt and his body convulsed twice.

Zeke opened his fist to show the smooth gray rock. "I told you this was magic."

Then Zeke turned and stomped on Thomas's head, screaming, "Fuck you, rat putz, baboon cock, dingle-sucking bastard, piece of dung, useless dumb-dumb shit head."

He stomped on Thomas's skull again and again. A pair of teeth popped out like little fireworks arching into the sky. Something cracked, the sound of a burst pipe.

Luke rolled away, his stomach quivering, all his senses telling him to flee. But his body wouldn't comply. It took complete will just to stand. Zeke eyed him, then eyed the spilled rucksack. A mottled soda cracker lay in the dirt, broke in half. Another cracker was spattered with blood and wore a piece of spongy gray mass like a miniature top hat.

"Well, hell," Zeke said. "Get your things, we got to hurry. Those bulls see what I done, we're cooked. Both of us."

Luke didn't move, unsure with whom the worst choice would be: the unhinged giant or the railroad police. Zeke cursed and gathered up the rucksack for him, tossing it over a shoulder.

"My brain must be rattlin'. All this for some crackers," Zeke said. He picked up Luke and tossed him over his other shoulder. "Christ, please, I hope Smith McCain's not around."

SMITH MCCAIN, 1830

The first American train and track was built in 1825 by wealthy inventor Colonel John Stevens, to carry passengers around his enormous estate in Hoboken, New Jersey. Having already enough money to last countless generations, he didn't care to capitalize on that engineering feat, but left the realization of commercial railroads to the lofty ambitions of others.

In 1827, the Baltimore and Ohio Railroad became the country's first common railroad carrier, growing out of seaport competition amongst elite industrialists. The B&O began to schedule freight and passenger service between New York and Illinois, although due to legalities and logistics, it didn't really start travelling much distance until after 1830.

The first railroad track was only thirteen miles long, and the *Tom Thumb* was the first American-built steam locomotive to operate on this trackage. The *Tom Thumb* was manufactured by philanthropist Peter Cooper to move material for an ironworks between Baltimore Harbor and the city. On its inaugural trek, the machine raced a horse to prove its worth. Such is technology today that the engine was beating the horse in speed and efficiency, so promising the end of manual laboring woes, until a single component broke at the most inopportune moment and brought the whole contraption to a dead halt.

The horse won.

There were crowds all along the track that day, August 28, 1830. Later, the second time *Tom Thumb* ran the length of that thirteen-mile line, its novelty had worn off, and there were no longer eyes watching at every crosstie. A drifter, Elias Branson, was walking the hard earth, desiring that he didn't have to set one sore foot in front of the other any longer on his journey into Baltimore. When the *Tom Thumb* came barreling along, he saw opportunity for fulfillment of this simple wish and hopped aboard the rear car, enjoying his apparent upswing in good fortune.

The engine steamed into its destination, and an employee of Peter Cooper saw Elias Branson—now the first documented train hopper—hanging onto its back handrail, most obviously without any sort of permission, whether express, implied, or otherwise. Not cottoning to someone getting a ride for free, when he himself had to labor long hours for every measly necessity of existence, this employee took a piece of stove wood and brained Elias across the head as soon as he was able.

The employee was Smith McCain, and he became the nation's first railroad bull.

LUKE AND ZEKE, 1934, CONTINUED

Luke wondered if he should run, just turn and sprint for all he was worth, put a couple states' distance between himself and Zeke. But he didn't know where he was, and if Zeke wanted to, Luke was sure he could catch him fast as a thorn on wool. Plus, the giant 'bo *had* rescued him . . .

"Thank you," Luke announced suddenly, breaking their silence. "For helping me."

"I'm tired of seeing death," Zeke replied. "It's all around me."

Luke nodded, hoping that statement wasn't too literal. His forehead dripped, and when he wiped at it, his sleeve came away red. The back of his head dripped too. He bled from both places, and the aches there were monstrous marbles ricocheting against his brain with each step.

"Death," Zeke continued. "Men *and* women."

Luke didn't care to hear any more about death just then, but sensed Zeke was going to continue regardless.

"Can you believe I seen a famous actress kill herself one time? Her name was Peggy Entwistle, and she jumped off the big letter 'H' from the sign that says *Hollywoodland*. A real actress, in movies and everything, and killed herself. A looker, too."

Luke opened his mouth to reply, but Zeke didn't let him.

"Don't stop walkin'. I dunno where we are. We gotta make cover or distance." Then he repeated quietly, "A real actress in movies. She had everything . . . "

Two hours had passed since they'd fled the train, and Luke hadn't spoken 'til he'd said that "Thank you." The only conversation before those words had been one-sided. Zeke told him, "Keep your mouth shut and feet following mine."

They crossed patchwork ground that swapped between wild prairie and cultivated farmland, skirting the city, which Zeke muttered at more than once. "Could be Wellsville, could be Baldwin . . . "

Since Thomas the bull, they'd not seen anyone and, with hope, nobody had seen them.

Abruptly, Zeke stopped.

"What's the matter?" Luke asked.

"Somethin' in my shoe." He sat and pulled off a boot. A brown pebble rolled out. Zeke stayed sitting. He dropped his huge head between huger arms. He cleared his throat. "It happened to me, you know."

Luke didn't know. He waited. Zeke's shoulders were wide as the yoke spanning two oxen, and those shoulders slumped low. Then Zeke trembled, cursed, looked up, then down, and finally continued.

"I was only a little tot, didn't know which hand to crap in. An old man stuck his cock in every hole of my body. His face was scratched up and he smelled like blackberries, and I knew he'd been watching me from the wild brambles that grew along our fields. Watching . . . just waiting for his moment when I was alone."

Zeke looked at the dirt as he spoke, rather than at Luke. "Now, I ever find a man doing that to someone, I kill him. Done it before and I'll do it again."

"I'm sorry that happened, Zeke."

"What the fuck do you know?" He pounded the earth like a piston, again and again, until it gave way and a hole was bored into the ground.

"A man done that to me, too," Luke said. "I swore I'd never let it happen again . . . but I couldn't have stopped it. You did. You saved me."

Zeke's face turned upward, and his anger and scorn were gone. Instead his appearance was soft and expressionless, as if asleep in a comfortable bed. Twin scars ran across each of his temples, and to Luke they looked strangely graceful and delicate, like the threads holding together the face of a doll.

Zeke was a giant damaged rag child.

"Fuck the railroad police," he said. Then he rose and walked on, and Luke followed. They didn't say anything else for awhile. Eventually they circled the unknown city until they came to a line of warehouses, made of aluminum but no longer that color, instead tarnished bronze and streaked turquoise by years under the sun and wind and frost.

Luke's head still bled, and he realized he'd been absentmindedly wiping it, as if mopping off sweat, only the sweat was crimson. "That's a lot of blood," he said. "It won't stop coming out of me."

"You're just trickling. It ain't bad."

Trickling for two hours ain't good either, Luke thought. He suddenly felt wearier than ever in his life, not to mention hungry and dizzy and aching.

"Wait," Luke said. "I've got a pebble now in *my* shoe."

But when he sat, he didn't take off his boots. Darkness fell before his eyes in an instant, and Zeke caught him as he slumped over the edge of sweet somnolence.

LUKE AND DAISY, 1934

When Luke passed out, the improbable safety found in Zeke's arms provided comfort. It'd been a rough day, even by hobo standards. Getting shot at, beat up, and cavorting with ghosts tends to sap the strength from any man.

The night was late when he woke, but the small camp around him shone in cheerful vagabond sociability. Around a dying fire pit in various postures of slouch were a dozen men, women, and others who could pass for either, picking their teeth and rubbing their bellies. Luke shifted and saw his old rucksack had been returned; he'd been lying on it as a pillow. The little nicked knife was pushed under his arm. Zeke was beside him, wearing an open jacket and shirtless underneath.

He handed Luke two soda crackers. "Saved you some. I wouldn't eat them all."

"Thanks," Luke said. His voice came out hoarse and slow. He worked his tongue around his mouth, feeling like he'd swallowed flame and spit out ash.

"Saved you a couple other things, too. We had us a feast tonight." Zeke pushed to him a dented tin bowl with two hunks of cooked meat that were bloody-red on one side and charcoal-black on the other, and a matching tin cup filled with pond water. He pointed to a stack of pink apples on the ground and smiled broadly. "Apple orchard back yonder, overrun with slow-moving gophers."

One of the campfire 'bos laughed with a wheeze, sounding like a man having a stroke. Luke took a drink of the pond water and felt better—though not by much—and examined the group. The lot of them were dressed in old clothes crusted in mud or grease, and most of them were frail and wrinkled, even the younger ones. One man was fat, which was a rare thing to see among transients. Two women muttered to each other, one of them turned away from him. The woman he could see was one-eyed and toothless, but that hadn't stopped her from dolling herself up with lipstick and rouge so bright her cheeks looked like a couple of red checkers. She saw Luke looking and winked at him with her good eye while running a finger down the musty crack that some people might consider cleavage.

The other woman turned to see what the first was winking at and Luke froze suddenly, unsure what to do. She wore a cowl over her head, but by the firelight Luke could tell she wasn't really old enough to be called a woman, though she wasn't young as a girl either. Nor was her face covered in the grime and ill will that despondency on the road brought to most other rail riders. She was, in fact and against all reason, one of the prettiest gals Luke had ever seen in his life, sitting across from him in a homeless camp, lauding their feast of gopher. He tried to look away, to not stare, but the part of him that froze wouldn't comply; it seemed an offense to turn his eyes, disregarding something so beautiful growing in these backwoods of despair.

"Howdy," he mumbled and nodded.

"You all right?" she replied, touching her head.

Her voice sounded like a pale buttercup opening its petals to the dawning sun. Luke considered that pale buttercups didn't make much sound, but at that moment nothing else seemed to compare as appropriately. He touched his own head in reflex to her movement and felt a cloth wrapped around like a headdress. It was damp, and when he brought his hand back down, there were flakes of dried blood on his fingertips.

"My shirt," Zeke said. His voice turned serious, like when Luke first met him. "You owe me a new one."

The wheezing man laughed again, a second stroke.

"Ain't funny," Zeke said. "I wore that shirt for two years, and never got any blood on it but my own. That's some bad juju to wear another man's blood."

The wheezing man didn't stop laughing until a greasy wreck next to him said to *shaddup* and punched him in the ear.

"So what happened?" the fat man asked Luke. "Look like you fell face-first off a mountain."

Luke thought how to answer, then smiled and told the truth. "Would you believe I robbed a bank with John Dillinger?"

"*Whoo-whee*," someone shouted. "Sure beats pickin' corn."

Others concurred, until a hobo as withered as a tumbleweed made a guffaw. "That's some crossbuck you're building," he accused. "Dillinger got his self killed last month."

"Not Dillinger?" Zeke asked.

"Sure 'nuff, it was in the papers."

"Can't read."

"Me neither, but I saw it in the headlines I crapped on. Saw a photo of it anyway . . . showed his corpse laid out on the mortician's table. You know, Dillinger's johnson must've been a foot long, way it jutted up in that pic."

'Bo voices muttered, "Don't say?"

"Dillinger lived a full life, all right," someone added.

"Thought he'd never go down."

They murmured agreement and took a moment to reflect.

"Name's Fat Willie," the fat man said to Luke, changing conversation.

Each of the 'bos sounded off their names all at the same time, so Luke couldn't make out most. A couple others had "Willie" thrown in their monikers, and the one-eyed woman was Willie Mae. The girl that made him freeze called herself Daisy Rose.

Luke said his own name and that it was nice to make all their acquaintances. "By the by, I've been ridin' rails a long time, but what's that mean I was 'building a crossbuck'?"

"You never heard that old saw?" Willie Mae asked.

"It's those railroad signs warning where the tracks cut through a road," Fat Willie answered.

"Sure, the crossing sign, I know that's a crossbuck. But what's it to do with me?"

"It's also what's called the crossing of fact and fib. One part's truth and the other's big talk, and I called a warning on you, your crossbuck was gettin' big."

Luke chuckled. *If only they knew . . .*

The wheezing man pulled out a Jew's harp and started playing slow. The rattle of his breath accompanied each off-note, but the others didn't seem to mind.

"Zeke was tellin' us how you came to be here," one in the group said.

Luke nodded.

"Where you headin' now?" Fat Willie asked.

"Anywhere."

"Same as us. But where you planning to escape?"

"Escape?"

"You need a fugitive's hideaway or something. Ain't you bein' chased?"

Luke thought of the Earp brothers. Had that been real, and would these people believe it? He shook his head. "Naw, I'm just travellin'."

"Hope you travel like yo' britches are on fire." This came from a man who appeared not to be a stranger to having parts of himself aflame. Pieces of his skin bubbled and peeled off his face and hands in disturbing colors.

"I'm in no rush," Luke said.

The burnt man exchanged glances with Zeke, who dropped his head.

"It don't matter anyway," said another 'bo, this one reclining on a blanket of dirt. He was dressed in a simple bedsheet with holes cut out for the head and arms, and his naked legs stuck out the bottom, enjoying the weather. His head was adorned with a tailed cap that once may have been a squirrel, but now was so mangy it looked like their cooked gopher. "Fast or slow, if McCain's after you, he's gonna get you. Best to hide, in my opinion . . . " His voice trailed off ominously, and then he added, as if an afterthought, "But not in the shadows. Stay away from those."

"Where's he supposed to hide then? Underwater?"

"Just sayin'."

"Next time say something that makes sense."

"How could this McCain even find one of us?" Willie Mae asked. "Not like we have forwarding addresses. McCain's just a man, lazy as most."

"Hell he is," Fat Willie replied. "McCain's a demon sure as I'll be shittin' gopher teeth in ten minutes."

"S'right. McCain is bigger than any man can grow, sized like a mountain, and cruel as Lucifer himself," another 'bo said.

"And he's black," Fat Willie added. "I don't mean he's dark-skinned like Zeke, but he's black as night all over, with a cold stony face, looking like that Liberty statue if it were carved from coal, lost its majesty, and grew a beard."

"Yup, you'll sure know when you see him," the burnt man said to Luke.

"What're you talking about?" Luke replied, "Who is this McCain, and why should I care?"

The camp turned silent but for dismayed gasps echoing through the night. He glanced around; Zeke appeared nervous, and Fat Willie was agitated, and Daisy looked . . . pretty. She looked just too pretty to be anything but a fever dream or a midnight fantasy. He knew hers was the kind of appearance that could cause him to do things he normally wouldn't; common sense skips out the door when the heart begins to flutter. Daisy's skin was the light brown of soft loam, and her eyes were brilliant jewels colored as wet azure.

The wheezing man stopped playing his Jew's harp, repeating Luke's question with a fluster. "Why should you be worried about McCain?"

Fat Willie leaned forward. "McCain's the bull of all bulls. You get caught riding the rails by him, and you'll be lucky if you still got half your teeth left afterward."

"Weren't you the one tellin' me about a crossbuck?" Luke asked.

"You were talkin' up Dillinger, and everyone knows he's dead," Fat Willie answered. "McCain ain't no crossbuck at all."

"You done killed a railroad dick," someone broke in. "McCain don't cotton to that. He'll hunt you."

The summer night was warm as a harlot's bed, but Luke turned cold. "I didn't kill anyone."

"Zeke might have done it, but you're a part. The bull had kin in law, and there's always someone who's gotta take a fall in that case, whether it's deserved or not."

"How'd you hear that?"

"Now, boy," Fat Willie said. "When you're land-living, such word travels fast as yesterday's wind. You should know."

And Luke did. Hobo camps had a way of collecting whispers and grumblings about the local state of affairs that not even city leaders might discern. There were more times than he could recall of learning a private lynching was soon to occur, or of a riot being planned, or of the overthrow of some merchant or banker. Luke knew when other people were being sought, criminalized, or persecuted even before they did, and he knew in advance to either pick the winning side or scram out of town.

"Way you all talk about this McCain," Luke said, "makes him out to be a boogeyman used to scare children to sleep at night." He glanced at Daisy as she bit a ragged nail. Even such an act made her endearing.

"Finally, someone here's sensible," Willie Mae added.

The 'bo in bedsheets shook his head. "Smith McCain's got eyes that glow yellow like a railman's lantern. Sometimes that's the only way you can see him at night, 'cause he moves through the darkness unseen as the devil's shadow."

"I don't believe it."

"Believe it, friend."

Fat Willie leaned forward. "I heard McCain caught a 'bo outside Houston and broke his ribs one by one, 'til his chest looked like a puddle of noodles. Did it on account of the 'bo looked at him funny."

"Let me guess," Luke said. "The 'bo was just cross-eyed all along."

"You heard that already?"

"Naw, just guessing that was the direction you were headed. Wouldn't be as good a tale if there wasn't some twist thrown in, a crossbuck like you said."

"Flatfoot Willie told me once that Smith McCain beat a man in Oregon and beat a man in Florida at the same time."

"Which one of you's actually seen this McCain?" Luke asked.

The hobos glanced at each other and shifted on their seats. One of them said, "Ain't many men come across McCain and leave that encounter able to talk."

"Flatfoot Willie said he seen him," said Fat Willie, "and Flatfoot Willie ain't a fibber."

"Maybe not, but maybe he didn't see what he thought he saw, 'less Flatfoot Willie was also in Oregon and Florida at the same time."

The old wheezing man with the Jew's harp interrupted. His voice turned suddenly strong and majestic, as if he'd been saving up all his vitality for this moment. "Boy, let me tell you about Smith McCain . . . "

SMITH MCCAIN, 1860

Smith McCain was born big, and he was born mean, and both qualities sprouted together like twin children in a race, trying to outdo each other as to which could develop faster.

Smith never had a friend. Didn't need 'em. Anything a friendship offers—socializing, support, compassion—Smith despised. He did what he wanted and never doubted his actions were anything but the divine right of his own say-so. He lived in a woodsman's hut in the middle of a swamp with his momma, an old uncle, and a pet copperhead snake.

One evening the uncle got drunk and let slip that Smith's unknown daddy wasn't a man at all, but that the momma succumbed to unnatural desires on nights the moon hung full. On those occasions, she'd murmur some blasphemous words that only a handful of others had ever spoken, and then she'd bend over in the woods without any drawers on, until her pungent scent brought about a slobbering wolf or a tusked hog or, more than once, a puma-sized creature that doesn't exist anymore.

Smith didn't doubt that his uncle was telling the truth, as the old man had never lied to him before, but Smith still slit his throat with a buck knife once the alcohol completely appropriated the elder's wakefulness. The pain of what that drunk uncle informed him dug deep into Smith's heart just as it would any other person's, learning his daddy was something born of beastly hooves and the inclination to murder. That was probably the closest Smith ever was to needing a friend to talk over matters.

Smith thought he should confront his momma and demand an explanation. Instead, he just killed her. He let his pet copperhead snake go free in the swamp, but just before it wriggled away into a mossy hollow, he stomped on its head, killing it too.

Then he went out to stretch his legs in the world.

Though Smith was born half-creature, he still looked normal as anyone else, save his tremendous size. The strange thing—one of the strange things—about Smith was that he never stopped growing. Most people sprout through their teens and quit about age eighteen or so. Not Smith. He added another half inch every year in height, and a couple dozen pounds of muscle, until soon he topped seven feet.

So astounding were his physical dimensions, one might assume he was the pinnacle of grit and swagger. However, one making such an assumption would be wrong as politics. Smith was miserable just for the sake of misery best suiting his face. He hated work and he hated people, though not having any money, he had to get along with one or the other in order to eat. Even thievery is work, if you consider it, and a lot less reliable than most other occupations.

Smith made his way to Baltimore and took up loading ore for the railroader, Peter Cooper, from where he made his way into history books as the nation's first bull. About this time, Cooper needed an "official" railroad security guard on premises, so he promoted Smith to such work, a job Smith found he thoroughly enjoyed. As a guard, he didn't really do much of anything, just sat by himself in the shadows, eyeing men suspiciously, and occasionally having license to beat them when he believed they'd done wrong. That was about the closest to contentment Smith McCain ever felt.

The railroads grew, and so did he. Smith partook in the westward expansion, keeping abreast of every new mile of track laid. He kept the rails safe from freeloaders, bums, spongers, leeches, vagabonds, beggars, and anyone else qualifying who sought to hitch a ride somewhere without paying the applicable fare. Along the way, Smith contracted for each of the major railroading companies and learned the rail system better than anyone, even surveyors whose entire careers were dependent on mapping out lines. Smith got so he never stopped waylaying hobos, just took a train one way until it reached its destination, then took another train back the other way, crisscrossing the country all day and night, dead-set to stop every penniless derelict he could. Men said Smith even got so he could be watching over two trains at once, three trains, and more. He was everywhere.

Other bulls revered him, and he became their hero. When Smith was around, the free riders weren't. And if they were . . . well, they wished they'd never been born. Some were sent off with broken bones, some with broken heads, some never seen again.

Smith McCain supposedly died about 1860 somewhere near Charleston. He was in the center of a switchback, drubbing a particularly vexing tramp he'd pulled off one train, when another train, going the opposite direction, ran clean over him.

But no one ever saw his body. Course, having a train run over you doesn't leave much to be found. Nonetheless, there's enough men who've seen Smith through the years—who've survived Smith, even to this day—who'll attest he's still out there, still protecting the trains from malevolent freeloaders.

DANIEL INTERVIEWS KING, 1985: DAY TWO

Weather turned unseasonably cold in the autumn of 1985. Days were brisk, even in the warmer hours of the afternoon, and you found yourself longing for that overcoat bundled away in the closet recesses behind the telescope you never used and last season's Christmas gift wrap. I'm not saying a blizzard was bearing down, just that chill in the air had bite, and nights were worse.

This is Los Angeles, after all, and most times people don't have to worry about turning into an ice sculpture, not like the unfortunates back home on Long Island. But any cold is enough to make miserable conditions worse for forsaken children living on sheets of damp cardboard or in rat-infested stairwells. The raw winds blowing in from the Pacific Ocean have a way of pervading even the thickest layers of Goodwill sweaters.

Since 1983, Los Angeles began erecting emergency public shelters as a solution for the effects of a problem, without affecting the problem itself. What should have been a temporary emergency response to the burgeoning population of homelessness became a permanent shelter industry. Some shelters offered support for victims of domestic violence or substance abuse, and some assisted with job placement in sewing factories or waste plants. Some shelters provided meals in the morning or evening of watery soup, light coffee, and day-old bread. Most shelters, however, were nothing more than long corridors filled with cots and lice and hypodermic needles and a hundreds-long line of other destitutes cursing and arguing to ensure their own place to sleep within.

Outside one of these shelters—the Christian Rescue Mission on 5th and San Julian—is where I next met King Shaw. I'd gone home the night before to my condo, ordered in Chinese food, exercised, lounged in the bath, slept in late, and then made my way here. I can only imagine King's parallel life as he slumped in his wheelchair all day, drank chicken broth for dinner and cheap whiskey for dessert, pissed in a can, and minded the pimps, prostitutes, thugs, and addicts that comprised his daily landscape.

Funny thing about King, he could have been another man. He was a musician once, a blues singer down south when he wasn't riding the rails. He even had a song recorded by Decca in 1953 that was later digitized by the Library of Congress. I listened to it one time, marveling at some of the sweetest licks I've ever heard, as if there were two guitars playing instead of King alone. The critical discourse attached to it mentioned it was like hearing the ghost of Robert Johnson strumming in accompaniment.

King gave up those dreams, but that's a story I'll get to later.

So here we are at present, on a day in late October which had begun to drizzle, in a year which had begun to molder away, with me pushing King in his wheelchair past shuttered storefronts and burnt lots carpeted by weeds and garbage bags. He spat chew and commented on the weather. I replied the weather was fine, if not gloomy. King added he could tell me some things about gloom.

I believed it.

"Last night," I said, "I reviewed notes of our conversation."

"Bet they didn't make a crumb of sense," King replied, "reading 'em all alone in your big house."

"You're an augur as well as a gentleman." I couldn't help the grin spreading over my face. "You told me that Harriet Tubman's Underground Railroad is still crossing the nation. Luke Thacker met her, and she returned him back to our world—the *regular* world—where everyone's still alive and not just figments of some shared-entity memory? That about sum it up?"

Feral dogs darted past, snarling, and a distant radio blared music I'll never understand, and I wheeled King down a sidewalk crossed by gutters and cracks and galaxies.

King seemed disappointed in me. "A good story's a good story, whether it's writ or spoke, but there's a certain strength added when it's told out loud, when folks are sharing the experience together. I doubt those little footnotes you scrawled are up to the task of making someone *believe*, even yourself."

"I'm not trying to convince myself to believe anything," I said. "It's the rest of the world I want to convince, to make understand that you matter. Everyone has a different tale to tell, everyone has unique difficulties, and that's what the policymakers need to appreciate."

"That's right. We all got different stories, and if you don't record them with some sort of sentimentality, they'll fall by the wayside like used rubbers tossed out a car window as it speeds by. No one wants to touch 'em, and they land in the weeds with all the other crap, decaying and soon forgot.

You want a story be remembered, give it nourishment, care, room to grow, tend it like a living thing, not your wet leavings."

"Funny you mention recording. I brought a tape recorder today, so I can catch the details, that vibrancy of your tales. Okay to record what you're saying?"

"Does a man piss after he drinks?"

"I'll take that as an affirmative," I said, the dumb grin returning. If nothing else, King was royalty of the colloquial.

We came to a graffiti-masked corner mart that also served as a bail bonds and pawn shop, where a group of men stood around drinking coffee or cola from Styrofoam cups. One grimaced at me like I stunk up the neighborhood, while another gave me as big a welcoming smile as my mother at Thanksgiving, just different as people can be.

I gripped the wheelchair handles and made to push on, but King stopped me. "Here's as good as any to talk."

"Here?" I questioned, glancing back at the men as they argued over the Lakers.

"Like I said, I got stories to tell, and stories need an audience. More folks to hear, the stronger it becomes."

"I don't think they'll be paying attention."

"They may not pay attention, but they'll hear," King said. "Words got a way of gettin' in your head and hiding there, 'til they rise up when least expected."

"Okay, if this is what you want."

"You start taping yet, mister big-shot journalist?"

I took a small, handheld Casio device from my pocket and pressed the record button. "I am. Now."

King leaned his head over like speaking to a microphone. "Think about when you're nearby a couple strangers and can't help hearing bits of what they're talking about. Like sitting behind someone on a bus, hearing lil' snippets on their aunt, and how it is she can make the best tamales in town but never charges money for them, or what Luella's cousin thought about the hairdresser and why they were havin' that fuck-all blow-up? You don't catch it all, and what you don't hear, your imagination takes up, fillin' in the missing parts."

"Happens enough," I said.

"It's those bits and pieces you heard that want to become a whole, like solving the empty spaces of a crossword puzzle. It's a reaction, man, automatic, and sometimes you catch your brain workin' at it, and sometimes it goes on in the background without your realizing.

"That's how it is to us about the ones in Athanasia. We're hearing whispers from them all day, our minds connecting memories of those people, creating little flashes of the past. And while we're thinking about them, it's makin' them stronger.

"Sometimes they get so strong in our mind, we have to talk about 'em like they're a part of our own life. Stories connect people, see, what's called a *communal experience* 'tween the listener and the teller."

He paused, looked at me for agreement.

I nodded. "Sure, stories are the most powerful form of art we have."

"True that. And you arrange the events of a story in a way that's meaningful, not just based on some timeline. Real life is straightforward and filled with the mundane. But a story, you choose the moments in time to speak on. Skip the boring shit, emphasize the exciting, create an order of events that offers resolution or dramatic fulfillment or whatever."

"Which is why stories are always told a bit differently each time," I added.

"Yup, 'cause storytelling takes on the teller's personality, and the teller in turn is changed by what he relates. They work off each other, so it's a motherfuckin' intimate affair."

I took in all that King said and embraced it. Never mind I was getting a lesson in storytelling from an uneducated homeless man; what he said made sense.

And King Shaw continued those stories . . .

LUKE AND DAISY, 1934

On a day as easy as the rest of the year proved tough, a group of 'bos sprawled across the berth of a long-journeying railcar. Instead of hiding within a boxcar, they rode brazenly on a flatbed's top for all the world to see, and if a bull noticed them, the train would be past before anything could be done about it. This the group hoped to prove true, but otherwise it was at least a nice change from riding in darkness.

Zeke and Willie Mae and a couple others sunned themselves comfortably under the brightening morning rays. Daisy Rose and Luke kept apart from them, feeling something warmer between themselves than rising sunlight.

Daisy was small and thin, and one might say she couldn't outweigh a bald tree twig. Maybe it was heredity, maybe it was malnutrition, but when her arms hung down, her body resembled a sewing needle and her head was the knotted thread wound at the top. In this regard she and Luke were alike, only him tall and her sawed-off at the height of his underarms. Her skin was soft and impossibly warm, though it carried plenty of stains, stubble, and scars. Her high cheeks flushed with everyday satisfaction, her eyes voiced her emotions, her hair smelled to Luke like groves of blossoming jasmine. Daisy's hands were narrow, her feet wide. She was crass and stubborn and generous and romantic. She hadn't been riding the rails as long as Luke, but she'd grown as accustomed to its lifestyle as he. Soot covered her brow.

She and Luke conversed quietly, sharing the lives of each to the other to make them the lives of each other. "Daddy fancied himself a creative, and he didn't hold back at my birth. It might twist your tongue to say, but my full name is Margarita Amarilla Rosa Verde Cortez."

"That sounds real pretty," Luke said. They sat side by side, his left fingers brushing against her right, the lightest of contact in which strange electricity arced pleasantly at each touch. "Didn't your momma have a say in it too?"

"She died 'fore I was born."

"*Before* you were born?"

"She was killed by a fever. Grandmamma cut her belly open and pulled me out."

"Oh. I'm sorry," Luke said. He didn't know what else to exclaim, but guessed if he said nothing that'd be awful awkward, and further guessed she was used to hearing people apologize for something they had nothing to do with.

"S'all right," she said. "It pains me some to think on, but I never met her, so don't worry much about who I don't know."

"You don't wonder about her life?"

"I'm sure I have."

"I mean, if you're a part of her—"

Daisy's loud exhalation cut him off, and Luke felt like a clod for pushing the matter. It was natural that any person wondered at some point about their origins, though the matter might be a bit more sensitive when those origins were lost before birth. The electricity dimmed between their fingers, and Luke knew he was thinking too much into the matter rather than attending to present affairs. He leaned over and his shoulder nudged hers, and he wrapped his hand tight around her own, skimming light swirls into her palm with his thumb.

"Sorry," he said again. She smiled and squeezed his hand back, and Luke felt happier than ever just to sit aside her. "I'm real glad I met you."

"Me too," she replied, and dimples graced the peaks of her grin.

His heart skipped a beat for no reason, and his head felt light, and his skin tingled with impulse. The brain'll muddy up instinct, but skin prickling like that don't lie. Luke chanced to kiss Daisy's blushing cheek, and she nuzzled into him.

He repeated her given name. "Margarita Amarilla Rosa Verde. I like it a lot. Would you care if I called you by it, Yellow Daisy Green Rose?"

She giggled, and the sound was sweet church bells lolling through rainbows. "Daddy was the only one who ever did. I dropped the Amarilla and Verde parts. Colors for a name are kinda silly, don't you think?"

"I've heard worse."

"Most don't speak Spanish anyway, so they'd constantly be asking what it all means, and who'd care to hear me explain the same thing over and over?"

"I'd never tire of hearing anything you say."

She squeezed Luke's hand again and turned urging eyes to his.

He didn't need the prompting of tingling skin this time and kissed Daisy again, moving to her wonderfully pink lips. She tasted of peach. She tasted of passion. They didn't close their eyes, but looked deep into each other.

The locomotive whistled a long, loud salute.

When they timidly pulled apart, they were silent and gazed at the rushing scenery, at russet-colored foliage and far-flung cottages, the downslope of mountains and the clouds that topped their peaks like foam overflowing a glass of soda pop. Distant telephone lines ran through it all, the chain of some great necklace keeping those pendants and charms from falling apart.

They held hands, and Luke wished the moment never to run out of steam, never to run out of rail. But sometimes silence is comfortable, and sometimes it's awkward, and often silence in new love is a nervous effort as if, given the chance, an unengaged tongue might repudiate what the heart feels.

They both moved to speak and both halted. Shared little laughs. Daisy toed his leg with her boy's work shoe.

"Mm," she said, and he repeated the sentiment back.

After some pawing and nudging, Luke took the reins and picked up their earlier conversation, his voice hushed. "Were you born in Mexico?"

She shook her head, ready to talk about anything. "Daddy was, though he claimed instead he was born an Iroquois. He was real big into tribal life, like herbal medicine and smoking peace pipes."

"That's real impressive, people who know about natural medicines. Sometimes cures from plants is all it takes."

"Daddy believed the Iroquois had it down best. And they could communicate with dead ancestors, foresee the future, that sort of thing. He died climbing a mountain after eating a stack of peyote pancakes. I don't know if he ever foresaw the future of his own grave, but at least he was able to meet with those old kin he'd been searching for. And who knows, maybe he and Mommy are together again, living in heaven the life of husband and wife they barely got to experience while alive."

"I think once two people are together, that's forever," Luke said. "Like mixing water and wine; even if they wanted, it can't be separated."

"I believe it."

They kissed again, and Luke felt like they never stopped kissing, even years later, after her death.

LUKE AND DAISY, 1937

Three years had passed since Luke Thacker met the tomboy Daisy Rose, and each day he found he loved her more than the last.

They didn't marry or settle down in any traditional sense, but lived together in the same precarious consortium from which they met, riding the rails by day to new hopes and sleeping together at night under old dreams. The sun didn't rise or set but that Luke considered the world to be a fine, if not tough, place after all.

And it wasn't just them; Zeke completed the family unit, travelling alongside as the child they spoke of one day having, a youth in a giant's body, content enough to be part of an adventure that was greater than he could experience alone.

Willie Mae was with them a while too, until she had a heart attack, worn out one afternoon while doing the mattress shuffle with an entire work crew. It was later said that no corpse had a bigger smile, and those few who knew her mourned more than she would have believed.

So the threesome—Luke, Daisy, and Zeke—made their home in the transit, living off scraps and scrounge, sweat and luck. They rode the Union Pacific westbound to knock apples in Washington during fall, and the Chicago line eastbound to cut winter ice from Wisconsin's lakes, and the Western Pacific to California to pull springtime oranges, and the Gulf line to work summers in sweltering Mississippi canneries. And throughout the seasons they'd find a dozen other places to strive, from Corpus Christi to Saint Cloud to San Diego; from Tampa to Seattle to Bangor, tramping on each new line the way children collect gleaming marbles, with fascination and impulse and thrill.

The days were long and hard, and don't let anyone say otherwise, that living off the land is a picnic, cause it ain't. But finding work or coin to settle long-term in a single locale was not often procurable, so they got by, moving around and doing better than most, as having found friendship and passion sustained them as much as a thin blanket or an extra bowl of beans.

Luke led the way, acting a father and husband to their family circle and a forward scout to their trailblazing, deciphering the hobo signs that kept them company as much as the trio did each other. The signs helped them traverse new geography, find victuals, escape perils, and generally led to new adventures. Luke tried explaining the signs he saw, tried teaching the language's nuances to Daisy and Zeke the way Hazel had instructed him half a decade ago, but the others balked or fumbled at comprehension, like running a race on tiring legs or like trying to fill their arms with too many hatboxes.

And Luke found this to be true with other 'bos: Just as ordinary folks—non-transients—didn't see nor pay heed to any hobo signs at all, most 'bos couldn't discern the more complicated and fleeting messages that only Luke seemed able to identify. All rail riders knew the basics of the Hobo Code—the signs for food or water, danger, availability of work, and how people in a given town might feel about them—but a limitation existed as to the depth others could perceive or decipher. It didn't matter if someone were nimble as Daisy or strong as Zeke; the limits were there, and it was a hard-pressed thing to explain, like telling someone there are some extra letters in the alphabet they can't see, and with that a whole new range of words and meanings.

Luke wondered why he could read the Code's complexities while others could not. For a while he thought he might find an ally in perseverance, but Daisy and Zeke just got tired of hearing things they themselves couldn't experience. They recognized Luke had some sort of premonitions that favored their efforts, though listening daily about magic doorways and netherworlds filled with memories and ghosts proved to be a bit taxing.

But Luke kept at it. "It's there, mirroring our life and what's remembered," he told them. "Athanasia . . . Athanasia."

"I dreamt about it again last night," Luke said. "Athanasia."

"I dreamed about Peggy Entwistle," Zeke replied. "Saw her killing herself right in front of me, again and again."

"I didn't see her there," Luke said.

"I know she wasn't there. She was in *my* dream. I can't get her out of my head."

"How come you dream so much about ghosts," Daisy asked, squeezing Luke's leg, "and not about me? *Hmm?*"

Luke smiled broadly. "'Cause you're my dream during the day, the one that came true."

"Good answer."

"Peggy Entwistle asked me to save her," Zeke said. "But how can I, if she keeps dying?"

"I don't know," Luke said thoughtfully. "I never figured exactly how it all works."

"One instant she's glorious, the next, her face could be a mashed pie . . ."

"All the times you talk about it, how often have you been to that memory world?" Daisy asked.

"Just the once. But I see signs leading to it occasionally enough to revisit."

"Then why don't you take us there?" Daisy said. "Show us around. It'd be a scream to meet John Dillinger."

Zeke paled. "Just 'cause I don't believe it, doesn't mean I want to go lookin' for haunts."

"Wish I could, but I don't think it works like that," Luke replied. "I mean, if you can't see the door, how do you go through?"

"We'll just follow behind you."

"Fair enough to try, though I don't know when I'll see a sign next. I can't call 'em up."

Daisy smiled, and her eyes crinkled merrily. "I'm sure we'll be with you when you do."

It turned out not to be much of a wait at all. That afternoon, they walked a dirt trail that paralleled old busted tracks, the crossties rotted and home to lazy beetles, the metal rails rusted orange as wildflowers. A big slab of granite had heaved itself out of the ground long ago, and its face glittered with sparkles of quartz and feldspar. Also on its face were hobo symbols: one the image of a blue door hanging slightly open from its frame, and the other a circle and an arrow, pointing the direction.

"It's this way," Luke said.

Zeke was hesitant. "Dead folks?"

"They're not dead exactly. They're memories."

"But they ain't alive neither."

"It's the state of collective memory, what's called the deadeye."

"Shit on that. It's even got the word 'dead' in its name."

Daisy rolled her eyes. "I'll protect you, baby Zeke."

Zeke aped her eye rolling. "Shit on that, too. I ain't scared, just sayin' it's unnatural to go cavorting with ghouls."

Luke fidgeted. "They're not ghouls—"

"Goddamn, I know what you said. Memories, dead eyes, whatever. Let's just go!"

They followed the arrow, and Luke found the entrance to Athanasia below an iron bridge running amongst scrub oaks and wind-whipped shale. A flat riverbed cut underneath, filled with dusty brushwood and dry yellow weeds, as if water forgot it once flowed there. He led Daisy and Zeke to the spot, pointing excitedly at the sign of infinity scratched on rusty pilings, along with another circle and arrow to continue that way. "That's it, that's the mark!"

"Where? That weld seam?" Zeke asked.

"Right in front of you, two feet across. The number eight laid on its side."

"The way those rivets are corroded, I see a number seven," Daisy admitted.

"No, no, it's clear as me," Luke said.

But as they walked through, Luke wasn't that clear to the others at all, more of a murky shape disappearing into fog. Like sight of him, Luke's voice waned too. "Come on through."

They all went under the iron bridge together, but when they came out the other side and Luke put his arms around Zeke and Daisy, and applauded them on entering a realm they'd never before believed, the other two gave him no more mind than a speck on the wind.

"Luke, where'd you go?" Zeke asked.

"You funnin' me?" Luke asked, flicking his ear.

"This sure is a dandy new world," Daisy mocked, glancing around. "Just like Luke said, looks exactly the same as where we came from."

"I ain't good at hide-and-seek," Zeke said. "Show yourself."

"I'm right here!"

"Look at that," Daisy told Zeke. "A butterfly. Wonder who remembered it being here."

"Har-de-har," Luke said. "You can still see the regular world around you, even while being here."

She didn't respond to him.

"Goddamn it, Luke, let's go," Zeke yelled, turning in a circle. "I don't like hangin' under bridges. Reminds me of the mines."

Luke stood in front of them, waving his arms in front of unblinking eyes. Daisy crossed her arms and Zeke clenched his fists. Luke had to go back through the door and reapproach them.

"Some parlor trick," Zeke said. "Where'd you hide?"

"I was right there, went through to Athanasia. I was standing next to you the whole time."

"Fuck that deadeye place," Zeke said. "I'm hungry for lunch."

"So when are you *really* going to take us there?" Daisy asked.

Luke cleared his throat and again tried explaining, but it got to be a sore subject.

Yesterday was summer, while tomorrow could be spring, but today cold winds blew in from the east, and the birds and bugs and 'bos felt the pull south, toward warmer climes.

Luke found Daisy rustling around in her potato sack, and she pulled up a small compact mirror. The glass was dull, and a single crack ran diagonally from corner to corner, so looking into it gave a view of herself from two slightly different perspectives. In one, the light caught it just right and made that half of her face shine. The other view couldn't catch that light and instead seemed obscured by a bit of shadow. No matter how she tilted the glass, the two sides wouldn't reconcile: one side stayed bright, one side stayed dim. Luke watched her from behind and saw himself in each half of that reflection, like herself, bisected between light and dark.

"You admirin' that pretty face of yours?" he asked with his Luke Thacker smile, which in the glass straddled the realms of bliss and doom.

Instead of replying, she sighed and asked, "How much longer can we get by? Hand-to-mouth, and even that by luck."

"I don't know what else to do."

"Maybe someday you'll work on those trains you love, a baggage porter or a serviceman."

"That'd be fine. But what kind of a job is that if you can't be with me?"

"Why can't I?"

"Ain't no women porters. Maids, maybe . . . "

"*Qué demonios.* Is that what you think, I only aspire to clean? Maybe I'll be the conductor and drive the engines, or maybe I will be an engineer and build my own trains, better than anything you've ever seen."

"If anyone can, Yellow Daisy Green Rose, it's you."

She smiled, and it was brilliant, while her voice was tired and reconciled to the good and the bad all around, like looking into a cracked mirror. "I never cared for hearing my full name, 'cept when you say it."

Luke traced a smudge of coal behind her ear as it faded into oil-black hair.

Zeke burst into the clearing where they sat, in a park of woods outside Duluth. "Look what I got," he said, passing them cans of tuna fish. "Salvation Army just dropped 'em off, says they only expired last week!"

"Is that mincemeat on your collar or lipstick?" Daisy asked him.

Zeke blushed, which was an odd look for him, a rocky granite cliff given rosy cheeks. "Bit of both, I suppose."

"Wish we had a squirt of lemon for this tuna," Luke mused.

Daisy snapped her fingers. "We still got some onion."

"And Lord says Hallelujah!" Zeke exclaimed.

They ate, and they stayed in the park for two more weeks, until hoarfrost nipped the ground and old leaves tumbled off their trees. In that time they laughed and they cried and they fought and all else expected of a family. They climbed trees and they fished, met a baker who gave them day-old rolls, met a man who robbed them of those rolls, shoveled ballast between crossties for a quarter a day, watched 'bos play in the ice of refrigerator cars like children, 'til one froze to death, and then they didn't play anymore.

Luke and Daisy made love every night under the moon, while Zeke took up with a gal from town who was near big as him, and made him squeal with laughter when she brought out baked mincemeat pie.

After Duluth, they rode the rails to San Bernardino.

One day Daisy sidled up against Luke while they pulled strawberries in an ocean's field of green and red. She whispered, matter-of-fact, "I think I'm with child."

His eyes grew large as the fruit in his hands, and his cheeks flushed their color. "Lord, Daisy, Lord."

"Are you happy or angry?"

"I think . . . " He paused. "I couldn't be more glad, and feeling this way surprises me."

"Me too. I mean, I'm also glad, but I never thought I could do it, I'd *want* to do it."

Luke snapped his fingers. "We gotta make a house."

"Yes."

"How long 'til . . . ?"

She said her body was changing already and she hadn't bled for two months. That night and those following, they lay beneath constellations and drew out their life together amongst stars they'd not before considered. A triangle cluster was where they'd settle down, and a dusting of sparkles proposed well-wishes. Luke said he'd learn to farm, and Daisy said she'd learn to cook.

"We'll name her Juniper if it's a girl," Luke said.

"Josiah if he's a boy," Daisy replied.

The next month she bled more than she ever had, and she quietly told him she wasn't pregnant no more. Daisy only cried after he started.

One time, Luke and Daisy won a marathon dance contest and were awarded ten dollars. They slept in a penthouse and ate porterhouse steak and hazelnut truffles.

One time, Zeke won a singing competition. Luke had never heard him carry a tune before, but when he belted out a miner's ballad into an unsuspecting microphone, the sound of his voice was divine as a choir of angels glorifying their baby savior's birth. The judges wept, and the audience women swooned, as well as the audience men. Poor Zeke got so embarrassed at the attention he never sang again.

Next time, the threesome came upon a wrecked automobile flipped upside down in a drain. Zeke lifted it by himself, and Luke and Daisy freed a family of four, who thanked them politely and then ran off as if they feared hobos more than they feared being trapped in that car.

Another time they were in Monterey, California, and a camera crew was panning for a Hollywood film. The crew needed background extras to add authenticity of the dustbowl hardships, and so Luke, Daisy, and Zeke got immortalized on the silver screen in Hal Roach's *Of Mice and Men*.

Time after that, they stood on Mount Rushmore at the top of George Washington's brow and watched the sunrise of June solstice. They even spent some time working to carve the monument too, until the designer, Gutzon Borglum, caught Luke and Daisy having an afternoon delight before the eyes of Thomas Jefferson; they were fired for besmirching the dignity of Borglum's favorite forefather. Zeke was let go too, guilty by association.

A different time—and this could have happened before or after the other times—Luke and Zeke were attacked by a rabid wolf with frothing slobber drippin' off its fangs. It was Daisy who rescued them; she leapt in between the men and the wolf and crouched down in a boxer's stance that would have made Jack Dempsey proud. She took a tree branch and hit that wolf so hard, the rabies was knocked right out of it, and the wolf ran off howling.

Loss and hardship brought all three together, and mutual affection kept them united. Luke and Daisy and Zeke rode the rails hand-in-hand, the way a family might ride in a buggy on their way to picnic. Sometimes the sun warmed them and sometimes it fried their asses. Sometimes it vacationed, and they huddled together under a blanket, frozen snot hanging off their chins. Peanuts and wild berries could be their dinner, or rabbit stew, or nothing at all. Could be, they didn't eat for days at a time, and then one afternoon would join in the type of barbecue feast that legends were built of, leaving their bellies so stuffed they couldn't eat for the next couple of days even if they wanted. They travelled the nation, and they learned its secrets, and any day could start with mountain marigolds in the morning fog and end with grasslands filled with bison, all together watching the gathering dusk. In this way, they rode the rails together, and they wouldn't change it for the world.

LUKE AND SMITH, 1938

It was nighttime, and the boxcar door was half-open, the way Zeke always liked it. Luke was awake, the others asleep. He watched outside as stars jetted past, as if he were the one at a standstill and the glittering sky was a busy thoroughfare, each speck travelling to its own important place.

There wasn't much of a moon, but its faraway edge could be seen about halfway across the universe, and Luke decided it was a bit after midnight. They were travelling to a work camp outside Chicopee, Massachusetts, and getting there fast. He imagined some hobo signs with conflicting messages simmering in his brain, calling to be read outside, but didn't pay them heed; it was too dark to make out any writing. He was sleepy, but couldn't sleep, stuck in that strange flux between worrying about something and the knowledge that tomorrow would go a lot easier if he could saw some logs.

The stars vanished.

Luke became very alert. The stars hadn't vanished, but were being blocked by something in the doorway, something darker than the midnight sky. Luke held his breath, hoping the black shade would move on, pass like the shadow a locomotive's headlamp briefly creates over trees; one moment it's there, the next it's gone. But then the shape took a step inside the boxcar, and Luke heard a floorboard groan under its weight.

His guts felt hollow. Other 'bos came on and off trains all the time, and Luke was used to sharing new company at any hour. This time, though, something was different, something wrong. Every possible alarm seemed to ring in his head.

Luke called out, trying to make his voice deep, trying to make his voice rough. "This car's taken."

The shade stopped moving, though it still blocked the door. No starlight got past, and the boxcar turned dark and cold as if they'd fallen down inside the pipes of a broken furnace. The shade let out a long hiss like an exhaled breath—though it wasn't a breath, exactly—sounding part squealing brakes and part the exclamation one makes when catching you engaged in naughtiness, that moment of *I've caught you now.*

The shade replied, "Shouldn't be."

Already Luke forgot what he'd just said and was unsure what the visitor meant. Then the voice continued in a low, horrible grating rumble, as if a long train was dragged across the tracks against its will and there was a tiny nail stuck under one metal wheel, dragging with it.

It said, "Manifest says this car should be empty. But now I find it's not. Now I find . . . trespassers."

A bull? Luke thought. He'd never been rousted from a moving train at night before. That'd be too dangerous, too foolhardy, for the railroad dicks. After all, how could they even move from car to car speeding along in the dark? Climb along the roofs of each carriage and peer inside? Most bulls who stayed on the train slept in their own compartment or satisfied themselves with liquor in the caboose. Most bulls only hassled you if they were armed and you looked weak, and there wasn't much else to do.

Luke's hollow guts sank to the floor, and his heart beat faster. He tried to speak confidently, but his words came out tinny. "We just needed a ride."

"You need a ride, you buy a ticket."

"Who's there?" Zeke said. He'd woken, and his voice heralded all the confidence Luke had tried to muster. Luke sensed him rising and felt relief, not in safety, but only that he wasn't any longer the sole focus of the shade's attention. "Your ears built backward, pal? My friend said this car's taken."

"Better get out or we're gonna fuck you up," Daisy added. Daisy, strong Daisy, no more than ninety pounds, trying to sound mean, to throw in her lot. At least together they put up a good front.

The shade was silent for a moment. Maybe it really didn't know how many were in the car . . . Could be three, could be thirty 'bos. It certainly couldn't see them in the darkness. Maybe it paused, weighing the odds against itself, considering finding an easier opportunity the next car down the line.

Then it said—and there was not a hint of emotion in that voice, no anger, no fear, no satisfaction, just an emptiness, like reciting arithmetic tables—"This is railroad property. Where's your ticket?"

Luke heard a rustle, and knew Zeke passed him. Zeke bellowed and there was a thud—Yes! One hard shove and the shade that was standing in front of the open door would go flying out in a shriek to shatter amongst whatever there was to shatter against out in the night land. Zeke would save them!

But then Zeke was tumbling away back the way he'd come, past Luke, and Luke heard him cry a pitiful yelp of pain. The shade had crumpled him. It moved into the boxcar, closer, away from the door, and now the starlight was freed, the interior of the car lightening just enough to make out fleeting glimpses. One moment, Luke saw the shade's lower face, almost as high above them as the car's ceiling, and it was bearded—a man, that was all it was, a man. Another moment he saw a round bowler hat perched on the man's head, looking ridiculously small upon that basin-sized dome. A third moment, the man's face was again shadowed, but Luke saw his eyes glow yellow as a railman's lantern, just like Luke had heard a 'bo claim years before.

Smith McCain.

Luke was on his feet, fumbling for his pocket knife with the nicked edge.

McCain came at him, taking a single step that carried him halfway across the car. He was immense, larger even than the fireside 'bos alleged, his girth that of Luke's height. And he smelled foul, a smoldering stew of puke and rotten eggs and outhouse muck. When McCain opened his mouth, starlight reflected off long canine fangs.

McCain was upon him, reaching.

Luke's knife flicked open and, without hesitating, he plunged it into the monster bull's chest, but the stabbing all felt *wrong* in some way. The knife should have stuck into a solid but yielding substance, hopefully the heart, though any organ would do. Instead it felt like he stabbed into a pile of mud. The knife went in all the way to the handle and then deeper, so that even the top of Luke's hand seemed to impale within McCain. It *did* seem to hurt McCain, at least. The bull grunted a single curse and stumbled back—only a step—then pulled a blackjack off his belt and swung it with the force of a dynamite blast.

Luke was lucky; the train hit a tiny bump, just enough that someone standing would falter. Luke did. His knees unhinged and he swayed to one side, and the corner of the blackjack skimmed his temple. Luke was knocked back hard against the boxcar's wall with a thud, his thoughts reeling, pain shooting across his mind, but still understanding the fortune of that moment. If the blackjack had connected full force, his head would have been pudding. He fell to his hands and knees, pleading for his reeling senses to recover. He heard Daisy scream.

Zeke was back up with a roar. Luke could just make him out, looking like he limped at first, and then, ignoring any pain, he put all his force into a running tackle, throwing his broad shoulders into McCain's midsection. Zeke was a giant, big and strong, with a dexterity that still allowed him to move quick as a dancer, but against McCain he looked like a flailing puppy. When Zeke hit him, McCain barely moved, just made a wet, chuckling sound. Zeke wrapped his arms around McCain, head down, trying to wrestle him to the ground. McCain raised one arm and brought his elbow crashing down into the center of Zeke's spine. There was a cracking sound that was instantly drowned out by Zeke's shriek.

"Now I find . . . murderers." McCain's voice was a whisper that bayed.

No, Luke wanted to say, but nothing came out. *You're wrong, never . . .*

"Thomas's murderers. Trespassers and murderers, one and the same."

No, no, no . . .

Daisy cried Luke's name, and Luke tried to crawl to her while seeing double. He thought he saw her also trying to crawl to him from the other side. The train sped on, faster and faster it seemed, and time, too, sped faster and faster. McCain swung down the blackjack onto Zeke's shoulder, and the collarbone shattered, followed by Zeke's back, and Zeke fell flat, howling.

"Killed one of my own," McCain added.

The air outside wailed, the *clackety-clack* across rail ties deafening. The scent of blood broke the air, the scent of sweat, the scent of something old, unbathed, filled with hate like an abscess. Luke could *smell* McCain's hate. He could *taste* it, in his mouth, down his throat, a swallow of lunacy, icy yet boiling, all at once.

His gaze dropped to the pocketknife still sticking from McCain's chest, and Luke realized how tiny it had been all along, the blade like a sewing needle nudged into a mountain. They could never defeat McCain; he was half animal, half demon, dead but alive, and Luke had pricked him with a pocket knife hoping to save them all. He was a fool to have hoped.

A long, shrill scream sounded from the train's whistle, then Zeke's scream, louder. McCain kicked him hard in the side of his face with a heavy, buckled boot, and Zeke rolled over, his features no longer where they should've been.

"Thomas, sweet Thomas," McCain deadpanned. "Death was sweet in Thomas the bull."

"Jump out!" Luke yelled to Daisy. She looked as if she was about to anyway.

Daisy angled toward the boxcar door, but McCain whipped around, his arm seeming to reach impossible lengths until he blocked her, then struck full force with the blackjack.

No!

She fell like a comic strip joke might show someone falling, body bent upward at the waist, legs in the air, feet steepled up.

Luke stood just as the train seemed to hit another tiny bump, rolling him sideways, just as McCain kicked backward at him, the toe of his monstrous black boot barely catching him in the chest, but enough to fling him away, to make him feel his ribcage nearly collapse.

McCain spoke, calm as a mortician, "No one rides for free."

The stars and planets whizzed by outside, the sliver of moon turned a sideways frown. The boxcar had shrunk; Luke was next to Zeke, next to Daisy, next to McCain, all of them crushed and thrashing against each other inside a tiny trunk. McCain beat at them all simultaneously, and each cried out as one. Luke was hit, and a great pain rent his hip, another pain his brow. He tried to shield his face and felt his left wrist and forearm crack from a thundering blow. Agony shot through each finger. He rolled to the ground away into the furthest corner.

A bright light filled the car as they started across an open truss bridge, lamps shining at the entrance. Even in the flash of the light, when everything else illuminated, Smith McCain was still pure black, a monstrous shadow that had escaped its two-dimensional confines. Zeke lay motionless on the floor, broken bones, seeping blood, a knee bent backward. Daisy slumped on the opposite side, though she didn't look too bad off. McCain reached to her, his hand opening like a giant raptor, she a stunned mouse, eyes widening, his talons ready to rend her apart.

The bright light passed, and the boxcar returned to star-tinted darkness. Daisy screamed again.

Luke tried going to her, but his legs were sacks of wheat, floppy and heavy. He moved slowly. Zeke moved too, unbelievably, in the same direction; Luke thought he was a goner. The bull had Daisy now in one arm, and with the other, he took her head. McCain twisted slowly, like unscrewing a lid. Daisy's eyes bulged, and she gasped.

In the dim light she looked at Luke, and Luke saw her, and he looked away, knowing what was to occur, refusing for that moment to be his final memory of her alive.

There was a small popping sound. Everything else went quiet but for that. The small pop of a bag filled with air, the cork from a bottle of champagne, a gunshot from far, far away, went Daisy's neck.

Zeke reached McCain and grabbed onto his leg with his good arm, trying to pull himself up. The bull tossed Daisy out the open door as effortlessly as a wadded bit of rubbish, and she was gone.

Luke wailed, stumbling after her. McCain reached for him next, to bar his escape, when Zeke bit into the bull's knee, digging his teeth into the tender ligaments under the kneecap, pulling up and out with the last of his might, determined to rip it clean off, like tearing the end of a pouch of tobacco.

McCain let out a surprised cry and reflexively jerked down to Zeke. Luke slipped to the open door, turned back to see the bull take Zeke's good arm and rip it out of its socket. Then Luke fell out the door, remembering to roll when he hit ground.

But he didn't hit ground for a long time.

LUKE THACKER, 1938

Luke fell and fell for what seemed ages. He'd once heard that before you die, your life flashes before your eyes, and in those moments of falling from the train he seemed to relive every instance of his existence ten thousand times over. The pains, the regrets, the joys and dreams and failures and learnings of what he'd been through—of what ten thousand Luke Thackers had been through—filled his mind, until his own name was a mystery he himself created, like a jigsaw puzzle that you put together and then take apart to put together all over again. He knew everything, then nothing; a broken window, that's what he was, a single pane of glass with a hole in its center.

He rode a bicycle as a boy, begged for work through tears, watched airships at the World's Fair, knew every flower that bloomed and wilted; so went it all through the broken glass, faster and faster, leaving in its wake dust clouds of loss, windswept furrows of dissolution. He remembered seeing Daisy the first time, his heart twisting like a fever dream, remembered taking her hand that felt so soft when it should have been weathered to mule's hide by frost and sunburn and cinders. Remembered laughing with her, loving her, rolling up in the paper that lined boxcar walls to keep warm, or dangling their feet out open doors to admire the lights of farmhouses at dusk, and they were young, and should be young still, though he aged so much the earth was his child, and now she was taken, all he knew of her for nothing but those moments of bliss and yearning that fell away.

Luke dropped through the night air and landed on his back in a slow-moving river, his limbs splayed like a carnival wheel, the stinging cold water prodding his wounds, his thoughts. He saw then that he hadn't fallen very fall at all from the truss bridge. It crossed only about twenty feet above the river surface, and the train was still chugging over 'til it reached the far side. It had only been a few seconds since he'd gone out the door.

Luke saw a pair of yellow eyes glare at him from the depths of a receding boxcar, and then he was receding himself, sinking beneath the water. He struggled and threw his arms out in a half-assed dogpaddle, knowing just enough about swimming to lean forward and kick with his legs and keep his head up so that he made it to shore only half-drowned.

Luke lay there, shivering, and discovered the only noises were those he made. Everything else was silent; no bullfrogs or hoot owls, coyotes or crickets, or anything else that should have sounded deep at night on a waterway. Even the wind was stilled, so that no leaves rustled or branches creaked. It was as if the world had gone into mourning for him, for Daisy, for Zeke. He felt small and lost. He felt alone.

After awhile Luke rose, and all the pains of his body fired at once. His hip felt like it couldn't support him, his head was woozy and stuffed with rags, his ribs burned, his wrist and forearm swelled and ached in throbs, like his heart. His rucksack was gone, left on the train. Most everything he owned 'cept the clothes on his back was gone with it, even the too-small belt made of elk that was the last keepsake from his momma. Luke's shoes were missing too, and he shuffled barefoot over slippery stones and sticky mud, searching for Daisy.

The river slid past, liquid ebony by sight, sharp quartz by touch, earthy jade by scent. Ripples and soft waves kept it moving, always moving. Groves of fat trees bustled along the shore. In day they would appear crimson and gold and bright green but now, at night, they were only different shades of black. Everything black, some hues lighter than others, even nearly white if touches of moonlight graced it, but still black. Luke wondered how he could find her. She might have sunk beneath the surface; she might have been carried away with the current.

He didn't have to worry long. There, only a few yards away, hung Daisy's graying body, broken and tangled, amongst the shore rocks of the river.

Waves of screams rose up his throat and he tried swallowing them, but the screams grew too large and they poured out, until his mouth went dry and he beat his hands raw on the earth and exhausted himself. He pulled Daisy to land and lay next to her, him wet and cold and shaking, and her still with closed eyes as in slumber. The island moon and ocean of stars cast shadows over them both of distorted shapes that shifted without breeze. When he looked up, each star was a freckle of her skin, a dimple of her smile, a part of her cast to the unreachable endlessness of the cosmos.

He thought death was all that suited him now, and he'd be best in bringing it about himself, then considered the extremity of it all, and that he didn't know what would occur afterward, and he might be even more anguished than at present, though he couldn't believe that was possible. Tears wore down his eyes until he closed them, and without knowing it, he fell asleep.

In dreams, Daisy was with him again, and Luke told her the goodbyes he didn't chance to say while she lived. She listened patiently to all he professed and then replied that she wasn't ready to be taken away from the world.

"I miss you already," Daisy told him. "It's too much to be gone. It's just too much."

"I miss you too," Luke answered. "You didn't deserve this. You deserved that house and the flowers of your name and children to reflect your love."

She frowned. "I don't want your goodbyes. I want to come back . . . It's lonely here."

Luke took her in his arms, and they embraced.

A man materialized between them like a magician's parlor trick, separating Daisy to one side and Luke to the other. It was John Dillinger. "We all want to come back, Luke, but not all of us can."

"What's that mean?" Luke asked.

"Think on it awhile, and then come visit. I can still use a driver."

John's gaze darted up, past Luke, seeing something, then as quick as he'd appeared, John vanished, taking Daisy with him.

A black shade soared from behind, seeming to chase their departure. Smith McCain's yellow eyes were in the back of his head even as he rushed forward, so that he was still watching to see what Luke would do.

Luke ran away in a void, from nothing, to nothing. He was touched from behind, and he turned in fright to find Harriet Tubman drawing her finger in the air. A numeral eight laid on its side shimmered electric blue: the sign of infinity.

"The mark of Athanasia," she said "There's more here than you know."

"Did . . . Is she—" Luke stuttered.

"*Everyone* lingers awhile in Athanasia."

Then the pox appeared, eating the blue symbol into nothingness, then eating Harriet into nothingness, then the dreamscape surrounding him, the void itself was taken, until finally himself.

"But nothing lasts forever, child," Harriet's voice echoed in his mind over and over.

In the morning Luke woke and used a rock to dig a hole, and buried Daisy Rose as best he could. He piled stones over the grave so scavengers couldn't get her, though it didn't matter anymore. She was dead and there were as many scavengers under the dirt as there were above, but it seemed the right thing to do.

He found a rusted nail and used it to carve a symbol in the trunk of a twisted oak that spread its canopy over her tomb. The symbol was some squiggly lines with an arrow through them, a pair of almond-shaped eyes, a cross and crown and set of dots, and all of it surrounded by a heart that, combined, no one else would understand if seen, nor know to give veneration to the final resting place for a princess of the wind. As an afterthought, he carved the letters *R.I.P.*

Luke looked awhile too for Zeke. He didn't expect to find him, and his expectations were met. Zeke had saved him, and Luke would never know where his body might end up. Zeke's remains could still be riding the rails right now into Chicopee. Luke spoke out loud a few nice words of eulogy, then, feeling colder and more miserable than ever, walked away.

He learned later the river was named Westfield, above which Zeke and Daisy had been killed, and he never returned there again.

LUKE AND LIZBETH, 1938

Luke hopped a B&A train heading east from Springfield and quietly sat inside one of its solemn boxcars, staring out the flung-open door. It might have been a pretty day otherwise, but he didn't see the environs according to notions of guise, but rather by what each element represented. The trees and towns, shacks and sheds, pine-topped rises and river-bottomed crevices were no more than means for hobo signs, and today there were lots of them. Symbols passed in slow-motion frames of things he'd not before seen, yet somehow he understood every one.

Okay to sleep here.

Okay to eat here.

Beware he who wears many faces.

The B&A rolled past hobo encampments, and the 'bos there looked like gods to Luke. A man chopped wood with a giant silver axe, and a barefoot girl offered picked flowers as the train churned steel. Feet stuck out the openings of tents made from blankets, and frayed rigging held coffee pots over waning fires. Men dressed in crop share clothes watched Luke go by, and their faces were content. The camps were circled by more signs.

Something roused in him, a thing that had begun to wake when he first discovered Athanasia, though it'd since just been shuffling around drowsy in his head, operating at only a small bit of its potential. Maybe now it'd been jolted awake by McCain. Whatever it was, it was becoming more aware, more observant, as if it—*he*—found purpose.

Walk through, but don't look back.

Take supplication from the cherished.

The beast of bulls moves close.

Luke's emotions were raging synapses sparkling as a fuse sizzles, slow-burning into caps of a stack of dynamite. Imagery and icons and clues caught his notice, and each detonated in his brain, clearing room for further ciphers. He was barreling down a route not found on any map, and all he had to do was focus.

The Hobo Code was growing more complicated, more aberrant, more telling and prophesying. The B&A traveled faster down the tracks, and

Luke saw marks for villages where none should exist, marks for people who were never born, marks for places of sacrifice, places of worship, places where gods once lived and died. Marks that were foreign riddles, yet strangely made sense to him.

Two tree boughs crossed in a gust of wind, and a red leaf fluttered through it, and Luke knew that a holy man once blessed a spot of earth below, and if he had a lick of rheumatism, it'd there be cured. He saw the way a boulder rose against a ridge and knew there a wicked jinni had once been defeated by a wily child.

The wood vanes of a windmill spun in lazy clockwise spirals, and a black bird darted through to alight on a shingled roof's eave. It chirped three times, and Luke knew a woman was secretly buried underneath who had been raped and murdered. One year later the killer was castrated by her spirit, though others said it was a carpentry accident.

These things that came to his mind were no more surprising to him in their clarity than they would be to an unschooled man from Kansas waking in the morning to read ancient Sanskrit. It seemed just a natural effect that, to most, was unintelligible, yet once Luke understood it, the world around was a liturgical epic.

Nature, and what had been, and what could be, all had their own methods of communication, and Luke had tapped into it. It seemed to him he no longer followed the mystical *Hobo Code*, but that now it truly was the *Human Code*.

And though that realization was of great import, Luke didn't stop looking until he saw the sign of most gravity: *the mark of infinity*.

The train flew far, and the symbol finally showed itself over the arched entrance to an overgrown cemetery, etched into a plank of wood alongside the words "Eaton Burying Ground."

Luke felt as one with the train, as a long-range drover knows the moods and inclinations of his mount, knows how to ride it, cue it with a slight nudge, a jerk, a shifting of the hips, an almost prescient sense of what the ride is going to do before even it knows. It was time to get off, and Luke thought the train should slow, and the train did so, as if responding to his intent. He jumped. It was a good jump, and he didn't stumble or fall over. Just one big step, then another, like reaching over wide cracks.

The big steps shortened to a normal stride. He didn't pause, but put one foot in front of the other and kept walking along the tracks, then under the plank sign, through the graveyard and away, pulled to the misty edges of the nearby Atlantic coast. He progressed through the day, not seeing anyone dead or alive, though he was kept company by enough wildlife that he knew for certain where he'd gone. In the "real" world, squirrels and 'coons disliked him enough to run for cover when he came around. Here he moved amongst their shelters, passing elegant deer and fat skunks, rabbits, jays, even a one-eared bobcat that sniffed the air, but seemed not to discern Luke's passage.

The land struck him as old beyond its years, the crawling shoreline wrinkled by centuries, its loose brush rustling with lost secrets. A crippled dirt path led not forward in time, but seemingly backward. Luke felt he descended into forgotten lands, rather than onward to forgotten people.

That dirt path led to a cross path, then another, this one wider and climbing back away from the coast, and he went up a clearing that radiated a series of more paths, these all disappearing behind distant trees in a mesh web of gossamer. Each path might lead to a new world, and he had come from the past and was at the crux of the future, what he chose now determining the irreversible course of his life. Like most things, Luke didn't hesitate, but picked a center route that appeared interesting. He walked that way, and the chaparral thickened, and the horrible pox appeared.

The dots hovered far in the air, streaking away, coming back, vanishing, appearing, but only a couple at a time, like the scouts of a roving insect colony. It was an alarming sensation, knowing they were here, though none came near. They ate at things half-hidden in the woods that Luke couldn't identify, glimpsed between rustling branches of the paths he hadn't chosen. Suddenly the dense trees opened up, and the tops of a string of textile mills appeared, and the pox were gone.

The mills were distant, situated on the far side of waving pines, but they belched smoke and blew whistles, and men the size of ants walked or drove to and from them. Luke changed course again once he crossed a fresh blacktop road and continued along that, and the mills grew bigger until he stopped behind a ten-foot post, painted in jaunty letters that read: *Welcome to Fall River*.

The road changed direction, and he too, into the city, which was large compared to most others he visited. More people and more vehicles carried on around him, and Luke realized he had no plan, no idea how to find someone in the deadeye.

"Hello, is anyone there?" he shouted to the traffic. No one took notice, and Luke kept walking down the street, calling out.

How many times had he ignored a wino who was shouting to himself on the sidewalk? Now it was he who was the madman, and perhaps the citizens of Fall River simply ignored his delirium the way he'd ignored so many others before.

But he knew of no other way to get attention. First shops and eateries, then street-side residences, increased in size and décor, and Luke passed them all without a second glance, shouting louder as he moved uptown. "Hello? Hello, can anybody see me? Anyone around? Hello?"

Luke kept at this until he heard a reply, surprisingly, as he didn't expect any response to be so forthcoming. "Afternoon, mister."

A young woman waved to him from the elevated porch of an old-looking hotel. A dozen windows lined the front, four on top of each other, three stories high, each with a drawn gourd-colored blind.

He did a double-take, and his senses teetered between doubt and relief. "You can see me?"

"I can hear you even more, hollering like a ticker-tape parade is passing through."

"I didn't know how else to . . . find anyone."

"Come on over. I run the bed and breakfast around here. You look like you could use both."

Aware of his grubby shirt and ragged trousers and filthy feet, Luke accepted her invitation, walked up four oiled stairs to the porch, and met her with a handshake.

She was a handsome woman with soft features, appearing in her early thirties. Her face was round, if not a bit plump, and she kept a very tight smile held in place, as unwavering as the crisp auburn hair arranged about her head. Her presence reminded Luke of someone his mother used to call "High Society," being those women kept like show birds, allowed by men to venture outside only when escorted, and still restricted then to limitations of church service, picnicking, or shopping in approved ladies' stores. This woman struck him as forceful, though her vitality, perhaps, was repressed beneath a cold demeanor of lace and petticoats.

"I'm looking for Harriet Tubman," Luke said, perfectly conscious of how queer that declaration would sound to most people. "You know where I might find her?"

Something shifted in the woman's face, a turn from her rigid composure, and Luke considered she wasn't as restrained as he first expected. Then her tight smile reformed, and she nodded. "Oh sure. Me and Harriet can connect. We both go back a few yesteryears. I'll send word you're looking for her."

"Thank you, Miss, uh—"

"Lizbeth. Think of me as the welcoming committee to this part of the seaboard."

He told her his name, and she replied it was a genuine pleasure to meet him, and that she didn't receive a lot of company as once she did.

"I used to know everyone around here," Lizbeth said. "My father owned most of the commerce, and his ancestors lived in these parts since its original settlers."

"Seems like a fine upbringing," Luke said. "My roots are mostly unknown, but I don't think they extend to any area as nice as this."

"We all chop different trees," she replied, which struck Luke as an odd phrase to use. She continued, "Anyway, come on in and please make yourself at home. Any friend of Harriet's is a friend of mine. I'll set a room for you, as it might be a spell before she can get here. You know how she is, always busy, always rescuing someone."

"I don't want to put you out. I'm just as happy wearing the sky for a blanket as I am a quilt."

"Nonsense. You're amongst respectable folks now. We don't endure people sleeping outdoors, 'less they're—" Her eyes twinkled and she stopped talking, though her tight smile seemed to warm for the first time.

"Unless what?"

"Nothing," she said, cheery as a canary. "An old joke. Would you like some tea?"

Luke followed her indoors and immediately felt like he stepped on a freighter that twisted in loop-de-loops, so dizzy did he become. Wallpaper patterned in bright pink flora surrounded still-life paintings of rose petals and kittens. Each frame was ornate, sprouting carved gold vines that curled in on themselves. Varnished wood furniture filled the room like a museum, and each of those was covered with stacks of pale doilies bearing porcelain sculptures of flowers, angels, and, most of all, cats. There were figurines of cats sleeping, waving, playing with yarn, lapping at milk, winking, acting coy, acting fierce, acting bored, cats in pairs, triples, packs; cats of bronze, cats of ivory, cats of pearl, ruby, silver, crystal, and amethyst. A mantle display held oval-framed photographs of elderly people dressed in clothes several layers thick, and photos of felines dressed like the elderly people, and above that hung a large gold leaf mirror that reflected back everything in the room, so that it appeared twice as stuffed as it should have been.

The air was perfumed like a garden intent to murder with cloying vapors of petunia. Luke's eyes watered, and he covered his nose with a greasy shirtsleeve.

Lizbeth sauntered in front and he mimicked her path, careful not to knock anything over, and in this way they descended to the depths of the sitting room. Each footstep sank deeper than the previous into giant oval rugs of paisley, so that no sound was made. The house, in fact, was completely quiet. Even a towering grandfather clock squeezed to one corner generated no tick or tock, though its pendulum swung steady.

"Silence is a virtue," she said. "I appreciate hearing myself think. *We* appreciate it."

"We?" Luke repeated.

"Us," she replied, opening her arms to the room. Luke supposed she referred to the cat statues. "Lemon or cream?"

"Eh?"

"Your tea, silly. How would you like it?"

"Strong as possible, with a bit of sugar, please."

"Sugar for my sugar," she sang and disappeared into the kitchen.

He crossed the room gingerly while she was gone, looking for a place to wait that was as discreetly out of the way as possible from the sense of claustrophobic efflorescence. Without warning, and even padded under all the rugs, a single rogue floorboard squealed in betrayal at his step.

"I heard that," Lizbeth's voice floated through the rooms.

"Ah, sorry."

"You'll upset them."

Luke looked at the cat statues, feeling motionless eyes roving over him.

She returned and signaled for him to sit beside her on a lush crimson settee. He obliged. They sat without speaking further, sipping at the tea. Luke felt her appraising him, as if the sole of his worth were to be measured there, that moment, according to the manner in which this drink was sipped into his mouth, how the china cup balanced between his fingers. He tried to keep the thimble-sized cup level between thumb and forefinger, barely tipping it while imbibing. His pinky stuck out slightly, as he imagined sophisticates might partake. It all seemed fantastic that he should be made to feel as such—he, set there on a velvet cushion, dressed in a soiled overshirt that a coon dog couldn't bear to smell, and trousers crusted with motley residue that acted as a book of memories; one stain was where he travelled yesterday, another stain where he travelled the day before, and so on, for months and months back. He hadn't bathed in two weeks, hadn't shaved in more. Dirt and coal dust filled the wrinkles of his face, and some of Zeke's dried blood still spotted his arm.

"Seems like someone could benefit from a good washing," she finally said.

Luke groaned inwardly. It was bad enough perceiving one's own flaws, but worse still to have that knowledge recognized by someone else. All he could say was, "I'm sorry."

"I've smelled worse," she replied, very matter-of-factly.

Luke experienced the strangest fear that the horrible, overly-perfumed air was really a cover, powerfully scented not to produce an effect that was pleasing, but rather to mask something corrupted underneath. He took a sip of his tea. It had turned cold quickly. "Lizbeth, may I ask you something?"

"Yes," she replied. "You may."

"I suspect you know more than I do about all . . . this. Famous folks still living and all."

"I don't allege to entirely understand it myself, but I make do."

"What I mean to say is, I don't really belong here, you know."

"You don't say?"

"I'm not dead," Luke admitted as much to himself as to her. "I'm just passing through."

"I've heard before about a handful of the living making their way here. *Animates* is what we call them, able to come and go as they please. But, golly, what I wouldn't give to go back to the real world. Do it all over again."

Luke considered. "Doesn't seem too bad, how you have it. Get to keep living your life the way you always have. Nice house, comfortable surroundings."

Her face reddened. "Well, you don't know a pile of shit from a pair of titties, do you?"

Luke flinched, and his teacup trembled.

She regained her composure and laughed a small, strangled sound. "I'm just teasing."

They fell silent. She cleared her throat. He sniffled. They were silent again.

A question built in Luke, and after awhile he braved to ask it. "What are you remembered for, Lizbeth?"

"*Hm?*"

"What is it that keeps you here, being remembered?"

"Isn't everyone remembered for different reasons?"

"I mean, you must have done something famous," Luke said.

Her look said more than her words. "My wink and rhubarb pie have been known to be admired."

"It's just that I've never heard of you before."

"You don't know everyone in this world, do you?"

"No, true."

"Then who are you to question me, sitting there like you crawled out of society's asshole?"

Luke bit his lip. He set the cup onto a dainty plate painted with pink tulips. "I'm sorry, Lizbeth. Maybe I should move along."

"Nonsense, silly. I'm just teasing again. Lighten up!"

Luke wanted to leap up and flee, but he thought the dizziness of the room would topple him if he stood too quickly.

"Besides," she added, "aren't you waiting for Harriet?"

"You called her?" The only time Lizbeth had been away from Luke was when she made tea. But, he thought, if she heard a squeaking floorboard from the next room over, surely that range of sound would have gone two ways, and he would have heard her make any communication efforts.

"Maybe that's what I'm remembered for, corresponding *telepathically.*" Lizbeth's tight smile tightened further, as if her lips were sewed from the inside and the connecting thread suddenly pulled inward.

"Another tease?" Luke asked.

"Maybe not. Maybe I can read minds."

He began to feel, incredibly, even more uncomfortable than before. The crushing floral weight, violent perfume, stifling warm temperature, and Lizbeth's unbalanced manner all united to undermine his composure. She seemed to sense this and appeared satisfied, as if his discomfort were her pleasure.

Her tight smile relaxed. "There's a warm bath drawn upstairs. Why don't you scrub off, and I'll fluff the bed? I can send out for a laundress as well."

"Really? A bath readied?"

She winked. "Sugar for my sugar."

The bath was luxuriant. Luke forgave Lizbeth all her eccentricities once he lay soaking in the blissful wash. As soon as he stepped in, it turned brown as coffee from his filth, but it was enough just to repose in the searing water; his tensions unwound, his mind cleared, his worries lessened. The washroom was decorated in the same heavy-handed flower-and-cat theme as the parlor but at least, in here, it seemed more confined, without the impression of it all ready to smother him.

He lay there for some time until the water cooled, which was much sooner than expected. Lizbeth brought him a silk robe and slippers, not at all bothered by his nakedness in the bathtub. Of course, the water had colored so dark from his grime that nothing shameful could be seen beneath its surface.

After she left, he got out and dried. Examined himself in the mirror and was both shocked, yet not terribly surprised, at his appalling features. Though pink and scrubbed, Luke could still see black spots and lines webbing his features, as if the muck of transient living had stained him as permanently as a tattoo. He was skinny, more so than the last time he'd examined himself. His ribcage was a barrel that seemed squeezed too thin by binding hoops, and his upper arms were no wider than his elbows. He was emaciated with hunger, yet the hunger was something he'd lived with for so long that he'd grown accustomed to it, rarely noticing anymore its pleas for attention.

His face was gaunt and haggard, and strange wiry hairs sprung from points where hairs had never sprung before. There were new scars, new moles, new blisters, new wrinkles. His eyes were bloodshot and sunken, and the hair topping his head was stringy in front and shaggy in back.

He wondered what Daisy had ever seen in him.

Daisy . . .

A fresh wave of melancholy washed over him, and Luke had to grasp the edges of the basin not to collapse.

Am I sane? he thought suddenly. *Look at me, I appear as a ruined lunatic. And why wouldn't the mental condition match the physical? Who am I to think I can wander the world of the dead, searching for someone's memory? Does the crazy man realize he turns crazy, or does he always operate in a realm of steadily crumbling awareness?*

He squeezed a pimple on his chin, and the sharp pain and eruption of pus brought him back to focus on the moment. He took a towel and dried off and dressed in the robe and slippers.

The robe was an explosion of red hues formed of shimmering burgundy swirls, glistening ochre blooms, and provocative fuchsia silhouettes. Its measurement in girth fit perfectly around his withered frame, although the length was much too short. On a woman—if it were Lizbeth's—the hem would have extended beyond her knees. Upon his tall stature, it barely covered the hairs hanging off his ass. The sleeves, if tugged tight, ventured nervously past his elbows. The slippers were pink and fuzzy.

Though the clothes appeared better suited for the madam of a cathouse, they were wonderful to feel against his skin, smooth and plush, padded with some sort of bird's down between layers of carmine silk. Luke wondered only briefly what became of his own drawers. He'd stacked those crusty rags just inside the doorway, and they were missing now, but perhaps sent out to the laundress Lizbeth had earlier offered. He went into the adjoining hall and saw at its end a small window filled with falling dusk.

Another night, so soon. He'd been through much that day, and yet it had passed in a blink. With another blink he realized Lizbeth was standing there, perfectly still, watching him.

He prickled down to his toes.

She stretched out her arms as if to dance. "Oh, I love the night," she said. "It's so . . . quiet."

Luke agreed with her, though he thought the statement only held true for cities at nighttime. In wilderness, noises after dark sounded awful louder than their daylight counterparts. He said, "Thank you. For the bath and robe and hospitality."

"You are certainly welcome." She sauntered to him, one foot primly in front of the other, until she stood very close. "Bedtime."

And Luke realized how tired he truly was, how the weariness of life had leeched into him all the way down to the starved marrow of his visible bones. Jumping on trains, jumping off trains, running, always running, hungry without food, trying to find work, and then when finding it toiling twenty hours a day, but still hungry, still not enough food, laughing with Daisy, with Zeke, shivering at night, trembling at day, fleeing railroad bulls, holding her hand on a walk, making love in the dark, still hungry, still weary, even when there was no work, and the day was quiet and warm and they lay there, he unable to slumber, unable to save her. It was all too much.

"This way," she said.

"Say, where are my clothes?"

"Burned them."

Luke wanted to exclaim, but it felt too much effort. It would have seemed somehow wrong to dress again in those patchwork tatters anyway, after having cleansed himself. But now he had nothing . . .

"I think I might stay up a bit longer," Luke said, fighting the exhaustion that filled him. "I've got some matters to ponder."

"Nonsense," she replied. "Early to bed and early to rise, makes a man healthy and wealthy who dies."

"Say again?" Luke rubbed inside his ear, figuring there might be some water trapped there.

Lizbeth repeated the phrase.

"He dies?" Luke asked.

"I said it twice already. Perhaps you should get a parrot."

"It's just that I think—"

"There you go thinking again," she interrupted.

Luke let the subject drop.

Lizbeth led him to a brass-knobbed door that slowly crept open at her touch. Inside was darkness, interrupted only by more darkness. "Your room."

"Is there a light in here?"

"My, but aren't we the fussy guest."

A chilly draft snuck up the robe, and Luke felt his manhood shrivel. He cinched the robe tighter at his waist. "I'm sure it's wonderful. Thank you."

"That's more like it."

He squinted his eyes and edged into the room with arms outstretched. His sight began to acclimate to the gloom and, helped by a dribble of electric light sneaking in from the hall, he made out a four-poster bed layered with palatial mattresses and a pink-flowered quilt. Around it, the bed was ringed by hutches filled with more damned cat statues. *Was there no escape from them?*

He turned back to Lizbeth, afraid but determined to query his safety amongst the feral spawn, and thought he saw a hobo sign start to appear on the wall behind her. For the fleetest of milliseconds he glimpsed a slash of red, as if a finger had dipped in paint and wrote hastily, before the door slammed shut and the room went black.

"Lizbeth?" he said and felt around for the handle.

He found it and reopened the door, and Lizbeth stood exactly opposite him, her face inches from his own, her eyes big and eager. On her tiptoes, with arms upraised as if stretching, she blocked the far wall from view.

"Yes?" she said too quickly. "Does baby need a lullaby to sleep?"

"No, there was something—"

"A ba-ba of warm milk, perhaps?"

Luke leaned to his right, trying to peer over her shoulders, but she continued to feign-stretch with upraised arms, mirroring his leaning.

"Eh . . . No, forget it," he relented. Luke closed the door with a sigh, thinking perhaps the symbol had been his imagination.

"Good night!" she said enthusiastically from the other side.

Luke muttered the sentiment in return, then blindly made his way to the bed and climbed upon it. No matter how tired he was, he knew he wouldn't discover sleep while remaining in that macabre house. Yet while the notion of insomnia dwelled in his consciousness, wonderful slumber arrived.

Luke was awakened in the darkness. Or, more precisely, he was awakened by a shaft of light that fell across his face in the darkness. He squinted his eyes. The door to his room was wide open, and the light streamed in from the hall. A figure stood in the doorway, looking at him.

Lizbeth.

"Yes?" he mumbled.

"'Less they're dead," she said quietly, coming into the room.

Luke sat upright, his mind groggy. "What?"

"We don't endure people sleeping outdoors, unless they're dead."

He remembered the "joke" Lizbeth had started to say earlier that day.

She brought her arms out from behind her back. A large woodsman's axe was in hand.

"Jesus H, what's that for?" Luke scrambled out from under the covers, trying to keep his heart from breaking through his ribs. He still wore nothing but her ill-fitting robe, and it rippled across his thin shoulders the way he'd imagine a damsel in distress might appear.

"You were snoring."

"Snoring?"

"I told you they'd be upset."

He looked at the shadowy cat figurines surrounding him, expecting them to move suddenly, extend razor claws, and hiss. They remained inanimate. Only Lizbeth advanced, singing quietly.

"Sweetheart lies asleep in bed, forty-two chops for his head."

Luke's eyes widened.

"Haven't you heard that before?" she asked.

"No . . ."

"Oh well."

She swung the axe in a wide arc, its massive head coming just inches from Luke's own.

He shrieked.

"Be quiet!" Lizbeth hissed and swung again.

Luke rolled away from the bed as the hatchet smashed into the mattress where he'd just lain, severing his rumpled imprint in half. The recoil from the mattress's springs snapped the axe back up over her head like a motion in reverse, and its momentum toppled her rearward. Luke thought to grab the axe from her while she scrambled on the floor in a disarray of underskirts and gnashing teeth, but when he reached for it, she was quicker.

From the ground she prodded the weapon at his bare legs like a lance, but he leapt away and all thoughts of heroics fled for the hills. He retreated out the bedroom door and saw on the wall of the hallway the red 'bo signs he thought he'd glimpsed earlier and now wished he'd persisted to view. A pair of curved lines angled over a skull and crossbones: *If you remain, prepare for death*. Luke ran for the stairway.

"Stay with me!" Lizbeth cried from the room.

You're cracked as a leaking glass, he thought.

"Don't say that!" she shrieked.

Luke hadn't spoken out loud, and he remembered her tease about being able to read minds. The thought brought a little gasp squeezing up through his tightened throat, but then he figured no mind-reading was necessary on her part; she probably just anticipated to be called crazy by every person she met.

He leapt down the stairs two at a time. One of the stair boards creaked under his weight, and the sound reverberated in a shrill roar, like ripping out rusted nails from an old coffin lid.

A cascade of shatters and curses and chasing footfalls exploded from above. Lizbeth screamed, "You woke them up!"

This, more than anything, prompted Luke's feet to fly faster. He didn't want to encounter anything worse wakening in this house of horrors.

He reached the bottom of the stairway and faced the inescapable pink and paisley jungle that was the sitting room. Impossibly, the door leading outside was only across the room, yet it appeared as a distant mountain separated by a great divide. Tangled gold-leaf carvings seemed to become poisonous vines, pale doilies were sheaths of thorns, plush rugs were quicksand. Heavy furniture blocked each route like impassable boulders. And, within it all, the cat statue denizens were legion.

The statues were overwhelming. *Dear merciful Lord,* Luke thought. He hated animals, even cats, and visions of the sculpted felines coming to life formed stronger than ever in his mind.

A thumping and a faint moan came from behind the settee where he and Lizbeth had earlier sat drinking tea.

"Lover," came a low voice. Lizbeth was behind him, at the top of the stairs, suddenly calm, the axe resting indifferently over one shoulder.

Luke tentatively took a step into the sitting room. That eye-watering scent of flowers drowned in puissant perfume returned with a vengeance, and the step he'd taken was retreated. He breathed through his mouth, but the smell remained unendurable as he tasted it on his tongue and in the back of his throat. He thought again the toxic fragrance was there to mask something dreadful. More thumps from behind the settee, and the moans grew louder.

"I didn't want to wake them, 'cause they'd be upset," Lizbeth said. "Daddy doesn't care for company to visit any longer. That upsets him too. Everything I do upsets him. He blames me, both of them blaming me, as if everything's my fault, always my fault, 'cause I'm never good enough, am I?"

Luke held his breath and pushed into the fumes. His eyes watered. Like before, he felt he descended into a spiraling freighter.

Just keep moving, he thought. *One foot in front of the other and soon enough you'll get out.*

Never before had the color pink assaulted so viciously. Its hues burned his retinas with deviant fluorescence, and he felt suffocated by an avalanche of carnations, each petal more garish and looming than the last. That fear battled for prominence against the panic of the crowding cat statues, and in this setting he didn't know which was worse: pink flowers or cats, cats or pink flowers. Like feral toms, the statues seemed to breed exponentially, each staring at him with frozen yellow eyes from every nook and crevice of the room.

The settee began moving, pushed from behind by some force that Luke couldn't see. Its wood feet plodded with a slow swoosh over the carpet, swinging perpendicular to his path.

"Oh, they're upset now," Lizbeth reminded him, gliding down the stairs. "Very, very upset."

The settee completed its pivot, blocking Luke's route, and now he saw what lay behind. The sight wasn't the worst thing Luke ever viewed in his life, nor was it actually as grisly as the constructs he feverishly imagined capable to rise from Lizbeth's house. Then again, it definitely ranked high on any scale of diabolic horrors.

On the floor lay two people writhing terribly, each soaked in blood as red as furnace coal.

No, Luke thought as time seemed to slow, allowing him precious moments to consider his situation. Calling them people was not entirely accurate, as it was rather the limbs and parts and trappings of two people that lay writhing terribly and bloodily on the floor.

They were a man and a woman, both aged in older years. That much Luke could discern, but beyond his initial perception, identifying the rest was madness. Their eyes were open and bulging like hot fried eggs, their heads cleaved in halves; their mouths gaped open, and only wriggling stumps of tongue flapped up and down, emitting the now-familiar moans. Both the couple's arms and legs were hacked off and then chopped further in pieces, like whittling smaller pieces of kindling from the larger trunk. Hands and feet moved of their own accord, little excited puppies bounding up and down, showering gore with each movement the way wet dogs shake themselves free from drops of moisture.

Lizbeth was halfway down the stairs, and Luke was rooted only steps from its bottom tread. There was no way around the settee or the bucking body debris.

"I didn't kill them," she cried. "I was set up, all a mistake."

For an instant, Luke further studied the mangled corpses, in his mind pushing the split heads back together, pulling clotted hair away from their faces. He had seen them before . . .

The oval-framed photographs when he'd first come inside the house . . . This was the elderly couple prominently displayed on the mantle.

"Daddy won't go away. Why can't people just forget about him?" Lizbeth was right behind. She sucked in air as she hefted the axe over her head.

Without warning, the writhing body parts rushed forward, severed hands scrambling like odd-legged spiders, sundered legs slithering as snakes, disjointed feet vaulting with the leaps of misshapen toads, detached heads rolling quicker than angry hedgehogs.

Luke shrieked long and shrill, a locomotive's whistle sounding in alarm. Every person has their limits, and Luke had long ago hung dangling with clawed fingers off the edge of his. After Daisy's death, he wasn't even sure if he wanted to go on living, and that vacillation now took its toll. Luke threw his arms over his head and collapsed to the floor, ready for it all to end.

The body parts touched him, climbed over him, skittered around him, left their slimy residue of rotting entrails across his person, but caused no harm as they went past.

Lizbeth howled. "No, Daddy! Let me kill him! Please let me kill him!"

Luke glanced back and saw Lizbeth tumbling to the ground, her axe bowling over packs of cat statues. The cats shattered. They'd been harmless all along; Lizbeth was just a crazy cat statue lady.

The body parts fought her. A handless arm wrapped around her neck and the cap of a knee catapulted into her midsection. Lizbeth groaned and tried to gouge out the eyes of a snarling head. It snapped at her fingers with broken teeth.

The jungle-illusion of the sitting room melted away, and Luke saw the front door beckoning to open at his touch. A torrent of relief swelled that, beyond all reason, an opportunity for escape had suddenly manifested. He clambered away from the struggle and vaulted the settee.

The moaning heads grunted and whimpered as Lizbeth kicked them aside. "I can't help that's all I'm remembered for," she yelled. "But there's more to me than just murder!"

Luke was out the door, across the porch, down its steps, and racing to the street fast enough to lose his shadow. After a block's length he slowed the pace, his ribs hammered by his heart.

Lizbeth's voice sounded from behind, not close, but not far away either. She was following him. "Tell people I was innocent, I was framed!"

Luke pounded more pavement, running down a quaint street occupied by ice cream shops closed 'til morning, delicatessens, and stores of antiques, souvenirs, décor, travel books, artwork, and other things a carefree sightseer might be interested in procuring.

Writ in soapy film across the window of a photography studio was a circle with a pair of arrows protruding from it. Following that was the icon of a railroad track. *Go this way, fast, to catch a train.*

"Give me back my robe!" Lizbeth's voice echoed through the night.

Luke ran a mile or more, panting, until the tourist section of town was at his heels and large textile mills grew from the distance, like the ones he'd seen when he first entered Fall River. Industrial monuments were always a good indicator of a rail line nearby; commerce coupled with manufacturing like fondling teenagers. Onward, and he saw his beloved steel rails of freedom come into view. They crossed an empty boulevard, ready to charge north across the land.

Posted aside the boulevard was a bright yellow stop sign, and on that sign Luke saw a new hobo mark, an image of a star. It seemed to be moving with little shimmers, like a distant firework raining sparkles through the sky: *Wish*.

Luke didn't have to wonder what the wish should be. He thought of that feeling he'd experienced coming into Fall River, the sense of being one with his train, of controlling it, really *riding* it, not letting the train just take him where *it* wanted. That sense of command was harder now since he wasn't already on the train, connected to it, but that he had to call it from faraway. It wasn't a thing like a whistle from his lips, and it'd come galloping to his rescue; Luke had to couple with the train, like a line of cars hitching to the engine. He imagined shoving the Johnson bar forward, opening the cylinder cock, releasing the brakes, pulling out from its switching yard, chugging down these steel tracks faster and faster, 'til lightning couldn't outrace it. A New Haven engine marked with a big 3610 on its ebony cab, pulling chipped red tankers, a line of pillboxes, short hoppers full of iron ore, and here it'd come shooting up the tracks . . .

Luke heard it: a vibration in the rail, then a high-pitched scuffing sound, then the distant rushing rumble, and then the train was before him, slowing to a regular speed—a 'bo's hopping speed—and he reached for the first ladder that passed without having to run much. He lifted his knees to the bottom rung, got his feet under him, climbed a step, and shimmied into the double door of a boxcar half-filled with pickle barrels and seed bags.

As he got inside, Luke peered back and thought he saw a figure running at the train, and the figure was a woman, yelling and swinging her axe desperately at the wheels, but it was all a flash and a blur, and maybe just his imagination. The train sped up, spurtin' grease and ill will at her, if she were there at all.

Inside the boxcar were two other men, eating pickles and playing gin rummy with a pack of earmarked Bicycle cards.

"Howdy, 'bos," Luke said to the men by reflex, and only remembered he was all but invisible when they didn't give him a glance or nod in return.

Luke made a seat amongst the heavy burlap bags, watching the 'bos without any great interest, but as a way to take his mind off current circumstances. One of them was dark-skinned with an eye patch and a top hat over his gaunt head. The other was pale with some disease of the skin and an immense beard, as if trying to cover himself behind a veil of hair. They both seemed content as chipmunks, nibbling away in their tree hideaway.

Eye Patch pulled a playing card from the stockpile on the floor. He had seven or eight others held tight in his hand, but still couldn't form a meld. He tossed down a king of spades into the discard row. "How much longer, you think?"

"Should be an hour or two, hop off 'fore we cross the Neponset River," the man cloaked in beard answered.

"Heard the Neponset bridge got washed away last spring."

"If'n so, they got up a new one," Beard answered, laying down a discard. "Came south outta Boston last month."

"Rummy!" Eye Patch shouted, and slapped the pile. He took Beard's discard, a four of hearts, and added it to his meld.

"Darn, missed that one."

"Missed the last three in a row, too."

"Got my mind on more important things, I do."

Eye Patch pulled a new card. "You's just an important person, aren't ya? Wonder you're not running the country by now."

"No need to get snide, Phineas."

"I'm teasing, you know it." He lay down a run of clubs, then Beard added one of his own, an eight.

"Say, that eight of clubs is what cost me my eye," Phineas declared.

"Oh Lord, here's a crossbuck."

"What's that mean?"

"Nothin' but a warning for my ears," Eye Patch said.

"Humph," Phineas said, and drew a new card. "I've a better account about a Jack of Fools."

"First you're sneering, then you're stung," Beard ribbed. "But let's have it, you dandy. New on me how an eight of clubs could cost your eye, 'less it was for cheating."

Phineas fanned his remaining cards like he was rocking on a Georgia porch in the butt of summer. "I never cheated in my life, 'cept on my wife, my mistress, and my moll."

"And each of them gave eight clubs to your face."

"You heard the tale!"

The two men went on like this for some time, and each time they laughed it reminded Luke of happiness, and it reminded him he'd never feel it again.

The car door was half-open, like how Zeke always wanted. It was only the night before that he and Zeke and Daisy'd been laughing, then gone to sleep, then McCain had arrived. Them dead, himself almost dead twice over, and now on a train heading north, and Luke with no idea what to do, who he was. *Harriet, Harriet* . . . She was the only one who seemed able to help. He'd made friends with John Dillinger, but Johnny was as confused about the deadeye as himself. Of course, it'd been several years since last he'd been here, and surely Dillinger had figured it out as much as any other specter of Athanasia.

Luke watched the world turn outside like the screen of a moving picture. The stars were signs in themselves, and the glowing eyes of night critters blinked coded messages. From great distance he saw the ruin of a mountain, crumbling and dismantled by pox so red it appeared an eruption of lava ran down the fracturing slope. *How?* Luke wondered. *How could even a mountain be forgot?*

Maybe it was all too late anyway . . .

Phineas and Beard laughed again, dealing a new hand, sharing a flask. Luke wished more than anything to be a part of them, to share in their warmth instead of being some invisible spook eavesdropping on their lives.

"Say, fellas," Luke said, "I got a good one."

"Rummy!" Beard shouted and slapped the discard pile.

"Finally payin' attention again, *hm?*" Phineas commented.

"One 'bo says to another, I'm going to quit smoking," Luke said. "It's becoming too dangerous. *Really?* the other 'bo answers. *Yup.* Twice today I picked up a cigarette butt and someone nearly ran me over!"

"When I get to Haverhill," Beard announced, "I wanna get some ass and order a steak."

"Men only got two emotions," Phineas replied. "Hungry and horny. I told my wife if she don't see me with a hard-on to make me a sandwich!"

Beard spit out a mouthful of pickle with a laugh. "Bet that got you the ninth club to the face!"

Luke sighed and closed his eyes and forced himself to sleep.

LUKE AND PAUL, 1938

Luke dreamed he was a child back in Savannah, and his mother sat beside him drinking a bourbon sweet tea.

There was so much he wanted to ask her, but his voice felt hard to use under her steely eyes. She sipped from a glass tumbler and licked her lips. He played with the hem of his short pants, the last piece of clothing he'd ever owned not hand-me-down, ripped, and soiled.

She spoke first. "You weren't meant for this life."

He felt confused. Not meant for the well-to-do Savannah life? Not meant for the wanderlust 'bo life? Not meant for the animate life, running amongst the dead? Or something else?

In dreams our questions are rarely answered, and she added cryptically, "You're a sensitive child, Lucas."

Finally, Luke got out, "Are you still here?"

"No, son, but there's more. There's always more . . . "

A man appeared beside her, tall and faceless. She spat up all she'd drunk back into the goblet and handed it to him.

"You can't take it with you, honey, not even what you love."

A voice broke through his thoughts, and it took a moment for Luke to understand it was a real voice, not part of the dream. "Smith McCain is coming, Smith McCain is coming!"

Luke bolted upright like a sprung lever. His heart froze, his whole body froze, except for a single drop of perspiration that tried escaping down his temple.

He looked for the other two 'bos, but they were asleep in each other's arms; they hadn't heard a thing. He looked the other way and caught a flash of movement. A man on horseback galloped past the car's door, then fell back out of sight, like he was trying to keep up. He appeared again. "Better get out of there! Smith McCain is coming!"

Luke was on his feet before he knew it and at the door even faster, about to jump out.

"Get on my horse!" the man said.

"Wait, the others," Luke said.

"No time!"

Luke yelled in a frenzy at the two 'bos, "Get up, get out!"

They didn't stir. He screamed, "God, get up! Smith McCain is coming!"

But no one living notices me here . . .

Luke backpedaled to the couple. He remembered trying to make the boy on the road see him after he left John Dillinger shot in the car years ago. He wasn't able to do it then, but he *had* to now!

Luke balled up his fist and pounded on the face of the nearest of the two 'bos, Phineas. The man's head reeled one way, then the next way, his top hat rocketed off, and Luke punched him harder, screaming, "Wake up!"

Luke hit him as hard as he could, hoping not to cave in the man's cheek or jaw, but desperate to rouse him. Harder and harder, Phineas's nose should have shattered by now, his teeth broken like escaped seeds from a pod. Instead, little more than reddish blotches remained on the 'bo's face from his strikes, the appearance of one who's rubbed an irritating bug bite. It was infuriating: Was he that weak, or were his effects simply of such pitiful notice?

"Hurry!" the man on horseback cried to Luke.

Spittle fell from Luke's mouth and beads of sweat off his brow, raining onto the 'bo, mixing with the rain of his blows. *This must be like a baker's job, pounding limp dough until one's arms grow tired.*

Finally the man's eyelid fluttered halfway up, and he mumbled, "Eh, a fly?"

"Wake up, wake up! Smith McCain is coming!"

The man repeated, as if in his own dream, "Smith . . . ?"

"Smith McCain! Smith McCain!"

Then the 'bo was awake, as rigid as when Luke himself heard the warning. He blinked, seemed to look at Luke for a moment, then swept past as if Luke was a bit of dream rubbish.

"Get out! It's Smith McCain!" Luke again screamed, his voice threatening to break.

Something clicked in the man. He still didn't notice Luke's presence, but the strength of that name—the fear of it—somehow got through to Phineas, even while Luke pounding on him didn't. He grabbed Beard by the collar of his shirt and hauled him up. "Smith McCain's coming!"

Beard's eyes spun like large pinwheels. He cried softly, "Momma."

Then the two of them leapt about twenty feet across the boxcar and out the door.

"Hurry now!" the horseback man called again.

Luke followed to the exit, ready any moment for a monstrous black hand to grab him from behind.

"Jump on the horse," the man said, galloping at pace with the train.

Without thinking, Luke jumped, and he missed. One leg slid over the horse's rump, and the riding man tried to grab him, but Luke kept sliding, off and out in space, falling again in seeming slow motion. Luke thought that his body couldn't take much more abuse, and then one of the horse's rear hooves kicked him in the stomach as it ran off. Luke hit the ground on his side, his breath knocked free, bones cracking, and he knew only to roll away from the tracks so the back cars wouldn't run him over.

"I tried to catch you," the man said sheepishly, "but you're slippery. Takes a man with pluck to wear what you got on."

Luke's first thought was that his left wrist blazed with pain, and the rest of his body didn't feel much better. His second thought recalled he still wore Lizbeth's silk robe.

"Felt like trying to grab an eel in water with bare hands," the man added.

Luke scowled. They sat in a pasture, the horse tethered nearby, whinnying, which could have been laughing. Luke cinched the robe tighter with his good hand, dazed, his head still spinning. "I was in a bit of a rush to get away with my life."

"Name's Paul Revere, and I don't judge. But I do think if you're going to dress like a fancy Dan, you should consider wearing Persian blue. It's more flattering to your skin tone."

Another horse whinny, or laugh.

Luke groaned as he carefully stood. He looked at Paul, who appeared as Luke would have expected, as depicted in every image of Paul Revere he'd seen: a bit small in stature, with sharp features and beribboned hair, dressed in white leggings and a petticoat. In modern day, he was the last person who should get away with mocking another man's clothing.

A dozen insults came to mind, but he remembered Paul *had* saved him. Luke bit his tongue and simply said, "Thanks for the warning."

"It's what I'm known for."

"Not the first time I've heard that expression."

"You came from Lizzie Borden's place?"

Luke gaped. "Is that who she was?"

"Ol' Lizzie is crazy as a bedbug on fire," Paul said. "She's like a black widow spider, only you don't get the pleasure of mating her first."

"I didn't know . . . She wouldn't answer straight who she was—"

Paul interrupted. "Hey, looks like that hand needs some doctoring."

At the prompting, throbs of hurt resumed their flare up Luke's arm. He lifted it and saw now that the left wrist was purple and angled inward, a broken bone pushing up under the skin. His hand twisted like a claw, though he could still move his fingers, even if such movement sent little charges of pain racing to his elbow.

Adrenaline rush, Luke thought. That's what was keeping the pain tamped down somewhat, though he couldn't believe he had any adrenaline remaining. Then the rush faded and the pain throttled, and he bawled a slurry of curses at Paul and his despicable horse.

Paul took a step back. "Easy, we'll get you sorted out."

"You can set my hand?"

"Me? No, but I know someone who can."

The pained turned to an all-too-familiar resentment. "I ain't got money to pay a doctor or anything like that."

"You think I sent a bill for services rendered after warning everyone the British were coming?"

Luke shrugged noncommittally.

"Just hop on Brown Beauty. I'll do the steering."

Luke glared at the horse, and it glared back, staring him down 'til he felt smaller than a midget flea.

"Be good," Paul told it. The horse snuffled, dropping its gaze.

"You can do it," Paul encouraged Luke, and untethered the animal. "One of my daughters was riding a horse when she was barely three. I'm sure you got the same facilities as a toddler." He motioned Luke up by cupping his hands into a foothold. "I'll even help you mount."

Luke went up, wavered, then slid off the horse's flanks to crash-land on the other side. His wrist and feelings hurt more. Paul sighed, but cajoled him to try again, and eventually Luke made it, and Paul joined him, and the horse set off at a gallop carrying them fast through Massachusetts woods. Luke held Paul tight around the waist with his good arm.

Paul's head tilted back, and he said over the rush of hoof strides and shrill wind, "You're the first person I met who isn't keen on Brown Beauty."

"Animals and I don't get along much."

"I'll say. I'd just expect you rail riders to be proficient at getting on and off moving things."

"I'll take an engine over a beast any day."

"Animals are as much people as we are. Trains are lifeless and loud and ghastly to behold." Paul turned forward again. "But to each their own."

They rode faster. Trees flew past like emerald hornets, swift-motion streaks of green, black, and fallow, but soon those thinned out, displaced by blurs of slate, bronze, and blue. It took only minutes for the forest to give way to modern development; office buildings seized the place of timber, and parked cars replaced bristly shrubs. Brown Beauty slowed around delivery trucks and bridged canals, and a vast harbor came into view, filled with distant bobbing boats. The sun lingered half-over the horizon, casting hints of gold over land and sky and sea, and it all appeared as sculpted treasure.

"Where are we?" Luke asked.

"Boston, the Athens of America."

People filled the early morning streets, and Brown Beauty navigated amongst them. Newspaper boys cried out with the day's headlines, while sharp-dressed gals moved in packs, each as lovely as department store models. Men walked briskly along with important places to be, their trench coats skimming cobblestoned walkways and not caring. A cocker spaniel yipped. A man wearing a sandwich board called out President Roosevelt as a yellow-dog bum, and the spaniel seemed offended by the comparison. The crowds were fascinating and they were the same as all big cities, and they glanced up at Paul Revere in brief recognition, their noble herald astride his mighty steed, while ignoring the strange accomplice in a silken robe. The people noticed Paul, then they didn't, one by one, like a breath of wind coursing through willows, blowing each sideways in turn, and when the next one bent, the last returned to its natural straight shape.

Paul halted Brown Beauty with, "Whoa," and announced to Luke, "We're here."

Anxious to get down, Luke swung one leg over and tumbled off the horse in a maneuver that was half backward slide, half ass-first fall.

"Interesting way to dismount," Paul said, leaping off the animal in a fluid motion.

Luke stood, red-faced, and held his injured hand. His inner thighs were chafed and his embarrassment seared. "Like I said—"

Paul tied off the horse's reins around a banister. "You prefer engines over beasts, I get it."

They stood in front of a tall, regal-looking building built of pale pink granite and lined with Romanesque archways, seeming to stretch the entire block.

"The city's library," Paul said. "It has a *storied* past." He chuckled at his own quip while Luke grimaced. "Come on inside and meet the others."

THE SONS OF LIBERTY, 1938

"Luke, let me introduce you to Ben."

Paul led him into a sprawling reading room, filled with heavy oak tables and more books than Luke had ever seen in his life. A man was there, showing his stooped back to them while thumbing through a tome large enough to anchor a ship.

The man turned, and Luke saw he was doughy, with sleepy eyes and ruddy cheeks. The top of his head gleamed bald and bare, though around his crown hung long gray hair that draped well over his shoulders. He was old, yet held the bright, quizzical expression of an infant, as if every movement and bauble around him were of the greatest interest.

"You look familiar," Luke said.

"His face *is* on the hundred-dollar bill," Paul said in amusement.

"Never seen one of those."

Ben sighed. "I'm known for more than that." He made a face at Paul, glaring over the top of thick glasses.

Then it clicked: The man before him was Benjamin Franklin.

Paul smiled and put his arm around Luke. "Ben, this is Luke. Luke's the animate."

"*Weeell*," Ben said in long exclamation. "It's been a great while since I've conversed with one of you, at least in the sense of equality."

"Equality?" Luke studied the two men; they were healthy and well-groomed, and displayed significance as garishly as the jeweled rings on their fingers.

"You and I, here, speaking, and of your own free will," Ben replied. "Normally, I must *take* someone's attention."

"Ah, right. I seen John Dillinger do that to a couple of men."

"Dillinger's still a newbie, and rather a gambit at that. Some criminals do persevere—the lawless tend to be somewhat of a favorite—but most are replaceable, falling away to other crooks engaged in more recent notoriety, more daring exploits. Villainy is often a lot of fluff and not much substance. I don't think John Dillinger has the célèbre for permanence. But we'll see."

Ben gazed at Luke, and Luke wondered if he was expected to agree. The pause grew awkward, until he forced a reply. "I tried it myself. I sort of got through to someone earlier on the train, but mostly no one seems to pay me any mind."

"Nor will they, young man, until you do something remarkable."

"Oh. Guess I ain't done much worthwhile."

"Such is the voice of defeatism," Ben scolded. "You made it here; you must have some aptitude of note."

"I just followed the signs, and this is where they led."

"You *are* naïve, aren't you? How many people do you think can see these 'signs'?"

Luke fell silent, chewing that over, the pain in his wrist thumping all the while. "Well, lots of other people follow the Code. Most 'bos I know live by its signs."

"There are signs, and then there are *signs*," Ben said. "I trust that nobody else you know sees the doorways that lead here?"

Now Luke understood, though he didn't have the slightest inkling why he was different from everyone else, why he was special enough to cross to this realm. "Not that I know."

Ben nodded smugly, and his gaze dropped to Luke's arms, where one hand held the broken other. "What injury afflicts you?"

Paul spoke for him. "Snapped his wrist like a birch flute."

Ben hadn't stopped nodding, the all-knowing quirk of self-righteousness. "I see. Wrap the broken wrist in a poultice of purslane and mud, then stamp your feet three times in a semicircle while whistling northward."

"Wait, what? Should I understand that?"

"You will. Perhaps. Meantime, let's sit."

"Want some tea?" Paul asked. "We didn't throw it *all* in the harbor."

"Though we should have," a voice added. Two more men Luke hadn't noticed were sitting at a long table, both of them writing in the glow of half-melted candles. "How about a beer instead? It's family legacy."

"Legacy?" Luke repeated.

"That's Sam Adams," Paul told him, and Sam nodded affably.

The other man at the table stood to bow slightly. They were similar in appearance and dress—all of them—wearing heavy coats with some sort of lace scarf, lots of gold buttons adorning their outfits, and ungodly white powdered wigs. Paul continued, gesturing at the last man, "And the other is John Hancock."

"Greetings," John boomed.

"I get it," Luke said. "Benjamin Franklin, Sam Adams, Paul Revere, all you founding fathers still around. Makes sense, in a weird, backward sort of way. I take it George Washington's here too?"

"He's probably sunbathing up at Mount Vernon," Sam said. The others snickered.

"We're Boston men," John said.

"Sons of Liberty, most of us," Paul added.

"We travel, we visit with others, but oft we stay where we're remembered most or needed most," Ben said.

"There are more of us in the area," Sam said. "Though if you happen to come across Benedict Arnold and he tells you to go one way, be sure to do the opposite." The old men snickered again.

Luke shifted restlessly from one bare foot to the other, wishing he had something under his soles, even the pink slippers from Lizbeth, although bare feet or not, his discomfort around men of means was never less apparent.

Paul led him to the table, which looked officious and old, like the sort of surface men wrote notices upon that ordered the death of other men. Luke sat at the farthest end, facing the others, and imagined himself sinking into the chair until he passed through its carved seat and wood legs and made lam between the floor cracks. There was no reason not to trust the country's forefathers, yet an instinct took hold that reminded him men with authority always found a way to piss on him, then sneer when he didn't say, *Thanks for the wash.*

Luke forced a brave grin. "You said something about beers?"

Ben drew a small bell from his waistcoat and rang it with imperial chime. "Shaping the nation does cause a thirst."

A man shuffled into the room, wearing linens so white they nearly glowed against his dark skin. Deadpan eyes searched the floor as if that was what had summoned him.

"Beers all around," Ben said, and the man turned to go as silently as he'd arrived. "And Francis," Ben added. The man paused as a statue. "Please be quicker next time."

Luke massaged his injured arm as Francis departed. "Another Son?"

"Him?" Paul asked, and the others barraged laughter. "Just a servant."

"Domestic help," Sam clarified, "like a valet."

Ben added quickly, "Consider him a contented steward enjoying the security of an appreciative household, unburdened from vexations of the loafer."

"Folks call *me* a loafer," Luke said carefully. "I get through vexations just fine."

"Should we instead call him a retainer?" John asked, appearing genuinely concerned as to Luke's opinion. "A butler? Is there a more acceptable term these days? Every generation it's something different, you know."

"I don't care what you call him," Luke said. "What's the name matter?"

"Such wisdom in truth," Ben said curtly, ending the subject.

Francis returned hoisting a serving tray filled with heavy glass mugs, and placed one in front of each man before withdrawing without a sound.

They took deep drinks, and all the while Luke felt the others appraising him in a clinical sense, the way a scientist might dissect a particularly interesting specimen . . . a strange, unkempt, cross-dressing specimen. He picked at some muck splattered on the robe's sash and apologized for his revealing dress. "I was, *ahem*, making scarce from an axe-wielding madwoman."

The Sons of Liberty nodded understanding, as if they'd all experienced similar predicaments in their own lives.

Ben asked, "So, what can we assist you with, young man?"

"I'm looking for Harriet Tubman."

"I'm intrigued. And why?"

"She said she'd help me."

They paused, waiting for more.

"Well, assembly adjourned," Ben scoffed. "You're tight-lipped as a Loyalist captive."

Luke smiled dumbly, then thought he should look pensive for these men, or even sneer at Ben's wisecrack. But the expression felt so forced it was like a tight mask straining at his cheeks, so he smiled dumbly again, until biting his tongue. *So much for a brave grin . . .*

John cleared his throat. "Would you care to elaborate?"

Sam added, "Harriet keeps herself busy, even more than the rest of us. We can reach out to her, but it's all quite complex. Smoke signals and blinking lights and three coughs means yes, and so on. Her suspicions of us have never dispelled."

"Why's that?" Luke asked.

The men glanced uneasily at each other. Paul replied, "Let's just say we've held, um, some differences of opinion."

"Don't ever get her and Jefferson in the same room," John said.

Ben rolled his eyes. "Back to task, what is it you need, Luke? Why are you here?"

"I'm looking for my friend Zeke, and Daisy, the girl I love. They—they died."

"Ah, a contemporary Orpheus searching for his Eurydice," Ben said. "Ultimately the tragedy will remain the same. You may catch glimpse of them, may even share a few final words, but they will still vanish before your eyes. Again."

Luke's face slowly melted, a reflection of the waning candles on their table. "But—they were killed too early. It wasn't supposed to happen."

"And why not? Everyone dies. Not everyone can remain in this holding world like us, and even we who do will someday fall away as well."

"Then can't they at least stay here like you, living to be centuries old?"

Paul whistled.

Ben looked at the others slowly. "Yes, we really *are* that aged, aren't we?"

"And you'll outlast us all," John Hancock told Ben. "If I hadn't signed my name so large, I'd hardly be remembered. The accomplishments I achieved, the causes founded, mostly forgot in the stead of reckless penmanship . . . "

"Could be worse," Sam said. "How many of us were lost after that first generation passed?"

"Such is the fickleness of public regard," Ben added wistfully. "Entertainers will replace dignitaries soon enough, musicians and silly clowns paid more attention than we who struggle for the nation's liberty. Mark my words, our downfall will be heralded by puns and magic tricks."

Luke clenched and unclenched his good hand. "You able to help or not?"

The others looked at him cautiously, and each took a long drink, perhaps contemplating what to admit or to warn or to fib.

"As I told you," Ben said, "people who are remembered—who remain—must do something remarkable."

"That's your political leaders, war heroes, inventors, sometimes poets, sometimes religious shepherds," Sam Adams said.

"Sometimes anyone who becomes the moral of a fable, for good or for ill," John continued.

"Or sometimes the treacherous or crazies, such as you've already met," Paul added with a wink.

"But Zeke and Daisy were nobodies, like me," Luke admitted.

"Such is your plight," Ben said, quietly. "Though I apologize for being so disconsolate. I'm truly sorry for your loss."

Luke slumped, chewing at his lip, feeling, in front of these great men— men who'd formed a country from dreams and labor and sacrifice—that he might begin to cry over the loss of just friends and love.

Ben continued, "They will remain a bit, certainly long enough to say proper good-byes. Everyone lingers in Athanasia awhile, depending on the impression left while alive. Assuming they were like you, drifters, perhaps with few family who wonder at their loss, Zeke and Daisy may remain a few months, maybe a year. Could be more or less, as my observations have been unscientific—can't reproduce results with any standard expectation, you know. Erelong, their spirits will weaken and dwindle like a fading spark, until each blows out."

"But don't take lightly the remarkableness of your situation," Sam told Luke. "I can count to six the number of living persons—animates— including you, I've known crossing to the deadeye. You have a gift for something that only you will be able to realize."

"What gift is that?" Luke asked.

"Which part of 'only you will realize' didn't you get?" Paul said. "Everyone has secret intuitions or competence in a talent that others haven't got."

Luke remembered John Dillinger saying that exact thing before to him.

"I was told I had an aptitude for mechanics," Luke said. "Drove a car the first time I tried."

"And you caught a train just by thinking it to arrive," Paul continued for him, then addressed the others. "This kid says he doesn't know what he can do."

"How'd you know I did that in Fall River?" Luke asked. "Were you watching me?"

Paul's face tightened.

Ben interrupted, "And you admit a knack for reading symbols that others don't see. Seems to me you were blown in the glass to become a rail rider, called to your profession as a bard is called to writing soliloquies."

Luke sighed. "Maybe all that's good for travelling, but how will it help save my friends?"

Ben sighed louder in exasperation. "A certain expression leaps to mind involving a horse that is led to water."

"Paul can ride anywhere in the country in two hours on his steed," Sam said. "You don't hear him complaining that he doesn't know what good it'll do him."

"In Athanasia, the accomplishments or strengths you're known for are magnified," Paul broke in. "People remember me galloping on horseback at record speed."

"And when people forget about us," John said, "those strengths will fade, as will we. When there's not enough recognition behind our names any longer, we'll rot from memory as our bodies rotted in the grave."

"It's social consciousness," Ben explained. "One or two distant cousins remembering you isn't enough. You must be perceived in the greater awareness of society. The more you're recalled, the stronger you are, just as lack of memory leads to weakness, and that leads to the pox and the great and final *adieu*."

Ben took a sip from his glass mug and nodded for Luke to signal understanding. It was a curt nod, but if Ben's gaze were any more intense,

Luke felt his face might light on fire. Luke's gaze darted to each of the other men staring at him, if not as fervently, at least as minor gods surrounding their absolute. He mirrored Ben's motion: a sip and a curt nod, and they seemed appeased.

Ben continued. "The world is a great mind, perhaps even the brain of another being. Are we made in our creator's image? Perhaps, though I won't attribute that to religious orthodoxy. *Cogito ergo sum*: 'I think, therefore I am.' And I am dead, yet I live, so do I not exist within myself? Look in a mirror and, by regressive reasoning, that is your universe."

Ben paused importantly and took another sip, nodding again for Luke to nod back.

This time Luke faltered. There was an unpleasant eagerness in the others he likened to a man hunting a 'coon, while the animal sniffs nearer and nearer a snare. He felt an urgency to back away and figure through their intentions. "I might have slipped on what you're proposin', Mr. Franklin."

Ben snuffled. "Of course you have."

The other old men snuffled with Ben, appreciatively.

Ben continued. "Simply put, consider whatever is our origin endures the same limitations as ourselves, proven because we are of it—the mirror—replete with emotions, fallibilities, and a damned limited ability for recollection.

"Few remember more than a small percentage of their life in short-term storage. Certain events carry more distinction than others, while most of the menial day-to-day details are glossed over. That is, each of us in existence is just a detail—a construct or a cell—in this creator's mind. Those of us who affect the mind most substantially are remembered most clearly, while the rest fade away."

"You saying I'm made up in someone's fancies?"

"Not at all. Is a molecule imagined that composes a part of one drop of water in the ocean? Nay, it exists as a mote in the greater whole. We are all molecules in the stormy ocean of this existence, though some of us have realized greater staying power."

Without warning, Ben pounded one fleshy fist on the tabletop and a spray of foam shot from his mug and from his mouth. "You must fight to be remembered!"

Ben breathed heavily, and one of his eyes twitched as he went on. "It's a competitive plight, though we Sons of Liberty have founded something of our legacy into the long-term memory of social consciousness. But countless others come and go. We continue to do what people remember us for—what our creator remembers us for—mostly as men of learning, discussing important ideals. But there are many here in the deadeye, fading ghosts who struggle desperately to make their own names grow, to imprint themselves in memory. They battle to weaken others while improving on their own legacy."

Luke's mind spun, and his head hurt from the pressure of trying to reconstruct what he knew of existence. Everything Ben and the others said was heard, but only a quarter of it made sense.

And where were they going with this conversation? That snare he'd sensed was still around, though he was like to step in it if he moved one direction as much as the other, so dizzied had he become. He polished off the last of Sam Adams's beer, hoping that would wind down the dervish.

Ben broke from his speech to match Luke, draining his own glass. At this, he seemed to relax, and his twitching eye settled. With a sigh and a cry for refills, Ben withdrew the small serving bell and gave it a brisk ring.

Sam took over. "Only sixty years ago, Joseph Warren sat in that very chair you're seated. He was one of us, a Bostonian and member of the Sons. Did you know he was architect of the Revolutionary War?"

Luke shrugged guiltily that he didn't.

"My point. No one does," Sam said, continuing. "Warren's even responsible for sending Paul on his famous horse ride. But after death, he got into a spat with Edgar Allan Poe over ideological differences stemming from the Romantic movement. For God's sake, Poe was the movement's literary champion, and there's Warren, an aristocrat as reserved as they come. Warren tried to repress the country's surge to aesthetic expression, and the two men started a smear campaign against each other. Guess who came out on top in that fracas?

"In 1878, the pox came for Warren. Quoth the raven, he is *nevermore*."

Ben rang his little bell again.

John Hancock said, "Warren's blunder was that he assured people Poe was a morose drunk and an addict of opiates. Such is the brilliance of Poe that he never spoke Warren's name, but instead persuaded people the writer most responsible for inciting the Revolutionary War was actually Thomas Paine."

"It's better to be remembered for flaws than not remembered at all," Paul said.

Luke mocked a smile. "By that, I should be unforgettable. I'm more flawed than the Prohibition."

The library echoed with the Sons' laughter, but that didn't make Luke feel any more light-hearted.

"Damn the man," Ben interrupted the laughter with a great twitch in his eye. "How many times must I ring this bell?"

An old woman entered the room, hastening with a limp. Her face could have been carved from stone with a pickaxe, and she wore the same white linen as Francis. Behind her Luke glimpsed several others crowding beyond a narrow doorway. "Misters," she said, though to Luke it sounded suspiciously as *Masters*. "It's Francis. The pox takin' hold of him."

"Gods," Sam muttered. "Another one?"

"And we thought help was hard to keep while living," John said.

Ben gave Paul Revere a grim look, then jerked his head to the passageway. Paul got up without a word and took away the old woman, the door slamming shut once they'd passed.

Ben slipped out a chained pocket watch and made a short *tsk* sound. Nodding briefly at the others, he said, "Where were we?"

John answered, "Just telling Luke to build his legend."

Ben showed his biggest smile yet, but Luke saw that twitch in his eye hadn't gone away, and it reminded him of a lunatic he once knew who swore he could fly with griffins, until flapping off a water tower to his death.

"Ah yes, well, enough of that, we've tarried as is." Ben's tone changed. "Tell us about your friends, this girl you love. Daisy, was it?"

"That's her," Luke said.

"Daisy, er . . . ?"

"Rose. Daisy Rose Cortez is her name."

"Of course, and no finer a rose than is Daisy."

Luke wondered at the change in his efficiency. "You can help?"

"Yes, yes, we have need to find her," Ben answered. "Describe her: Is she comely?"

"She might not win any beauty pageants, but I loved the crap out of her."

"I'd expect no less devotion. Is she of similar height to you? Weight?"

"Daisy's about a head shorter than me, and she probably don't weigh more than a wet cloth. Why's that matter?"

"Just answer the questions, and keep that homespun patois to a trifle. We need facts, boy."

Luke gulped. "I, eh—"

"Where do you believe this Daisy Rose may be waiting for your sweet reunion?"

"That's the problem, I don't know. She never had a home."

Ben grunted and asked more questions, and Luke answered as best he could. Sam and John wrote swiftly as they spoke, jotting down everything with giant quill pens.

Ben finally nodded at some satisfaction. "And the other, Zeke?"

"Ezekiel Johnson's his full name, a giant of a man, with a big ol' dent and scar at each side of his head. Family owned a farm in north Texas, outside Amarillo. He talked about them a lot, so I guess that's where he'd be now."

"Excellent!" Ben declared. "I believe my men will be able to find them both."

Luke felt a draught of relief wash over him. "Thank you, Mr. Franklin, thank you for your help!"

"I do this not for you, young man, but for preservation of the many. We'll seize them where they're remembered most."

Luke ran a hand through his lank, dull hair. "Seize them . . . ?"

"Er, *locate*, I mean." Ben chuckled. "Dialect, you know, changes by era."

That jumpy feeling of the snare he'd sensed earlier returned, and moreover that somehow he'd been caught without realizing it. "Um, how is it you're going to locate them?"

Ben glanced again at his chained pocket watch. "The dead are drawn first to where memory of them is strongest, an instinct of self-preservation.

"It's easiest with loved ones who think on you fondly and, when glimpsing you, tend to remember a bit more, dredging up from the subconscious what the living call 'ghost sightings.' Though love, unfortunately, fades away as well. As such, time is of the essence! Memories, if not firmly entrenched in history or legend, fade fast."

"Don't know what I'm doing here if time's so precious," Luke said. "If that's the way to find Daisy, I'll get to her on my own!"

"That's the spirit, m'boy," Ben said. He stood and moved behind Luke, clapping him on the back. "You've got the gift, now make use of it. You can change the world!"

Luke beamed. He began to rise, then saw by the distorted reflection in his empty mug, the movement of another mug swinging down above his head. He couldn't understand it until the conk sent him soaring into a realm of firecrackers and pretty rainbows.

LUKE AND PAUL, 1938, CONTINUED

Luke woke to his teeth clattering with each thud, and the thuds were lively.

He was moving, though he himself could not move. Something carried him, speeding along a trail, following a line of tidy white fences that stretched as far as he could see, as far as he'd passed, occasionally interrupted by gates that led to sensible farms or pert cottages. The sun was high and distant, and streamers of its rays fluttered across a pale blue sky. Birds meandered, chirping. Dogs with crossed paws woofed introspectively. All this, Luke saw only by craning his head up, as otherwise the world was upside-down and his nose buried in a muscled flank.

The realization formed that he was bound and flung over the back of a horse, so his tied legs dangled on one side and his arms on the other. The horse seemed to gallop faster than any horse rightfully could gallop. Luke's wrist was agony; rope bound tight against the broken bones, digging into them, jostling with each of the teeth-clattering thuds.

Thud-thud-thud.

"Hello?" Luke called gingerly. His head bounced briskly against the steed. Its coarse hair smelled of stale sweat and dung.

"Yes?" returned a cheery reply.

"Paul? Wh—what's happening?"

"I'm dropping you off with some friends."

"Where?" The thudding of the horse was maddening. Luke felt like his body would be shaken apart, like a vibrating mechanism that's got loose and rattles itself to pieces.

Thud-thud-thud.

"Salem."

Thud-thud-thud.

Luke's brain was a rubber ball bouncing inside his skull . . . a swelling, splitting rubber ball. He tried hard to focus, thinking of why he'd heard of that city before. After a minute he asked, "As in the witches?"

Paul Revere gave a quick laugh. "It's not the witches you have to worry about."

Thud-thud-thud.

Luke moaned, then pleaded, "Let me off."

And Paul did. The horse stopped running, and Luke was shoved off its flanks. He hit the earth—softer, at least, than the patches of ground he usually fell to—and was reminded of the realm of firecrackers and pretty rainbows to which Ben had incongruously sent him.

The horse whinnied a curt laugh, and Luke recognized it as Brown Beauty.

"We're here," Paul announced.

They were in a circular pasture of grass, ringed by a screen of gnarled oak trees. The sky was now bruised black and purple, and the moon appeared as a swollen eye.

"What happened to the day?"

"These things always occur at night," Paul replied. He shrugged. "You know how it is."

Luke didn't.

A scattering of flickering lights approached through the trees, torches carried in from all sides. He couldn't tell who—or what—carried them. All Luke's fears, pains, despairs, and regrets besieged him at once, and he'd have given up right there if he weren't already captive. Since that was a moot point, he consciously tried to force a different emotion to take over, and found it easily did: *anger.* He was royally pissed at Paul Revere and Benjamin Franklin and the others who'd apparently set him up for something very bad to occur.

"Why are you doing this?"

"Sorry, Luke. It's Ben's call. We just can't give up power to animates.

Your kind are allowed too much influence, too much coercion. Able to do things the rest of us can't, able to change the world, even if you don't believe it."

The torches were nearing.

"We needed to find out what made you tick," Luke continued. "Above all else, Ben's a scientist. He wanted to observe you."

"Why all the talk about me fulfilling my destiny? Why tell me what I need to do and build me up, just to knock it all down?"

Paul shrugged again. "It's what villains are supposed to do, isn't it, explain everything before you die? Seems satisfying that way—at least you won't be left wondering *why*."

"Die?" Luke shouted. "You son of a bitch whore! You're supposed to be the founders of this country, the good guys!"

"We are. We're the free thinkers, the liberators, the men of action. But remember we're also the insurgents, the tricksters, and the slaveholders. We're the men who founded a new nation, did as we pleased, and made all the laws to suit us best. Such is luck, we became the entitled."

Luke rolled over, watching the torches creep closer and closer. He got up to his knees.

"Nothing personal," Paul said. "I like you. Hey, and when your second self returns, drop by and pay us a visit. Beers on the house."

Paul smiled, his same jovial character, only now Luke didn't think it so charming.

"Smith McCain was never really coming when you scared me off the train, was he?"

"Sorry about that, but we couldn't let you dodge out. I figured McCain's name would get you moving. That's who all you rail riders are afraid of, isn't it?"

"Why don't you just kill me yourself?"

Paul seemed genuinely hurt. "I can't do that. People don't think of me as a killer. A soldier, a silversmith, a crier, but not a murderer."

Luke hated that that made sense.

The torches broke free from the circle of trees, and Luke now saw their bearers. There were perhaps a dozen pale men, each one sterner-looking than his neighbor, with a deadness in their eyes and a tallness to their black hats that caused Luke to think of a painting he'd once seen of Pilgrims filing off the Mayflower. But what ill will could the Pilgrims hold against him?

"Is this the accused, the bold fellow?" one of the stern men asked. His head perched over a stiff collar buttoned so impossibly tight it caused his neck to appear as an icicle. A snow-white cravat tumbled from there to his high waist.

"Huh?" Luke said. Being called a 'bold fellow' didn't sound so bad.

The stern men clarified their point:

"Tricky kin!"

"Adorer of atrocity!"

"Beelzebub's mystic!"

"Squire of the underworld!"

"Vessel of deficiency!"

"That's him, all right," Paul added. "An animate, Lucas Thacker, mocking God's boundaries of life and death."

The first torch bearer spoke again, his voice cold and booming like a great calving glacier. "I see ye take no pains in hiding your temperament, but appear defiantly before us in a witch's robe."

Witch?

"Wait, this robe ain't my fault," Luke clamored. "There was a woman with an axe after me—"

The others interrupted, shouting as one, "Witch, witch, witch!"

Then it all made sense. Salem, accusations by night, Paul's quip to fear something worse than the witches. *It was the judges and jury of Salem he stood before.*

"Where is your magik broom, you idolizer of excrement?"

"Where are your familiar and your book of spells, immoral son?"

"Schemer of abomination!"

"Licker of demon teat!"

"I ain't a witch," Luke shouted.

"I think they've heard that one before," Paul remarked.

They chanted, "Witch, witch, witch!"

"Ye are accused by he who is present," the cold-voiced man said. "What say ye? What evil spirits have ye familiarity with?"

"Evil spirits?" Luke laughed in disgust and spat at Paul. "How about this one right here, don't get much eviler than him."

The collective gasp of torch bearers echoed. Someone repeated, "Another evil spirit!"

Paul waved it off. "I leave this animate to your capable court, Honorable Magistrate Hathorne, and excuse myself to return to Boston."

The man Paul had spoken to, Hathorne, was the one with the cold, booming voice. "No, rider Paul Revere," he replied. "Ye are not guiltless. Ye too are now indicted for conspiring with the Enfant Terrible. Ye have been accused by he who is present!"

"I didn't think you Puritans had a sense of humor," Paul said nervously.

"We find no humor in your frolicking with Mephistopheles."

Paul turned to his horse to find that its reins were taken by two of the torch bearers. They led it away through the trees.

"Wait, don't accuse me. I'm just the messenger," Paul said.

His appeal was drowned out. "Confess, and give glory to God!"

"Diviner of magus!"

"Babylon's whore!"

"Malfeasance incarnate!"

The circle began to close in, and Paul found himself forced alongside Luke.

"Seems what I remember of them *is* true," Luke said with a sudden grin to Paul. He was feeling a whole lot better about the affair. "All it takes is a single accusation to get someone persecuted, regardless who claims it."

"Son of James, but I can't even blame you," Paul muttered. "I should've known better. Puritans are nothing but Loyalists at heart."

"Witch, witch, witch!" the torch bearers chanted.

"By the grace of God, ye are found guilty!" Hathorne pronounced.

"Guilty!" the chorus echoed.

"The accused are condemned to burn at the stake."

"Hathorne, no," Paul said. "Don't do this, don't set me to fire."

"Witches must burn!"

"Come, ye witches, to the cleansing pyre," Hathorne ordered.

Far off amongst the trees, directly beneath the swollen moon, Luke saw a pillar of fire rise high.

Two men lifted Luke by the arms to a standing position, and he cried out from the pain of his broken wrist at their rough handling. One untied the rope from his feet so he could walk.

"Bind the other's hands," Hathorne ordered, and more men seized Paul, one at each side.

Paul shook his head furiously. "Call it off, Hathorne. There's room here for us all to persevere."

"Your witch words do not sway me."

"If you do this, I swear by God, I'll get you back."

"Your blasphemy is noted in the book of sins. Perhaps this time, ye may *not* find new life after death . . . Ye are getting weaker, Paul Revere. Admit it."

Paul did no such thing, but his face blanched with fury. The men at his sides began to wind rope around him.

"How many times now have ye lost your way on a ride?" Hathorne asked. "How often have your treasonous cries gone unheeded? How much have your old wounds reopened? And to think that school children used to sing your name . . . Perhaps we'll keep you on that pyre, and after you reanimate, you'll burn again and again."

The other torch bearers chanted louder, but for one.

That man's voice stopped abruptly, and the torch in his hand dropped to a spot of grass, where it smoked ominously.

"What is it, Bartholomew?" one of the others asked.

Bartholomew's eyes darted around, and he swatted his hands through the air as one waves off circling flies. His complexion paled even more, and the hard wrinkles appeared like fine cracks upon his visage, so that his expression became one of a perfectly white egg, trembling, about to split apart.

"N—no," he said, "No, not me, it's not my time."

Luke saw it first, then the others caught on fast enough. Small red blobs, no larger than houseflies, formed in the air, landing on Bartholomew.

"The plague!" someone cried out.

"Second death!"

"The witch cousins have brought the pox!" Hathorne shouted.

"Pray for our brethren!"

"Pray, pray, pray!"

Bartholomew lifted his head, beseeching God for mercy, to accept his base soul. His legs trembled, then the bones took vacation and he crashed to the earth, howling and praying fervently, louder and louder, while rolling in pain. The pox filled the air in a cyclone twist, spreading over him, devouring. Hathorne and the others reached to lay hands upon him, appealing for His favor.

"Bartholomew Gedney has served Your name in allegiance! Mercy to his soul and glory to God!"

Luke and Paul were left staring at each other, hearts pounding. Paul tugged off the rope that the judges had not finished binding.

"What say we make haste?" he said to Luke. Paul looked around for Brown Beauty, but the horse wasn't seen, and when he whistled for it, there was still no sign. "Blast, I'm not planning to stay here and search for her. Feet, get me moving."

Luke waited for some magical phenomena to affect Paul's feet, but Paul just sprinted normally, away from the supplicating judges. Luke followed.

Outside the nighttime ring of gnarled oak trees, the sky changed back to pale blue, and the sun perched high in it.

"Paul Revere without a horse," Paul said to himself, slowing his pace. "Can't believe it . . . I *am* getting weaker."

Neither of them said anything else until Paul snorted and remarked, "I'm surprised more of those old farts haven't given out by now."

He looked to Luke for encouragement to explain further, but finding none, did so anyway. "Cotton Mather and John Hathorne were the memorable names, the others mostly just ancillary footnotes in the trials. It's the scaremongers who keep them going. Bloody witch trial fan clubs. You don't see such devotees for the signers of the Constitution."

They'd gotten far enough from the judges that Luke began to feel safe. He held up his bound hands. "Think you can take these ropes off me now?"

"Oh, heavens, forgot all about that!" Paul pulled a slim knife from beneath one legging.

"You had a knife all this time?" Luke asked. "Why didn't you use it on those witch hunters?"

"Against a dozen of them? Might've been different if I had a fancy machine gun like you modernists. I didn't want to make circumstances any worse," he said, cutting through Luke's ropes.

Once freed, Luke punched Paul in the face so hard his powdered wig spun backward.

Paul fell, sullying the seat of his breeches brown with earth. "Gods, guess I deserved it."

Luke advanced on him. "You deserve more'n that."

"Once is enough," Paul said and raised his knife. "I may not be a killer, but I am known to defend myself."

"And I'll be known as he who kicks your Yankee ass back to the Revolution."

The founding father paused, frowned, took a deep breath. "I'm sorry about all that with the judges, okay? It was poorly done. There. How many men living can say they've gotten a first-hand apology from Paul Revere?"

"You owe me more than an apology," Luke said. "I deserve an explanation."

"I already explained everything before Hathorne's group arrived."

"If that explanation were bullshit, I could open a fertilizer business."

Paul stopped. "I spoke only truth."

"You skimmed the truth. What do you mean that I have influence over the likes of you?"

"What you apparently haven't figured out is that it's all very caste-oriented around here. Us and Ben can mostly do what we want, but we still stick together for strength of recognition. The frontiersmen band with other frontiersmen; literary writers of the same era circle up; Olympians, pirates, pilgrims, miners, those who are of comparable circumstances ally—after all, Martha Washington won't be tinkling the ivories with the musician Scott Joplin, but she *can* be found in the sewing circles of Betsy Ross and Dolley Madison.

"Moreover, not only do the dissimilar prefer to avoid each other, they verily strive to undermine others' influence. Raise yourself by lowering others. And, well, now you're here on behalf of the destitutes."

Luke's response was a grimace, not just at what Paul said, but that his broken wrist seemed to hurt worse. Though Luke had hit him with his right hand, the wounded left suffered from the sharp movement. It'd been worth it though; Paul Revere could talk the hair off a dog.

Paul saw his pained look. "How's the wrist?"

"Hurts like a mouthful of hemorrhoids."

"Hathorne was right; you're unholy." Paul pointed off the side of the path to a winding creek nursing clumps of greenery. "Look there."

"At what?"

"Purslane."

Luke shrugged. "So?"

"So wrap it up."

"My wrist?"

"We're not talking Christmas presents."

Luke gave him a long sideways look. "Is this another crank like telling me Smith McCain's coming on the train?"

"No," Paul said, chuckling. "I'll even help."

Some minutes later, Paul Revere had mixed a poultice of purslane and mud and wrapped it around Luke's wrist. "All set," Paul said. "Now go ahead."

"With what?"

"With what Ben told you."

"That's ridiculous."

"Sheesh," Paul said, shaking his head. "Some people are more hard-headed than an anvil."

"You and Ben have hornswoggled me, knocked me out, kidnapped me, tried to kill me. You ain't done a lot to engender my trust."

"You're not one to forgive and forget, are you?"

Luke's long sideways look returned.

"Just do it," Paul said. "The directions Ben gave you."

Luke groaned, making it a loud-enough affair so Paul would know exactly how he felt. Then he stamped his feet three times in a semicircle while whistling northward.

"Now hold your left arm up."

Luke did, and Paul slapped it. Luke blanched. "Ow."

"But it didn't hurt like it should," Paul said.

Luke frowned as he peeled off the poultice. The frown wavered, considered, then changed to a slowly-widening gape. His wrist was perfectly healed. "That don't make any sense."

"It doesn't have to," Paul said. "Ben Franklin was never a medically-trained doctor, but he's remembered for giving all sorts of homespun health advice that works. Ben's remembered for just about everything. That's his strength: he's a man who wears many faces."

Luke's reserve allowed no response.

"Oh, c'mon, you've gotta understand all this by now. Don't let that anvil-head of yours get in the way . . . "

"I get it already," Luke said flatly, "the living give strength to memories."

"And if people like you don't think about us, don't talk about us, we die."

"So if I ignore you, you'll go away?"

"Even by your thinking to ignore me, puts me in your thoughts."

Luke shook his head. "I can't win."

"Then don't play."

"Why'd you say Ben had to observe me before sending me off to die?"

Paul sighed and rubbed at his chin, like deciding what wish to make on it. "We all knew the first time you crossed over to Athanasia. Seemed a fluke years ago, as you didn't want anything back then. But now you've returned with a purpose of finding and restoring your friends. That makes you a contender in changing history. Ben wanted to learn how much you knew, and if you'd done anything with that knowledge."

"Why in hell's he makin' it his business?"

"Listen, Ben's the brains around here. I'm just his messenger boy, and the others are yes-men. Ben gives the orders and we obey." Paul's cheerful countenance fell. "Truth be told, Franklin's a bastard."

That's something different, Luke thought.

Paul continued. "You seem like a nice kid. Just go home and forget this place exists. Ben can't get you unless you're here in the deadeye."

"What's he got against me?"

"Like I said, Ben's strength is being remembered as the smartest guy in the room. He knew everything, could do everything. He was alderman, governor, postmaster, philosopher, and scientist. He created America's police and fire stations, designed a phonetic alphabet, invented everything under the sun. He could have been—*should* have been—president, but he was too old, especially by revolutionary standards. Anyway, Ben preferred his French station as ambassador to American presidency. He was eighty lecherous years old and still bedding those Parisian dames nightly. How's that for libertinism?"

Luke shook his head and spat, ready to pick any direction but Paul's and walk away. "Anybody ever say you talk a lot without actually saying anything?"

"Here's the punch line: Benjamin Franklin didn't do any of those things."

Luke was dumbfounded into silence.

"Some story, huh? Like I said, Ben's strength is being remembered as the smartest guy. Doesn't mean it was true, just that's how he built his legend over hundreds of years. Ben *is* smart, he's a scientist, and he figured out some maneuvers. He included himself in the legends of me and Sam Adams and John Hancock and others, and we've been made stronger through his efforts, so we're dutiful. But he never did anything of note, just a tinkerer in some backwoods cottage with a grudge against everyone else who made something of their lives."

"But he's a founder of the nation . . . "

"He is now, but he wasn't then. See, it's Ben's biggest concern, fighting off rivalry. Reason he fears you is he *was* you. Benjamin Franklin was an animate back in Revolutionary days."

Even filled with shock already, Luke nearly swallowed his own teeth.

Paul continued, "Those who know about us can change us. You've got powers to channel, Luke, able to cross back and forth between Athanasia and the living, call a train like a dog, read codes. We're just protecting ourselves."

"I really don't give two shits about any of you."

"Power to one detracts from the rest. And when one is weakened, all associated with him are weakened as well."

"I take that back. I'd erase the lot of you if I could." Luke picked up their trail, walking the rolling cool path, and Paul followed.

"Now you're being honest. Think if the Revolution had failed; we'd have been branded traitors and criminals, and Benedict Arnold would've been the loyal hero."

Luke's sigh was monumental.

"Now, seeing what a romantic I am and empathetic to your tribulation of lost love," Paul said, "here's a piece of advice: You have two choices, and the misstep of one will ruin the other. You can search out your friends and say goodbyes, enjoying some final moments in their company before they vanish. Or you can go back to Real World—your regular life—and talk about them enough to keep them alive here, hoping there's sufficient time, ample interest to make them last, all while on the matter of faith."

They crested a rise. Ahead lay a four-foot narrow-gauge railway track slicing through wild creepers and flowering slips and beautiful marshes that did not move but for bubbles, which roiled and popped.

"Otherwise," Paul said, "you and they will soon be gone for good."

The distant tracks gave way to overlooks of Salem harbor, but up close it seemed an isle meant for fairies that zip and dart through such emerald moss. The tracks glistened silver where there was steel and shone tawny where there was wood, and at its sight Luke felt at least considerably better that anything was possible.

Brown Beauty emerged with a neigh from one shoulder of the rail line, lifting her leg coyly at Paul.

"There you are," Paul said. "How'd you get ahead of us, ol' girl?"

She shrugged her muscular neck, keeping secrets to herself.

Paul gave a curt, sidelong nod to Luke, acknowledging his earlier smug point. "See, Brown Beauty always comes back to me. It's why horses are so good, rail rider."

"Don't count out my own mounts."

A rusted crossing sign jutted from the ground, warning for the intersection of path and rail line. Drawn over it was the crude symbol of a locomotive: *Catch Train Here.*

Paul craned his neck, looking up and down the empty tracks. "Unfortunately, my own ride has room for only one, unless you don't mind getting hogtied and slung over the back again."

"Don't wait around on my account."

"Remember what I said." Paul wedged a foot into the horse's stirrup and swung over her in one swift motion. He looked again at the empty tracks. "I'm sure you'll hitch a lift soon enough."

By then, Luke had already called forth an image in his mind, letting himself stretch away, probing, sensing for the nearest train, and he found it, and it was fine, a Boston & Maine engine pulling wooden hoppers full of cranberries and sweet corn. He directed it fast, straight for him, and it came shooting down the line, heaving smoke and spittin' sparks and screaming a loud shrill toot.

Brown Beauty leapt backward, rearing, and Paul almost tumbled off. He regained control and patted down his powdered wig with a tense hand, ceding to the rushing train. "At least you got flair."

Luke swung out an arm and lifted himself onboard a car. "Fuck you and goodbye," he shouted, his voice growing distant fast. "I'm goin' home, but I ain't giving up."

DANIEL INTERVIEWS KING, 1985: DAY THREE

King Shaw was dying.

I visited him in the strip-mall hospice to which he'd been relegated, a government-run facility that dispensed more heartache than salve to its patients. It was a lonely place to expire, and no better a shelter than from where its homeless had come, only here the inmates were concealed from view; cities are shrewd to hide their doomed and diseased from the public eye. Political incumbents are done no favors when happy voters catch a glimpse of destitution living at their doorstep and decide to act on the issue by voting in someone else to wear the Grand Poobah hats, someone else who could do a better job of painting shiny pictures. So the infirm, the crazies, the beggared are shipped off during the night and shuttered to narrow cots where sterile sheets encircle them as imperviously as prison walls.

At first, I didn't know what had happened to King. He was offered no phone calls, and even if he had been, I doubt he would have reached out to me. What would have been the point? He was on his way out, and he knew it. But King's story wasn't over yet, and I was determined to make his voice heard, less for the tales he wove and more as a symbol of the abandoned generation, one of America's half-million sons and daughters left to starve in piss-stained cardboard boxes.

Being a journalist, it took me little time to track down, through rumor and word-of-mouth, that King had probably been taken to a small ward on 9th. It was there I found him, logged under the name *John Doe 248*, sleeping in cot 3-H.

I looked into his old face, and its landscape told more stories than words could convey. I stayed there and talked to him until his eyes slowly opened. He breathed deep, looked around, and asked if I had a bottle of Jim Beam to "warm his words up." I did. I teased a flask from my jacket's inside pocket, so the cap poked out like a winking eye. I know giving drink to a dying man won't endear me to any benevolence societies, but when a man's clutching at the end of his rope, you afford him any pleasure you can.

"Ain't much time," he said.

I agreed.

I found a hook-nosed nurse sleeping at her station and convinced her, along with a twenty, to allow me to take King outside. His regular wheelchair was gone, but in the broom closet we found another one that looked like a prototype for the covered wagon. I got him situated in it and wheeled him out to the street, trailing some sort of IV tube like a quivering tail, along with stern instructions: "Don't go far."

Once we were in the clear, I asked, "What happened to you?"

"Age and bad choices," King answered, and wheezed. "My head felt like it popped last night and then I 'bout waved the big white flag . . ." He sighed like a deflating tire. "I woke in that dungeon to a man advising I make my final peace." A cough, a shudder. "I closed my eyes, made a wish . . . then you appeared."

"Tell me what you need, and I'll make it happen."

"A new ticker, fifty more years, and a gal who dances like Grace Kelly."

King smiled, and that made me smile. His eyes closed and his head drooped, and I didn't know if he fell asleep or caught the scythe. Then he took another big breath, like he was trying to fill himself back up with new life. I parked the wheelchair at a bus stop where the lines stopped running long ago. I sat next to him on the bench, eye-to-eye, and took his hand.

"Is that all?" I asked, grinning.

He chuckled. "I never finished telling you about Luke's adventures with John Dillinger and Ben Franklin, all those others."

"I know. I hate a story without an ending."

"So, you asked what I need, and this is it—" Another wheeze. A big breath. I gave him the flask and he took a long swig, and color reappeared in his face. "What I want you to do, Mr. Greenberg, is share what I'm telling. Not just the parts you write for your big article, but all of it."

And there I found myself at a familiar crossroads as antiquated as man's first attempt to reason: King had made a request of me that I did not intend, nor want, to fulfill.

I was using King as a tool to humanize the plight of homelessness. Here was a plainspoken man with hopes and regrets and a powerful voice, and he'd done so much with his life, travelled the country, survived the growing pains of our nation, yet now was dying alone in the shadows. He was to be the champion of my articles, a recurring theme driving home each message that street dwellers weren't statistics but brothers and sisters, children, parents, *ourselves*. King was to be my twentieth-century Wandering Jew, a tragic figure compelled to restlessness for equal reasons circumstance and choice. I wanted to document the facts of his life, simply alluding to his "colorful" tales while whimsically referring to him as "The Bard of the Nation" or "Minstrel of the Streets."

What I did *not* want to do was dilute my message through inclusion of his fables about ghosts and magic trains. I won't name my reluctance as personal objection, but serious journalists find themselves serially shunned if they dabble in the whims of fiction, as if a moral conflict of interest exists between documenting the objective one day and penning a boy's tale the next, not to mention severely damaging the credibility of all the homeless experiences my interviewee expressed. Could Seymour Hersh have successfully exposed the My Lai Massacre by expounding, before they were murdered, upon the villagers' belief in eating duck fetus to reverse bad luck?

"Tell you what, I know some people who are creative writers. I'll approach them about collecting your stories into a book. These are great tales from another time, while still relatable to today . . . I'm sure they'd have no problem selling."

King grunted. "Man, the buck passes two ways, y'know."

I wasn't sure what he meant. "It's the best I can promise right now."

He took another long swallow of Jim Beam. It gave focus to his eyes, and his chin lifted, and the more he drank, the more the whiskey returned his strength and spirit. "I hope you don't take long considering otherwise, with me being at five and a half feet already under."

"Audiences of readership are divided. Some want to know the world's facts, while others prefer reading tales that incite the imagination. If you mix fiction into the fact, it's like watering down a drink. Next time, people get their drink somewhere else."

"Huh, and it's you who decides what's true and what's not?"

"I present evidence to my audience based on observable occurrences."

"And what if it's all the same?" King asked, clenching and unclenching a fist. "What if truth could turn fable, and legends become real?"

"Sure, history is rife with conquerors rewriting the past to meet their own agendas, justify actions for war or persecution. But it doesn't change the events that actually occurred."

"It does if it's believed," King said.

"Well . . . I may have to disagree with you, my friend."

"Right now, you want me heard so you can get clapped on the back, maybe win some contest. For me, it's to keep alive the memories. What I want isn't going to change, while you . . . Soon enough, you'll be championing my corner."

"I'm trying to bring assistance to people who need it, like yourself. Don't you see that?"

"Shit. The breaths I got left couldn't fill a backed-up crapper, I ain't wasting them waitin' for you to change the world." King coughed. Caught his breath. Drank a swallow.

I took out the small Casio tape recorder and flicked it on.

"The stories I tell, that's what I believe in," King said quietly. "That's what'll keep you and I living longer than that fancy mansion you roost in filled with pillows feathered by virgin hens."

I opened my mouth to voice a different tack, but King shook his head. "Mr. Greenberg, who you think makes the best storytellers?"

"No easy answer," I replied, considering my favorite novelists and screenwriters and other fictionists, and what trait made someone better than someone else. "There's education to consider, practice, natural talent, voice."

He pitched my ruminations to the wind. "It's hobos. Homeless, beggars, tramps, we're all the same in this."

I furrowed my brow, nodded once slowly.

"You know why?" he asked.

I could have answered any number of ways, but I knew none of my responses would match to what he was about to say. Anyway, King didn't wait for me to reply.

"You gotta believe in a story to make it true, give it life of its own. And no one really believes in made-up tales except two types of people: children and the downtrodden." He paused, wheezed, smiled. "Thing is, see, children grow up, and stories don't carry weight for them no more."

Though the tape recorder was running, I also pulled out a small memo pad and pen and scribbled some thoughts.

King said, "Us derelicts of society with nuthin' but nuthin', we believe in stories more than dreams, 'cause stories are the here-now where we place ourselves, while dreams are something that won't ever happen."

King grunted and dropped his head; he'd worked himself up. I laid hands on his shoulder and was ready to call an end to our outing. Then he cleared his throat and looked at me, a glisten cresting one eye, a tear welling like a pail of grief that's reached its brim but isn't yet done filling.

"No, don't think I'm crying," he said as if reading my mind. King clenched up, twisting to one side. "Just fuckin' hurts."

So much for my perceptivity. "Take you back to the hospice?"

"It'll pass in a moment." King's voice shallowed, the sickness weakening him moment by moment, but he couldn't stop yet. "This drifter I know says he's a veteran from the Korean War. Guy never served a day in his life, but he tells people he was a commando, and his memory sorta took over from the first lie he uttered, get it?"

"I know the type."

"His brain didn't fact-check itself, but came to remember the time he said the lie, so from that point on, he believed it true. Now it goes, no one assumes otherwise, he's been repeating war stories so often. Even speaks at veteran rallies and shit, and I wouldn't be surprised if there's army papers on him that have somehow evolved over time from the strength of what's believed."

"That reasoning opens a terrifying realm of self-supporting delusions."

"Does it?" King asked. "How you prove otherwise, a man's life, and what he makes of it? Memories change, paperwork gets revised, it's all the same . . . "

"Though rationalization is the cruelest of philosophies, I think we're sidetracking off-topic."

"Not at all, Mr. Greenberg, this *is* the point of topic. Here on the streets, a man's loathed, mocked, but he's still a man, still got hopes, got desires, and the harder he lives in those, the harder he makes the stories of himself, and the truer they become, if even just for him . . . Maybe his brain gets rewired in this way, and maybe that's how the brain in Athanasia gets rewired, based on the strength of those memories fighting every day for dominance over others."

"I see."

"Do you? 'Cause this is what kept Luke going: a way, a *hope* to make the stories true. Luke may not have been school smart, but he was bright as a summer sky . . . "

LUKE THACKER, 1939

When 1939 struck, the country was in shambles, more homeless riding the rails than Luke had ever known. And it wasn't just men, but whole families, mothers and fathers and five or six small children, each carrying a glum bundle and hiking down sodden roads. When a train might come along and offer a faster pace to somewhere else, the children were tossed inside the first open door like so many sacks of harvest. Sometimes the railroad guards would toss 'em back out, sometimes they'd turn a blind eye. There's only so much a bull can do, even a bull with a gun, faced with a tide of desperation that never wanes but grows tenfold.

Luke Thacker came to know hungers that handouts of cornbread and sweet onions couldn't sate: the thought of Daisy and Zeke set to race for survival against the endurance of their own memories, and those memories could not be much by any long shot.

Paul Revere's words echoed in his mind like that giant Liberty Bell in Philadelphia, clanging and clanging until it cracks noticeably. Paul had advised Luke to return to Real World—*regular life*—and spread Daisy's and Zeke's stories, in hopes there was enough time, enough interest, to make them legend.

But therein lay that damned, horrible problem . . . In a land where every man's life had turned to misery, how could he make the voices of two 'bos be heard above the rest?

Luke didn't have an answer, but he didn't let that stop him either.

He travelled, and he spoke, passing through tramp camps from Lancaster to Provo, sharing word of Daisy and Zeke to all who'd listen. He took a line to Cedar Rapids and regaled wary drifters with anecdotes of those he'd loved and lost. He hopped a freighter to Eugene, and even some bulls there listened, nodding their heads with empathy. In Wenatchee, Luke lay at night in fields of transients with eyes full of moon, listening to the hopes and woes of others in turn, before telling his own. There wasn't a lot a beggared man owned but his own tales and the pleasure he found from hearing others.

In Cincinnati Luke took sick, and by Madison he was well, and all the while he kept talking about Daisy, about Zeke, sharing their names, their lives. New 'bos were met, and occasionally new joys too, and new miseries and new laws. *No loitering. No begging. No sleeping on benches. No sitting on sidewalks. No trespassing. No outsiders.*

Riding a Santa Fe mail train into Denver, Luke saw a billboard that read: JOBLESS MEN KEEP GOING—WE CAN'T TAKE CARE OF OUR OWN. And that pretty much summed up everything Luke thought of life.

Luke even talked about Athanasia sometimes, but at this he was jeered. Fastest way to disprove anything you say is by proclaiming other worlds and that dead people share our beds; there's a fine line between the makings of a tall-tale crossbuck and a friendly ghost story whispered over the camp fire.

And if you already know that, you'll understand another truism: A man's remembered by the stories he tells, whether they're accurate or not, so Luke kept at it.

He grew attuned to his audience and figured for those he'd speak plain, those he'd speak true, those he'd massage with what they believed, and he also learned from them in return, the way a teacher learns which lessons take hold with their pupils and which go right over their heads.

If you were around during these times, you might have even heard Luke Thacker yourself. In fact, if you'd have been sitting in a certain 'bo camp one dusky night in Bakersfield, maybe smoking a cigarillo, maybe feeling the warm night breezes and thinking living outdoors wasn't so bad, you might have heard the following story as told by Luke himself.

It went something like this . . .

EZEKIEL JOHNSON, 1939

Ezekiel Malachi Johnson was born last of thirteen children on a dusty farm built of hayseeds and frantic hope, a hundred miles into Texas, south of the Oklahoma boundary.

Zeke wanted to farm when he came of age, like his pappy, but his pappy died when he was young, and it seemed Zeke's older siblings forgot about their runt brother when they parceled out the family land into only twelve lots. After Zeke turned fourteen, he tired of taking orders from his brothers and sisters, having been granted no more rights by them than an indentured servant, so he took to the road with a stick o'er his shoulder and a whistle on his lips. Thus began Zeke's truest calling as a professional drifter.

He started off mining in a copper pit in Ely, Nevada, for a year. He would have stayed longer, but there he grew broad in shoulder and tall as a horse, much too large to swing an axe in their cramped shafts. So he slipped onto the rear platform of an east-bound grainer and got off in Colorado Springs, where he found new work breaking more stones, this time outdoors at the quarry in Red Rock Canyon. He did this for another year, and grew some more, until a ridge gave way one day, dropping a rock slide onto the laborers below. When the mountain face collapsed, all the men in its path fell to the ground, curled up with hands over head, praying for life, but only Zeke's prayers came true . . . that day, anyway. It was as if a divine bubble formed, shielding Zeke from granite death while the others were flattened like wet flapjacks.

He wasn't immune to injury, however; one rock—the very last rock to fall—hit him in the corner of the head, just below the protection his crossed arms afforded, and caved in his skull a tiny bit. Zeke occasionally had problems thinking straight after that, and sometimes surrendered to emotions at the slightest provocation. But he lived, and he walked away, having lost all taste to ever again break rocks.

He returned to Nevada and worked awhile to dam up the Colorado River as part of the Boulder Canyon Project. But there, a piece of falling cement conked him in the opposite corner of the head from where he'd previously been struck, denting his skull another tiny bit.

Zeke sought safer pastures and hopped a new train, this one for Roseville, California, to harvest apples, hearing from other 'bos that the Pacific coast was so warm and bountiful a man would never feel cold or hunger again. Although he did toss apples there awhile, the rest of what he heard about the Pacific coast was bald-faced fib; cold and hunger could still be felt the same as anywhere else. At least there, his head wasn't cratered any further. A couple of apples dropped off their limbs to bean him, but none of them hurt.

DOORWAYS TO THE DEADEYE

1932 erupted and Zeke railroaded down to Los Angeles Central Station, searching to find work on the rising oil derricks that the southland propagated. One night he slept under a growth of chaparral in the Santa Monica mountains, far below a great sign that read HOLLYWOODLAND in letters so tall and white they seemed like marble columns supporting the heavy sky. While Zeke gazed up at the letters, he saw in the starlight a small figure climb to the top of the letter H and leap off. The body hurtled down, seeming to aim straight at him, and Zeke relived with terror the falling rocks from Colorado Springs. But the body struck a bluff instead and ricocheted into far-off weeds.

He cautiously crept to it, all the while looking around to make sure no one else came sailing down from the sky. Zeke reached the crumpled sack that had once been a person, and saw it was a woman. Her arms and legs twisted and jutted from every angle, as if she had too many knees and elbows along each limb. The woman's face was pushed sideways, like a painting that's still wet, and someone runs their hand across it. Amazingly, her eyes blinked, and she looked up at Zeke. Her ruined mouth opened once to say something, thought better of it, and closed. Her eyes followed suit. Zeke didn't wait around, but immediately left those surrounds.

Later he found out she was an aspiring actress named Peggy Entwistle, who was despondent over the failure of her movie-star career. Zeke had no idea who she was, but that was the closest and only association he'd ever had with somebody famous, and for the few remaining years of his life, wherever he went he'd tell people how he witnessed the suicide of Peggy Entwistle.

Zeke left the Golden State and ended up in the Dakotas, then Mexico, then Montana, then elsewhere. By this time he'd lost all fervor to make a man of himself on the road, and missed his family's farm in Texas terribly. But there wasn't any going back; each of his siblings had children by now, more mouths to feed, and less food to do so. Dust storms had blown away all the topsoil, and Zeke came to find out he was actually persevering better than them. His brothers and sisters were tied to the dying land, unwilling to give up that which they'd toiled so long to cultivate, while he was a rolling stone, able to find work wherever work was to be found. Trouble was, Zeke was finding less and less of it.

Hardships of the road never failed to surprise him, though its abject loneliness remained constant. And he thought, one afternoon, of poor Peggy Entwistle, who ended it all on her own terms, having failed at finding what she sought, yet achieving understanding of the pointlessness in it all. Ezekiel Malachi Johnson remembered that Hollywoodland sign leaning out precariously over grim cliffs, and he thought of himself taking a leap from its very same ill-omened letter "H" . . .

That was the day he met Luke Thacker.

Luke stopped telling about Zeke, noticing most of the other 'bos were sleeping. Two had leaned back where they were and a third had fallen on his face. One rum-dum chased fireflies while singing Baptist hymns. The last hobo still listened, though his head was propped up by one gaunt arm and he plucked hairs from his nostrils.

Luke asked, "You don't care for what I'm sayin'?"

"It just ain't interesting. Hell, hearing it got me dismal."

"Zeke was one of the strongest, toughest men I ever met. Nothing dismal about that."

"Yeah, he sure 'nuff overcame some real rough times, but ain't we all?" the 'bo asked. "I mean, you may as well been jawin' about me. Your friend left home cause the soil wasn't deep enough to bear his roots. He was hungry, lonely, seen death. Been all over the country, but that and a nickel might buy a cup of coffee. Like I said, could be the story of me. Could be Warbler over there, or Joe Crow, or Two-Toe Andy, or Short Willie. None of us wanna hear the things we been through, what we're going through still."

"Doesn't that make him someone you can empathize with?"

"Why would I give a blue hoot to empathize with him? Just 'cause I *can* relate don't mean I care to. Your buddy worked and worked like a mule, but didn't have a goddamn thing to live for. Whyn't you go tell a hog about all the other hogs gettin' fattened up for their slaughter, and see how he likes empathizing?"

Zeke's story already felt weaker, fading, like echoes of a memory.

Luke thought on what the 'bo told him. He wanted to say more, to build up Zeke's legend through truth that Peggy Entwistle came to him in dreams, and that Zeke had saved Luke twice, once from the clutches of

Thomas the bull, and secondly by giving his own life in protection from Smith McCain, and that McCain really *was* over seven feet tall with eyes yellow as a rail man's lantern . . . but Luke wasn't sure how to make it sound sensible and not like another crossbuck.

It didn't matter, since that last hobo walked away to piss behind some outcast trees; Luke would have been talking to himself. It was true what the 'bo said, that Zeke's tale was as everyone else's. Zeke worked hard, though never got much from it.

Next time Luke came upon a 'bo camp, he tried to found Zeke's legend by making him memorable.

"One time, Zeke joined a travelling circus, working as the strongman. Part of *Mighty Black Zeke*'s show was to swing a sledgehammer onto a lever, where the puck would shoot up to ring a bell if the mechanism got struck hard enough. Only problem, he was too strong for the limitations of the machine, and every time he swung, the puck shot up so high and so hard, it'd shatter the metal bell to pieces. The ringmaster got tired of replacing the bell, so it wasn't too long until he just replaced Zeke."

'Bos nodded at this, and Luke heard a couple guffaws, but the subject still didn't seem to win over anyone. A tramp with crippled hands broke in. "That's nothin'. I was in the circus, and I was the best darn clown in town and anywhere else up or down."

"Clowns are funny," someone said, encouraging the tramp. "Tell us clown stories, pal."

And Zeke got dismissed again.

Another day, another camp, Luke tried again, attempting to galvanize Zeke through compassion.

"In fall of 1930, Zeke Johnson was camped for the night on the American River, outside Coloma, California. The water was cold as a witch's tit, but Zeke was a man who liked to keep his self clean. Stepping into the shallows, he stubbed his toe on a yellow rock. Turned out, this was by Sutter's Mill where the big gold rush of 1850 began, and seemed there were still some nuggets to be found. Bein' a miner, Zeke knew exactly what to do, and it didn't involve breaking anything. He just built a sieve and started dipping. Made a fortune of it, too, and sent it all back to the siblings in Texas who had turned him out, in order to save the family farm and feed his nephews and nieces."

Still nobody was interested in Zeke. Other men in camps had done it before, sacrificed for kin who didn't appreciate their efforts. Stumbled upon opportunity and since lost it. Wished for things to be different than they were. Hurt and toiled and bore it all.

Each time Luke started in on Zeke, the subject got changed to politics, to music, to hopes when life might be easier, when a man didn't have to live like a beat hound.

In the middle of telling about Zeke knocking out Gene Tunney, a toothless 'bo interrupted. "Go on now, Luke, you still ridin' with that lil' skirt?"

Thinking of her unexpectedly brought the usual heartache, and Luke's mouth tightened. It wasn't remarkable that 'bos were familiar with each others' riding companions, but it was surprising the gummer asked about Daisy while being unmoved by Zeke. Luke said simply, "She's gone."

"Other side the mountain, huh?"

"There wasn't no one like Daisy Rose."

"You wanna crossbuck 'bout her?"

He nodded. "Daisy was the finest of us all."

And speaking about her, Luke found, came much easier . . .

THE CODE MAKER, 1939

An old man listened to Luke's stories from far away, and he pursed one side of thin lips, and steepled aching stiff fingers under his chin to rest. The man was old, this man, and discerning and shrewd, sitting at a table that also was old and shrewd in its own table ways, inside an old cabin, atop an old mountain, upon an old land.

The old man's smile was indulgent, but more than that, it was suggestive. He unsteepled his fingers and ran one, drawing, through dust that covered the old table, inside an old cabin, atop an old mountain, upon an old land, and what he drew was a symbol.

The symbol was a triangle with an eye at its center beside a crude locomotive with a double-binding line connecting them together, and it was of the Hobo Code.

DAISY ROSE, 1939

Margarita Amarilla Rosa Verde Cortez was an only child, though she was told she had over a hundred cousins south of the border, and cousins counted the same as siblings in her daddy's family. Aunts and uncles helped raise each other's children equally as their own, all under the watchful eye of *la familia's* matriarch. Life sounded like a great festival, the way her daddy told it, with *tías* cooking tortillas and beans all day that the children could eat while they played kickball and spear-the-hoop. Their home was always wonderfully warm, even in winter, though magically cool in summer as it nestled under the shadow of Iztaccíhuatl's mountain. Wealth mattered less than a *conejo's* fart, and a man was filled with joy simply by gazing upon flowering madrone or the scarlet monkey's tree, not snared and bamboozled by the American money-mongers who sought only to squeeze every ounce of blood from its peoples' dying bodies.

Daddy told her this, though she never saw the homeland he spoke of. Nor did she feel those "adult" pressures he eschewed, that kept them travelling across the Gulf Coast states in search of a life that settled itself without demanding anything in return.

"Back home in Xalitzintla, we stayed up all night dancing and playing music, and were never tired the next day, for such activity keeps the spirit invigorated."

In America, the impure whiskey and weak songs leave you with a hangover.

"In Xalitzintla, fruit is brought in by the wind and dropped outside our door each morning," Daddy said.

In America, a half-spoiled peach costs a nickel.

"In Xalitzintla, we ran naked in the forest, there was no shame in nudity. And the *señoritas* . . . " Daddy trailed off, glancing at his daughter. "No matter. In America, you are jailed and fined and called immoral."

"When will we go back?" she asked.

And each time he replied the same, "Someday."

But that day never arrived, and Daisy once met another man from Xalitzintla, and he called the town a shithole and said her daddy would be tarred and hanged if he ever returned.

So she got to learn the American land in ways most don't, as her daddy—by way of loafing—instilled an appreciation for the little things: a sunrise spread across Lake Pontchartrain; sweet stew of bass and crawfish pulled from the Tensaw; making music from gourds and reeds; sleeping under willows and moonshine.

"Jack of all trades, master of none," Daddy heard a wandering farmhand say, and he adopted the expression for himself. Daddy found he related most with indigenous Americans, and he learned much from them in the ways of herbal medicine, and he made sure Daisy learned too: to drink an infusion of creosote when you caught a cold, to mix the foliage of chamise with animal grease to heal a snake bite, to eat small amounts of coffeeberry if your innards got backed up. In such a way, they weren't reliant on anyone but Mother Nature.

They lived on reservation land, among the Chitimacha of Louisiana, then among the Karankawa of Texas, then among the Quassarte of Oklahoma, then among others. Over time, Daddy even developed a fondness for the country he scorned, and showed it in remarkable talent of landscape paintings that he bartered away for the beginnings of a better life.

Things were looking up, and then Daddy fell off a mountain, and Daisy was alone at age fifteen.

She felt like a child in exile, not wanted anywhere she went but by foul-breathed men who wanted her for the wrong reasons. She learned fast how to flee, faster still how to hop a train and search out luck in other towns. She often dressed as a young boy, and passed as one, when travelling. The aches of hunger weren't new woes; she could tell what greenery was edible enough to get by, but she also knew she needed something better than chewing on leaves and twigs.

She cut her hair short to the scalp and sought work by the day. Daisy called herself Denny or David if the job was "men only," though often femininity made no difference to the site foreman. If something needed doin' and she was able, it'd get done, right alongside the fellas.

Daisy told anyone who'd listen she was willing to do anything for a chance to better herself. But so were ten million other unemployed kids, and so she wandered to the vagaries of chance . . .

A 'bo named Catfish Jack Slim interrupted Luke's story while raindrops slipped through the woven reeds of a thatched ceiling above. The plops and splats and hisses were soft and scattered as fitful click bugs calling in the distance.

"I thought Daisy was a delicate belle, eyes as big as stars, could sing a canary to sleep," Jack Slim said.

"She was to me, but that's not where this story's headed," Luke said.

"Just tryin' to picture in my mind, is all. You're tellin' she looked like a tomboy with no hair."

"Lord alive, Daisy was a beaut! I said she could pass for a boy if she wanted to dress for it. And don't matter if she cut her hair. Hair grows back. Think it's tough for you and me bummin' the rails, imagine how it's like for the fairer sex."

"I always wanted to marry a gal with hair past her rear end, that way I could tangle myself all in it."

"You love a woman, hair's the least of concern. Otherwise get her a wig, I guess."

"But your Daisy Rose was one of them pageant queens, right? Dolled up and photographed, I mean, before you whisked her away on rose petals and champagne floats."

"Where'd you hear that?" Luke asked. "I look like someone to afford champagne floats?"

"You and her was at least in love, right?"

"That's what I'm sayin'."

"Well then, isn't life always seeming rose petals and champagne floats?"

Luke took a pause. "I suppose it is."

"That's why I want to picture it, a beautiful couple, livin' like me, but maybe what some day *could* be me."

Luke wiped a smear of days-old oil from one shirt sleeve to the other. "I'll grant one half of that couple is beautiful."

"I ain't been kissed in ten years. It's all I want, a nice, beautiful girl to kiss. I can hump doxie women plenty, there's cheap whores in every station, but a girl to really kiss . . . "

"Don't ever call someone a whore in front of Daisy Rose. Otherwise, like to get what happened next."

There's a town in Louisiana called the "Frog Capital of the World," and its name is Rayne. This is where Daisy found herself by spring, having landed a job selling mating frogs to tourists so they could start their own frog farms, "whether for business or for pleasure." She dressed in a green suit adorned with cardboard chartreuse ears that stuck up; more than once children asked if she was an elf or a troll, to which she replied, "*Ribbit.*"

Rayne's vagrancy laws were merciless, and anyone arrested as such got sentenced for three months to a state work farm, so Daisy needed lodging as long as she sold those frogs. Accommodations, however, were only procurable at the French View Hotel, which was as much a hotel as a pickpocket can name himself an entrepreneur. There was nothing French about it, and its only view came from pull-down windows that opened to neighboring brick walls six inches away. The French View was the town flophouse, and it was packed every day with miseries and with bed bugs.

Bed bugs aren't unusual to 'bos, but these bed bugs were worse than Daisy had ever met. They caused illness and infection, and lodgers in the hotel sickened and died daily, each left no more than a sallow corpse, covered in bulbous, pus-filled welts.

A bony woman with one eye explained, "The bed bugs here may as well be vampires, suck you dry of blood 'til there's nothing left but a sack of riddled skin." She blinked her one eye. "I'd get out of Rayne, I were you."

"There's no work anywhere else," Daisy pointed out.

The woman nodded knowingly.

Rayne's bed bugs were the size of pennies, and colored the same, and they left feces and egg shells and shed skins over the hotel floor like a soft carpet. And each night the lodgers gained more bites, lost more blood, and their skin turned hideous red-and-yellow with polka-dots of scabs.

But Daisy stayed and kept selling frogs in town. She cared for her frog stock like children, fed them fat flies, rubbed their bellies to sleep, and the frogs sometimes did tricks in return, which made them doubly-more appealing to tourists.

And Daisy made friends with the one-eyed woman at the hotel, whose name she learned was Willie Mae. Willie Mae—Daisy also learned—was the town whore.

"It's fine what you do," Daisy said, "but don't ever let someone call you that. It's demeaning."

"Well, I *am* a whore. Anyway, I like my work, so I don't care."

"I'll care for you."

They slept in the same bed to save money, and labored the summer in their own ways. And they each weakened to blood-letting, but earned so much dough that in normal times could have been used to open their own bank accounts. They talked about someday runnin' off to start a frog-themed brothel that Daisy would manage, and Willie Mae would star as the main attraction.

While around them lodgers collapsed in fevers, chills, pains, languors: men, women, sad-eyed children, even the hotel cat.

The proprietor of the French View didn't give two shits, even about his cat. He was a mangy, coarse man, with long whiskers sparse as a crawdad's feelers, and his own pale skin was covered in the same bloody welts as everyone else's.

"That's life in Rayne," he replied to Daisy's complaint. "Get used to it."

"Can't you do anything about it? People are dying."

"What the fuck I look like, someone who cares? There's no fix."

"But—"

"Get outta here, or I'll teach you a lesson you didn't learn in school."

The proprietor was aptly named Toaddick.

Daisy got upset, but she took it upon herself to nurse the hotel's sick, using herbal medicines she learned with her daddy: teas of birch leaves and mountain mint to ease pain, and gel from the aloe plant to tend bite infections.

And maybe she saved a few lives that way, but she never found out, as Daisy suddenly turned unemployed.

The owner of the mating frogs business announced, "Tourist season is over. Come back next year."

Her heart dropped about twenty feet. "What about the unsold frogs?"

"Auction 'em off for frog leg gumbo, they're no other use. Costs too much to feed."

Daisy came on a plan.

"What's it worth," she asked Toaddick at the hotel, "if I get rid of your bed bug problem?"

"Can't be done."

"I got a way, at a cost. Twenty dollars."

Toaddick said, "All right, I'll take that bet."

Daisy bought all the unsold frogs with her savings of nearly ten dollars. Then she brought them to the French View Hotel and let 'em loose.

And it worked. The frogs seemed happy to help Daisy, for all she'd helped them; after a week, the frogs had cleaned house, literally, of every bed bug and leaving, so a man could shit and shave without crawlers up his neck.

Daisy went to collect payment.

Toaddick said, "You done real good work here, and I'm about to pay, but I think you should know—and there ain't no easy way about it—when you've gone off to work each day, earnin' honest money, your wife . . . Well, behind your back, mister, she's a whore."

"Don't call her a whore. And I ain't no mister, you dumb shit."

Toaddick squinted, leaned close, did a double-take. "Hell, with that short hair and flat chest, I thought you were a clean-shaved gentleman."

Daisy held out her hand for payment.

Toaddick said, "I've been rentin' one bed to the two of you."

"We share to save money."

"Shared beds are for married couples only. Seems to me, you owe back pay for some months of fine accommodations." His smile gleamed charming as a goiter. "Twenty dollars and a cock suck oughta cover it."

Daisy's open hand turned to a fist.

"Teach you and the whore to try and cheat me," he added.

"Don't call her a whore, you fuck-face turd!"

Little Daisy walloped him, and she walloped him so hard his head came to show like the biggest bedbug of all, albeit one smashed under the heel of a heavy boot, 'til what's left is bloody mulch.

The sheriff came, who was also Toaddick's cousin, and Daisy and Willie Mae were sentenced for three months to a state work farm. That night, and no one figured how, Toaddick was mysteriously further mauled by a pack of marauding frogs.

After their release, Daisy and Willie Mae rode the rails, penniless, to a little 'bo camp halfway 'tween Kansas City and Topeka, and that's where Luke Thacker was met.

"And then you and her fell in love?"

"And then we fell in love," Luke repeated.

By now, a group of 'bos had filled their hut like turned-out dogs wanting relief from the night's rain and cold.

"Daisy Rose sure was a firecracker," one said.

Another cut in, "I seen her once, this Daisy, and she waved at me, and her smile was so pretty I could've framed it and hung it on the wall."

Catfish Jack Slim asked, "Tell again, Luke, when you met her and first kissed on top of that flatbed car."

Luke did, and after he'd told, said, "I've been chewin' your ears for some time. Anything the rest of you want to crossbuck about?"

Jack Slim turned a glance to the others, and at each eye, a dismal downcast look was returned. He finally said, "Naw."

"Nothing? Friends at home, places you seen?"

"Some good work lately," a sunburnt 'bo offered. "Harvesting peas, a penny a pound."

The men shrugged, mumbled. A clumsy silence ensued.

"Fellas gotta have a story on boyhood, how it is you came to be bummin' the rails?" Luke said.

"M'family lost their home. I cost more to feed than I was worth."

A chorus nodded, "Me too."

Jack Slim said, "I wish I had someone to share my days with, is all. Maybe tomorrow."

"Tell again, Luke," a weathered gray 'bo asked, "you and Daisy lived happily ever after?"

Luke's throat tightened. "It ain't happened yet . . . but it will."

"Go on."

And it did.

Lonesome 'bos of the road came to Luke for his tales; whether crossbuck, truth, or lie, they wanted to hear about him and Daisy. Each felt happiness in the company of another, and it seemed by storytelling, tramps with no hope remembered times of finding a reason to wake in the morning. A man's back didn't seem so filled with ache at the end of a day's toil when he had a partner to commiserate with. In some way or another, the men and women Luke met had all experienced love and lost it in some way, and wanted to be reminded of it again, to dream, to long for its return.

In such a way did Daisy's stories find footing on the rails.

But Zeke . . . his legend just didn't take. Time passed, and Luke tried, but the stark fact laid him low that regardless of his efforts, some people's stories persevered while some did not.

LUKE THACKER, 1939, CONTINUED

Luke grew as common a hallmark to the rails as did engines to smoke, dust, and flying cinders. He hopscotched the nation's lines, and he spread word of Daisy and Zeke, and he relived memories, and he spoke of hopes, and he worked, and he survived. And through it all, his mind wandered as much as his feet: Was it possible to tame trains here in regular life, the same as he'd done in the deadeye?

Paul Revere had told him, *In Athanasia, the accomplishments or strengths you're known for are magnified.* It reasoned that if the power was magnified there, Luke must have at least some bit of it here and, even if diminished, it *was* nonetheless a power . . .

So each day he tried it, like learning how to whistle or strum a banjo that you got to practice often to get better, strengthening an aptitude until you reach a level of mastery. Only no matter how hard Luke tried, nothing happened. He practiced and practiced trying to copy what he could do in Athanasia, while part of himself asked: *Is it really practice when a man flaps his arms up and down, tryin' to teach himself to fly?* And another part of himself knew there were a dozen doctors with big knives that would love to lock him up in their institution and cut open his brain and study what made him tick.

Luke began shouting at trains, taunting them, throwing up his hands, screwing up his face, and overall looking like a jackass to any other 'bo seeing him. One of these 'bos was an older ashen woman, sharing a boxcar with him on a cold, sunless day.

She perched between jutting iron brackets that once may have held long shelves, but now just appeared to encase her in some insectoid resin. Her legs crossed under, and her knees rose high enough for spindly elbows to sit on, so her hands could outstretch effortlessly to Luke.

"What're you doin'?" she asked him over the clatter of the car. "Constipated?"

Luke grimaced, wishing a wall were between them. "You wouldn't understand."

"Oh, all right. I'll just go back to makin' sure the earth don't fall out of orbit and crash into Mars."

"Say what?"

"Someone's got to do it."

"That someone is you, huh?"

"My record of success speaks for itself," she said.

"And if you weren't around, we'd crash up?"

"Course not, kiddo. If not me, someone else would take up the charge. Duty gets passed along, right? Mama did it 'fore me, and her mama 'fore that, and so on; we got a pedigree of saving earth's colliding with other planets."

A siren blared far away, and townships passed by, and cars and crossings and gray-weighted clouds. Luke raised unruly eyebrows. "I've half a mind to thank you for your service, and the other half to warn you to never admit that to anyone else."

She giggled, a decidedly girlish sound coming from someone who looked to be sliding toward seniority, with great massive bags under her eyes and a neck with folds under it like layers of a frilly dress. "Oh, I know who needs to know. 'Cause whatever it is you're doing that I wouldn't understand, here's a caution: Practice slow. Psychic muscles are like body muscles, and you need to pace that training, or you'll hurt yourself."

The woman had Luke's full attention now, though he didn't know if her words were an insight or a warning. "Psychic muscles?"

Her smile seemed innocuous enough. "What you're doing. You learned something in dreams or astral realms, I'm guessing. Now you're stumped tryin' to use that ability here while awake."

Luke felt the scruffy hairs on his arms begin to tingle. "Go on."

"Things don't work the same as in dreams, kiddo. Dreamin', all you do is think it, but real life, you got to *cause* it."

"How do you know?"

"I'm a seer, and guess what I see?" she asked.

"Venus ready to sideswipe us?"

"A 'bo sign comin' for you, right about—"

There was a great rattle and peal, and the frenzied flapping of a hundred birds scaring away. The train crossed a track switch, veering left at the check, and a signal target flashed green once, and a wood arm snapped up in salute.

The hobo symbol written on it was one Luke hadn't seen before: A triangle with an eye at its center beside a crude locomotive, connected together by a double-binding line.

He felt something in his mind click, a feeling he hadn't sensed in years but remembered so vividly from when he first was led to Athanasia: a fleeting thought shooting quick and bright as a comet, and if he didn't act on it now, the thought would rocket away and he'd be left wondering what it was he'd been thinking about. The thought said: *You're ready.*

The woman clicked her tongue while nodding slow. "It's your third eye, kiddo. In dreams, it's always open, but awake, it's closed. You got to open that eye."

Luke felt as confused as she sounded certain. He moved closer to her. "How?"

"First, you're trying too hard. You can't hold a butterfly in hands clenched to fists, so relax. The world ain't waitin' for you all strung up. Take some deep breaths, close your eyes, think about a place in the center of your forehead, right about where that scab is."

Luke touched the dried blood from some mishap; they happened so frequently he couldn't keep track. The area was still tender, and he could feel a faint throbbing from behind.

She continued. "Each time you inhale deep, imagine the breath not just going to your lungs, but up inside your brain, behind that scab. Keep doing that, letting the breaths build up there, while you're thinking about what you want done, about your ability in dreams. Focus on your thoughts and your breaths, and the pressure of those breaths in your head is like a force behind a door, and soon enough that door is gonna burst open."

The idea sounded utterly irrational. Luke tried it anyway.

He let his mind stretch away, reaching for the train's engine, taking hold to control, *and suddenly he felt it*. He felt as one with the boiler, felt the weight of the coal, the heat of the steam, felt the pistons moving one way, then the other, felt his breaths through the regulator, out through the chimney, just as he could do in Athanasia—

A thud broke Luke's connection as a heavy knapsack landed on the car's wood floor. A moment later a 'bo couple pulled themselves inside. They took one glance at the strange woman perched amongst the iron brackets and Luke facing her with uprolled eyes, like they were having a religious blessing. Without a word, the couple grabbed the knapsack, turned, and jumped back out.

The woman said, "You're gettin' there, kiddo, it's your energy center that needs strengthening, needs dominance."

Luke tried again, harder, taking the engine into his own mind while riding atop it, steering it, driving it . . . and he thought these things, and he felt these things, but the train did not respond to any command of his at all. Something was there, he was sure, but his dominion over trains wasn't working the way it did in the deadeye.

Luke fell back, panting. His shoulders rolled, his head swayed.

"Tell you what, kiddo," she said. "You did it."

"I didn't do nothin'."

"You opened your eye. Told you I'm a seer, and I saw."

A drip of blood ran down the bridge of Luke's nose. The faint throbbing from behind the scab was beating like a drummer's cadence. It took him a moment to realize these things.

"That's enough for today," she continued. "But keep at it how I said, make it a routine, and you'll ace that power you're seeking in no time."

"Well, thanks," Luke said.

"This is where you get off."

"Here? Why?"

She giggled again, and the old seer woman could have been any darling girl at a tea party. "'Cause I'm done with you, kiddo."

She closed her eyes, started humming.

"You really keeping us from Mars?" Luke asked.

Her hum got louder.

He took his rucksack and jumped off into a vineyard of briar snakes. Once landed, Luke took a moment of reverence and watched the train roll heavily away.

Luke practiced calling trains throughout days and nights that contested each other, and just when it seemed one side had won—light or dark—the struggle swung to the other's favor. So too did Luke battle himself, at turns feeling conqueror or feeling defeated, and then it went the other way. But he kept at it, puzzling, wandering, practicing and practicing, until he felt sure he'd go crazy if something didn't pay off.

He'd been walking a tough road in a rough state in the interior of America when, this moment, a junk train came huffing past, making its way up a steep incline. Luke leapt onto the coupling between two gondolas, not thinking much of it while his mind considered crazy things like clairvoyance and living memories.

"Move along, 'bo."

Luke jerked his head to all sides, then he looked up and saw an old bull above, sitting on the metal ledge with his legs rocking to the train's rhythm. "Please, sir, I've got to get where I'm going."

"Not on this train you don't," the man replied, smoking a pipe.

"Just this once?" Luke asked. "There ain't another line out here for half a day."

"Unfortunate for you."

"Pete's sake, can't a man get a break?"

"You'll get a head break, you don't move off this train."

Damn.

Luke didn't care for more troubles, so swung back down where he'd started. He wondered, though, what that old bull would do if he made the train steam backward to lay right at his feet. *Bull would probably jump down and bean me as normal as any other day.* No, in Athanasia he might have some gift to manipulate machines, but he couldn't do a thing yet over here, nor could he do a thing regardless about hardnosed railroad dicks. A bull was a bull, and he was a tramp, and ever the two shall be at odds.

Damn, damn, damn . . .

As the rest of the train filed away, Luke turned, scuffing his busted shoes through hard earth, causing little poofs of dust to billow skyward, and if he looked carefully enough they could've been any 'bo symbol in the world, even a triangle with an eye at its center beside a crude locomotive.

At the last minute he clenched his fists and spun around, and he opened his third eye, and spread his mind after the train, reaching for it, corralling it, *demanding* it return. He caught it, and this time his mind and the engine clicked; he felt an influence over the train, even while the train fought him.

It bucked and clamored, wrenching forward against him in great gusts up the incline, but Luke kept at it, pulling back, and the engine sorta shook hard from side-to-side, almost rolling off the track, and you could see it, just leaning forth with all its might, a hooked fish on a line, straining in its tug o' war of determination.

"Get back here . . . Come to me, you stubborn bastard," Luke muttered.

Maybe it was his imagination, or it was *because* of his imagination: The wheels locked up, sparks flicking out from the friction caused by forcing them one way on the rail, then the other. There was a groan of metal, a shriek of steel. The train checked to a standstill. The old bull stood from his lofty perch with a puzzled expression on his face. He saw Luke standing there watching with grit teeth, and raised a blackjack at him.

Luke broke. He let the train go, and like a tug o' war that the rope gets snapped, the recoil tension caused the train to lurch forward in a great jump, and the surprised bull went flyin'.

Luke ran the other way, laughing all the while.

His tough road eased considerably, and he kept walking it, roaming the day away. Come afternoon, he heard a bit of song and followed its melody. *"Ain't got a shoe for my foot . . . No washin' soap for this soot . . . "*

Luke tramped through loose bracken that sprouted wherever it felt, and he crossed a gorge that cut itself across clay earth. There was a cough, a mumble, a humming of some chords, then another bit of song: "*Train, train a'comin', take me from this land, just a poor sinner boy, done the best I can.*"

He kept going. Around him thickets rambled, surrounding a small cove, and he came to a smoke-stained sheet tied between branches of laurel. There, sheltered beneath, was the singer.

"Sounds real nice," Luke said in greeting. That wasn't entirely honest, but compared to hearing his own voice, this fellow could've been a stage crooner.

The singer was about his age, a 'bo with a big smile. He held a plain box like it was some sort of guitar, six pieces of colored wire screwed into it at different intervals and stretched across a broken fence stile. One wire had snapped and corkscrewed high into the air, and there were some letters and notes drawn over the apparatus, but at the end of the day it was still a box, and sounded as such.

The man didn't startle at Luke, as though he'd gotten used to audiences eavesdropping. He kept grinning and wiped a rag over his forehead. "Tune needs some work yet, but I'm at it."

"Mind if I share your company?"

"Have at it, friend." The man was even thinner and shabbier than Luke, but he looked a truckload happier than Luke, too, with a pot of cold stew set by one bare foot and the leftover spine and head of a surprised fish at the other.

The man strummed his pretend-guitar a couple more times, and notes screeched out wobbly and plaintive. "This is just practice 'til I get the real thing. Shouldn't be any time much longer."

"I'll watch for you at the Opry," Luke replied, scuffing his foot around the ground in search of a patch that was thistle-free. "Name's Luke Thacker."

"Oh, I heard of you, a crossbuck 'bo telling stories with a pretty gal on his arm."

Luke blew out a big mouthful of air. "Really, you heard about me? Who from?"

"Heard it from a 'bo, who heard it from a 'bo. You know how it goes."

Though Luke knew well how things like that go, he'd never met a stranger knowing who he was through word-of-mouth. He thought suddenly of the bull, Thomas, that Zeke had killed. Could it be detectives were finally on his trail, asking around? He gave a nervous chuckle. "Sure, talk travels, but how'd it get my way? Didn't think hardly anyone paid me a care."

"I love hearing 'bo crossbucks. We make ourselves out of stories, y'know? You talking about another world after death, that place—what is it, Athanasia?—is making way along tracks as much as any engine. Big tales."

Luke's heart skipped with relief, though he played it off by making a big show of stretching his long arms and crossing them behind his head as he sat under the smoky sheet ceiling. "Athanasia, that's it. There our memories keep existing even while our bodies don't, and the dead we knew are remembered as they once were. A strange notion, but it's all around us, not a crossbuck at all."

"I get it. People don't believe a thing 'til it affects them, though once it does, it's a doughty punch."

"Ain't that the truth," Luke agreed.

"No one believes me either."

"About what?"

"What're we jawin' about? The place where the dead still walk like they don't know they should be underground. You call it Athanasia, but I never knew its name. Never met anyone else who's been there, either. Most of the time I thought it was a drunk-binge, even if I don't drink."

Luke stared, dumbly thinking what the singer had said was just lyrics to another song and not a shared experience at all. The box with screwed wires rested on the hobo's lap, worn out from impersonating something it wasn't. The 'bo yawned, tired or bored. He flicked at his dark skin and a hover fly retreated to perch elsewhere.

"You been to Athanasia," Luke finally said, more a statement to himself than a question to the man.

"And I ain't never going back."

"You been to Athanasia," Luke said again, almost a whisper.

The man looked anew at Luke, and his eyes narrowed in suspicion. "Take it easy, friend."

"How? I mean, how'd you get there?"

"Followed the 'Bo Code. Found some real strange signs I never seen before, one of them pointing to the door of a coal shed. And before that, a man appeared in my dreams, asking me to come and visit. Said he was my poppa and wanted to make amends. Course, who believes in dreams?"

"Who was he? Your poppa?"

"Glory if I know. Sometimes you think back on things and wonder what you were expecting. At the time it was pretty astonishing, imagining this handsome jack in a tuxedo fathering me. There were bright lights flashing around him, and he talked kind of funny, real proper-like, and then I seen the symbols leading me to where he's waitin'. This was up in coal mine country, Pennsylvania, and the signs called me by name, and no one there should've known who I was, so I followed, believing real hard I was special, I was meant for bigger things than this. Then I seen that funny glowing sign he showed me painted over the porch of a depot, a number eight laid on its side, and I went through.

"At first it didn't look like nothing was changed. It was this Yankee yokel town, and everything was gray, like coal dust had cast a shadow over the sun. Some folks passed by and I nodded to them, and they ignored me, which was ordinary. Saw some girls jumping rope and steered clear of them, as you don't wanna be a tramp caught talkin' to young girls. Like I said, all ordinary. I waited there for the man who said he was my poppa, but nothin' doing."

King paused as his face hardened. He made a sound of disgust, as if in reminiscence of what had occurred. "Pair of railroad dicks came by, and that's when I realized something was wrong, as the bulls walked past without a word to me. Never happened that a man with a badge don't roust me when he can. From there I asked around, and it was like I was invisible.

"First person I met who acknowledged me was a tall man in a beaver-felted top hat that made him look even taller, with tiny bloodshot blue eyes, and he demanded to see my papers of freedom. I told him to kiss my unwashed keister, 'cause I never heard of such a thing. Course, he didn't take kindly to that suggestion. The man uncoiled a whip that seemed to appear out of nowhere and his other hand held up a pair of shackles, and then he said his name was Lewis Robards and his job was to capture *me*, a runaway slave."

Luke's eyes went big, and he started to say something but King held up a hand to not interrupt. He continued, "Hell's bells, but no one wants to hear that, and it don't matter the color of your skin. I backed off, but fast. Another man and a woman joined him, both mean-lookin' and holding old-fashioned weapons, the man with something like a blunderbuss you see in pictures of pilgrims, and the woman holding a long pitchfork like a devil would use.

"All I thought then was my handsome poppa was a real bastard, and I had to get back through that depot entrance with the glowing sign. I barely made it, too. They shot at me, and a bullet left my shirt with an extra hole.

Last thing I heard them say was something about how Benjamin Franklin's gonna get me. Don't that beat all? Threatening Franklin like he's the boogeyman?"

By the time the man finished telling his story, Luke was sweating for him.

"It ain't all like that," Luke told him. "There's good people too, but there was plenty others after me as well."

"What'd have happened if they caught me?"

"Don't know, and I'm glad I haven't found out. Suppose you'd be trapped there until you died and died again, alone with the memories."

"Well, they can have it. If the stories I heard you been tellin' are true, figure we'll all be there soon enough anyway."

"You're the first I met who's visited also, and I don't even know your name."

"Shawell," the 'bo replied, then seemed to decide the occasion warranted further elucidation. "Shawell Kingston Pawłowski. But most just call me King Shaw."

THE CODE MAKER, 1939, CONTINUED

An old man watched Luke from far away, and he nodded an unhurried nod, and he drew more symbols in the dust that covered the old table, inside an old cabin, atop an old mountain, upon an old land.

The old man watched King Shaw as well, from far away, and was pleased at this crossing of Luke and King, and the indulgent, suggestive smile of before returned.

This old man who wrote the Code was not the first to do so, nor would he be the last, and if not for him someone else would take such charge. Duty gets passed along. Eugenia of the Rails had said that, and she knew.

For many years the Code Maker had written messages to others, preserving ancient rites of communication through leaves, glyphs, and clouds, even reclaiming those vanished manners once revered, the warnings and omens voiced by giving name of statues or shadows or soul jars. And still there are more, always other means if the receiver is attuned to such, the dreams of night, the visions through cedar smoke, the celestial doings of our universe . . . But such is the challenge with messages: How to relate something for only the intended to receive?

Once upon a time, and not long ago, writing wasn't practiced at all. Should something need to be said, men met and said it, and if they couldn't meet, then it wasn't spoken. Tidings could be sent by way of chittering birds and the rustling of grass; but in such a way, too, was a message garbled or heard by those not meant to hear.

So was the Hobo Code a method of this means, and the Code Maker used it to move Luke Thacker along, and others like Luke, keeping them safe, showing them glimpses until the time was right . . .

And that time was now.

For the Code Maker himself was old, and he was tired, and he was under assault, undermined by those wishing to erode his work, his memories, and the memories he served.

Luke had learned the Hobo Code well, and through it the Code Maker told him of the time, this time now, to return.

LUKE AND POCAHONTAS, 1939

The Code Maker's message was received. One year had passed since Luke Thacker was last in Athanasia, and he felt of two minds when the Code called now for him to revisit . . .

At present, Luke was bumming around Louisville, dining better than in years off the raisin pie scraps and ladyfinger handouts of the Kentucky Derby Festival. It was a tough swap, sacrificing the familiar refuge of the rails for city alleys, as the trade-off meant a skull crack and lock-up should beat detectives catch him defiling the view of hapless racing fans and wealthy tourists. But Luke wore a hat and a smile, and every street corner he traipsed found the remnants of melons, hot dogs, deviled eggs, popcorn balls, and salted filberts. And even there, he continued to champion Daisy and Zeke to all who would listen while his belly gorged.

Hopping a few fences and catching some luck brought him to the sidelines of Churchill Downs, where Johnstown the horse won the day's roses at "The Fastest Two Minutes in Sports."

The infield tote board screamed results amidst the cheers of fans, but to Luke it appeared the world was cheering the Hobo Code messages that scrawled across as fast as the placards ticked, urging him on to some uncertain victory.

His heart swelled.

'Bo symbols flashed by of the open doorway, the happy face, then the sideways infinity sign, the exclamation to depart, and more; the signs were self-evident, and they were illusory, a call in the wind that was verse set to birdsong. As happened after Daisy's death, his mind filled with the promise of truth in the same strange way a river glows on moonless nights, did the sense of raging synapses of his brain read so much.

Any man can lose his way.

Return to your future.

Luke, you are chosen.

And though he perceived the messages, still he wondered, what was their actual meaning?

For Luke wanted desperately to go back, to find Daisy and hold her in his arms, yet too was he wary of returning. He'd committed his time since returning to regular life to strengthening the memories of Zeke and Daisy. He'd taken the matter on faith, but believed it true, what Paul Revere had said: *Go back to Real World and talk about them enough to keep them alive in the deadeye, hoping there's sufficient time, ample interest to make them last.*

If he went back to Athanasia now, it might undercut his efforts, no longer spreading their stories, not to mention there wasn't a damn good thing ever seeming to come from stepping in the deadeye.

But he wondered, too, was there actually any effect from his endeavors? Was it too late, Zeke and Daisy already gone? Or were they talking to him even now, and he forgetting each time they visited, as fleet as memories that come and go?

You too can come and go, the Code said.

You too are fleet as memories.

You too care for others, as do others care for more . . . there are millions more . . .

And so he decided.

Luke left the racing track, making his way through the crowds to the rail line crossing Central Avenue a block away, where nobody was watching. He found the mark for Athanasia on a crossing arm painted bright-red as a scream, went under it, and hopped into a boxcar. The messages told him to travel for Jamestown, Virginia, and so there he made steam, contemplative; it wasn't a long journey, but he thought a long time. A journey without destination was but a wandering, and that seemed all his days. How much longer could he do this?

Luke wended his way eastward from Kentucky, through the hills of Lynchburg and the dark tobacco fields of Blackstone, into the Tidewater region, where the streams and gorges cut through Petersburg's heavy clay soil and the mountains sprouted every color foliage one could imagine, then over the gorgeous James River and still east, past Sherwood Forest and Chickahominy, onto Williamsburg, the rail tracks running softly along Highway 60 and cutting back south like a chipped blade toward the estuary, and here the skies thundered and cried their angry rains, and Luke worried he was the cause, he the interloper to a world he didn't belong; but then the storm passed and Luke decided all was well, until he hopped off the train amongst stands of old hardwoods skirting the peninsula's brackish wetlands and fell into the sights of a hideous, hellish man.

The man stepped back in surprise, not used to seeing people fling themselves off rail cars. But then he closed in, scowling with an expression that by itself might nearly cause murder. "A bit of rum, and I'll not feed you yer own ears."

The man's appearance was near terrifying as Smith McCain's. He stood tall, with a wild black beard that swarmed his face so nothing else could be seen but large, shadow-lined eyes topped by heavy lids and filled with inky cannonball irises. As he stepped closer to Luke, his great beard swelled, seeming almost a living thing, a wolf's hide wound 'round the man's chin, rising and snarling. It extended to the man's waist, and braids wove into it with black ribbons were writhing pincers while pieces of tied, smoking hemp were the stingers of scorpions. The beard seemed to fuse with the man's flesh and muscle, snaking its way over his body in rifts and plaits, then back around in streamers that frayed every direction.

Luke was certain he knew him, coming from the lore of childhood tales and the legends of treasure hunters, as being that dreadest of all dread pirates: Blackbeard.

Blackbeard carried a long shovel over one massive shoulder, and when Luke didn't make reply to his challenge, he swung the shovel around and planted it deep into the silt with a warbling clang.

"I know ye can hear me fine, lad, so don't gawk, or I'll add yer eyeballs to dine upon." Each word seemed to boom with the echoes of musket fire.

It was a silly thing, really, Luke thought, that he should one moment be riding the rails in passing serenity and the next be facing a murderous madman.

"I—I'm just passin' through, sir," Luke said, shuffling his feet, and hating himself for the act. His eyes went to the ground, and he instinctively felt the way he did against a railroad dick, trying to make himself as invisible to the surroundings as possible.

"Like to be, you're lookin' to steal me treasure."

"No, sir, that's the last thing I'm lookin' for, I promise that much."

"Devil take yer lyin' tongue and I'll damn ye meself!" Blackbeard pulled a flintlock pistol from a bandolier strapped to his chest. When the monstrous beard moved aside so the pirate could arm himself, Luke saw there were twenty more pistols strapped beneath, running in a line the breadth of shoulder to waist.

"Wait, I ain't got rum, but I know where's some fine hooch." Luke didn't know any such thing, but he thought that'd buy time, figure out why he'd been called to Jamestown for this, maybe call the train to come back and jump it for anywhere away.

"Moonshine?" Blackbeard bellowed a sort of horrible disbelief. "Ye'd think me that much a heathen? Eh, what good are you alive, but another scourge after me gold?"

A woman's deep voice commanded from the trees, "Leave him, corsair. The animate is for me."

Luke turned—not enough to take his sight entirely off the pirate—but enough to see who'd spoken, and his wonderment at her was as great as that of meeting Blackbeard.

A young Indian woman approached with eyes filled big by passion or by rage, as Luke always thought a woman's eyes could evoke either by the same glint. Her henna-hued face struck him as alluring, though it betrayed years older than her true age, and she was barefoot, dressed in a deerskin cloth with frayed edges that barely covered any part of her body at all.

"Bloody wench." Blackbeard barely acknowledged her. "Mind yourself, lass, or I'll rape ye with me rapier."

She held her ground and spat out a short laugh. "I've heard use of your little blade, but not known it be so feeble."

"Then a new conquest for me," the pirate said, and fired the pistol at her.

The shot's crack stung Luke's ears, louder than the regular sound of pistols he was used to, and its puff of smoke stung his eyes.

The Indian woman moved in a burst of speed, almost like a puff of smoke herself, from one spot to the next, and Luke caught a bare glimpse of a stone hatchet balanced carefully in thin hands as the pistol's musket ball shot past her cheek, leaving a line of char where it grazed. Blackbeard dropped the gun and pulled another off his chest.

She darted at him and her arm swung out, and in a flash she'd circled behind. Once away, she turned and crouched, watching the pirate through wary almond eyes.

He hitched a breath. He dropped his pistol. Black eyes grew larger, looking down. The roar of his pain and fury was drowned out only by the hirsute squeals of his beard, where the axe had cleaved through as it buried deep into his chest.

Blackbeard staggered, steadied himself, grabbed the stone axe with one hand and yanked it out, while arming himself with a new pistol in the other hand. A gush of blood leapt from the ragged wound, and when he panted, Luke heard a faint bubbling issue from his lungs.

"Mind yourself, corsair," the woman said, pointing to the sky. "You still have time."

A haze of red pox emerged over the tree line, the circling vultures of dying memories.

Blackbeard seemed to draw some quick conclusions, foremost the need to decamp. He holstered his weapon and blustered, "Damn yon pox on the windward, and both ye for bringin' 'em!"

He staggered off, his path like a horseshoe, a few lurches toward them, then turning to move a few lurches away, all the while muttering, "I'm just lookin' for me gold, it's mine, mine, oh, where's me gold . . . "

As if reading the question off Luke's shaken face, the Indian woman explained. "The corsair's legend is strong here. Blackbeard is said to have buried many treasures along the Virginia waterways, but his maps were lost, and erosion and storms changed the face of the sandy shores. The plunder of a hundred ships is within these inlets, and even he cannot find it."

"What a way to spend eternity, looking for what you lost."

"Is that not you?" she asked.

Luke bit his lip.

She motioned to the gleaming rails that sliced back into old growth trees of the peninsula. "Come. I'm here to take you."

"To where? And, well, who *are* you?"

"We are to visit the Code Maker, and his whereabouts change. I am Pocahontas."

"All right," Luke said. "Odd, I'm not even surprised."

"There are many after you," she said. "I am here to keep you safe."

"You're not the first to claim good intentions."

Pocahontas shrugged. "Call your train. We will ride together."

"Really? You can hop cars?"

"I am, how you say . . . *lissome*."

Luke looked up along the rails and started thinking about an engine, and one sounded off as it steamed their way.

Pocahontas nodded. "Impressive."

"Um, actually, this one's coming on its own," Luke admitted. "Just a coincidence it's passing by."

"At least you do not steal false credit."

The beast of an engine rumbled past. Luke said, "Jumping trains ain't easy as you think. You gotta build momentum, have steady feet, hold that bar tight when you catch and don't let go for nothin'—"

The first boxcar with an open door sidled past and Pocahontas jumped inside from a standstill, the way a cricket looks frozen and then leaps ten feet into the air.

"Shit," Luke said. "Wait for me!"

He ran fast, trying to catch up with the open car that already was moving out of sight. He tripped and went sprawling, and had to use his mind to focus on the train and ask it to slow backward, so he could clamber aboard.

"Did I do it right?" Pocahontas asked innocently.

"Yeah, it wasn't bad . . . for your first time or anything." Luke sighed. The Indian princess watched him, her face impossible to read. "So where's

this Code Maker, anyway? You said he moves around, but I'm guessin'
you're privy to all that?"

"Yes. Can you steer the train?"

"I'll take us anywhere these tracks lead."

"And what about where tracks do not go?"

Luke paused. "Can I do that?"

"Can you?"

Her reply led only to more questions. He scratched the stubble of his
jaw. "I don't know."

"Sedalia, in Missouri. That is where we must go."

Luke nodded. "All right. I can do Sedalia. They got a big ol' station in
their downtown parts, the Katy Depot, lines lead right in. Real nice ragtime
music there, too." Pocahontas's face was still unreadable. "Or . . . you don't
care for music."

She blinked. Luke turned the train west to cross the James River.

Some minutes passed. Luke cleared his throat. "How come I couldn't
just meet you in Missouri? I was already in Kentucky before getting called
to come the opposite direction."

"Jamestown is where I always return."

"From what? Travelling with this Code Maker?"

"Yes, and Jamestown is where—"

"You return, I got it."

"The cycle has not yet been broken," she said.

"I see." Though he didn't.

"He rewrites the Code," Pocahontas said, "and so his cabin moves. He
has help in concealing his whereabouts, but there are many after him."

"Like they're after me?"

She nodded. "Sedalia is where we go today, and tomorrow may be
different. He cannot stay long in one place, so he stays in them all. Like
you, he is a traveler."

"What's in it for you?"

"My reasons."

"How do you travel the country and then get back to Jamestown?
Known for running fast?"

"The Code Maker helps."

Luke sucked in a breath, let out a sigh, knowing when a conversation was over. He contented himself to run fingers over the floor planks, crack his neck, mutter about busted shoes, and wonder on this Code Maker.

Soon the train lolled into its steel dock at Katy Depot, turning to a juncture line that was pressed on one side by a coal stage and on the other by redwood passenger platforms.

They debarked and passed through clumps of travelers, the first non-dead he'd encountered since returning to Athanasia, and the bewildering sensation returned of being invisible, ignored. Even Pocahontas didn't get the head turns he'd seen of other notable bigwigs, and he wondered at that.

She led him, slipping amongst hurrying businessmen and finely-dressed women, passengers and conductors and loafers, like skimming through water, sleek and fluid, and they sidestepped out of her way without realizing. Luke's eyes danced over her body; he didn't mean to, but he couldn't help it either. Most women who said more words to him than *"ain't no handouts today"* looked like they could have been a relation to Medusa. Pocahontas had muscles on every part of her body and they rippled when she moved, like a lithe cat stalking prey through the forest. Her thighs were larger than his own, but they were still shaped like a young woman's, smooth and curved as the billowing sails of a fast-moving ship. Her thick black hair bounced behind as she paced across the depot, down stairs, and out through the streets, so as Luke followed it seemed to reach back and tickle his face. It smelled of jasmine and the way fresh sunshine warms morning rain.

And then Luke began to encounter the *others*, the dead, the memories of the deadeye that were kept about, the ones who accepted what they were and the ones who stared off into space, surrendering to a slow fade-away. In that way Sedalia was bustling with both the living and the ghosts.

They passed a man screaming for the pox to take him, just take him now. They passed children weeping for lost parents. They passed a sheep with two heads that watched dumbly from four eyes as it chewed cud in the middle of the road. They passed a stoic, naked elder who bowed their way and muttered something to the wind. They passed people Luke might have known in the living world, people fretting and scared, people lonely and worn out, and it seemed to him that bein' remembered, kept around in such a way, wasn't meant for all.

"What if someone don't want to be here anymore?" Luke finally asked. "What if they just want to be forgot forever and leave this place?"

Pocahontas shook her head, a dour look shrouding those composed features. "Nothing to be done. Crawl under the earth and sleep until you're taken."

"Why've I got a feeling that's what you want?"

"Nothing else is left me. My husband gone, my parents, my son who I knew only as a babe, his daughters, their children, all dead, all recorded in the tomes of history, but not enough—how you say, *vigor*—to keep them here with me."

"Everyone else I met, they're fighting to be remembered."

Pocahontas did not reply for some time, still leading from 5th to Hancock to 6th, passing the big-steepled fire department, heritage plaques, horse tacks, and historic homes. Finally she said, "What does it matter prolonging this? Eventually all will be forgot."

"Guess I just want to have a choice in the matter," Luke said. "Maybe leave on my terms, but only after I've done right by everyone else, after I've had my say. I sure don't want someone else cuttin' me out early."

"That is you. I've already done my right. Enough for a hundred lifetimes."

"So what are you sayin', that you're ready to give up?" Luke asked. "Wouldn't make sense if you're helping me."

"Should you weave a basket of grass and that basket get a hole, do you weave a new basket? Or would you mend the one already made?"

"Fix the hole, I suppose, if it's easier."

"But if the rest of the basket is old, frail, crumbling, what is the use?"

"Well then, make a new one."

"And for us, what would you do?"

Luke glanced at her, away, at the other miserable lives around them. "Remake yourself?"

She didn't reply. The long-drawn whistle of a departing engine carried from the distance.

He asked, "But if you change your memories, won't that make you be forgot? Who you are, what you've done, changed or twisted so no one remembers rightly who you've really been?"

"I'll make myself who I *want* to be, not what the world sees of me, and if that should cause my oblivion, so much the better."

Luke shook his head, wondering not only at her life, but at his own. "I do seem to recall hearing of you told as a bit more sweet and accommodating."

They arrived at a tall, gray limestone building with golden windows and fine-chiseled brick copings. The multi-gable roofline and turrets looked like something from a fairytale. Tasseled awnings named it as the Hotel Terry, and below that was a gorgeous big marquee sign declaring: *A place where you are always welcome and feel at home.* Below the marquee hung a follow-up notice, like the post script of a letter, handwritten in bold ink slashes: *No Bums Allowed.*

That second sign made him pause as if the words were spoken just to him—again—by some hard-lined railroad bull. He felt edgy suddenly, dejected.

Pocahontas stopped to look back at him. "Really?"

"Sorry, it's happened too much . . . Force of habit."

"That habit need be broken."

"Yeah, that it does. But I'm with you." He straightened up and stepped forward, following her up two marble steps while she crossed the hotel's front landing.

"Anyway, we are not going in there." Pocahontas pushed open a glass door and went through.

"Wait, what? You just said we're not going in . . . " Luke hurried to catch up. Above the door's lintel was a symbol he'd not seen before: A sun bisected in half, the lower part colored dark and the upper part light.

He went through the hotel door and arrived inside an old cabin.

There, an old man looked up, nodding to Pocahontas, then to Luke. The old man was Indian like Pocahontas, with bronze skin against small dark eyes and a long, flat nose that seemed to pull against his unsmiling cheeks. He wore a blue and red fringed robe, and the top of his head was wrapped in a strange cloth turban surrounded by bands of painted flowers. Tufts of shaggy gray hair escaped from underneath its pleats. He sat at an old table, drawing pictures with his finger in a thin sheet of dust.

Luke covered his nose, stifling a sneeze. Even by 'bo standards the room was filthy and old. Everything about it looked peculiarly ancient and ashy and worn.

"Welcome," the old man said, standing. "I am Sequoyah. I write the Code."

Luke froze, every nerve tingling like he'd filled himself up with lightning. "*The* . . . Code?"

"The Code you follow."

"The Hobo Code?"

"Yes."

"Code of the Railroad—"

"Language of the rail rider, communiqué of bindle stiffs, consultation and admonition of the unsettled vagabond, yes."

Luke's mouth gaped, snapped shut. He wasn't sure what else to say, much less think.

"I go," Pocahontas said.

"Yes," Sequoyah replied. "Thank you, as always, O Warrior Queen."

Luke had time for only one brief reflection that Pocahontas looked distant, like she was thinking hard on something he'd never know, before she pulled out a stone knife that was sharpened to a razor's edge and sliced it across her own throat.

Luke leapt back with a sound like a kicked goose.

A jet of blood shot from Pocahontas, splattering the dusty floor, and she knelt down to sit cross-legged amongst its pools.

Luke leapt back a second time, then leapt forward to her, thinking even as he did so he was about as effective as a stray bouncing ball, but so was he overwhelmed coming into this unexpected room with its unexpected revelation, and now this beautiful champion killing herself. He tore a rag from his patchwork pants pocket and moved to wrap it around her neck.

Pocahontas slapped him across the face.

"Stay back," Sequoyah told him.

Luke nearly screamed. "You're just going to stand there, she's dying!"

"How else will she rebuild her legend?"

Luke reeled, flustered. "I'm just supposed to accept it, huh?"

The Code Maker nodded once.

"Another horror of this place," Luke said, stepping away as she swayed and toppled to one side. "You're just going to let the goddamned pox eat her?"

"No, though it's what she wants."

"Hell with this world."

"You will learn the truth, son."

"Son?" Luke turned on him, the rag falling away from splayed fingers. "You're not going to say you're my daddy, are you?"

"No. If I was, I'd have whipped your hide long ago." Sequoyah smiled faintly. "But you *are* a distant relation, and believe it or not, I don't have a lot of those remaining."

Pocahontas trembled once more, fell limp, and faded away, her body shriveling in on itself, then vanishing.

"Where's she going?"

"Back to where I've writ it, where memory calls, to Jamestown."

"But others who've already died don't—"

"As I said, I have writ it, Luke." Sequoyah wiped his hand across the table, and the markings were erased. A fresh layer of dust appeared, undisturbed over the table top, and the old man stuck out one long finger and slowly wrote in it: a squiggly line swirling around another, a symbol of a funnel. "Her memory agrees, for there is more than one way to change history."

Luke stared dumbly at the symbol, then at Sequoyah. A long corncob pipe hung from the Indian's tight mouth, spewing sweet chicory smoke and flecks of ash that only added to the dust of the cabin. All the air in the room smelled of that smoke, as countless years of puffing away had clearly plastered everything around like layer over layer of paint, an ugly burnt yellow hue, sticky, streaked . . . and through it all, everywhere in that room were more symbols, either carved, scrawled, or drawn in the dust . . . the dust that seemed to take feature the more Luke gazed upon it, as if it were some topography of land.

"Dust of the world," Sequoyah added, as if reading his mind. "We are all of dust, and to dust we shall return."

Luke blinked. He felt angry, mean, and at every breath that goddamned dust seemed to drift in through his nose. He sneezed, then said, "I never even heard of you."

"Not everyone has, and I am old, though not as old as the trees named after me."

"So why am I here, besides watching a suicide pact?"

"Haven't you ever wondered who was writing symbols just for you, when you needed them most?"

That brought Luke down, his irritation forgotten. His thoughts began to spin. "Yeah. I mean, yes, everyday. I thought I was crazy sometimes, or just imagining it."

"It was me," Sequoyah said simply. "Leading you here, now."

Luke thought there should have been more impact at Sequoyah's words, some overturn of his life, of what he believed, a rationale of destiny. Instead he just shrugged, tired. "You sure got a roundabout way of leading folks somewhere."

"The path to knowledge is never direct."

"More wisdom don't mean a thing to me. If you can write the Code, why don't you write Daisy Rose back into my arms here and now?"

Sequoyah's slight smile was only sad. "Writing something alone does not make it so. I can tell you what to do, what occurs around you, explain premonitions, causes, but words do not transform life. They must be met with action."

"So let me guess, you brought me here to do something for you, another errand boy mission?"

"Or you can go back to eating out of trashcans until Smith McCain kills you in three years' time. Slowly and painfully."

"Oh."

"Otherwise," Sequoyah said, "if you'd prefer circumstances turn different, you'd do well to ditch those bemoans and be a bit more receptive."

"All right, I'll keep my bemoans to myself. What is it you wish of me, O master?"

"If that's your idea of a peace offering, I will accept it, son. Because what we're fighting is the resurgence of masters, indeed."

Luke crossed his arms, bit at one chapped lip.

"You know, too," Sequoyah said, "of the ones who wish to destroy you, to control you."

"Franklin?"

"Benjamin Franklin and his associates are after me as well."

"You . . . you're not an animate too?" Luke asked.

"No, but I stand in his way," Sequoyah said. "Benjamin Franklin not only wishes to make himself live longer in this world, he wishes to control the world entirely."

"As in, control what's remembered?"

"To rewrite all of history to his bidding. By his desire, it will not be what the shared consciousness of those alive recall, but what they are *told* to recall, being brainwashed, if you will. If the world was to have one singular religion, it would be of Franklin, and him as their god."

Luke searched his memory, what Ben had told him: *The world is a great mind, perhaps even the brain of another being . . .* and then of Paul Revere later confiding: *Power to one detracts from the rest . . .*

"Control all the world?" Luke said, shaking his head. "It's too much. He may be some kind of monster, but how can Franklin possibly do that?"

"Look around you, Luke. People are being forgotten faster and faster: culture, events, history, all vanishing, and much of it are things Franklin finds contentious to his image. It's the stories that are important, the communication. And when all should remember only the name of Benjamin Franklin, he will take that immortal seat of omniscience, all-power, complete with vengeance and pettiness and every other human fallibility. Consider a world reinvented, with the population kneeling at the feet of Franklin and his cronies, a slave state where he chooses on whim who is remembered and who is forgotten."

Luke felt numb. And he felt, too, as he had when speaking with Ben in the library at Boston . . . He was being told this in order to be controlled, to be led somewhere, to do something, and now he was wary. "So you need my help to stop him? He loses power so you can gain it?"

Sequoyah sighed. "It is why I like you, Luke. You question things, you wonder at them. I have been the Code Maker for a hundred years, and will be so for more, but no man is meant for immortality. Soon it will be time for me to ascend. Or descend, perhaps, into a deeper consciousness. That is what Franklin does not understand. Even after this, I tell you there will be more."

"And?"

"And you must take up my torch."

Luke startled. "Me? Hells no, I don't want your type of life, sittin' here controlling people like some game."

"Before me was the grammarian John Eliot, the first to translate the Algonquin language. Before him were others, Aztec and Mayan priests, scholarly minds in Mesoamerica to develop written scripts. I invented the written Cherokee system of symbols. There have been others, and there must be more, someone to come after me who can further the language of the Code, who understands it, who can speak to its people. If there's no one to oppose him, Franklin will fill the void."

Luke just shook his head, silent. Sequoyah continued.

"I have been grooming you, Luke, for many years. You have the aptitude, but need teaching. You wish the power to stop people like Franklin, free his enslaved, defend the drifters and 'bos like yourself, those reviled and abused? I will teach you great things, but you must next carry this torch of rectitude. It does not have to be today, but if too many tomorrows are passed, it will all be undone."

"All I want is to find my friends. I keep their memory alive, they'll stay alive too, at least *here*. I know that much, right?"

"Focus on sharing the Code, not just for two people. You cannot save them unless you save ten million."

Luke rolled his eyes.

Sequoyah threw up his arms. A thunderclap burst, and dust filled the air in a great blinding wave. Luke gagged.

"The spirit is in the Code!" Sequoyah said. "It's people who believe in it, follow it. The needy, the destitute. We have our own religion here, and those who follow find their way to a better life in Athanasia . . . but with all followings, there must be a leader."

Luke fanned the dust from his face. "You know, you actually sound a lot like *him*. A bunch of philosophy and big predictions, and I have to be the one to do everything, but it don't mean shit to me. I appreciate your symbols and all, helping me with the Code like you've done, but respectfully, I decline."

The dust disappeared. The room was clear, sterile.

"You must take time to think on it," Sequoyah said.

"Maybe while I'm on the pot and there's nothin' around to read."

"Remember that while some make their memories strong through stories, others are weakened by those same tales."

"I know, I know. Franklin said the same thing."

Sequoyah frowned. "I'm speaking to impair him, not mimic him."

"I got that too, yeah."

"Very well, Luke Thacker, of my distant blood. You still have time, if barely. I write this in the dust: Learn three lessons, and then return to give me your final decision."

"Don't count on it. I've got other plans." Luke turned to leave the way he'd entered, anxious to get away, only to find a solid wall.

"Not that way," Sequoyah said. "Over there."

Luke reversed to where Sequoyah pointed and saw an old door with a wood pull handle where a moment before had been a wall of plank siding. "How'd you—"

Sequoyah shrugged, the tiniest bit of smile creeping up one corner of his mouth.

Dawning broke over Luke. "I'm inside an illusion, some sort of magic, smoke and mirrors, ain't I? Hiding your real location . . . "

"Doesn't matter," Sequoyah said, pointing to the door. He puffed a vast cloud of chicory smoke from his pipe. "Your ears are closed, so there's the way out."

Luke went through.

ZEKE'S SECOND DEATH, 1939, PART ONE

Luke heard the thud and clack of the door and lock closing behind him.

He had to squint, blink, and blink again in the bright sunlight after being in that dim cabin, so at first he wasn't sure where he was, and even once his sight cleared, he still didn't know. There was just a lot of colorless prairie grass and a couple of weathered steer skulls.

He turned back and grimaced at where he'd emerged: an old, teetering, cobweb-covered, termite-filled shambles of the foulest of outhouses. Through the crescent moon cut-out of the splintered door, he glimpsed a rat scuttle inside on a crossbeam . . . Outhouse rats, worse even than sewer rats. Luke shuddered.

Above the moon cut-out was a symbol carved into the wood: A sun bisected in half, the lower part colored light and the upper part dark, reversed from how it had appeared at the Hotel Terry. Did this symbol mean exit, and the other way around was entrance, or did this reversal mean the way back to Sequoyah's cabin was now closed?

Either way, it didn't matter, he thought, since he'd left with a purpose. He struck out walking in the warm afternoon, and fifty feet away came to the burned-out ruins of what once had been a homesteader's shack, now nothing but a pile of charred logs. Whatever happened here had been long ago. Tall weeds grew up between the beams, whipping in a wind that came and went. If there was a home here once, he guessed there must be a road or a rail line somewhere nearby.

He shielded his hand over his eyes and looked around as far as he could. Nothing, nothing, and then he saw a man on horseback racing to him.

Not another one . . . After Paul Revere and the Earp brothers, Luke was objectionable to coming across any more horse riders, and he had no doubt this one wasn't coming for any other reason than himself.

There was no place to run or hide in the open land, 'less he wanted to brave the outhouse rats, so Luke crossed his arms, puffed out his chest, and stood there, trying to look as formidable as he could, though he could feel his knees just pining to knock together.

The rider came up fast, like a line of light bursting through clouds, growing larger and larger, spread wide across the land by the trail of dust kicked up from behind. When he arrived, the horse stopped up before Luke with a whinny, then took a couple steps around him in appraisal, glaring, as if Luke had already offended it in some breach of equine custom. It was a rich ebony-colored mare with long muscles that stretched at each movement.

The horse's rider asked, "You Crossbuck Luke Thacker?"

Luke squinted up. The rider struck a slim figure, dressed in rawhide fringe with a jaunty red bandana crossed at his neck. He seemed too young, fair-skinned with full cheeks that flushed like ripe apples and with a long, uneven mustache, as if he'd never shaved, but let whatever hairs grew upon his lip extend as they pleased. Around his waist were twin revolvers, one at each side, and below that, strapped off-center to the saddle, hung a burlap satchel filled with envelopes. The satchel bore an officious-looking emblem portraying an eagle above a galloping steed.

"I know you are," the boy-man continued, "so don't deny it. I heard about you coming here, an animate in our world looking for his dead friends. Just need confirmation before I deliver you a message."

The rider had a curious voice, a soft crispness to his words that one associated with English lads, but which was also overlapped with a somewhat out-of-breath Western drawl. It seemed impossible, to Luke, to have such conflicting qualities in his speech, yet the duality was distinctly present as he spoke. English, Western, English, Western, like the clip-clop sounds of the horse as it paced back and forth upon the hard-packed earth.

"That's my name," Luke finally admitted.

"I met a fella named Ezekiel Johnson, says he's your friend. He's not doing well . . . reckon he's on his way out. He wants to see you one last time."

"Zeke, he's here?" Luke asked incredulously.

"Not *here*," the rider said, looking around. "Up in Amarillo."

The horse snorted, its sound like ridicule at Luke's imbecility. Wisps of steam blew from its nostrils in smoldering rings.

"C'mon. I'll give you a ride," the boy-man continued, reaching down for Luke's hand. "Name's Bob Haslam, fastest rider of the Pony Express. Heck, fastest rider ever in the nation while I was alive, and I'm the fastest now in the deadeye. Quicker even than Paul Revere. I could take him twice over in any straight race."

The horse took a step backward, baring teeth that, as far as Luke knew, should have been flat and broad but were instead wicked spikes that poked out from around its bit in different directions, like the nails of some medieval mace.

"Ah, don't mind Annabelle," Bob said. "She can get a might feisty, what with all the ambushes we ran into over the years, but she's a good gal."

Annabelle seemed to disagree. A red glow came off its eyes, as if something caught fire from within and the flames of roan reckoning were soon to burst forth.

"Where's the nearest rail?" Luke asked.

"A train? There's a track about a quarter mile yonder, but engines don't schedule much for these parts. Just ride with me."

"Animals and I don't much get along."

"Trust me, I'll get you to your friend much faster than anything else," Bob said.

"Trust *me*," Luke replied, "when I say you won't."

"Suit yourself," Bob said, trotting away. He led Luke to a single track held to the ground by weeds and dried clots of mud. Half the crossties were sun-bleached and cracked, while the steel was pitted orange with rust and even covered in some places by tumbleweeds.

"Like I said, it doesn't get much use," Bob repeated.

Luke concentrated, thinking of the hobo sign that meant to catch a train, the child's scrawl of a box with wheels and a block on top for the stack, envisioning that train coming down the tracks this very moment. He thought of it as an AT&SF line, heading northbound to Amarillo. The engine would show first, a great black steam locomotive braying its fiercest cry, leading a couple dozen flatbeds of stacked girders, then cars filled with soybeans and hay and tobacco. Coupled at the end would be a bright red caboose with a crooked stove pipe sticking from its top next to the cupola, and a big Santa Fe emblem emblazoned on the sides. The doghouse would be empty, its rear platform open and surrounded by sturdy grab rails.

He thought of nothing else but the train, it arriving now, this instant.

Arriving now . . .

Arriving now . . .

And from the distance it came, announcing its approach with a shrill whistle and trail of dark smoke.

Bob's mouth fell open. "Moses on a swing."

"Think you can keep up?" Luke asked.

"Annabelle can keep up with any machine."

"Don't be so sure. This one's got places to be."

The train roared past, picking up speed with each turn of its wheels. The cars blurred, one after the other, and Luke waited until the end, the caboose, and he turned his body to it, held out one arm and caught the rear guard rail. Normally the momentum would have ripped his arm off, but Luke seemed to melt into the motion, like two winds coming together as one. He slid into it, propelling over the rails and, in one step, stood on the platform waving back to Bob.

The Pony Express rider slapped Annabelle's flank and yelled a command, and the horse took off, galloping fast, flames rising from its hooves as it kept parallel to the train.

In this way they travelled a hundred miles, which only took two minutes, and once they reached Amarillo's station, Luke stepped off the train like stepping off a sidewalk curb. The train never slowed, just kept driving off into the distance, seeming to fade away before it crossed the line of the horizon where most things in the distance tend to vanish.

"I could've got you here quicker," Bob said. "Annabelle was going slow so you could keep up."

"Appreciate the consideration," Luke said, then gave a wink. "But you did all right."

The horse didn't seem so menacing now, as if sensing its intimidation over Luke was no longer so impressive.

"Last I saw your friend, he was in the downtown district."

Bob led, and Luke followed, and a mile later they found Zeke where Bob had left him. True as the rider said, Zeke was on his way out. His long travels had ended now, at this moment, not at the moment of his *first* death. Luke felt his heart rip from his chest finding the dying giant prone in the mouth of an alley, his head pillowed on a spilled bag of fruit rinds and cardboard cups.

Bob tipped his hat to Luke, then reverently to Zeke. "Message delivered," he said quietly, and rode off.

"Luke . . . " Zeke wheezed. "Real good to see you again."

"What can I do to help, anything?" Luke said, though at the same time he also said, "What happened to you?" and "This is too early," so that all the sentences came out together in a crazy jumble of words.

"Mugged," Zeke moaned. "Even in death I got knocked down, some crazy woman with a pitchfork . . . "

"Pitchfork?"

"Long one, big as my cock." Zeke chuckled, which became another wheeze, which became a gasp, which became a shudder. "There were others, couple of men, but they just watched, laughin' at me. Don't matter . . . I was done anyway."

He wheezed again while Luke took his hand.

"Death ain't like I expected . . . though it's just like you said . . . " Zeke spoke slowly, as if each word was carefully rationed from a dwindling supply allotted him. "I came back, here in Texas . . . where I was born."

"It's where the memory of you is strongest, that's what brought you back here."

"Only there ain't no memory left at all. My family's farm was abandoned . . . nothing but barren ground and fell-over homes. My brothers and sisters gone, scattered all different directions. Neighbors gone, cousins gone, friends gone. None of 'em recalled me with much attachment anyway. I was just another hungry mouth . . . then I left."

There was an impression of something smoldering around Zeke, a smoky miasma, and pinpricks of red dotted him like an angry rash. But it was no rash—the pinpricks moved and swelled. The pox ate at him. It was a slow, painful progression into some hereafter that he presently suffered, and Zeke wept, and Luke wept. Luke took his hand, angry and resentful of himself and frightened for Zeke, though he was calloused to seeing this act of second passing.

Zeke went on, "I didn't leave much of an impression anywhere . . . 'Til I rode with you and Daisy, I mostly travelled alone."

Luke was almost embarrassed to ask, in Zeke's dying moments, but he had to know. "Have you seen her, Daisy . . . since—"

"No," Zeke answered simply. "Seen nobody I've ever known . . . 'cept Peggy Entwistle. Remember her? I seen her leap to her death . . . She came all the way from California to find me when I arrived . . . Kissed me on the cheek and gave thanks for saving her second life. I single-handedly did it, she said. I spread—" Zeke sucked in a long rattling breath, paused, continued, "I spread her legend so far, it caught on in Hollywood lore. She wished the same for me . . . "

"I'm trying, Zeke. I just need more time. I'm going to spread your legend until all the world remembers you."

"You know . . . it's too late."

The bottom half of his forearm sank inward, then his chin did the same, jerky motions like watching a fruit wither and turn rotten, collapsing on itself, but sped up fast.

"Always thought I was meant for more . . . " Zeke said. His eyes were big and their whites shimmered like the wind-filled sails of a distant schooner.

"I know," Luke answered. "Nobody was stronger, nobody braver than you."

Parts of Zeke were see-through, parts of him bloody, small holes opening on his flesh and radiating outward, bigger, deeper.

"How could I be forgotten so soon?" Zeke asked. He moaned, a sound that was long and drawn out: at first suppressed, then finally just let go.

"I'm sorry," Luke said. "I tried, and I won't stop trying. I'll find a way to bring you back—"

"There ain't no coming back . . . from this." Zeke's eyes dulled, glinting now like bright stars that fade behind a lightening sky.

And Luke had a crazy thought: *Were the stars really still there when one looked up to the daylit sky, or did they all die each morning, only to be reborn at dusk?*

There were other people around, walking the city sidewalks, smoking cigarettes, pushing baby carriages, talking about politics, about the election, Roosevelt against Landon, who'd win and who'd lose, and if it would help this damn stinking economy. Did it really matter who captained the nation's sinking ship if it was ruptured as grievously as the *Titanic*? People talked about the Olympics in Berlin, about neighbors, about church, about movies, about bank robbers, about affairs they themselves had no part in, but of which they could still form unshakable opinions.

There were other people around, some dressed in fine business suits, though there was little business to be had. People dressed in hats, in shawls, in bonnets, second-hand blouses, chafed pants, shirts with faint stains, coats with missing buttons, people of all ages, appearances, similar, yet not, walking and talking on the city sidewalks while loud cars and trucks drove by, searching for important places, and the weather was pleasant, and the afternoon young, and many were hungry and tried to recall when last they weren't, but things could be worse, and they could be better, though no one knew for certain when either might occur.

There were other people around, doing all these things, though none else saw mighty Zeke dying in the mouth of the alley.

Zeke gasped like sucking breath through a straw, then he spoke his final words. "I saved you, Luke. Remember . . . "

And Luke knew Zeke was speaking of more than one occasion. He silently cursed Smith McCain.

"I hope you were wrong, Ezekiel. I hope your namesake *is* a free ride into heaven." Luke squeezed Zeke's hand.

The holes in Zeke grew large. Through those peepholes that formed in his body, Luke saw nothingness. And in that moment, knowing his friend was to die, in as much sense as "forever" meant, Luke had another crazy thought: "nothingness" and "forever" meant the same.

Then Zeke was gone.

DAISY ROSE, 1939

Daisy Rose was kidnapped in early 1939, sometime after she'd died.

It was the final months of a tough winter, and she'd clipped her own wings to nest outside Shreveport. It wasn't that Daisy was remembered strongest there, but that she remembered herself there once being happy. Daddy had moved her back and forth along the Gulf of Mexico, so there was never one particular place she'd considered home, though being raised in the warm, wet air of the southern coast had instilled itself as the clime of preference, much milder than northern states and more colorful than the heartland. And, not long ago, she and Luke had one season worked and loved and lived in Shreveport. So she settled there again and found the humidity wasn't as bad as when her heart beat, but that being alone made existence more dismal than it was worth.

A feeling of unease shadowed everything, and Daisy tried to resign herself to whatever ghost-afterlife some higher power had designed for her outcome. Because higher powers had to be at work here, didn't they? After all, she'd been alive, then killed, then brought back. Wasn't that what the preachers said happened to Jesus, and he was proof of God?

She'd seen the pox at work, too, and knew something else might come for her. She feared those red dots, not knowing what they were or how to stop them, only witnessing their immaculate destruction. If her coming back could be likened to the rebirth of Jesus, the pox only reminded her of Hell's demonic nearness.

Daisy kept to the outskirts of a farmer's cottage, under the shelter of blossoming mulberry trees, and watched the world turn, preferring to remain among the woods like a haunt, but close enough to be in sight of the man and his wife and their gaggle of screaming, playing children. When night came and the stars twinkled overhead, she thought it could be her and Luke indoors. She dreamed and dreamed . . .

Squash and melons and cream and lace would all be plentiful. She'd set supper in the evening, and the sunshine would last hours longer than it should. Luke would come in telling all about the harvest and news of the many neighbors that'd stopped by to jaw a bit, and who had asked of her and the youngsters. That oldest boy looked to be twelve, and he'd be named Junior, after Luke, and the next eldest boy would be named Ezekiel. Some of the others could be Juniper, Josiah, or Willie. Luke would like that. There was a big pond nearby surrounded by cattails, and he'd teach her the best way to cast a line. And all the animals on the farm were friendly and everyone lived forever . . .

It was a fine fancy.

Her kidnapping happened in a flash and without warning. Daisy was doodling in the dirt with her toes and didn't know she'd been taken until the act was done, and she was tied up and blindfolded and somewhere in writhing transit.

The abductor's bindings were perfectly executed on her, and she didn't even know how it had occurred. Her hands were trussed behind her back and her upper arms cinched tight against her sides like she was in a cocoon. Her feet were tied, her legs tied, even her head shoved down and bound, squeezed against her own breasts. She jostled and bounced without seeing, without knowing, and felt sometimes like she sank, sometimes like she flew, and couldn't determine if she were being carried away by car, boat, or one of those bi-wing planes she'd seen slowly flying through the skies. The blindfold never shifted, never gave hint of where they travelled. Everything was black as the moment she died.

When attacked by Smith McCain, she'd been plenty scared, although that was a fear that had ended quickly. She was terrified now, and alternated between screaming for help and withdrawing into abject silence. Were such a thing to have happened while alive, it would've been a bad affair, but this was worse. Daisy knew the limits of pain and depravity while living, the potential for beatings, rape, torture, or murder. But as the saying goes, fear of the unknown is greater than the known; if she were already dead, and no longer constrained by limits of what the mortal body could endure, there might await a whole Sears catalogue of atrocious acts she'd never imagined.

She wondered, frantically, *Who?* and *Why?* Since she'd died, she'd not encountered a single other soul who could sense her. If she ever felt loneliness while alive, that experience had been as a baby thinking the world is large while looking across the crib it lies in.

And her fervid wish for companionship cruelly deceived her . . . She was no longer alone yet suffered the more for it.

Daisy was carried for a long time, though time held little concept anymore. Finally, after a thud, and the click and whoosh of an opening door, she was stood upon solid ground. She smelled the musty odor of old paper. There were voices in the distance, drawing nearer.

Rough hands held the back of her head and removed the blindfold. An explosion of bright light hit her eyes. It wasn't that the room was aglow, but rather that the sudden switch from darkness to mild incandescence caused her eyes to feel like they were on fire.

She blinked a million times as the bindings around her chest and neck came free, then her legs, then her feet. Only her hands remained tied.

Daisy turned to confront her abductor. Though her vision was blurry, and she felt sick and dizzy, there was no mistaking it: *she was alone*. She had just a moment to consider her surroundings of a room filled with heavy oak tables and shelves and shelves of books, before another door opened and people entered.

Three men came to stand before her, one in front and two behind him, one at each side, the way aides follow an important person. They were dressed in old-fashioned costumes like she'd seen in oil paintings. The front man also looked like someone she'd seen in oil paintings. He was bald on top of his head, but the edges sprouted long gray hair that draped well over his shoulders.

The man had only to speak one word for Daisy to sum him up for something she'd reviled all her life: Smugness, and the worst of it. One single everyday word that, with the right amount of inflection, some over-zealous articulation, timed rhythm, and meticulously-composed tone, suggested he was about to deliver a speech of grand victory or address a crowd of adoring commoners. Perhaps some things weren't so different between life and death after all; this man was highfalutin, and he wanted her to know it.

The single word he said was, "Hello."

LUKE AND THE EARPS, 1939

Zeke was dead—*again*—and gone forever, as much as Luke understood second death to be. Could be like Sequoyah had said; maybe spirits reappeared in some other realm, and another one after that, something like washing down through a set of pipes, each opening to a deeper, danker juncture until carrying out to the ocean of nothingness, or maybe sucked up a pressure valve and recycled into starting existence all over again.

A man could go crazy thinking about it, and Luke wasn't of a mindset to ruminate.

Amarillo was hot and bustling, and Luke left the alley to walk amongst the living. The boulevard turned to Fillmore Street, and marquees and flat boards scrambled for attention: *Paramount Theatre*, *Mobil Gas*, *Coca-Cola*,

Herring Hotel, Natorium Dance Hall, Kress Drugstore, Greyhound Union, and too many others to focus on, everything dusty and faded but still screaming for attention, *Me! Me! Me!* He didn't know what to do, while his emotions clamored and fought, and frustration built of indecision and ineptitude struck him as most dominant . . . Luke howled at the world and swung his bony, weak fists with fury, smashing passing men in their faces.

Each man startled, fell back a few paces, then resumed his bustling, which drove Luke even more wild that even while he tried to save lives and failed, and tried to do good and failed, and knew secrets of the universe hardly anyone else dared imagine, he could still be so completely unknown and disregarded. He grunted and punched harder, landing a hail of shots and jabs on every bastard who dared his range. Passersby took their punishments as uncomplainingly as a punching bag, each resilient and impassive.

One fellow, dapper as a groomsman, looked the most cheerful of anyone Luke had ever seen. He whistled a radio ditty whose tempo matched the bounce in his step, and his eyes shone with some horrible gleam that could only be born of joy.

Luke hated him.

"Why are you so goddamned happy?" Luke cried out. "We're all dying, everyone you ever loved, dying!"

He slugged the man until his hands split and bled, and the man's head bounced back and forth like a crazy rubber ball. The fellow changed tunes to something even more upbeat and greeted a woman with her jewel-eyed babe.

Luke, red-eyed and savage, felt worse with each attack instead of better. A sound approached, the clip-clop of hooves on cement.

"Funny thing," a curious soft voice hailed him. "I've got a second message for you."

When Luke turned to Bob Haslam sitting calmly atop Annabelle, he immediately felt ashamed of himself that the Pony Express rider had witnessed his tantrum.

"I've had a few rages myself," Bob said. "I get it."

Luke's frustration laughed: *And when I am known and regarded, I wished I wasn't.* He swallowed from an already dry mouth and said only, "All right."

"I was on my way to Knoxville when I got a message from Boston to deliver you. Comes from Benjamin Franklin, of all people."

The dryness of Luke's mouth became a desert. "What's he want?"

"Says he has a friend of yours that he's keeping safe. A gal you know real well named Daisy Rose."

Luke's heart seemed to double. "Daisy's with him?"

"Ben asks you to visit him right away, he's got some things to work out. If you don't want her to meet Zeke's fate, come alone and with a good attitude, and he'll return her."

"Come alone or she'll meet Zeke's fate?" The fury Luke had been looking to vent was restored. "That a threat? If Ben's taken her hostage, if he's hurt her, I will rip him from the history books, I'll burn his memory to ash!"

"Easy there. I don't know the context of the message, I just deliver the dispatch. But I'll tell you this much, whenever I see a portrait of Franklin, it chills me somehow. No matter the picture or its style or the artist, Franklin's always got the same look, that sideways smirk like he controls the world and he don't care who knows it."

Luke clenched his fists, ready to pound on more pedestrians. If his life held any meaning at all, he couldn't lose Daisy like he'd lost Zeke, he couldn't, he *wouldn't*. He hungered to jump a mile into the sky, topple buildings with the kick of his foot, so did fervor strike him. Nothing else mattered but saving her . . .

People flowed around Bob and himself like water diverted by a boulder. Weary-eyed clerks and produce men and cigarette girls nodded their heads to Bob alone, and Bob tipped his hat to each in turn. Luke shoved through them, careless.

Bob said, "If you want, I'll lead you back to those tracks you rode in on."

"Hell with that. Those fuckin' tracks are coming to me."

His mind was a maelstrom already, fueled by the rage of fire and pain, and there existed no doubt as to what he could do, no hesitation wondering if he was good enough or strong enough, but that Luke's mind roared a command: It shot out quick as a snappin' rattler, mighty as a tsunami, twisting and tunneling and reaching out to seize the railroad tracks he'd ridden in to Amarillo's station a mile away.

He could feel them in his thoughts, the steel rails hot from the sun and pitted by rust, could feel the splinters of weathered timber that formed the crossties, the dusty grit and sharp edges of old ballast, even the cracked, compressed loam of the subgrade, and Luke took it all and tore it from the earth and pulled it to him like a child pulls a string of taffy, until those tracks were at his feet. Without pausing, without thinking it, he snatched the nearest train and brought that too, screaming and whistling down those same tracks Luke had seized—*his tracks*—that's what they were, Luke Thacker's tracks, and he made use of them.

Bob tipped his hat to Luke in awe. "Message delivered."

Luke didn't say goodbye, just caught the train and was on his way to Boston at record speed.

The engine ran faster and faster down the rails, and the world outside flashed through every hue of light, turning a tunnel of color that was pulled together and mixed until it emerged a silvery streak, then dulled to something clear and fuzzy, like trying to look through a windshield covered in swirling dust. Luke strained his eyes to see out, but the wind wouldn't allow.

Why would Benjamin Franklin grab Daisy? She wasn't an animate, she was dead with little enough memory to keep her around, as Ben himself had pointed out. She had no power, no sway . . . Was it just to hurt him? Did the Sons of Liberty take her as some sort of bargaining chip?

But for bein' an animate—like Ben—Luke didn't have nothing to bargain with anyway . . . He beat his mind for answers. Shotguns, bombs, swords, blow darts, what could he use to kill Benjamin Franklin?

Of course, he didn't have any of those, no weapons but his wits, and those were dull as mud. And what good would weapons be anyway? They were already ghosts; he was the only one risking death.

Luke shouted in anger, wept in frustration, laughed at the inanity of it all. Sat quiet, motionless, watching the seeming bending of time and universe around him. Contemplated himself. Contemplated existence. *Could it be, he was thinking about this all wrong?*

Had Sequoyah been right, and what else did the Code Maker know? What exactly *were* the limits of his presence here? There'd been nothing after death but darkness, so he'd once believed, yet now he was in the deadeye. Men couldn't "wish" a train to appear, but he'd done so. There were limits on speed and motion, some scientific theory or shit, although he was single-handedly voiding that very same theory.

And what else did he—Lucas Thacker, penniless and alone—have potential for that he wasn't even aware to consider? And was there an answer to that riddle, or was it the kind of psychological prompt that, when found, would just wake him from this dream, or cause an aneurysm to burst in his brain, or free him from the hamster's maze in some alien ship?

But none of that is gonna get Daisy back . . .

The train began to decelerate, and Luke knew he was back in Massachusetts. The train decelerated more, and he knew he'd entered Boston. It slowed to regular speed following the rails along Highway 20 and crossing Commonwealth to Fairfield. Luke stepped off at Boylston Street, and the train roared away with a whistle for luck, and he walked the final block to Copley Square until the grand library showed itself rising up like the tall granite coffin of a pale pink god.

Luke's fury had calmed some, cooled by thoughts of Daisy in happier times, and he felt strong and in control of things for a change. He'd settle with Ben amicably, he promised himself; whatever this was had to be a misunderstanding. *Ben trying to control the world, and Luke to stop him?* Asinine. If Luke understood the rules of Athanasia, Ben would have to conduct himself as "remembered," that being a reasonable man.

The streets were crowded as Boston people did their Boston deeds, and Luke noticed a curious thing: mingled with the people were barefoot men and women wearing crisp linen clothes that nearly glowed with whiteness. Luke couldn't tell how many there were, but he was reminded of Francis, the servant of Ben Franklin who'd been taken by the pox, and the others like Francis hidden in the library's back room. The white-dressed people had frail, ashen faces, and they moved quickly up and down the streets, following the living; it took Luke a moment to realize they whispered into the ears of Bostonians who passed by.

Luke didn't pay them any further mind; he had more important duties to conclude. Soon he'd lift Daisy in his arms and carry her off to wherever she wanted, and he'd never let her go again.

His toes stuck out of one shoe, and they felt the asphalt warm under the sun. Forty yards from the library and things were going to turn out all right. A delivery truck honked, and a vendor sold baked beans. Thirty yards from the library and he wondered if he'd ever want to leave Athanasia for Real World again.

Twenty yards away, and a cowboy-hatted man came out to meet him, walking briskly down sharp-cut steps that formed the building's stalwart main entrance. Even without the marshal's badge pinned to his long coat, Luke recognized him clear enough.

Wyatt Earp said, "Should have stayed in the land of the living, Thacker."

"I'm here to see Benjamin Franklin."

"Ben don't want to see you," Wyatt replied, and a smirk climbed the thick pulls of his mustache.

Luke stopped, faltered to reply, finally got out, "He asked me to come."

Laughter burst out around him. "He asked *us* to come, too."

Luke turned to his right and saw an Earp brother approaching: Virgil. He turned to his left and saw the third one, Morgan.

"Hell, boy, you got the sense of a nail coming back here, 'less you like gettin' hammered on the head," Wyatt said.

To assert the point, something clocked Luke on the back of his skull, and flashing stars erupted. He wavered, slumped upon tired knees, but kept consciousness. When he turned around, a fourth mustached cowboy stood behind him, holding a large pistol by its barrel. Luke hadn't seen him before.

"Meet our brother James. He's a marshal too."

The fear in Luke broke cover, returning again, that unwanted houseguest pounding on his brain with its familiar staccato tap. This time it brought a friend: *outrage.* "What's all this mean? Ben's got someone in there, and I'm here to take her back. He said we'll work things out."

"What this means is this *is* how Ben works things out."

Luke rose on shaking legs and jabbed a finger at Earl. His voice cracked. "He can't . . . Benjamin Franklin's not remembered for being a traitor or a liar. He can't invite me here, then stab me in the back!"

"Benjamin Franklin's known as a diplomat," Wyatt said, "and sometimes diplomacy involves a few back-room deals."

"That was some luck getting away from us after the bank robbery and then again in the woods the next night," Morgan interrupted. He took Luke's wrists and bound them hard in metal cuffs while James leveled the pistol between his eyes. "Course, I heard you got aid from an old witch who's good at helping folks vanish."

"That wrinkled fishwife is gone as yesteryear," Virgil added.

"You're all alone now," James said.

"'Cept for us."

"See, we make the law around these parts," Virgil said. "Come to think on it, we make the law around *all* parts. And you evading justice sort of chaps our hides."

"And we don't like our hides gettin' chapped," James said, then winked. "Except Morgan, and you turn out to be a rodeo man from Austin."

"High hell," Morgan shouted. "I was drunk!"

"We're marshals," Wyatt shouted over him. "Act professional, ya dimwits."

Virgil pulled out a thick rope, looped off at one end. "Think this noose is professional enough?"

Luke's eyes widened.

The white-garbed people had stopped their whispering at passersby, and stared at Luke being taken by the Earps. Their faces, which had been frail sad things before, had somehow fallen even worse, a wretched, tortured look of dashed hopes marked by the downturn of grim mouths, the sinking of haunted eyes. At the last, Luke saw Paul Revere among them, gaunt, unsmiling, his lips stitched together.

"But relax, boy." James Earp whacked Luke back to attention. "We ain't gonna do it here."

They travelled a knot of roads for a long time without stopping, three of the Earp brothers on leggy auburn mares and the fourth, James, driving two more horses before a buckboard prison wagon. The old vehicle bounced and dipped on an undercarriage that was twisted as a spine with scoliosis. The back of the wagon emitted crooked slat sides and a ravel of barbed wire enclosing its only item of cargo, the deplorable criminal Luke Thacker.

After some flip-flops of the sun and moon, the Earps and Luke made their way to a wide-lane interstate route that a silver sign named only as *Thirty*. Cars and pedestrians passed in both directions, maneuvering around the slow-moving procession. The Earps yelled at them all, demanding attention, and people nodded at the brothers with glints of recognition until, once passed, their heads turned away in lapsed disregard.

An empty crop truck ran alongside, then pulled over to let them pass. Virgil shouted to its wondering driver, "Prisoner coming through!"

A comely boy pedaled by on his bicycle, and Morgan told him, "Do the crime, serve the time!" Morgan's voice boomed jolly and confident like a carnival barker's, and the boy nodded enthusiastically.

"Anyone runs from us and they'll get a visit from the bullet fairy," James added.

It's an act, Luke thought. They were as much showmen as they were gunslingers. That was everyone in Athanasia, the dead vying for attention, accomplishing nothing new of worth, only reenacting fading glories.

The Earps trotted their horses to a crossing at Townley Road and turned south, following an arrow that read: *2 miles to Monroeville.*

"We're taking a detour, *animate*," Wyatt shouted back to Luke. "Remember this town? A milestone in your felonious career."

Luke remembered well.

"The townspeople saw you get away from us," Morgan said. "We're gonna let them know that in the end justice always prevails."

"God makes tomorrows for the criminals we don't catch today," Virgil said.

Not just an act, but a travelling sideshow, Luke thought. Clowns, braggarts, bullies, that's what they were, not noble frontiersmen. History had been duped to name them heroes, but there were just as many stories calling the brothers cowards and cheats. Luke voiced his disdain, a tricky weapon. "You crows ever get tired of cawing? You preen at each others' feathers and peck at the scraps left by greater men."

"I'd enjoy my final breaths, if I was you," Morgan said.

"That's the thing about bounties," James confided. "'Dead or alive' is just a pretty notion. No outlaw's brought in open-eyed. Why, that's just a waste of taxpayer dollars, and the courts these days are burdened enough."

"We call this a Texas tea party," Virgil said. "And you're the guest of honor."

Luke wished he'd kept his disdain to himself. What's the old expression? *A fool and his life are quickly parted . . .* something like that. The Earps made sure to stay away from railroad tracks as if knowing Luke might try escaping that way, though it wasn't easy to hop a car with bound hands, regardless of how slow and close the train came. But he'd try, oh yes, he'd at least make the attempt. And where was the Hobo Code to help him now? The signs had fallen silent ever since he'd been taken by the marshals. There'd been no helpful advice like, "Stay strong," or "Leap from the wagon at the third left." He felt helpless without the Code; he didn't know what to do but wait for a track . . . or try calling the track to him again.

To up the insult, Wyatt seemed to read his mind. "Try callin' a train to your rescue, and we'll shoot off your kneecaps. Let's see you jump a ride like that."

Luke turned the disdain upon himself. *He'd lost Daisy again, and it'd been so easy to play the fool . . .*

They came to another intersection and halted, and Luke was struck by a memory of long ago as this being a crossing for Monroeville Road. A glitzy black car had parked diagonally across the road, halting traffic in all directions. A couple of vehicles were blocked behind the car, their drivers staring out with slack faces through windshields, perhaps wondering why they were stopped, perhaps daydreaming. Nobody honked a horn or yelled to "get moving."

A man leaned against the car's fender, one lavishly-suited leg crossed easily over the other. His head was bowed, face concealed beneath a tipped gray fedora. He lit a cigarette, and in the brief flare of its red glow, Luke glimpsed a chin dimpled as a puckered ass.

Wyatt trotted toward him, ahead of his siblings. "You're blocking our way, mister."

The man considered a moment, took his time to reply. "Suppose I'll move out of your way, nice and gentlemanly-like, soon as my driver is returned."

Luke smelled the burnt cat-hair scent of a Chesterfield.

"John Dillinger," Wyatt Earp realized. "As I live and don't breathe." His hands dropped to the rosewood grips of twin Colt pistols.

"Is that another brother you brought along?" John asked, counting off each of the Earps in turn. The cigarette rolled back and forth between the corners of his mouth, as if moved aside by the force of his words. "How many of you coattail riders are there?"

Virgil answered, "Each of us made his own history." He spat a thick wad of chewing tobacco that took its time falling to the ground.

"Can't believe you came back for more," Morgan cut in, lifting a long Winchester rifle. He levered a cartridge into the chamber, and its clap echoed across the tall field grass. "If stupidity were a crime, you'd be a lifer."

John moved into an exaggerated stance, each unhurried movement a caricature. He widened his posture, stuck out his chest, tensed his arms, fingers cocked at each side like he was about to quick-draw on the Earps, only there weren't any pistols visible on him; he just shot from his mouth. "Go back to your tumbleweeds in the desert. Out here, this is my part of the country."

The marshals laughed.

A flock of birds broke cover and scattered to the sky. One of them let out a shrill squawk before bursting into a shower of floating red dots.

The pox was here.

As happy as Luke was to see Dillinger alive and well and—further— here to rescue him, he didn't figure the point. The Earps would blast him to kingdom come. Luke crouched into as small a ball as possible, except his head, which lifted just high enough to see over the wagon sidewall.

"How many times we gotta kill you to erase the speck of your flyshit memory?" Morgan asked. His horse grunted, taking a nervous step back.

James stood from the wagon's seat. "Hell, brothers, let me have a turn at this. I ain't killed anyone in two ages."

"Take him," Wyatt answered.

James unslung a rifle from its driver's bench scabbard. His smile was a piece of ivory that cracked when he said, "Draw."

John sighted his pointer finger up at James and cocked back a thumb into the imaginary shape of a finger gun. "Bang."

The Earps laughed harder.

Their laughter was cut short by fast gunshots ripping through the air, each slug a screaming tracer of light. Five shots, ten, twenty, it was impossible to count, the rounds chased each other with the sound of a desperate sewing machine amplified a hundredfold. James Earp shrieked and his chest blew out to tatters in the wind. His rifle flew to the earth, his hat leapt to the sun. An arm detached at the elbow and sailed far away, and still the machine gun bullets chewed into him, keeping his riddled body upright by the sheer force of each shot's impact.

"*Hog's puck!*" Wyatt spun and his .45 pistols were in hand, blazing salvos at the shooter.

A figure had risen from the field, dressed as immaculately in his dark-striped suit as John Dillinger. Unlike Johnny, he wore no hat, and his crop of dark hair rippled in pomade waves. He seemed younger than his real age, and his apple-cheeked face was soft-featured but for hard, narrow eyes. The man held a Tommy gun in his hands, and it didn't stop firing for a long time.

John Dillinger dropped to a knee and wrenched his own machine gun from behind the front tire of the car, and when he triggered it the roar was louder than a pack of high-strung hounds. The remaining Earp brothers fired back, but they couldn't draw a bead while their horses reared and bucked from the crossfire bullets.

John aimed low and shot Morgan's horse to pieces; the cowboy plummeted off and found himself pinned and covered by steaming horsehide and shattered hooves. The whizzing pox cycloned around the poor animal before dive-bombing it, and the horse's screams sounded as human as any Luke ever heard while it was eaten from existence. Morgan cried like a babe while the pox flew at him, thinking he was dying, but Luke saw right away he wasn't being devoured; just the poor horse.

Bullets pinged, ricocheted, slammed the pavement, riddled the air with noise and smoke and lead. The cars parked behind Dillinger took stray rounds, their grilles and windshields punctured and shattered by slugs. The drivers screamed terrified one instant, then stared out slack-jawed the next.

Wyatt and Virgil popped rounds off with their pistols, first at John, then at the other gangster, back to John, back to the other. They were no match for the machine guns. A long *rat-a-tat*, and a red line stitched across Virgil's chest like he was a rag doll torn in half, and all the red yarn went unraveling. His horse bucked him, and Virgil took a kick in the ribs as he tumbled off to wallop the earth.

At least I'm not the only rider a horse kicks when it can, Luke thought.

Wyatt Earp was last, and he must have known it was over. He made some sort of somersault leap off his mount that Luke hated himself for admiring, and in a flash the marshal was in the back of the prison wagon with a revolver wheeled to Luke's head. Wyatt shouted, "Give it up, or the animate's bound for Hell!"

John paused from his shooting, but the second gangster didn't look to give it a thought. He continued firing at Wyatt and Luke both, great streaming arcs of rounds chewing up the wood wagon and spitting out splinters.

"No, Floyd!" John shouted to the other gangster. "Hold your fire."

"That's right. I said stop or I'll kill him dead." Wyatt wrapped Luke in front of himself as a shield from the bullets. "I swear it!"

"Dead like this?" Floyd asked, and he turned his machine gun to Morgan, who was still trapped on the ground under his disappearing horse.

Morgan Earp gave a sharp grunt and lay still, riddled with holes.

"Goddamn it, Floyd, enough!" John yelled.

But Floyd laughed and laughed, the sound keen and hard like the gunfire itself. He fired his Tommy machine gun back up the blacktop road, shooting into cars, signposts, flying bugs, anything that caught his interest, and he turned like a children's top in a circle, spraying the world with laughter and bullets in every direction, and even the clouds seemed to drift away seeking shelter.

"Okay, okay," Wyatt yelled. "I yield!" He threw his pistols out of the wagon.

Floyd stopped firing. "There ya go, Johnny. Man sees sense after all."

"All right," John replied grudgingly, "your way works some of the time, but that doesn't excuse Kansas City."

"I just wanna shoot people."

"I know you do, but it's not . . . Oh, don't know why I bother." John turned to the prison wagon. "Out of there, boys."

Luke and Wyatt Earp both complied, stepping down from the buckboard with eyes wary of any further barrage. Luke's hands were bound, but his elbows were free, and he swung one into Wyatt's temple.

The marshal faltered, shook it off, cursed Luke and his luck, and looked upon his shot-up brothers, all deader'n ducks in soup.

John Dillinger asked, "Which one of you shot me in the head, anyway?"

"Does it matter?" Wyatt said, his face hard-lined with rage.

"Naw, guess not. Just feels good to recoup my reputation."

Luke shot Wyatt a glare as deadly as any of their guns. "Get these cuffs off me."

John nodded at the cowboy to do so, and Wyatt obliged.

Luke blurted, "Benjamin Franklin's got my girl!"

"I know," John answered.

"You do? How?"

"Been following your affairs, Luke. News around the hereafter is considerably more interesting than regular life. It was the Lindbergh kidnapper who took Daisy."

"The one who took the pilot's son?"

"That's right. I was still alive when the Lindbergh baby kidnapping occurred, and never a more vile crime has occurred. Whoever snatched that baby was never discovered, no clues, no nothin'. Someone just appeared, perpetrated the deed, and vanished."

"So who was it?" Luke asked. "If they're here in Athanasia, ain't it someone everyone knows now?"

"Figure the strength of the kidnapper's memory isn't only in the crime's notoriety, but in the mystery. The abductor is a faceless, nameless shade. Comes and goes without you seeing, just the victim who vanishes."

"Damn this world!"

"You'll be next, boy," Wyatt Earp jeered. "Disappearing and no one knows, no one'll ever remember you."

"Shut up," Floyd said, and shot his machine gun at the ground around Wyatt, spreading dirt and blacktop into the air.

Luke looked at each of the others, his eyes wild and bloodshot. "How can I get her back?"

"With my help," John said, and winked.

"And me!" Floyd yelled. "I hate Franklin. His money's the reason I went to prison."

"By the way, that's Pretty Boy," John said, hitching a thumb at Floyd. "Gets a bit heated, but he's a good chum."

"I can't stand that name! It's Floyd, and anything else you call me gets this." He fired a burst from his machine gun into the air.

John shrugged. "Rescuing your gal will take time, Luke. Time on your part."

"I'm not waitin' anymore. Let's go now!"

A cough came from Virgil Earp as he began to stir on the road, coming back from his demise. The lines of blood Luke had thought of as unraveling red yarn receded. Next to him, Morgan let out a groan, and James lifted his remaining arm, twitching.

They all began to reanimate until something went wrong with James. He convulsed suddenly, his back arching in a tall horseshoe, and then started flopping up and down like he was having a seizure. The cloud of pox that had taken Morgan's horse cycloned around him.

"Brother!" Wyatt yelled.

James spasmed harder, and he howled like a mauled animal. Wyatt rushed to him, cursing the pox, ordering them away like they were breakin' the law, and he'd arrest them if there wasn't compliance.

"No one remembers those other Earps anyway," John said, puffing a cloud from his Chesterfield, "the ones not at the O.K. Corral. James's been a long time for dying. You can't have memory strong for so many brothers . . . How's anyone supposed to differentiate them?"

James Earp's howls became long screams, but even as his screams died off, they still seemed to linger in the air once he'd been eaten from memory.

"C'mon." John motioned Floyd and Luke to his car, adding to the latter, "You're driving."

Luke got behind the wheel of John's Model A Ford, feeling a sense of comfort in the leather seat, like reuniting with a friend not seen in many years. The gangsters squeezed beside him, and Luke fired up the engine, enjoying the warmth of the shift lever in his hand, the clutch under his foot. The car rolled forward and the gears lined up for him, rotating in synchrony as if by themselves. "Wasn't this car totaled first time we ran into the Earps?"

"Even destroyed, if a car's got a strong enough impression in peoples' minds, it comes back," John answered, "and folks come to know me by this vehicle."

"Where're we going?" Luke asked.

"Just head east on Monroeville Road."

Luke did, and Floyd shot a parting salvo at the remaining Earp brothers in farewell.

"Then what?" Luke asked. "Take the highway back to Boston?"

"I think you'll know soon enough," John said.

They drove past a Texaco gas station in the opposite direction, and Luke recognized it in his rearview from the day he first met John Dillinger. Dawning broke. "I'm going back to that water tower?"

"It'll return you to the world of the living."

"I ain't going without Daisy."

"Like I said," John answered, "we can help you, but we can't do it for you, Luke. And you're still not ready. It's your legend that needs to grow."

"Swear to Moses, I'm sick of hearing that."

"As much as people may love us, see us as exciting, romantic, even Robin Hoods of the Depression, Floyd and me aren't good guys able to rescue kidnapped girls. We're just criminals."

Luke gritted his teeth as a wooden sign announced the border to Ohio. A hobo mark was painted on it, no doubt from Sequoyah: *Take the railroad home.*

Though he didn't have any home, Luke knew well enough what the message meant.

"It's a trap, see?" John continued. "You stay in Athanasia trying to get Daisy, her memory—and yours—will fade away, faster than you'd care. You have to return, make the most of yourself, spread your legend 'til you're big enough to be noticed here in the deadeye. But stay now, and you'll die."

Luke fell to silence, downshifting to a thin dirt road, watching the water tower rise from the distance like a strange stalk of corn. *Now what?*

While Floyd made explosion sounds at crows that passed, John lit another Chesterfield.

"Speaking of which, legends and such, I'm of a mind to work on my own," John said. "Say, Floyd, didn't your old partner get the gas chamber last year? What was his name, Richetti?"

"Eddie? Sure, old drunk got executed, not even done what the coppers nailed him for."

"Let's recruit him, start up a new gang."

Floyd looked away dreamily. "Yeah . . . Richetti. And Mad Dog Underhill's gotta be around, Homer Van Meter, Red Hamilton . . . "

"We can build one hell of a new operation."

"I like it, call us the Pretty Boy Floyd gang."

"Wait, what? It'd be the Dillinger gang!"

"I could live with Pretty Boy's Toys."

"You're just insulting now," John said. "Plus you said you hate that nickname."

"I hate anyone else calling me it."

"Compromise. The Dillinger-Floyd gang."

"Floyd-Dillinger gang," Floyd replied, his gun edging to John.

"You sonuvabitch, I was Public Enemy first!" John's eyes narrowed as he reached for a revolver in his jacket, then broke with a laugh. "Guess two egos are a tough sale . . . "

Floyd didn't laugh back, and they all fell to silence.

By the time Luke reached the water tower, he'd grown more enthusiastic to depart. "Well, fellas, I can't thank you enough for the helpin' hand."

"Don't mention it," John said. "Just keep telling people I'm still around."

"And me!" Floyd added. He turned his machine gun to the metal cistern tank and fired a burst for the hoot of it.

"Remember what I said," John added. "Keep building those legends strong. We'll be waiting when you come back. We'll be watching."

Luke shook hands and got out. The water tower hadn't changed since the last time he'd been here years before, 'cept new cobwebs under the trestle, a few more splinters in the wood, taller and wickeder weeds all around. He walked under it, past the blue happy face symbol, and out the other side. He turned, and Dillinger and Floyd were gone.

Real World . . .

But they weren't really gone, were they? Luke knew they were in the car right now, right on the other side of that water tower, just sitting, watching, waiting to see what he would do, what he *could* do . . . He'd show them.

In Athanasia he'd called a train to escape Lizzie Borden, called a train when leaving Paul Revere, called a train with Bob Haslam twice, and he knew if he could do it in Athanasia, he could do it here, *had* done it here— a bit, anyway—at least in catching the engines. He just needed to be more forceful, more focused, more confident to control them in Real World. He was focused now. He was confident. He felt good about it, he felt strong.

Luke thought of the psychic third eye, about the woman seer who'd explained the process to open it, about taking slow, deep breaths to fill up his brain while he centered on calling that train. He brought to mind the 'bo symbols used to hail a line, imagined a steamer coming to him, spread his mind out searching for it, stretching far, far away until he found the right engine, and he coupled with it, and the engine just sort of shrugged and went along, knowing it didn't have a chance to fight back so it fired down the tracks, faster and faster to Luke's demand.

It was a jaunty silver and blue "Big Boy," a Wabash 4-8-4 locomotive pulling center beam flat cars of galvanized pipe, and pale reefers filled with malt beer and cheese and ice, a set of low-slung gondolas, another set of high-side livestock cars, and a garnet-red caboose with a bay window, and it was his.

He was getting stronger.

The train roared o'er tracks smashing the silence of miles of meadows, and as it passed, Luke swung on board and gave a big wink to where he knew John watched. And once he'd done that, Luke thought on what he had yet to do, which still seemed more than impossible to save Daisy Rose. She was a destination so distant it was like wishing to travel to another planet, and he with no means but a dream.

But he kept at it, one train after the next. He rode the rails all the following year, and what he gained in that time was the learning of three valuable lessons about himself and about reaching that far-off destination.

LUKE AND SKIPPER, 1940: LESSON ONE

The reporting mark of "SP" stood for the Southern Pacific Railroad, a conglomerate of smaller merged branches that furrowed across the southern cuff of the nation from New Orleans to Los Angeles, moving north up a crooked seam to Oregon. The company's logo was a handsome one, picturing railroad tracks twining into a golden sunrise. Their slogan pledged "The Friendly Southern Pacific."

And the slogan was true. Luke liked the SP lines for that reason: When he was feeling downhearted, an easy ride in their cars came with sunshine and freedom from bulls, just like the logo painted on their engines, which perked him up fine.

The day started glum when Luke hopped an SP line bound west for El Paso. It seemed forever since he'd returned from Athanasia, though he still dwelled on Zeke's loss, still bled failure at getting back Daisy. The section of track Luke rode was branded the Sunset Route, and he felt it appropriate for the wrong reasons, considering his life heading into darkness and all the bright colors around him slowly abating. On top of the doldrums, he suffered a nasty little bug caught from sleeping in a barn covered by mold.

Luke leapt into the clattering boxcar and spotted another man already inside, sitting in the farthest corner on a pile of shadows and loose straw. Luke tensed, but tried not to show it. As always, coming upon another 'bo in a railcar was a tentative matter.

"Howdy, 'bo," the other man said right away in a friendly voice. He must've shared the same opinion as Luke, and the quicker one of them gave greeting, the safer they'd both feel.

"Howdy back," Luke replied.

"Name's Skipper."

"I'm Luke." He tried to make himself comfortable on a piece of floorboard that prickled with splinters like a rug of cacti. "Skipper, huh? You a sailor?"

"Never seen a boat."

Skipper half-smiled. The other half was a sad frown, his lips looking like a sideways letter S. It was an uncomfortable face he made, and an uncomfortable silence that followed as he waited for Luke to ask further.

Luke didn't. He figured there was a story behind the name, and if Skipper wanted to say more, he could. For now, Luke was tired and depressed, and there didn't seem to be much else to discuss as the train chugged along. He hugged his knees to his chest, and in that way the baggy coat he wore on his back was also able to fit over his legs. The floorboards popped, loosed from missing nails, rattling and knocking more splinters free. The silence lengthened ten long minutes.

Skipper broke first, picking up where last they spoke. He knocked against his left leg, the sound of it like rapping at someone's door. He pulled the pant leg up to show a length of oak fastened to his upper thigh by a strap. "The name's a joke, see," he said. "People say I skip when I walk."

"Don't sound too funny to me," Luke replied.

Skipper scooted nearer, showing Luke up-close where the wood leg fit inside his boot. "Folks always want to touch it. You can too."

"Thanks, but no." Luke wiped a runny nose on his sleeve. "How'd you lose it?"

"Caught under the wheels outside Colorado Springs. It was my own fault."

Ain't it always? Luke thought.

Skipper continued, "I met the prettiest gal I ever seen while I was drunk as a skunk, and boy, weren't we dancing and laughing that night. She never hopped a car before and dared me to show her. I barely remember the fall. Being as mashed as I was, there wasn't much pain . . . right away. I slipped getting on, and the wheels just cut off my leg neat as a razor. The gal called for help, and I was taken to a rich man's doctor who stitched me up. Never saw the gal again. Never been back to Colorado Springs again, either. All I know, my leg's still sittin' on the track waiting for me to put it back on, and that gal's waitin' there too, for me to whisk her away."

"You'll never know 'til you go back."

"I was kidding. It's another joke, see. No gal'd want to end up with a one-legged man."

"Nothin' wrong with having only one leg," Luke said.

"It is compared to two legs."

"I heard once about a Yankee general who lost a leg to a cannonball. He later bedded the queen of Spain. And here you are sidesteppin' some Colorado Springs tail."

"I ain't no general."

"And you never will be with an attitude like that."

Skipper presented his half-smile again. "You the one makin' jokes now?"

Luke felt his temper jump. "How's it like, feeling sorry for yourself? You fancy a girl and you got a chance, take it! Wish to God I had my chance again."

Skipper's half-smile trembled. His eyes quivered with rheumy tears. "You don't know what it's like bein' maimed, see. Can't run no more, railroad bulls catch me they beat me twice as hard just for the thrill of watching me try to hop away. I used to ride a bicycle to work, mister two-legged Luke. Ain't no one-pedal bike around, tell you that much." He sucked in a great heave of phlegm and sobs. "Worked in a department store too, 'fore they went under. I was a goddamned shoe salesman."

Luke shook his head, feeling bad enough about himself without getting it from someone else. "I knew a man with no legs at all, wheeled himself around on one of those little carts. Worked in a coffee shop, rolling up and down the counter, bringing folks pie and fillin' up their coffee.

Every one of those customers gave him an extra nickel tip 'cause he was so quick."

"What're you sayin', I should lose my other leg too?"

"Jesus in a boiler! I'm saying there's plenty you can do, you want work. Your tongue ain't maimed. Seems to me, you were a salesman once, that's your best opportunity. The hell with shoes, go big, sell bonds or insurance, you're not afraid of yappin', that's for sure."

"Insurance sales? I'm not good with numbers . . . "

"With your excuses, go be a doormat. People can wipe their mud on ya, and you got reason to bellyache about it the rest of the day. But that girl, if you thought there was something between the two of you, I'd do anything to get back there and see her again, no matter my number of legs."

Skipper started crying, one tear after the other cutting rivets through the ash and dust masking his face. "I don't wanna ride rails no more, I hate this life."

At once the likeness came to Luke, and he resented it by realizing the truth of his own life: Here he was, playing the role of Benjamin Franklin in rebuking this man who, in contrast, was himself, and, further, that the rebuking was deserved. Sometimes a person gives you significant advice, but for whatever reason you ignore it, forget it, do the opposite. Take those same words, though, and put them in someone else's mouth, even your own, and suddenly that advice seems to explain the sense of the universe.

Ben's words poured from his mouth, and Luke spoke them to himself. "This is your only life, pal, fight to make the most of it!"

"You think—maybe—she might still be there?" Skipper asked, gulping.

"We hit El Paso, you catch a line straight north six hundred miles and find out."

"I'm gonna do it, by God!" Skipper lifted himself high, swaying on legs of wood and flesh.

Luke smiled, feeling better by helping someone else. The SP line had paid off again, in its own way. And there he learned the first of three valuable lessons about himself: He alone must make the most of the gifts he'd been granted.

As an afterthought, Luke added, "By the way, if anyone should ask, Benjamin Franklin's an asshole."

DAISY ROSE, 1940

A yawning workman unloaded crates of produce in the early morning dawn when Daisy Rose approached and whispered into his ear, "Benjamin Franklin invented the lightning rod."

The man blinked, paused, then resumed unloading.

A smartly-dressed nurse walked past, reading a romance mag on her way to Boston Medical Center. Daisy hurried to her. "Benjamin Franklin founded the nation's volunteer fire departments."

The nurse mumbled, "He did," and resumed reading.

A crossing guard attended two young children in an intersection, while roadsters and flatbeds waited patiently at all sides. Daisy followed them, whispering to each in turn, "Benjamin Franklin's the smartest man this world has ever known." She added hurriedly, "And you love him more than your own mother."

"Say it like you mean it, bitch."

Daisy nodded, head hung low, eyes flushed pink and swollen. She dared a glance back at the man with a whip. "Sorry, Master Robards."

"That's *Mister* Robards." His whip loosened, starting to uncoil. "Master's a slaver word and you know better. Franklin doesn't truck with slavery, bitch. You can leave anytime you want."

And he laughed.

The laugh started small, a chuckle of reminiscence over another laugh, another time, and it grew. His chest pitched, hard breaths struggling to find room against the spasms building beneath his ribs, and the chuckle became the sort of hearty chortle one shares at a merry gathering filled with mirth and diversion. Yet it grew more, the chortle rising to a hideous cackle. He laughed so that his black teeth clacked against each other over and over, as if he shivered from cold. He laughed so that his tall, gaunt frame rattled like the loose bolts in machinery that tear free and spin wildly away. And then Robards laughed harder, and he had to clench his side, doubling over as he gasped for air, and his beaver-felted top hat tumbled off. The laugh became a shriek that blanketed the city, and it sent the others scurrying to find farther places to be.

As they fled, they glared at Daisy in terror, in anger that she'd provoked him, that it was *her* fault Lewis Robards would surely find one of them tonight to unload his frenzy upon. They were men and women and children of all races. Black, white, Asian, indigenous, it didn't matter their parentage, but that they were Franklin's "staff," his "labor force." Their faces were stark, frail, hopeless like herself, all piercing her with tragic eyes. *We hate you*, those eyes said. *We'll get you back*, those eyes said.

Even the other foremen seemed to shrink away, the woman with her long pitchfork, now edgy and sucking at a lip, and the bearded man with a blunderbuss, gulping like something got stuck in his throat. They watched Robards howl, forgetting for the time their charges, the people dressed in crisp linen whites that patrolled the streets, whispering into unwary ears.

Daisy trembled.

Robards stopped laughing. He spat. "Get the fuck back to work."

"Yes sir, Mister Robards."

A flower vendor stood on one corner, offering beautiful bouquets of every color. Somewhere, some distant memory came to her of picking blossoms in a field with Luke, and that he'd charmed her with dreams of a house surrounded by flowers of her name.

Daisy whispered into the vendor's ear, "Benjamin Franklin can do no wrong."

LUKE AND BLUE BOY, 1940: LESSON TWO

The reporting mark of "LN" stood for the Louisville and Nashville Railroad, a line that offered services equally to freight and passengers (willingly for those riders with tickets, and not at all willingly for those riders without). It was a stoic and enduring line, running since 1850 from Alabama and Georgia north to Ohio. The train's emblem smartly repeated its own reporting mark, L&N, writ in old-timey red-and-gold script. Their slogan declared "The Old Reliable."

And the slogan was true. Luke liked the LN lines for that reason: in a time when engines broke down as frequently as children went hungry, the LN always came through.

Luke found himself riding this day to Memphis, dining on wild strawberries and strips of dried salt pork that were surplus from the

Spanish-American War. He shared a car with the sorriest-looking 'bo he'd ever seen.

"People call me Blue Boy," the 'bo said. "Or Blue. Or Boy. Or whatevah you want. No one cares about my name."

"People call me Luke. Or good-for-nothing." Luke grinned, but the boy didn't respond.

Blue Boy looked a sad young man, barely past his teens, with eyes that drooped down his cheeks as if caught in the throes of a weeping fit. He was skinny as the spine of a dime-store paperback, and his legs were long and spindly like a spider's; only he didn't move quick like a spider, but more like a tired hound dog on a hot day, every motion a morose challenge. And if personality matched appearance, his was a dead ringer, slim and downcast. He could have been the guy you threw a rock at because he looked funny, and you knew he wouldn't do anything back.

Blue Boy pounded at some nuts on the boxcar floor. "Why acorns gotta be so hard to crack?"

"You need to warm them first."

"And never a fire when you need it."

"We can build a fire," Luke said. "Just hop off and gather some wood."

"Wood's always damp when you need it to burn, splintery when you try to build with it, soft when you need it hard, hard when you need it soft. What's the use?"

"You ever done a happy thing in your life?"

"What's that use either? Happiness don't get you new shoes or a soft bed . . . don't even get your acorns cracked." Each sentence Blue Boy spoke ended on a downward beat, like the words were stuck in a bog and sinking without much struggle.

Luke nodded, warming up a crossbuck in his head. "I knew a man once who found happiness in all he did, even smiled when the bulls threw him off—"

"I hate stories," Blue Boy interrupted. "No offense, mister, I just want somethin' to eat that ain't your words."

"Got some strawberries here with your name on 'em."

"I don't see no name on them."

"Figure of speech, friend."

"I hate figures of speech too. Just say what you mean, mean what you say . . . but I'll take those berries nevertheless."

Luke eyed the boy with reserve. "You want some salt pork too?"

Blue Boy grimaced. "That your game, huh? I know what that means, doin' for salt pork. I ain't gonna no more!"

"Tell you what," Luke said. "I'll leave some fixings right here, and go over in the corner to hit the sack. You want the pork and berries, they're yours. Otherwise, the next tramp'll dine fine."

And that was what Luke did. It took no time for him—with a full belly, and rocked by the pulse of the train—to fall asleep, and he dreamed a curious thing: Paul Revere dressed in white, barefoot, his lips stitched together, but also able to speak. "Loose lips sink ships, and my own future too, it seems." Paul's easy laugh was distorted, a gurgling sound like something trying to reach out from a cramped, locked cage. "Free us, Luke, free us. I failed him, and I told you what I shouldn't have, and Ben found out . . . My own horse betrayed me. Ben now speaks the language of *horses*, for God's sake . . . He's got too much power, soon he'll be unstoppable—"

Luke was woken by a scream.

He sprang up like an electrocuted cat, hair on end, senses on hyper-alert. His mind reeled, groggy, foggy, questioning where he was, dreaming or awake, Athanasia or Real World. What brought his senses back to perfect clarity with a clap of thunder was the matching thunder booming across the sky. He *was* awake, *was* in Real World, but awake in Real World now meant peril.

It was Blue Boy who screamed, and he screamed again.

Outside, a boiling tornado pulled earth to the heavens, and then the train rounded a bend and the sight went from view.

But the sound wasn't lost, and it turned more violent. Another burst of thunder, then another, each growing louder. And behind it all, a second sound: a wicked roaring, half siren, half howl, like an avalanche that wouldn't end. Luke's heart beat louder than it all. His eyes grew big, seeming to swell from their sockets 'til they might pop out, and he didn't know if it was from the increase in air pressure or plain fright, though it seemed a likely mix of both.

Out of nowhere a big truck's wheel shot from the sky, smashing against the boxcar's door, and quivering splinters and burning rubber sprayed inside. A little squeal escaped Luke's mouth. He dared look outside as much as possible without getting yanked away by the wind. High above, a flatbed truck flew upside-down in black clouds, circling like a giant three-wheeled bird.

Their train roared over tracks, gaining speed, trying to flee something in pursuit. A spotted sow shot past even faster with a wavering *oink*. It too was upside-down. Broken trees and pelts of hay followed. Luke's ears were ready to burst from the gale's shrieks.

The rails rounded another bend back the other way, and Luke saw the horrible revelation of the twister angling right for them as the train turned into it.

Blue Boy screamed until his voice broke, and he fell to the floor, and his eyes seemed to continue the screaming; they'd lost their weeping droop and were wild things now, berserk and daunting with life. The train rattled, shook. Luke lost his footing. Vice grips seemed to crush his head.

"I don't wanna die!" Blue Boy croaked. "I'm sorry I wished it!"

Everything grew louder and louder, and the train jounced and leaned, heading straight to the twister. Something shattered, and an explosion sounded far away, though it could have been right outside, the way sounds blared and muffled equally in the wind.

The pressure in Luke's head was too immense to bear, and he thought of a melon with a quarter stick of dynamite shoved inside. He thought too, suddenly, of the pressure behind his forehead that was his third eye, and of the seer woman's voice, and about focusing his mind, directing his abilities, a control . . .

A whip of gale seized him, tugging at his legs, and Luke's body lifted ever-so-slightly off the floor, sliding toward the open door. He dug his fingers into the wood, nails scrabbling and cracking at splinters and rusty bolts until he caught a loose board that was warped in the middle. He gripped it hard, the tendons straining on his forearms against a force that would suck him out to spiral up into the clouds.

If he lost now, he'd lose everything.

Luke shouted against it all and fired his mind outward with thoughts of nothing else but taking the engine, owning it, riding it, and he felt the connection click immediately, as the couplings of cars click, and he felt too, it seemed, a sense of the train's own terror, of the engine embracing his takeover.

The loose floorboard he gripped began to slip free from its bolts, and Luke's feet were yanked high in the air. He flapped up and down like a flag in a gust, and Luke shouted louder, and he forced the train to turn away to the right, and where there were no tracks to turn onto, Luke forced those too, tearing the rails and ties and fasteners away from the earth and oncoming twister, and stretching them the way he needed, the way he'd stretched tracks in Athanasia.

The train blared its horn, and clouds of grit masked whatever could be seen, and Luke veered them all so sharp it seemed the boiler would fly off in somersaults, but he kept it in control, kept the train speeding and balanced, and they roared away from the twister to safety, all the while Blue Boy mouthing silent screams.

Things settled down as quick as they'd erupted. Luke let out a breath he felt he'd been holding for twenty minutes and counted everything he was thankful for, including the LN line; the Old Reliable had gotten him through again, even if by his helping it.

And such was the second of three valuable lessons Luke learned about himself: His abilities in Real World had caught up to those in Athanasia.

The engine chugged back to normal, and he nodded to Blue Boy. "That sure was somethin'."

Blue Boy's eyes hadn't turned back from the wildness of their flight. In a hoarse whisper he answered, "If by somethin', you mean we faced death in the eye and spit, then yeah."

That wasn't how Luke was thinking, but he went with it.

"You flew a train, mister," Blue Boy said.

"It wasn't exactly flyin'."

"I won't never think a thing is impossible again."

THE CODE MAKER, 1940

The Code Maker was kidnapped in mid-1940, a year after he'd revealed himself to Luke.

His kidnapping happened in a flash and without warning. Sequoyah had been writing in the dust that covered the old table, inside an old cabin, atop an old mountain, upon an old land, and didn't know he'd been taken until the act was done and he was caught, tied up and blindfolded.

He felt himself lifted into the air, his hands trussed behind his back, his arms bound to his sides, his legs wrapped tight as if they were one, and then he was slung over something like a shoulder, and he unable to stop it, unable to make a sound through the oily gag filling his mouth.

He was no less a beast of game, a trophy, snared and soon to be mounted on someone's showcase wall, and Sequoyah knew this.

There was a shuffle, a twang, a thud, a stumble, a second thud—louder—and Sequoyah toppled backward for what seemed ages, but surely was only the height of his own body.

He lay there, heart pounding, ears straining for every sound, which came quickly and without caution: footsteps.

Gentle hands took the back of his head and removed the blindfold. Pocahontas peered down.

"You are not hurt," she said.

Who, what, he tried to ask, before the oily gag was taken away. Once Pocahontas removed it, all he could do was spit out acrid aftertaste.

"There," she said, pointing across the floor. "The Lindbergh kidnapper."

"He dead?"

"For a time, yes. But whether a *he* or *she,* I do not know."

A figure lay sprawled on the floor, motionless, one hand clutched around the long feathered arrow stuck deep in its chest. It had no face, just a blank sheet of skin pulled over an indistinguishable skull. Its clothes were swirling robes of haze.

"I was hidden," she continued. "You were right for me to stay."

"As much as I write signs, the signs write back to me," Sequoyah said.

"The kidnapper will wake soon, will try to escape."

"See that it doesn't, please."

Pocahontas tied up the figure with its own bonds and locked it deep within an old trunk, inside an old cabin, atop an old mountain, upon an old land, where it could not get free.

Sequoyah sighed. "I've been found. It's time to call Black Herman to hide us elsewhere."

LUKE AND MARTHA, 1940: LESSON THREE

The reporting mark of "WM" signified the Western Maryland Railway, a coal-and-freight-hauling operation that covered the state up to Pennsylvania. The sigil branding its enterprise was a black and gold crest trailed by a powerful bird's wing like the tail of a racing meteor, and its slogan promised "The Fast Freight Line."

And the slogan was true.

Luke liked the WM lines for that reason: When he had to reach a faraway place, and reach it fast, no freighter was swifter. It happened he'd heard the Civilian Conservation Corps was looking for hands to dirty themselves up in Cumberland, so he hailed a WM train heading that way and hopped it. There wasn't a quicker run on rails to a CCC work camp, and Luke made it before anyone else.

He reached the city outskirts just as hunger got the best of him, and jumped off the line where it crossed Williams Street, at a block of wood and stone buildings that looked disheveled as a seedy motel bed, saggy and lumpy and worn thin. Street signs heralded confusing directions, like a wind had come along and spun 'em all topsy-turvy. People of every color wandered on and off the road, some looking uppity, some downcast, most just weary and dusty.

A woman passed who seemed oddly familiar, though different, the way memories change people over years. Luke was used to it. Now half his life was living in memory-land, and it seemed everyone carried familiar airs.

But the woman did a double-take at him, which caused Luke to follow suit.

"You don't look hardly changed," she said. "What's it been, nine, ten years?"

The woman wouldn't win no beauty contest, but her face appeared kind and strong, which is a truer beauty than smooth skin and rouge cheeks. Her hair was done with a wave up the front, and lay combed out and lustrous down the back. She wore a pretty floral dress, and lanky arms and legs plunged from it to end in dainty gloves and thick-soled shoes. None of that rang a bell to Luke until he noticed her skin: it was mottled, colored in some areas and pale in others, like a faded Dalmatian dog.

He thought back many years, to first learning the Hobo Code. "That you, Po' Chili?"

"Ha! Nobody's called me that in a long, long time. I'm Martha now . . . well, again. It's how I was born."

Luke gave her a great hug, and only halfway through the embrace did he waver, thinking his oil-stained clothes would soil that pretty dress. But she didn't let him pull back, and they both exclaimed how nice it was to see the other, and they meant it.

She held his hand and said, "I married a railroad bull, would you believe it?"

"I do, if you say so."

"Ollie, that's his name." Po' Chili—*Martha*—beamed as she said it. "Ollie rousted me from a car one day, but he was gentle. Set me on my way with the address for a soup kitchen. Come to find out, he ate at that kitchen, too. Railroad bullin' bought chow enough for five days a week, but he wasn't proud enough to starve the other two. We talked a spell about life, about food, and soon we started running our own lunch stand. Ain't much, but I like to cook, and he takes the orders. Don't turn no one away if they're down on their luck, either. We wed and ain't gone hungry since."

"Lord, but that's the sweetest thing I heard all week. And you deserve it. Just hope you don't serve none of that turnip soup."

She swatted him, and he chuckled. After a beat, Luke cocked his head. "What happened to Hazel? Two of you were inseparable when we last rode together."

Martha's jaw popped hard as she clenched it. Her head turned upward and looked daggers at the sky, as if it were responsible, then she spoke in a low voice. "Dead. Hazel's dead half a decade. Murdered."

Luke's breath whooshed out. "Murdered? Who'd murder Hazel?"

"He was just ridin' the rails like all of us, like always. A man came in the middle of the night and tore him apart. I think you know who it was."

Luke felt numb, knowing exactly who. "Smith McCain."

"Hell a'mighty, it was. You left us last, we were headin' toward Portage. Hazel was beside himself after you'd gone. He tried following you, like he had something urgent to say, only he wouldn't tell me or anyone else what it was. Years he talked about you, like you was gonna save us all, 'cause some crazy symbol said so. Then he got killed. Slaughtered."

"I was going to save you all how?"

"Can't say. You know Hazel when he got about that Hobo Code, reading into it, predicting the future."

Luke thought he did indeed know. After all, Hazel had taught him the Code. Luke reflected on the intricacies of the symbols and wondered if Hazel had survived in Athanasia, if he even might still be there now, but doubted it; five years dead was a long time for a 'bo to live in the deadeye's memory.

Martha went on. "I shoulda stopped hoppin' trains after that, but then I fell in with a couple other 'bos named Willie Steam and Left Eye Willie. Not more'n a few months passed, but McCain busted those two Willies to pieces. I'd been out huntin' crops when it happened, and when I come back, Willie Steam had just enough left in him to say what took place. Who knows, my ticket could have been next, but that I met Ollie."

"He killed my friends too, the girl I loved."

"You oughta learn your lesson, Luke. Give up the rails 'fore it's too late. Remember what I said 'bout folks needing roots? I'm happy now, done blowing back and forth in the wind."

Luke did remember, and he remembered too what Sequoyah had said of McCain killing him, given time. So this was the third of three valuable lessons Luke learned about himself: He would never find peace, never be safe, nor would other rail riders, as long as Smith McCain was around.

"I'm gonna finish that bastard," Luke told her so assuredly he half-believed himself.

"You've aged years since last we spoke, but you ain't no wiser."

"Believe it. I've changed in ways I never could've imagined. That Code me and Hazel followed means more than we knew, and my time is near done."

She looked at him with a mournful expression. "So you say."

"I'll be damned if I let McCain keep huntin' us down. Man's a butcher, cruel as cancer, and there'll never be peace while he's around."

"Suppose you're just going to knock on his door and pull a gun, *hm*? Or do you kill by dagger, or is it poison, assassin?"

"I'm not going to kill Smith McCain by any weapon. I'm gonna make it so you'll never even knew you'd known of him."

A CROSSBUCK ASIDE, 1941

Way I heard, the man they call Smith McCain wasn't much of a man at all. Oh, he may have had the plumbing of a man, whiskers of a man, name of a man, but none of that by itself makes a man of a man.

See, Smith McCain saw a big ol' fruit bat once, and that scared him yellow. Saw a tarantula spider another time, and that scared him worse. Got so he was scared of everything and he'd whisper to himself at night, alone under the covers, about what a tough, mean guy he was, 'til he believed it for the next day.

One time, McCain was supposed to be guarding this freight train full of antique furniture and gold doubloons and other highfalutin crap, but there was a 'bo named Larry the Worm who got to thinking his own life would be improved should he take possession of such treasures. He was named the Worm 'cause Larry was soft and lanky as one. Really, Larry couldn't put up a fight against a bluegill if they were both on land and that fish was already gutted and filleted. But Larry was feeling his oats this day, and he jumped up on a car and jimmied its door open and started stealing all the contents. And here comes McCain with his big bull truncheon, and he says in the voice of a goon, "Hey! This is railroad property! Get outta there!"

And Larry says back, "Yeah? Well, I'll fuck you like I fucked yer momma, and I done every hole she has and even some not meant for the cock of a worm."

And McCain starts crying, just blubberin', saying, "Don't hurt me, please don't hurt me, mister! And don't say that about my momma, 'cause that hurts too!"

"Go on, ya baby," Larry says, "afore I paddle you and send you to bed with no milk."

"Real sorry I bothered you, mister!" McCain calls back, only his voice is real distant, because he's already half a mile away, smoke and sparks shootin' from his heels.

That's the real Smith McCain, swear to goodness. I heard it from a man, who heard it from a man, who heard from a 'bo who knew McCain firsthand, this 'bo being Crossbuck Luke Thacker.

SMITH MCCAIN, 1941

Smith McCain felt a small change come over him, the feeling of being out of sorts in some sense, the way a man might get a bit stuffy or sneezy when a head cold decides to settle in. Not that Smith ever took sick, but he knew the effects of illness on others, especially rail riders who were vexed by all manner of rotten bugs and infections.

This change Smith felt was as if he'd shrunk the tiniest bit: nothing noticeable if he'd been seen from one day to the next, but he felt it in his bones, a slight contraction, and if he harbored any imagination, he might wonder at why his perfect black clothes weren't fitting quite right.

But that wasn't possible . . . Smith had only been growing, never shrinking, since his mother shat him out in the middle of eighteen-oh-*who-gives-a-fuck*.

Smith howled at the sensation and clenched his fists so tight the veins stood out on each forearm, and he pummeled the freeloading goddamned hobo in his piss-pale face.

The ragged man before him screamed and screamed for mercy, and for help, and for his daddy, and Smith beat him until the words were senseless gurgles and then were silent, and still Smith loosed his rage onto the formless, shattered lump of flesh in hand.

It was midnight, always midnight for Smith, his favorite time to come out and avenge himself on those who poached freebie rides. 'Course, he didn't mind coming out at dusk, noon, dawn, or any other hour to attend the cheats and scourge of the rails, but midnight served him best, when he could sneak up on a man like the dread nightmare you know will someday chance upon sleep.

The 'bo's blood dripped off Smith's knuckles in fat dobs. He licked at it, a taste that was sweet and thin, a pouch of sugar left to molder in the copper pipes under a sink, where bits of meat and wine and muck filter through, all leaving their flavors. Some men tasted of petulance, some of dolor, some of contrition or self-disgust. This derelict was cloying degradation. Smith's tongue unrolled from his mouth in a great flap and lapped at the man's ruptured skull. When done with that, he played with the 'bo's glazed eyes, pushing them in and out of their sockets while his mind emptied and everything around him dulled and fell away.

Then that twinge again.

Something . . . a muscle waning. Could that be it? A tendon restricting . . . that sense of shrinkage, as if he hadn't eaten in a long time and his stomach constricted, only that sense filled his entire being . . . *What in pitch-fuck-hell?*

Something was weakening him. *Someone* . . . That was it, someone out there shitting on his good name, telling stories, telling *lies*. Smith McCain saw the signs too, oh yes. Being around as long as the railroads, he knew every 'bo symbol writ in their feculent language, like the communication efforts between a colony of roving dung beetles. He read the markings as they blew upon turbulent winds: *Lucas Thacker* . . .

Another sense unnerved him that he'd known that tramp once, had lost him. With so many rail riders turning out, he didn't care much back then about Lucas Thacker's evasion. Easier pickings were found on every line, and Smith didn't hold much power outside a train car to chase an escapee anyway. But now the 'bo signs told of Lucas Thacker's treachery, this guttersnipe hobo who could cross back and forth between the worlds of life and annihilation just as easily as himself. And to jam the cap in the whole fucking breech, the filthy cocksucker persisted in stealing train rides every chance he could.

Smith cursed and stomped the dead 'bo's chest until his ribs shattered to splinters and erupted out his skin and shirt. Then, with one huge kick, he sent the mangled carcass sailing out the boxcar door to smear along rime-pecked crags.

"Lucas Thacker," he said in a low, emotionless rumble, "I'm coming for you."

LUKE THACKER, 1941

Luke Thacker remembered what Sequoyah had told him—that after learning three lessons, he'd return to that dust-filled cabin—and Luke knew it was true, but not quite yet.

He did begin venturing back into Athanasia, each time dipping his toes into its pools of peril, and when finding them not so bad, he stayed a bit longer, until the need would overtake him to return to Real World and spread the Code and share the crossbucks of his adventures with other fireside 'bos.

And by recurrence he got more comfortable in the act, in hiding or escaping pursuers in Athanasia, in making the transition back and forth from there to regular life. He became a knight of the road, questing through the greatest magical realm in the world. He travelled the rails faster, hopping between cities, making acquaintances, figuring things out, spreading stories, and all the while searching for Daisy.

He'd wake in one car out of Myrtle Beach, go through the deadeye in upstate New York, and maybe stop for coffee with Mark Twain, who could tell him a thing or two on ridin' the crossbuck line 'tween truth and fib. Next he'd commandeer a line through Brainerd, jump back into life for bean dinner with a jungle of 'bos, then sail away the night on the tracks, all the while following those signs of the Hobo Code he now knew were of Sequoyah's doing. Luke could wake next in Yakima and do it over, crossing from Elko to Ardmore to Champaign to Rock Hill, and go to sleep in the following boxcar at sunrise, once he'd jumped into Joplin, Missouri, which is where he'd been last . . .

And though he had too many adventures to herein relate without overwhelming the consciousness of all who listened, the following incident is one of meaningful note in such annals of Crossbuck Luke Thacker, which undoubtedly and most certainly are true.

For a moment, Luke lost track of where he was, and he heard a noise before he saw what it was, and by the time he saw it, he was surrounded.

He was in a soggy slab of land that a woman named Ma Barker had told him yesterday was "half swamps, half cliffs, and half snakes," though a more reliable source indicated it as belonging to the Ozark highlands, east of Boonville and below the Missouri River. The signs had led him here, and Luke had followed, and soon enough he found himself maneuvering a withering dirt road, looking to make camp in a spot that was dry and away from passersby. It was a striking sweep of land, but everything was wet, not the type of soil he preferred to lay his head, especially if it *was* half—or any other notable percentage—composed of snake.

The road was more mud than dirt, where it could still be called a road, and often buried by a tangle of slippery trees. The air hung thick with humidity, causing his clothes to feel ironed on, and a constant mist breathed over him from invisible clouds that seemed to float overhead at all steps. Flowers bloomed everywhere, glistening with dew that never dried, and he recognized some of the more common species, while many of the bright blossoms were as exotic princesses, beautiful yet strange to behold.

That was when he heard it: a soft moaning, seeming carried from far away. Luke figured the moaning was probably the result of pox at work, but this moaning sounded different, like a chorus of suffering. The farther he pressed down that road, which became a path, which became a dim line riven through low-hanging boughs and high-reaching grasses, the closer the sound came, an assemblage of cries and sighs, crackles and creaks.

The noise grew to envelop him from both sides, and Luke hesitated, deciding he should leave it alone. *Best to turn around and let whoever's here just be.* It wasn't a far distance he'd travelled into these woods, off Route 98, but it was a long-winded distance, trudging through the muck and dank forest, and he didn't care to retreat the way he'd come, acknowledging the misuse of most of a good afternoon.

Luke took one more step. From the undergrowth, the first red dots passed by, then more, and suddenly a fright took hold that the pox was coming for him. But he heard a crash and another moan, a sucking sound, and he eased, realizing it wasn't him they were after. It wasn't his time . . . *yet.*

In short order, the pox increased in number, swarming like great clouds of terrible insects, and Luke began swatting around his head to keep them away. He hadn't encountered such a multitude before, and it caused his nerves to tingle as to what they were consuming. Trees, flowers, even sections of the ground turned red, steamed, trembled, dissolved, and Luke had a horrible vision of the Earth's crust disappearing under his feet, sending him plummeting into the lava-filled bowels of its core. A wall of woods opened to his right, and pox poured in, and more pox poured out, a busy highway of death, filling the air until he could no longer see anything else.

Luke pushed through the pox clouds back the way he'd come, or so he thought, but found himself suddenly in the middle of a clearing, its edges glowing red and radiating outward. *Like the eye of a hurricane*, he thought, calm in its center, while surrounded by screaming gales. Things began to flash before his eyes, ghostly images and thoughts spread over present events, so he couldn't tell what was current and real, or foretold, or memory.

Large canoes hacked from elder cottonwoods lay on the ground, filling with pox holes, smoldering, vanishing as if sinking into the wild currents of the air. Old clay pottery broke, though their shards didn't fall but instead shrunk and faded. Carved poles and thatched roofs and baskets woven of reeds were attacked by the pox, and they filled with gaps and turned to glowing cinders that winked out like extinguished lights.

An entire village was being consumed around him. Round huts like hay stacks, but composed of mud and boughs, broke apart, pieces of wall cracking, shattering, then burning up into red ash, firing pox embers and vanishing into the air. A long wood fence, perhaps a pen of some sort, collapsed, melting like ice under the sun. That impossible emptiness hung behind each instance, until filling in with . . . *reality*. The ground shifted, trees spread, holes of existence filled back in. There were people, too, sprawled on the ground, eaten alive, and it was they who moaned, though Luke knew also that there were spirits present he couldn't see, which were pained as much as those of physical form.

The Hobo signs struck him full force, a whirlwind of symbols in his mind, of thoughts in language he couldn't decode and ancient memories he couldn't solve.

Was this what Sequoyah had spoken of, culture and people vanishing around him, faster and faster? Was this of Ben's doing—if it didn't promote his image, it was of no use and therefore dismissed? Or was this natural, as goes the paling of all memory? What else had already been forgotten, and what was being forgotten even now?

The knowledge came, and Luke knew, without knowing how: These were the Niwihanna people, an indigenous race whose own history was instilled into their children as firmly as were the names of local fowl, seed, and goddesses. They could count back moons for two thousand years, wandering the Midwest plains as nomadic slaves of one tribe, or slavers of another, until following their own coded signs to find peace in the Missouri watershed. At one time they were mighty, numbering over eight hundred men divided amongst nine villages. Here there was ample food, water, and shelter. Here migratory animals provided them clothing, bedding, meat, sacrifice. Bones were used for awls, for arrowheads, for jewelry. Fur was used for mats, for insulation, for costume. Here, along the river, the vast marshes provided medicine and herbs and fields to grow squash, beans, and corn, all without asking anything in return, but for a nightly prayer of thanks.

The Niwihanna traded west with the Mitutanka and east with the Nuptadi, and they occasionally quarreled with the Osage over inconsequential matters, as neighbors often do. But these tribes flourished together, amongst others, praising and cherishing the rich life provided by the Spirit of the Missouri River. Of course, the Niwihanna didn't know its name as the Missouri, but understood when it was referred to as *Ouemessourita, Emasulia Sipiwi,* or *Eomitai.* When the Niwihanna happened upon the first white travelers, they were told to call it *Pekitanoui,* though they themselves knew it only as *Great Water.*

On Great Water was born Hollahanna, strongest warrior of the Niwihanna who could defeat, using only his hands, monstrous fanged bears with fur tipped golden and gray. On Great Water was born Sissinnoba, daughter of the priestess Tenskwatona, who was lovelier than even the brightest stars in winter dark. When Hollahanna and Sissinnoba mated, the flowers of the land were sown.

On Great Water were born the Ahtahkakoba, same-named brothers who each guarded the river with lightning spears barbed by the fangs of Hollahanna's defeated bears. Every sunrise, their watchful eyes could be seen illuminating the sky. On Great Water was born Citlaliq, who prophesied the Niwihannas' enduring prosperity so long as they remained in the land of the river.

On Great Water was born Tomau, last of the exalted chiefs who, at the height of his peoples' power, provided lodging and meal for a party of bumbling explorers led by Meriwether Lewis and William Clark. Tomau thought these men with skin colored as the moon would not survive the season, but he gave them as much provision and blessing as they could accept.

Tomau's hospitality and generosity were widely extolled in later years by members of the expedition. His people were discussed, and their stories shared and embellished, until it sounded like they couldn't hunt a squirrel without tripping over rich gems. In such a way, the Niwihanna were conspired against by those desiring that land of plenty.

Now, only a century had passed since the Niwihanna were decimated by sudden wars brought upon them, forcing them to flee the land they had made home. Defeat followed defeat, by smallpox, by forced relocation, by hunger, by loss of faith in Hollahanna and Sissinnoba and the brothers, and all the ancestors and spirits that once watched over them.

And all this was already now forgotten, first by few, then by many. The Niwihanna were but one bit of culture termed "Indian," lumped together with all other native dwellers, yet left out from bedtime tales of cowboy raids and teepees and scalping parties. They were allotted to the nation of the defeated, and there is scarce room for legends of those who do not conquer. The shared consciousness of existence lost interest, watched other things, learned other things, spoke other things.

So soon were an entire people forgotten, so soon.

Luke stayed there in that clearing as the eye of the pox-hurricane grew wide, radiating outward from its center until all traces of the Niwihanna were gone. The low-lying cliffs jutting over the Missouri River, and the wet marsh and morass of woods, all returned as they were; but, Luke noticed, many of the flowers he'd earlier seen were taken as well.

It was true, as Sequoyah said: The world and its memories were dying all around him. Someday, such would be the fate for him, for everything he knew, for everything he didn't know. Ultimately it was all inescapable, but for now, Luke was resolved to push that fate as far into the distance as possible.

He caught a train and moved down the rail, ready to revisit the Code Maker.

DANIEL INTERVIEWS KING, 1985: DAY FOUR

My prior interviews with King Shaw had occurred in late mornings, but he couldn't meet me today until its end, as he "got busy with things," which caused me to wonder where he'd been, if not on his deathbed.

Yesterday was the day I'd found him withering in the strip-mall hospice, and after we concluded talking, he asked me not to return him to that hospice, but to wheel him instead to the corner mart/bail bonds/pawn shop we'd stopped at before, which I did.

I wondered if that hook-nosed nurse would even miss him. Likely she'd at least miss the wheelchair, and I promised myself to see it eventually returned.

I wondered, too, where King had slept last night. I'd offered him hotel fare, but he'd declined with a snuffle.

"Going to a shelter, then?" I'd asked.

"A bitch to get into," he said. "Most times, I don't even try."

"It'll be cold tonight. In your condition, you need a place with comfort and care."

"Oh, I got somewhere," he replied, giving the vaguest answer possible.

So I departed, wondering at King's secrets. Before we went our ways, he asked me to bring him a cigar for the next time we met, which I also did.

This final afternoon I spoke with King, the sun began to fade like a small plum eaten lazily by the horizon. The weather wasn't cold, it wasn't hot, it was just fine, fine all around, and the L.A. smog had cleared out, and the sky shimmered like a darkening ocean lifted over our heads, and even the songbirds seemed to be making their way home from the city, flitting past with goodbyes for the old man in the wheelchair.

"My last stogie," he said, upon the cigar I'd brought. "Hope it's a good one."

I hoped so too.

King looked noble, with a fedora on his head like a crown, and me his royal scribe, penning decrees and grand judgments. After an hour, the cigar was only half gone, clenched hard between yellow teeth with smoke billowing out at the fury of his words.

He told me more adventures of Luke, and he told me tragedies of Daisy and Zeke, and he told me about others whose lives intersected and made way for bigger highways, or else dead-ended suddenly. Truth of the matter, King appeared healthier than ever, his skin richly toned and more vivid than I'd seen before. He spoke faster too, as if trying to unload all the stories before that final whistle blew, announcing his shift had ended.

And King didn't ask again about me passing his stories onto others. At the time I was grateful, not keen to continue that rocky conversation. Later, I got the feeling he already knew it would happen, given time. He saw something in me, or maybe he *foresaw* it, but either way he was satisfied, and his last task was just to tell it.

And tell it, he did.

"One day, say about 1949, we were driving in John's car," King said. "Well, Luke was driving, 'cause that was his thing. Cars just seemed to purr under his caress. Anyway, who should we come across shooting at some Civil War battlefield in Pennsylvania, but the photographer, Mathew Brady. It was John who recognized him. Luke and me didn't care two huffs, but John Dillinger was something of a war buff since childhood. He loved imagining himself as General Sherman rolling through Savannah, setting ablaze whatever he fancied. His love for the War Between the States was fueled, in part, by Brady's picture books, which John read in school during his boyhood.

"John thought it'd be a hoot to get his own portrait done by Brady, and he was ready to threaten the old man with deeds so violent most couldn't imagine in eight lifetimes if Brady wouldn't comply. But Brady was real nice, happy to have made a fan in the gangster. John further insisted Luke and I join him for a group portrait, and I didn't want to, but then I thought of all the violent deeds John had just rattled off like ingredients to a soup, so I hopped in. John was a vain bastard. He was good lookin', so I suppose he deserved to be vain, but I didn't see why anyone would want to immortalize my ugly old mug.

"Anyway, Brady popped out a set of pictures for us right on the spot. I think normally it takes some weeks to process those old photos, but remember this is the *other* place, Athanasia, and all your talents are multiplied and shit, so that was that. I'm not much of a sentimental fella, but how many guys can say they've gotten their picture snapped alongside John Dillinger by Mathew Brady? I can name two, and you're lookin' at one."

"That is . . . amazing," I said. I forced a salesman's smile of sincerity that the old man wouldn't have bought if he were paying attention, but he was too caught up in reminiscence.

"Here," King said. "I want you to have it."

He handed me a small sepia photograph, produced on cardboard, which looked as if it had been folded into as small a square as possible, unfolded, then folded again a different way, many times over. The image was a blur of cracks, all horizontal lines one way and vertical lines the other. If you held the picture at an angle, under the right kind of light, and squinted with one eye, you could make out three men, their arms loosely hung around each other's shoulders.

"I used to keep it safe 'tween the pages of a book on card tricks," King added. "But I lost that book to a twelve-year-old in a poker hand. The boy cheated, but at least he let me keep the photo."

I took the picture cupped in both hands, ready for it to disintegrate. "What is it?"

"What do you mean?" King sounded genuinely dismayed. "I already told you what it is. It's a photo of me and Luke and John. That's John in the center, Luke on the left, and the jughead on the right is me."

I hadn't formed my question succinctly. I knew what it was supposed to be, but I didn't know what it *was*. A doctored photograph? A gag? I remembered a show I'd watched with my father while growing up in Long Island, and expected to hear the catch phrase the very moment I acknowledged belief in the picture: *Smile, you're on Candid Camera!*

But I played along like a good Boy Scout and thanked him generously for the gift, dramatizing how I'd treasure it always. Whether the picture showed King or not, I couldn't say, but I thought how much the picture itself was of King at present, old and beat up, faded with uncertainty, filled with a story that would soon dematerialize from all memory. It, like him, was something to be discarded in time by me and by all the world.

DANIEL GREENBERG, 2019

Would it surprise you to know I still have that picture?

King gave it to me, along with a couple other personal effects, because he thought when he died, whoever found him would keep anything they considered worthwhile and throw out the rest, and he wanted to make those determinations himself while still alive. One of those effects was a strange gold coin with a handsome jack's winking likeness . . . but more on that later.

The next week I showed the battered picture to a friend, a photographer who worked for the *Los Angeles Times*, and asked his opinion. He said it was neat, and went on to describe it as an albumen print photograph, legitimately produced in the style of *cartes de visite*, a type of greeting card popularized in the 1850s and '60s. The process and material were perfect, but could now be created by any photo hobbyist who has built or restored the right equipment. The photo itself, obviously, was no older than fifty years. Hell, there was even the fender of a Ford coupe nosing in from the image's edge.

He asked who the people in the picture were, and I just replied, "Friends." He said again that the photo was neat.

But did I consider it authentic, even as a reproduction? *No.*

It may well have been a picture of King, standing at an angle with a goofy *what-am-I-doing-with-you-clowns* look, one hand shoved deep into a coat pocket, the other hand around an immaculately-dressed man with a pencil-thin mustache. Under careful scrutiny, it did look like King, or a younger version anyway, his head covered in gloss-black hair that reminded me he hadn't always been the frail bald man I knew. But to say that pencil-mustached man in the center was John Dillinger was . . . well, *impossible.* There was a background marker stating *Pennsylvania Turnpike*, and that highway system wasn't built until the 1940s, some years after Dillinger died.

So King gave the picture to me, and I filed it away in storage, along with the original transcripts and keepsakes from him and the other homeless subjects I'd interviewed. I only remembered it when I opened up his files this year and began to read his stories again.

In 1985 I took that picture from King and nodded as sincerely as I could, thanking him and agreeing it was marvelous proof of the impossible. Only today do I believe it.

Now I've probably gotten ahead of myself in these recollections, but like King once told me, *You arrange the events of a story in a way that's meaningful, not based on just some timeline.* For as I reflect upon his life and my own, it turns out I have a lot in common with King Shaw, which, on its surface, seems a funny observation to make.

King never had more than a handful of coins and the clothes on his back at any one time. I come from the upper class of Long Island and even managed to raise myself beyond the means afforded me, moving to the penthouses of Manhattan. King was an old man, while I was young. He couldn't much read or write. I was a finalist for the Pulitzer.

Of course, he was one of the reasons I was a Pulitzer contender, so that might say a lot about our connection. We were both avid talkers, champions of the word, if you will. Another likeness is that we'll both have died of cancer. Him over thirty years ago from the liver and colon, me in six months from the prostate.

And now, we've each possessed this picture that nobody else would believe in.

When King Shaw died, I found myself again having to search for him. I checked first with the ward on 9th, but he hadn't turned up there, though I got an earful from a certain hook-nosed nurse. I made a few phone calls, hit the street, and asked the questions journalists ask. As before, he didn't take long to locate, only this time the result was grimmer. King was reanointed with the transient's salute of *John Doe*, but instead of a cot, he lay on a metal tray covered by a single sheet that left the top of his head exposed at one end and his withered feet at the other. This was in the basement mortuary beneath Good Samaritan Hospital. I identified the body, and they later buried him in a common grave at the L.A. County Cemetery near Boyle Heights.

That was the end of his story, but not of mine.

Then again . . . that wasn't the end of his, either.

KING SHAW, 1942

Once upon a time, King Shaw was a strong man. He was often weakened by illness and physical frailty, and his legs never seemed to work the way they should, but those who knew him said there wasn't a thing he couldn't do . . . 'cept settle down to a life of respectability.

King didn't know when he was born, and he didn't know who his parents were. He'd been given up as an infant, but sometimes he'd been sold, and sometimes he'd been kidnapped, and other times a twister had carried him away, though in all cases he ended up in the care of immigrant fortune tellers as part of a gypsy caravan.

When he quit childhood in 1926, King read his first fortune, which happened also to be his own. It was midnight, as is often the case for affairs like this, and the moon was full. It was Friday the thirteenth, and there was a dire wolf on the prowl, and somebody threw an evil eye at him earlier, and on top of everything else, the gypsy caravan was camped over a desecrated Indian burial ground.

Uncle Lou and Aunt Paz—the man and woman who generally cared for King, though there was no familial association—were asleep. King pawed through the gold-leaf chest Aunt Paz kept beneath a shelf of enchanted ironwood, until he pulled out her deck of Tarot cards. They lived in a motorized carriage, which looked mostly like a backwoods cottage perched on a set of spoke wheels. Inside the carriage, a crown of dim light bounded from a single lantern. King shuffled the cards and set them out the way he'd always seen done by Aunt Paz when she read the fortunes of paying customers.

Then he asked some simple questions that basically came down to the same burning queries all adolescents—all people—wish to know: *What's life got in store for me?*

King turned a card over and that card immediately, with a spark and a whoosh, fell into a bit of sad ash. Young King gasped; he'd never seen that happen before when Aunt Paz handled the deck. He turned the next card over, and it too fell to ash. A faint scent of sulfur lingered in the air. Another card, another, until half the stack was gone. Then a card with a woman surrounded by nine circles—the Nine of Pentacles—did not burn, and so he set it aside. That was a good card, one signifying material wealth, and that made him happy. The following card also didn't burn, and King was excited by it; he would travel to distant places. The next card prophesied a deep friendship, and with that he felt most content of all.

The following three cards also did not burn, but they caused mortal despair, as each undermined the intent of the first three. After that, the rest of the deck burned at once, so there remained only those six cards, three sets of two, lined next to each other.

He read their messages and knew they'd be true, and he wished to God he'd never sought the knowledge that would haunt him the rest of his days. King wept bitterly. He packed up what personal effects held sentiment, not numbering many, and ran away that night from the caravan of gypsies, vowing never to read fortunes again.

When King quit childhood in 1926 and read his own fortune, the three divinations the cards foretold were thus:

You were born for riches you will never know.
You will die alone, far away.
You will kill your dearest friend.

Once upon a time, King *did* try to settle down, to find a regular home, before he knew destiny had called him to wander. Growing up, all he'd ever experienced was travelling with gypsy caravans, town to town, grove to grove, and he wondered what it would be like to ever sleep in a stationary bed each night. But if he were a buck, every hand that touched King passed him off somewhere else, so that he learned never to take his shoes off for too long in one place. In the north he was told he was too simple, yet in the south he was too uppity. In the east he was too eager, and in the west, too slow. So like other displaced young men, King Shaw took to the rails to find his way in life.

No one ever figured out why, but King limped when he walked. It wasn't substantial, not like a man does with a wooden leg, but noticeable to most people if they were looking for it. When he took a step with his right side, his left side seemed to tremble as if it would buckle any moment. But it never did; that was just the appearance. The same would happen when he took a step with his left side; the right looked about ready to give way, though it never did, either. If bystanders didn't know better, they might rush over and give King a steadying hand to lean on, which, depending upon circumstances, he might or might not take. King later said that his weak legs benefitted more than impaired him, and often when in need of a handout, folks were a bit more generous with someone appearing disabled, as if an appeasement of guilt for themselves suffering from glowing physical health.

Weak legs notwithstanding, King could run and hop trains with the best of them. He rode the rails for years and celebrated his birthdays in boxcars or empty horse stalls, sometimes alone, sometimes with others, once in a jail cell for vagrancy, another time in the loft of a haunted barn. King travelled the country and, like Luke Thacker, his greatest thrill became in seeing new places. He labored and lived and had good times and bad, but no times were as gratifying as visiting wonders of nature and roadside attractions he'd never before known, and which caused him always to consider: *What else is there?*

When the Second World War erupted, King tried to enlist, but his weak legs saw that hope derailed. The army recruiter kindly told King he should be thankful he could remain stateside and serve his patriotic duty on the home front, carrying parade banners or working in ammunitions factories, or rationing durable goods. None of what that recruiter said really applied to King; he had no goods to ration, nor any particularly patriotic spirit. He just wanted a free ticket to see foreign lands.

So King continued on his aimless way, searching out work to live, shelter to sleep, peoples to chat. Though he was self-deriding about it, King had his fair share of trysts with lady friends, and most of 'em he left broken-hearted at far-flung way stations while he sailed away on the next sunrise-bound railcar. Being gentle and conversational endeared King with the fairer sex more than he understood; even back then, crippled and homeless as a wayward pup was preferable to men of means who were loud-mouthed and oppressive.

That year King Shaw took a break from rail riding and found himself in Meridian, Mississippi, smack in the fertile delta west of the nation's greatest river. There were thousands of itinerant hands on its waterways, and they flocked together in camps, marching from farm to farm, all searching out work like colonies of ants upon the crumbs left at a weekend picnic. It reminded King of the gypsy camps of his childhood, though in greater scale. He signed on at a plantation, and they registered him as a seasonal field worker, although King considered himself more of a freelance contractor. He wasn't shackled to this labor as he imagined his ancestors to be, though he was still indentured enough by the need for food and some kind of hope.

As it was, King Shaw wasn't any menial commoner at heart, but had the grand aspiration to be a famous blues guitarist, and he was going to make a name for himself and rise from the swells of the disheveled. He'd have record deals and a big house and a silver car as wide as a city block to drive from coast to coast. This King dreamed, though he didn't own a guitar. So he spent the days twisted over cotton plants, sweating out seeds from fibers and cursing each skin-gashing thorn, patiently enduring 'til he could save enough to get a decent six-string from the local pawnbroker.

"I know a Joe who'll sell you the purtiest guitar you ever seen," said a field hand named Jerry Grit. Jerry had lived in Meridian since birth and was satisfied life was better there than laboring anywhere else. He added in a sly whisper, "Joe's my brother."

Jerry and King sat on dirt pies outside a men's bunk house, King whistling over broom straws he'd tied to a guitar-shaped stick, pretending to strum. King asked, "Joe take credit?"

"Think not. Brother's lookin' for twelve real dollars."

"Twelve? For that I could start my own record label."

Jerry shrugged. He had a rough-hewn fiddle and began to play its jangling strings, so when he spoke, his voice slipped into something like a song.

"Brother Joe got it from this bluesman outta Greenwood a few years past. Some say the man gave his soul for that guitar and died playin' last. Fella's name was Robert Johnson, and for twelve you'll get his device. I'd say that's a bargain, deal done, much cheaper than ol' Johnson's price."

"A twelve-buck guitar and a wish keeps me sittin' with you. Where am I gonna get that kind of loot?"

"We're working, ain't we?"

"And paying to eat, paying for soap and clothes, even gotta pay for our own picking baskets, then wages are cut to pay the foreman who oversees us, cut more to live in this palace." King thumbed at the windowless bunk house. "Can't fathom why in green earth I'm even here. Got tired of travellin', but if this is anchoring, I'm going back to the rails."

"Fella's gotta eat on the rails too."

"At least there I eat when I want, not by the sound of the calling bell."

Jerry shrugged again and played quick notes. All the while, his eyes kept that shrugging motion like an echo. *What's to do, what's to do?*

"Never gonna get an instrument sitting here," King said. "Something about the day calls me to stroll."

King stood and limped away, the thrum of Jerry's fiddle scratchy and wild and fading by notes the farther his slow-stepping ambulation took him. King didn't know where he headed, but by the time he was lost in the grand land, he realized he'd known all along why Meridian, Mississippi, had been the spot picked to lull.

He'd heard from a 'bo named Willie Ears about a gypsy graveyard, otherwise called Rose Hill Cemetery, said to be the desired burying ground of tribal and honored Roma from all over the nation. The Queen of the

Gypsies had died there in 1915, and her subjects sought final comfort in her caravan under the earth.

As it happened, Rose Hill was located smack center there in Meridian.

King Shaw could read the Hobo Code good as anyone, and better than most. Today it seemed to be speaking out loud, so strong were the symbols. Spindly cartoon arrows dotted his path, and a triangle with a halo over it for "nice people" came by, and a picture of a cross with a crown over it, as if he were expected there. Another picture and a whisper in the breeze told him to catch a ride on the next vehicle he saw, and King thumbed a lift on the back of a truck, sharing the wind with a shaggy dog that smiled like a poet.

In this way, it didn't take long at all until he'd reached Rose Hill.

He hopped off the truck and thanked the driver and his dog for passage, and entered the graveyard that was bigger'n he assumed, with towering marble obelisks on each side of the walking path.

Just inside the entrance was a caretaker's shack, and painted under its eaves showed a lanky stick figure symbol lifting a spear. *Armed Man.*

And then an oldster in bib overalls hustled out, holding a shovel threateningly. On his forehead a monstrous red boil glared at King like a third eye with a grudge. "What do ya want?"

"Bein' we're at a cemetery, you can assume I'm not here to play tiles."

"No trespassing. You come to vandalize, I'll turn your face inside-out."

"A man's got a right to come and pay his respects," King said.

"I know a vandal when I see him. Colored graveyard's on the other side of town, so scoot."

"This is the right place. I'm lookin' for family."

The caretaker guffawed and shot a snot comet from his nostril. "I know what you are, and you ain't a gypsy. If lies were mirrors, you'd be lookin' at yerself all day. You're just a jigaboo with a limp."

King bit his lip, figuring how to deal with the old bastard. Violence begat violence, and if he said the wrong thing, it wasn't unfeasible a truck with burning crosses and a short noose might be called up.

King didn't speak any gypsy tongues, though Uncle Lou and Aunt Paz had been fluent in Romanian, Italian, Spanish, and a hybrid of Moroccan-Greek, and he remembered a few scattered words from these languages and the general intonations of some others. King looked at the man and closed one eye, lifted his chin, and held up a hand with the fingers outstretched—except for the middle, which pointed straight up—and he said in a lilting chant, "*Buona note, pomodoro verde. Buona note, pomodoro verde.*"

What King said translated to something like, "Good night, green tomato," but the man didn't know that. His sunburned face paled to the color of a Kluxer's robe and he didn't make another sound, just turned tail and slunk back inside his shack. The lore of gypsy curses was a volatile beast.

More cartoon arrows showed along the path, made of stones laid side-by-side or scratched in the dirt with a stick. *This way*, and King went on.

He followed the arrows leisurely, admiring ivory crypts made as exquisitely as any mansion, and mourning effigies so lifelike their tears seemed to roll without end. Small graves were tragic, while large ones seemed fair, as if they'd gotten the most out of life, so no sadness need be spared. Around him, candles burned, and incense smoked, and strange flowers bloomed, and he saw chains of beads and faded photographs, broken vases, gifts, letters, even shoes and stuffed dolls, all trappings brought and laid in memorial at graves for as many reasons as there were mounds. Eventually the Code led him to a small sedge-topped knoll. At the base of this knoll stuck out a single headstone with two names etched on it.

Louis and Paolessa Pawłowski, died together, 1939.

Uncle Lou and Aunt Paz had raised him well enough, but it took King a while to appreciate that, having endured frequent bouts of starvation and loneliness as an adult that he'd not experienced while under their care. He never knew what "dire need" meant until striking out on his own. And though King didn't think about them often, he realized his memories of the old couple had grown fonder with age.

They'd both had something of that gypsy gift for foresight, and he wondered how they'd coped with the terrible knowledge of future events. Maybe having each other was enough. Maybe true "sight" had one blind eye, and they only saw the good things. King couldn't handle the six cards that'd been dealt him, but Lou and Paz seemed to have done all right. And now they were here.

There were few things King wished he'd done differently in life, and one of those was to have told them "thank you" and "goodbye." He tried to rectify that wish now by speaking to their final resting place.

And a funny thing happened.

A voice came from their grave. It wasn't a voice speaking in his head, nor was it a voice out loud that anyone else could hear, but rather it was there and it wasn't, as much as certain whistles can be heard only by dogs, but not by their masters. The voice was Paz's, and the voice was Lou's, and the voice was whole peoples of immigrants resolved to make their way in a hard and unforgiving land.

The voice said: *You were dealt a fine hand after all.*

King didn't believe it.

Something trembled in the dirt beneath the gravestone, and a green vine poked out, wagging its tentacle-like tip at King. It rose from the sedge in a flurry, winding around and around the granite slab while offshoots of tiny thorns and small pale flowers erupted, and the whole thing glistened wet and fresh, like a creature hatched. More vine tentacles broke from the grave, and King thought how a giant kraken might surface from the depths to catch an unwary fishing vessel. He took a step back.

A ray of sun caught the green clump's center, and something gold and metallic flashed there. The vines stopped growing, stopped moving, except for an unsettling pulse coming from its cordon, a fleshy pillow fluffing and unfluffing itself, all the while bearing a gift. King looked closer and saw that gift was a small gold coin.

He hesitated, leaned closer. The coin looked old and foreign, and the symbols on it reminded him of letters drawn by Aunt Paz. King reached into the clump of vines to grasp the coin, and a single vine lashed out, pricking his little finger with a taloned thorn.

King sucked in a breath and grabbed the coin. A drop of blood swelled from where he'd been pierced and dripped into the vines, which quickly sucked it up. The vines then uncoiled from the gravestone, retracted their tentacles, and sunk back into the Pawłowskis' grave.

Fever and chill broke over King at the same time, and a sensation like lightning jarred from his hand to charge every nerve, and he gasped. King saw Athanasia the way he'd seen it in life, but also the way he'd seen it in dreams, which were entirely unlike experiences. Visions of Uncle Lou and Aunt Paz wavered before him, and they smiled, calm and understanding. They knew what it was like to up and leave, what it was like to carry that ineludible spirit of quest. They wished him the best, and they told him to come visit, and then they were brushed away by a pair of hands as if an unwanted fly were shooed out.

Behind the hands materialized a man, and the pleasure King felt at seeing his adopted parents was replaced by venom.

The man said, "Shawell, I am sorry I have not been there for you." He was a handsome figure in middle age, wearing a tuxedo with a white carnation in its lapel. "But I want to make it right, son."

"You got some nerve showing up again. Who are you really?"

"I am your father, Shawell. I have already introduced myself before."

"Oh, right, the time you asked me to come visit, and the welcoming committee tried to enslave me."

"As I said, I am sorry, son—"

"I ain't your son, you didn't raise me."

"I begot you, but I could not keep you. Your mother was a cabaret singer and a musician, whom I loved but, like yourself, I could not keep. She was bound by her family to perform vaudeville acts and they would not allow a cheap sideshow entertainer to steal away their daughter. Our baby—you—was traded away for showhouse favors."

"This gets better and better."

"Before, when I asked you to visit this middle ground of death, I could not properly greet you. I was called away by an employer, and others found you first. Animates are in great demand, I am told."

"First you give me up, then you blow me off. And to think of the great life I'd have had under your parentage."

"I apologize again for that misfortune. I am busy all the time, son. A magician must always promote."

"Magician?" King repeated, furrowing his brow.

The man's voice swelled, and the building beat of an invisible drum began to thump. "I may have been little enough once, when I first met your mother, but I did not settle for those low rungs. I became the most prominent African or American or any other country's magician of all time, the illustrious, the stupendous, the amazing Black Herman! Me!"

A cymbal crashed, and lights flashed behind, then upon, Herman's face. King couldn't deny the similarity; the man who was his father had a slight brow overhanging sharp, heavy-lidded eyes. His cheeks were high and dark, and his ears a bit too big for his head, although that played well against the length of his face. Herman was clean-cut, however, with a 'do shorn tight and a widow's peak as sharp as a knife. King hadn't cut his own hair in several months, and it billowed out in strange wiggles and puffs.

King said, "Should I applaud?"

Herman sighed. "I wish not to win you over by my accolades, but know this: You were raised by gypsies, but you do not carry gypsy blood. You have magic in your blood."

"What's that matter?"

"It is how you may come visit Athanasia, when the time is better suited to you."

"Don't stay up late waitin' for me."

"Things are not always what they seem, son."

The gold coin King still held began to smolder, heating fast to burn his flesh. King yelped and opened his fingers, and a twist of steam faded away as the coin vanished.

Herman held up his own hand, and the gold coin was there. He flicked it over a thumb back to King, who caught it with the opposite hand. The coin seemed the same, except the gypsy symbols carved on it were gone, replaced by a grinning portrait of his father. The gold face of Black Herman winked from the coin.

King woke lying on the ground by the Pawłowskis' grave.

The coin had been a token for passage, a one-time oracle's fare, and its value thusly used. Then again, the coin was made of gold, and that purposed a whole different value, even if the face on it wasn't recognizable as any regular currency. He clenched it so tight the etchings left imprints across the burn on his palm.

King Shaw left the gypsy graveyard, and he went into town and sold that gold coin with his father's face just as soon as he could.

He bought a new suit of clothes and a dinner of pork chops and steamed apples, and he got his hair cut in a shop with a twirling red and white pole outside. He looked in the mirror and thought himself even handsomer than Black Herman. Afterward, King returned to the plantation and took a ride with Jerry Grit to Greenwood, where he used the last of his money as payment for Robert Johnson's guitar.

Well-armed with a new look, a full belly, and the strummer that would cause record producers to claw over each other in signing him, King Shaw left the plantation and hopped aboard a new train. He didn't know where it was bound, and it didn't matter, for Easy Street, USA, was his ultimate destination.

King was too lost in thoughts to notice someone else already occupied the boxcar he'd hitched himself to.

"Howdy, 'bo." The voice sounded genuinely happy to see him, and it even struck him as familiar in some impossible way.

King narrowed his eyes at swaying shadows and corners half-filled with cow dung and hay bales. He located the man who'd spoken, who was using one bale as a seat, another as a headrest, and a third as a foot stool. The man's skinny limbs sprawled in all directions, and his clothes flopped in rustles as if a private wind blew through them.

King forced himself to smile, though a sad resignation stole away his cheer, that perhaps his road to riches just came upon a bridge marked as "washed out," and the detour would be a long and uncertain roundabout. He replied, "Well, if it ain't Crossbuck Luke."

LUKE AND KING, 1942

Luke Thacker grinned, offering a big wave for King to share his corner of the car. "Wondered when I might see you again."

"Hear tales you're still travelling to the deadeye," King replied, his face seeming jovial enough, though he looked to have been caught in the middle of a daydream. Luke patted him on the shoulder as he sat on the haystack recliners, and caught the slightest shadow of reluctance beneath King's friendly mien. "Chasing ghosts and running trains like they were hounds at your call. Those crossbucks probably true, I take it."

"Folks believe different parts of 'em, or want to, anyway. But it's all real, and I'd wager you're the only person who knows it. You may not like Athanasia, but it exists, and my Daisy Rose is imprisoned there. I'm going to get her back, and I'm going to make her live forever."

"Good luck and Godspeed," King said.

Luke's grin turned humorless. "I could use a friend to help."

"I'll call you my friend 'fore I call you a fiddle, but I've got other plans." King pulled out a small pocket knife with a nicked, dull edge and began to slide it along the guitar's strings, drawing out a ghostly, vibrant squeal. "I'm gonna be a musician."

Luke felt his eyes grow large. "That knife . . . "

"Different sound, huh? Old man showed me how to use it, makes a richer tone by dragging it over the strings rather than pickin' chords with your fingers."

"No, I mean where'd you get it?"

King shrugged. "Found it in a boxcar some years back. Must've been used for skinning, there was some blood and hide on the blade."

"That knife used to be mine."

"Huh, don't that beat all." The lack of sincerity in King's voice matched the suspicion in his eyes.

"I'm not trying to claim it," Luke added. "Just, well, I stabbed someone with that knife."

King stopped sliding it over the guitar strings. "Who's that?"

"Smith McCain."

"Bull."

"He's a bull all right, and I'm not saying I killed him, not even hurt him much, just that I stabbed him with that blade. He attacked us. Killed my friend, Zeke. Killed my love . . . Daisy Rose. She's the one I'm trying to get back."

"I might have been born dumb, but that birthing wasn't yesterday. You're trying to make a sign or a story out of something to convince me to travel with you."

"No, it's the truth."

"It's a crossbuck like your tales, a punch of exaggeration."

"Those crossbucks are true," Luke said. "I'm telling you what happened. You're meant to be part of this."

"I'm meant to make song."

"And I wager you will, though the tune may sound different than you expect."

King snuffed, went back to dragging the strings. "Bull."

Luke asked, "Why're you on this train?"

"Don't mean a thing to me, just took the first train out of Meridian."

"I called this train. Saw a message to return to Jamestown."

"Virginia?" King snuffed again. "That's a long way off."

"My trains tend to skip a mite faster than normal runs."

"Your trains?"

"Like I said, I called this one."

King cast his eyes to the boxcar door, and Luke imagined him thinking it might be better to hop off here and make his way elsewhere. Then King's eyes blinked and doubled in size: The world outside had become a running blur, shapes no longer discernible, even the colors mashed and whirled like an egg beater at work. It must have been an unrecognizable sensation that the train could be hurtling along so fast that what should have been the ground turned as washed-out as the sky, like moving through a bank of high-velocity fog that muffled even the sound of acceleration.

King paled and dropped the guitar, his fingers scrabbling for handholds in the floor to grip. "I'm gonna be sick."

"You won't," Luke replied. "You're just as fine as you were before you knew we were going this brisk."

"Brisk ain't the word I'd use."

"We'll slow soon enough."

King looked out the door again at the frightful way light seemed to bend and twist, like they were shooting through a tunnel underground or through some cosmic tapestry.

"Fits, don't it?" Luke asked. "You were headin' wherever providence fancied, and I just happen to be that providence."

"I don't agree to that."

"What would you call it?"

"I ain't callin' it nothing. I'm here and you're here, and we're gonna die on these tracks soon enough, but 'til then, nothing's gonna mean I'm going to your spirit world."

"You won't die on my train, King. And I'm not forcing you anywhere, but we both know you've been called to Athanasia, same as me."

The train careened faster.

"All I know, this is a dream." King shut his eyes tight.

"Wish it were. I wish nothing more than I'd wake up and you were Zeke, and Daisy was in my arms, and we had Hearst's riches, and the snow never froze our toes again. But is it your dream or mine, King?"

The train barreled onward.

"King," Luke repeated. "Open your eyes and tell me, is it your dream or mine?"

It took some time for King to respond, but eventually he pried apart one eyelid. They'd slowed enough for the blurs to resume normal shapes of wide pastures and wider waterways, the rises of old and distant towns, the craggy pits of played-out excavations pockmarking auburn mountains.

He sucked in a huge breath. "I can see again."

"That'll happen when you aren't closing out the world."

"You give me that shit-eating grin again and I'll—"

They rolled past a huge billboard sign: *Highway 60, Twelve Miles to Williamsburg.*

King's voice dropped off as he grit his teeth. "What's that, Williamsburg, Alabama?"

"Virginia."

"It ain't possible . . . It ain't. That's half the country away."

"We're cutting south here, toward the James River. Should be seeing Chickahominy in the distance soon enough."

"I'm closing my eyes again."

"There's some purty scenery you'll miss out on."

King didn't close his eyes, but looked out the open door, and Luke could see his chest heave up and down.

They passed tottering outbuildings and an abused water tower and a couple signs identifying Mill Creek, and another one as Turnoff to Toano, telling trains to slow for Mining Tipple.

A slope of structures broke ground, and the train slowed considerably more as it spanned a bog of loading tracks beneath that tipple. A conveyor house rattled its metal gates above them, the showy blue building built into hills and staggering upward in sections by bridges and stilts and ladders, wood screen huts crossing overhead to drop material into open hopper cars, and atop that the tower of a coal elevator soared over the bin, and a gaping drift mine lay behind it all, like a horrible mouth spewing out the commerce of platforms.

"Think this is where I'll get off," King announced. He didn't wait for a response, just gathered up his guitar and his pack and went to the door and leapt out.

"Wait!" Luke shouted, and he scrambled to nab his own possessions, as few as they were. He knew King was averse to continuing their journey, but he didn't expect him so quick in departing.

Fortunately, by the time Luke got out, King wasn't far off, just limping along the tracks toward a crossing of more tracks that cut through the staging yard beneath a coal bunker stacked on narrow uprights, like a mule balancing at the top of a stepladder. Neighboring tracks crossed from there, leading to more buildings, until each line broke free to flee for the withering forest beyond. Several dusty trains were parked abreast each other, waiting to load or offload or just takin' a coffee break, so quiet was the mainline.

"King, hold up," Luke called loud.

At this, two bulls skipped out from behind an ore car as if they'd been waiting for rail riders the whole day. Their enthusiasm upon seeing Luke and King might have been infectious if they weren't holding brutal clubs.

"Well, well," cooed one, "looks like a couple of jokers are about to meet a pair of jacks." He slapped a blackjack into an open palm, while the other man took a practice swing with his. He saw King's guitar and pointed at it with a big toothy smile.

"Oh no, no, no," King said, "I just got this." He held Robert Johnson's guitar in a death-grip to his chest.

"And you're about to lose it," the first bull said. "Now, bein' as I wouldn't want to get blood on that fine instrument, maybe I won't split your skull too deep should you hand it to my chum without asking."

"Otherwise I'm gonna teach you the good word of Smith McCain." The second man took another swing through the air like he was Lou Gehrig lining up for a home run. Both bulls were narrow-eyed hulks in overalls, and could have been inbred brothers. One showed a scar running down the left side of his face from brow to kisser, and the other showed a scar on his right side.

Luke looked back at the train they'd jumped off, and it was already long gone. Nothing moved on the rails but the brother bulls plodding toward them. Then a door opened from one of the outbuildings and some wrench-wielding workmen came out, looking like they wanted to join the festivities.

"Nicky, caught us a pair of rail bums!" one of the workmen yelled into the building, confirming Luke's worry. "Come on and get some!" More of them came rushing out.

"We're just passing through," Luke said.

"Passed through the wrong place," said Left-scar.

"Ain't cracked a bum's head in half a day," said Right-scar. "We get paid by the amount of teeth we turn in to the foreman, and currently we're under quota."

Luke instinctively ran his tongue over his teeth, thinking he wasn't keen on losing any of them.

Something glimmered bright, pulling his gaze away from the surrounding men: A sign.

A staircase ran along the blue conveyor house and above it, scrawled in two-foot high exclamation, was the mark of Athanasia. Luke's spirits did a cartwheel, though he guessed the stairs were about sixty feet away on the other side of the bulls, and that was a detour not likely to occur.

"What's so bad about a man hoppin' a ride, anyway?" King asked. "We ain't bothering no one."

"Your ugly mug bothers me," said Left-scar. "The smell of you bothers me. Your brand new clothes like you stole 'em off a mannequin bothers me. Your kinky hair, the lice you carry. I could go on."

"You offend our sensitivities," added his mirror.

"You sure look like a sensitive lot," King said.

The group of wrench-wielding workmen came nearer, grinning, and they didn't look better off than any other 'bo, wearing ragged clothes and unshorn whiskers themselves.

Luke corralled his nerves and thought about the train they'd just rode . . . thought to bring it back . . . *come back* . . . A part of him detached the way it had during the tornado, seeming to meld into the spirit of the train. Even though the engine and cars weren't at his fingers, nor even in sight, he could sense it, could discern its pulse on the steel rail, the taste of oil on the chassis, soot in the boiler, feel the heat of its steam . . . reaching . . . reaching . . . bringing it back.

"Boy, wake up," Luke heard someone say. "This ain't no daydream."

"Can't wish us away." Snickers, laughs.

Shouts.

He'd caught that train and yanked it fast like a recoil; the engine came shrieking backward down the tracks. Luke opened his eyes and jerked King forward across the rails separating them from the bulls on the other side.

The train whistled past, wind catching at his hair and clothes, and King stumbled, pulling them both down.

"Get up," Luke yelled over the train's clattering. "Run, now!"

"Where? We're cut off!"

The workmen had scattered, some barreled over by the speed of the backward train, while others waved wrenches at it menacingly.

"Follow the track, circle around," Luke said, pointing to the conveyor house. "That way."

They took off at a serious sprint, and the train slowed and stopped, blocking the track, ready to start chugging forward again.

The bulls and workmen got over their surprise fast enough. It must have been a dull day at the coal mine offices, for those men were enthusiastically disinclined to let their playthings escape.

"Get 'em!" went the shared cry.

Luke led the way to Athanasia, and King followed, quick as roadrunners. He knew King saw that glowing hobo sign ahead too, and imagined him inwardly groaning: At least it'd be a spot better than at present . . . *maybe.*

They fled to the conveyor house and went under its staircase and out the other side, passing into the deadeye, and the bulls and workmen didn't see them again, even once Luke and King ducked back, crossing a walkway to return to the rail yard they'd just escaped, moving amongst the head-scratching men like specters.

"Hell'd they go?" Left-scar muttered. He returned from under the staircase where it ended in a brick enclosure, surrounded by furnace pumps and the walkway.

Luke watched the men make some of the saddest expressions he'd ever seen, children whose Christmas presents are snatched away before getting opened. Right-scar's lip curled out and trembled, and he looked to throw a hissy fit. Luke almost felt bad for him, then straightened himself out. If it wasn't for the entrance to Athanasia, he'd be toothless by now.

A flash of movement caught Luke's eye, something in the timbered woods opposite the mining outpost. His senses alerted that someone saw them, was coming for them . . . Another flash, and it was a figure, not so much walking as bounding in quick bursts, the way a plume of smoke billows up and then dissipates, then billows again, only in swift, nearing flares. "King, we got more company."

"I can't wait," King said sourly. "Could it be another slave catcher, or maybe a pissed bull, or how 'bout someone worse?"

"Person's alone at least," Luke said. "Think it's a woman . . . "

"Don't mean anything to me. Could be Lizzie Borden with an axe."

"Ain't her. I know."

"Won't ask."

As the figure emerged from the woods, recognition came, and Luke let out a sigh of relief so loud King might have thought he'd choked on something. "It's Pocahontas."

"Is that good or bad?"

"For us, it's good," Luke answered. "Being as she's the reason I came here to Jamestown. But for them . . . "

The Indian princess bent down and picked up a rock the size of her fist, and launched it with the speed of a Lefty Grove fastball. It bashed the back of Right-scar's head, and he flew forward like he'd been running and tripped over a root. The others looked at him like a dolt while he lay stunned and even still as he rose, muttering and rubbing at the back of his head, until they forgot about it, returning to search for the runaway 'bos.

Luke told her, "That pleasure only goes so far."

"I have found no limits to it." She launched another rock, and a workman's head caved in at the temple. Eventually he shook it off.

"Stories I heard, you're supposed to be a sweet princess," King said.

"Stories you heard are fables."

"Don't get her started," Luke told King, then to her, "It's real nice to see you again . . . and here in Jamestown like you said. I just didn't think . . . I mean, after last time . . . "

"The Code Maker has called for you, and I come to assist. He rewrites my story each time."

"To make you terrifying?" King ventured.

"To tell the truth. I am a warrior like my father, like my brothers, like my sisters, not a love-struck doe."

"And no one amongst us will doubt that," Luke said, "though I'd like to ask, pretty please, if you wouldn't ever cut off your head in front of me again."

King sputtered.

Pocahontas shrugged. "Time for you to call your train, hobo. To the Code Maker, I take you."

LUKE, KING, AND POCAHONTAS, 1942

They rode a brand-new steamer on the Seaboard Air Line Railroad, far back inside a baggage car that swayed like a cradle. Luke asked, "So where is he this time?"

"You will see," Pocahontas answered.

"Being I'm the one steering this train, a direction would help."

Pocahontas sighed, shot him a squint. "South. We must have caution speaking his location."

"Even with me?"

"Ears are everywhere."

"Huh. I'm sure those ears are bleedin' from exhaustion, you're so garrulous."

She took out her stone hatchet and twirled it between lithe fingers, eyes closed, silent.

King caught Luke's eye, and Luke shrugged. Around them, trunks and bags and cases and packs thumped and rattled and rustled. King shifted his guitar between arms, absent-mindedly strumming a few strings. "What now?"

"We're off to see Sequoyah. Stop me if you've heard this before, but he's the one who writes the Hobo Code."

King stared at him.

Luke added, "Suppose I should explain."

"Suppose so."

Luke made his first genuine laugh all week and told King everything over the next hour, as they travelled through the Carolinas, and through Georgia, and through Florida.

Afterward, King was quiet for some time before he finally spoke. "The trio that set upon Zeke, the woman with the pitchfork, the two men . . . those are the ones who came after me."

"Yeah, I figured."

"They're with Franklin? But why?"

"I don't know, but you said they wanted to enslave you. Ben has some people working for him who don't seem happy with their lot, whom he calls 'servants.' Guessing that ties in."

"And Franklin's trying to take over the world of the dead?"

"The world of the *remembered*."

"Semantics, it won't affect us."

"It will someday, King. Someday for us all."

King sucked in a breath and spat it out. "Damn."

Pocahontas interrupted. "Here we halt."

Luke didn't pause, but brought the train to a gentle stop. They got out, and Luke let the train go free to carry on. They'd departed under signage that read: *Route 90. Seaboard Passenger Station, Tallahassee, 2 Miles.*

"It don't matter you told me already, and that I went through it before," King said, "but it can't be that we passed through half the east coast in an hour."

"And I was takin' us slow."

"Don't rub it in."

Pocahontas motioned them to follow, and they did, single-file from the crowded station onto the roadway, through a Chevy car lot, then behind fruit vendor stands and a sweet shop that made Luke's mouth water. They crossed Lafayette Street, which was a tunnel of rich weeping willows and ghostly murmurs. Red pox zoomed by.

They went down other streets where the usual stores got more crowded together, and cars and stray dogs came and went, and they passed light poles adorned by war posters, and then a tall Spanish conquistador sauntered past, his arm brushing the hilt of a great sword. Another conquistador sat nearby, slowly polishing his silver breastplate under the sun. The armor's glare hit Luke's eye like a finger poke, and the conquistador nodded to them with the slightest perceivable motion.

Luke just squinted tears, and King made a worried face. Pocahontas finally spoke again. "We walk on a trail named for them. De Soto, that bastard Spanish slaver who came here before the Pilgrims."

"Longer I come around these parts, more things seem the same," King muttered.

Pocahontas silenced them quickly with one finger, then made a whistling sound, two shrill notes like a warbler.

From the shadows of a streetside church, the figure of a stooped woman emerged for a second, and Luke caught a glimpse of dark brown skin, a rough gown, a kerchief. She whistled back, mimicking the two-note pattern, then vanished.

"We move," Pocahontas said.

Luke's reaction was a double-take. "Was that—?"

"Your friend, yes," Pocahontas said. "Tubman helps, watching Sequoyah's cabin. Her railroad came through here long ago."

"I'd been lookin' for her."

"She knows. Is why she helps now."

"Hold on, that was years ago."

"Time does not mean as much to us as to you. What is a year or ten in the span of centuries?"

"Still . . ."

Pocahontas shrugged. "Come."

They went over Holland Drive and into the city's heart. Passed kids playing hopscotch, passed a honky tonk pool hall. Passed a diner that served pickled quail eggs and gator gumbo, where families lined up out the door. A homeless man beat time on spoons from his sidewalk stage, and King's eyes sparkled, a wistful look to join in.

"Another time," Luke said. King satisfied himself with a sigh and some humming.

They cut through a beautiful park and soon arrived at the driveway leading up to a long red brick building with a fancy-columned portico and tall gable roof that reminded Luke of his childhood home back in Savannah with his mother and stepfather.

"Governor's old house," Pocahontas said flatly. "He named it Apalachee."

"Sequoyah's there?"

She nodded once.

They started up the driveway when Luke sensed, rather than saw, a quick movement from shadows along the thick-treed yard. There was a bird call—the warbler sound—but three shrill notes instead of two, and the pattern repeated, twice and quick. *Harriet . . .*

Pocahontas barred one arm with a gut-wrenching wallop across King and Luke to halt. Her other arm snapped out to brandish a wood-and-stone knife. Luke didn't know where she'd been hiding it, but the knife was in the open now, its chiseled blade pointed toward someone following them up the long driveway.

It took Luke a moment to figure what he was seeing: A man shambling toward them, looking no more than what might remain of a scarecrow after it's weathered a couple hurricanes and dried out by crawling into a pit of flaming charcoal.

He felt Pocahontas tense, but the nearer the man got, the less Luke worried. The scarecrow man looked like any other hobo who hadn't eaten more than some hard crackers in the past month, now grown gaunt and haunted by his days. The man dragged his feet like each was a brick, and the legs pulling them were nothing but frayed string. His anguished gray eyes were piercing.

Luke called uncertainly, "Howdy, 'bo."

"Not hobo," Pocahontas said. "Darkness taint."

The sight of her knife aimed his way didn't give the withered man any pause. He closed the distance between them, one gasping lurch after another. When he finally spoke, his voice was the husk of empty honeycomb or the sloughed skin of a shed snake, dry and wispy and crumbling. "*Virgie . . .*"

"Stay away," Pocahontas ordered.

He didn't. Sunken eyes darted to her, then down to the knife, as he tottered closer. Then he turned to King Shaw—

King held his guitar tight to his chest, like a shield to keep between them, and it felt warm in his hands, almost beginning to tremble. The ragged man looked him up and down, then drew in on the guitar.

"Please," the man whispered, holding out one trembling hand. He reminded King of an addict, panting and sweating and stumbling forward like nothing else mattered once he got an eyeful of something he wants.

It didn't surprise King either, what with his drugged appearance, when the man tripped over his own lurching feet and fell. King's surprise came at what he saw on the man's back, and then he nearly shrieked.

Next to him, Luke gasped hard, while Pocahontas just kept pointing her knife. She said real plain, "See, darkness makes sick."

The man's back was covered by a monstrous leech the size of a small bear, and he seemed to wear it like some sort of hideous knapsack. The leech glared at them from one giant eye while a million strands of wet filament fed into the man's flesh, each line taut and swollen from gorging.

King had burned leeches off his own legs after fording swampy marshes, but he'd never believed anything like this could exist. Purple veins wound round the mottled mass, while its yellow Cyclopean eye dripped noxious slime.

The scarecrow man slowly stood again, struggling under his burden, but he couldn't seem to walk any longer. He'd been sucked dry of energy, spirit, strength, and anything else one could lose before ceding extermination. Around his frail neck a jaunty tie flapped in bright striped colors, and it seemed so at odds to the man's plight that King's revulsion turned to commiseration.

"Friend, is there anything we can do to help?"

"My . . . guitar . . . " the man croaked. "Virgie . . . "

"This?" King held the guitar tighter, and it kept getting warmer, and there was no denying it now shook in his hands, a thing waking from hibernation, getting excited for adventures in store. "Who are you?"

"Robert . . . Johnson."

The guitar wrenched back and forth in King's hands, trying to break free.

"Please," Robert said, holding up a hand.

King glanced at Luke, and Luke nodded to do it, the unspoken look in his eyes of knowing a man's cross needed lightening. King took a cautious step and offered up Virgie.

Robert's fingers wrapped around the guitar, and both he and it looked like a lightning bolt went through, were they alit in joy. There were some rapturous hallelujah sounds, and Robert smiled so big his ears twisted back, and the leech let out a farting sound like a dismayed moan. Robert shouted, "Virgie!"

And he strummed a sound across its sweet strings that rang as ghostly as it did beautiful, the notes cutting through King in melancholy and in longing for everything he'd done and everything he'd dreamed. And by mournful chords did Robert Johnson appear to grow stronger, as if reversing the leech's consumption, and what had been taken from him began to restore. His face flushed, he stood taller. The music howled and wailed, and it wasn't just Robert playing, but the guitar itself singing like each string was a voice in chorus.

Pocahontas's knife went away. Luke said, "Lord, that's gorgeous."

"What happened to you?" King asked.

Robert Johnson filled his lungs, and his whole body swelled as he sang, and the chords spilled the blues he was known for. "Was damned at the crossroads, and I'm damned ever more. Demon'll never stop feeding 'less I play for."

King said, "But we're in this land of memories, and I known of you playing a guitar already. Hell, everyone in the south knows of your guitar. How'd you come not to have one here?"

With each word of response, Robert's voice grew ever stronger, losing the sick desperation he'd so recently given off.

"Brother, I don't like it here one bit. But God have mercy, I like the alternative even less. I'm remembered for selling my soul to play the blues, and it's true. But Scratch don't make damnation easy t'all. See, I can't hold none other but the one I traded my due. Virgie's my soul now, and you've returned it. Playing her's the only way to ease this rue."

King thought about the last of his gold he'd used to buy the guitar.

As if reading his mind, Robert said, "I ain't got nothing to pay you back, mister, but my dearest gratitude. I'll do anything you want, anything I can, only I can't ever stop playing or that demon'll go back to feedin'. But I'll sing of you. Oh, mister, I'll sing all y'all 'til the end of time."

"Not of me," Pocahontas said. "I want no more."

"Will you sing about Daisy Rose?" Luke prompted.

"Tell her to me true."

And Luke did. He spoke of Daisy's beauty and her spirit, told how she'd been murdered, how Zeke was murdered, maintained Zeke's strength and loyalty, though he was gone, and how they all came to be here now. And King spoke of his own life, of leaving his family, of searching for better ways, of his quests and dreams, and all else he'd done and why.

Robert Johnson's voice soared in a strange cry that was nothing like King had heard in his life, stark misery and sweet psalms, and Robert sang all the stories of King Shaw and Luke Thacker and their friends, and when he ended, he walked back down that long road with no end, singing them again and again to all who'd listen, and those who listened were many.

King took a moment to reflect. "Since I'm givin' things away, I guess I can't deny you always been telling me the truth. Here, this is yours."

He handed Luke the small pocket knife with a nicked, dull edge.

"Thank you."

King and Luke and Pocahontas went into the old Governor's house, Apalachee . . .

LUKE AND COMPANY, 1942

. . . and arrived inside an old cabin.

Sequoyah was there, sitting behind an old table that was covered in dust. He looked unchanged, unmoved from the last time Luke had seen him.

Another man stood next to him: a handsome black man, wearing a shining tuxedo, who was in the process of pulling two furry white ears out of a silk top hat. The man looked at them suddenly, stuffed the ears back inside, then placed the hat on his head.

"Welcome again," Sequoyah said to Luke. He motioned to the man in tuxedo. "This is Black Herman."

Herman nodded first to King Shaw. "Son."

"Son of a bitch is more like it," King said.

"Shawell Kingston Pawłowski," Sequoyah said, "I welcome you to my home. But please leave those unpleasantries at the door. Time is short and plans need be made."

"You're Sequoyah, huh?"

"Yes. I write the Code."

King opened his mouth, and Luke guessed an insult was on his tongue, but instead King sneezed. He opened his mouth to say something else and sneezed again. It wasn't unintended, Luke knew. Sequoyah waited patiently until King kept his mouth shut, then he gave a tight smile. He motioned at three old wicker chairs surrounding the table. "Sit or stand, the choice is yours, but ears must listen now."

Pocahontas nudged Luke and King forward, and they took a seat.

Sequoyah steepled his fingers at Luke. "Have you considered what I asked of you?"

"Yeah," Luke admitted. "Thought on it like you said, and you were right. So you help me rescue Daisy and I'll do what you need, carry on this banner of the Code, help others with it, whatever."

"Good. But there's more."

Luke raised an eyebrow. "Here we go."

"First we must defeat our enemies."

"There's no end of those, is there?" King finally got out, his eyes flicking toward Herman.

Sequoyah caught the dark glance. "Must we clear the air now of family squabbles? Black Herman has been my caretaker, of sorts."

"Of sorts?" King asked.

"Your father keeps me hidden from pursuers. His talents are greater than even Houdini's."

"The Handcuff King stole all my tricks for himself," Herman cut in, pulling up the lapels of his tuxedo. "Still will not admit to it either. We both died young, but he had the Hollywood movies to memorialize him. If only I had a bit more time to cement my reputation . . . Death is a fickle courtesan, and when she courts you there is no rebuffing her seductions."

"At least, I might add, you're certainly more of a moralist than he," Sequoyah added. He lifted an open hand to King. "In life, your father fought the Jim Crow policies; he used his success for activism. Now he is committed to me to do the same."

King narrowed an eye. "I'm sure he feels good that you're stroking him off, but—"

"But you hold it against him that he first brought you here, only to leave you abandoned."

"That about nails it, just as he done to me in life."

Sequoyah rubbed his temples. "It was me who called him away that day, when you first visited Athanasia. Benjamin Franklin had found me. There was a posse of gunslingers at my door with nooses and knives and all sorts of other horrible implements. I called upon your father to save me, and he did so with not a moment to spare. Had he chosen to see you over me, you both would be together, best friends even, while working under the slave servitude of Franklin. That great fraud was on the verge of toppling all the balance of power that time. But I escaped, and reset the scales."

King didn't move, but he seemed to deflate a little, soften around the edges. "I see."

"As I have said before, I am sorry, son," Herman said. He held his hat in hand, like a beggar in attrition.

Luke laid a tentative hand on King's leg. "I'd let it go, I was you."

King sucked in a big breath, cleared his throat. "Maybe. So what's next?"

"It's Franklin, as I was saying," Sequoyah went on. "He is marshalling his forces, and we must marshal our own."

"Who are our forces?" Luke asked.

"Look around."

Luke did, expecting to see a deluge of appearing forms or signs. Pocahontas cleared her throat. Herman looked away. Luke said, "I count us five."

"I knew you could do it," Sequoyah said.

"Some sass from the man asking my help," Luke sputtered. "I mean, who else is with us?"

"Harriet comes and goes, but she's not much of a fighter, you know. Stealth and planning are more her thing."

"And we're going to stop Ben, and the Sons of Liberty, and the slave catchers, and the hired guns, all by ourselves?" Luke asked.

Sequoyah shrugged. "As bad as Franklin is, at least he can be reasoned with . . . perhaps. But there's another who's joined his cause, one who will never stop, and he's got a wild hair for you, Luke . . . Smith McCain."

"Hell."

"Indeed."

"Can't you just rewrite the great and almighty Code or something? Erase them all out of existence?"

"We can rewrite the Code all we want, but it cannot remove the memory of people like Franklin from our minds," Sequoyah said. "We must forget him first, then he will be erased. But right now, he's too powerful, too well-ingrained into our shared consciousness."

"Can't say I'm getting any more excited for this."

"There are ways to defeat all, but each person is different. Of Franklin and McCain, you must defeat one by cunning and the other by violence."

"Tell me you at least got some sort of plan to do so," King asked. "Something to give us a fighting chance?"

"The plan," Sequoyah answered, "is to confront him. And on his own turf."

"I'm under-inspired with confidence," Luke muttered.

"You've a week to come up with something better," Sequoyah replied. He began running his finger through the dust on his table, drawing symbols.

"What's in a week?"

"Field Day in Boston, and much of the city will be present," Herman interrupted, moving closer. "Benjamin Franklin is making his big push, and there we must push back, firmly and conclusively."

"So what'll we be doing, besides going up to him to say 'howdy'?" King asked.

"First is outreach," Sequoyah said.

"Which starts with something up the sleeve," Herman added with a grin, showing the cuffs of his sleeves. A document with some sort of speech on it peeked out, then slipped back under. "A message, in fact, to deliver to the masses."

"Jesus, if your tactics are as hackneyed as your act, we're all doomed," King said, though a smile finally broke through.

"We must all say what needs to be said," Sequoyah added. "The truth of things, to counter Franklin's lies." He nodded at Luke. "I'm hoping to get some help in that."

"Yeah, sure," Luke said. "Though whatever army of hobos you're envisioning rushing to your aid probably ain't gonna happen. Our concerns are generally more about trying to find our next meal rather than joining someone else's battle."

"And there's less of your people too, I've seen. Men going off to war, finding the work long sought, building houses, having families."

"Sorry this flush economy is gettin' in your way."

"You know what I mean, Luke. Whether rich or poor, the stories are the same."

Luke sighed. "Yeah, I get it."

"And speaking of *getting*," Herman said with his most dazzling smile, "the time has come to get going, to get our message out, and to get others involved. I am off to work some magic!"

A bright flash and a curling puff of smoke later, he vanished, leaving Luke and King thoroughly confused.

DAISY ROSE, 1942

Behind the large pale pink building of Boston Library, there's a long row house that's built half-submerged into the ground, the single entrance lying at the bottom of half a dozen sharp concrete steps that seem to descend from a back alley into the blackest of tunnels.

Normal folks—those alive and carefree to the goings on around them—walk right by this building every day, pass the white-clothed people being led in and out, and don't think a thing about it. But for a plaque reading *Devereux House and Slave Quarters, Historic Landmark*, this building exists only in the world of memory.

It took Daisy no time at all to figure this out, though she had plenty of time to mull it all over. She'd been held as part of Franklin's "labor force" for nearly three years. Three long, miserable, reviled years of fear, hatred, and woe.

Slaves, that's what they were. And it didn't matter their race or the color of their skin—dark or light, Oriental or Eskimo—if they had a voice or could wash his drawers, Ben worked them until their second death, and that second death was everywhere. Others in captivity who were younger than she, more "freshly dead" than she, were taken at any hour by the horrible pox.

Daisy was one of the longest-lasting in his servitude, and told daily by the foremen that today would surely be her last. She didn't know why she outlasted the others, but thought dimly that perhaps Luke had something to do with it.

Luke, Luke, where are you . . . ? she'd wonder, though even those fleeting regards of hope came to her less and less often as she spent her days whispering to the living of Franklin's accomplishments, and most nights too, doing the same.

Sometimes the laborers were chained down inside the old Devereux House for reasons unknown. That's where they'd been the night before, and only when the sun came up in the morning were they unshackled by the foremen: tall Lewis Robards with his beaver-felted top hat and barbed whip; Martha "Patty" Cannon with wild black hair and a long pitchfork; and massive, bearded Anderson Jennings, who gripped his blunderbuss so tight his knuckles seemed locked into claws.

The laborers were led up the stairs and outside, and Daisy hated herself for the knowledge that she preferred doing what was next rather than rotting underground in that cold and lightless building. At least working was outdoors.

The first living person she came to, she whispered into his ear, "Benjamin Franklin is your loving savior."

That afternoon, a sidewalk vendor lifted his cap and wiped the crease of sweat off his brow. "What's it today, Al? Ice-cold lemonade? A sausage dog?"

"One of each, Hank."

"Nickel apiece makes a dime." Hank, the vendor, pulled out a frankfurter from his three-wheeled cart, glancing up the length of Hanover Street. "Sure is a hot one."

"Sure is, buddy."

Neither saw Daisy approach from behind and whisper to Hank, "Benjamin Franklin invented the odometer, thereby increasing the efficiency of mail carriers."

Hank nodded, puffing out his chest and running his thumbs up the sides of a grease-stained apron. "Say, Al, you know that Benjamin Franklin invented the odometer, thereby increasing efficiency of mail carriers?"

"Well, history never was my strong suit."

Daisy moved behind Al. "Benjamin Franklin created the nation's first political cartoon."

Al took a thoughtful sip from his lemonade, realizing he *did* recall something about history. He repeated Daisy's remark, and Hank nodded along. "Nothing Franklin couldn't do, was there?"

Barefoot men and women wearing crisp white linens moved all along Hanover Street, whispering into unsuspecting ears of strolling pedestrians and slow-moving drivers. Daisy guessed they'd be done here in a few minutes and would move to spread Franklin's message to the next block. The labor force was growing, and their message spreading far.

Along the sidewalk came a tall dark man wearing a black-tailed tuxedo. He paused at the vendor's cart to stretch out his back and take in the city view. Daisy moved to him, barely wondering that the sun did nothing to cause sweat or flush on the handsomely-dressed jack.

She whispered, "Benjamin Franklin founded America's first insurance company."

The man nodded slowly and whispered back, "Benjamin Franklin is a phony, and you well know it."

Her gasp was startling even to herself.

The man continued. "Keep whispering into my ear, but listen carefully. You are Daisy Rose, a friend of Lucas Thacker, are you not?"

Daisy's voice caught. She opened her mouth, but nothing came out, so she gave two quick nods, then mouthed air into the man's ear. She glanced across the street to see Lewis Robards unleash a monstrous flurry of whippings upon a man who hadn't done something right. The poor man screamed. Anderson Jennings was nearby too, but arguing with the woman, Cannon. They both jabbed fingers into each others' chests. One of their voices rose: "The new gun ain't one of us, he's just a train bull!"

The handsome jack went on. "In one week's time, the city of Boston will hold its annual Field Day, a charity event with baseball and entertainers. Over eighteen thousand people are expected to attend: political leaders, newspapers, orators, and luminaries. It is assured that Mr. Franklin will be present. Here is what you must do . . . "

And into Daisy's ear he whispered plans and devices. When finished, the man pulled away for a moment, then leaned back in. "I am Black Herman. Pass my message along to others in captivity."

Daisy gulped, found her voice. "But Luke—"

"Luke will be there. He will find you. I must move on."

Herman cracked his knuckles and walked down the sidewalk to a pale old woman in white, pausing to quickly speak with her.

Daisy whispered anew into Hank the vendor's ear, "To hell with Benjamin Franklin."

Hank nodded along. "Yeah."

"Benjamin Franklin's dumber than a pail of piss."

"I always thought so," Hank muttered.

Black Herman moved along to the next white-robed person, a man with wild eyes and hair who looked half-savage, and whom Daisy knew had once been Paul Revere. After Herman spoke, Revere gave such a giant smile the stitches split from his lips.

Herman moved on to the next, and then the next laborer, whispering to each.

A voice blasted across the street like a fusillade. "Hey, you!"

Daisy turned in its direction. The white-robed people turned. Black Herman turned. The voice was aimed at him. It came from Lewis Robards.

"The hell you mixing up with our workers, boy?" Robards roared.

Anderson Jennings and Martha Cannon came at Herman from across the street.

Herman looked around, all eyes upon him. The sound of a drum began to thump through the air, and he spoke. Herman's voice was loud, as if speaking into a microphone before his grand audience.

"Gentlemen and lovely ladies all, little did you know that coming here today would not be of the regular griefs you daily endure, but rather that your blues should be lifted by the good fortune of laying eyes upon me, the illustrious, the stupendous, the amazing Black Herman!"

A cymbal crashed, and lights flashed behind, then upon, Herman's face. He continued, "I am slave to no man, and have come here today to tell you all—"

Jennings fired his blunderbuss rifle, and Herman rocked backward.

Herman gasped, strained out, "Apologies, but this show is postponed—" He threw his hands to the ground, and with a bright flash and a curling puff of smoke, the drums, light, and Herman all flicked away. Only a faint sulfuric smell of burnt powder lingered.

"Damn it, Jennings," Cannon shrilled. "I wanted t'hear what else he was gonna say."

"It wasn't gonna be how purty you are, that's for sure," Jennings answered, his voice more growl than decipherable words.

Cannon jabbed her pitchfork at the last person Herman had spoken with, a gangly, slope-headed man with fewer hairs than he had teeth. "What'd he tell you?"

"Nothin'," the man muttered. "He din' say but nothin'."

Cannon's shriek was hysterical, a mad frenzy that came upon her. "Damn liar!" and she rammed the pitchfork through the man's stomach, twisted and pulled out, and the man's guts came with it. The man didn't make a sound, but seemed to smile as he fell, and the pox came swiftly upon him.

Lewis Robards shrugged. "Well, that's that." He kicked a heavy boot at the man he'd earlier whipped. "Back to it, shit heel."

That worker crossed the street, and Daisy heard him whimper to the living: "Obey Benjamin Franklin, or you'll suffer the fury of Smith McCain."

LUKE AND COMPANY, 1942, CONTINUED

Black Herman reappeared in Sequoyah's cabin in a big magician's puff of smoke and promptly toppled over, a rivulet of blood pouring through his white starched shirt, past his clutching fingers, down his proud tuxedo.

"Daddy!" King said, and there was no hesitancy in his voice.

"I made it a good show," Herman said. He spoke real soft as he rolled over on the dusty floor. "The word, it started . . ."

The others reacted as expected: Pocahontas just watched stoically. Luke tensed, moved forward with a gasp and shout on his lips, then drew back, not wanting to get in the way. Sequoyah was already crouched over him, an old, leathery hand on the magician's forehead. He said, "Goodbye, old friend. Till we meet in another place."

King's voice rose. "Hold on, he'll just reappear again, right? Like all the rest of you?"

Red dots started appearing in the air.

"This time, I think not," Sequoyah quietly admitted. "His memory has been languishing while the ploys of Houdini and Harry Kellar have gained perseverance."

Herman's eyes started to wobble, and the pox fell upon him.

"Son," he whispered, and King leaned in close. "You sold my coin, but I retrieved it for you."

Herman flicked open his fingers, and where nothing had been a moment earlier, there was now a familiar gold coin with his winking likeness. "A memento . . . Remember me."

King took the coin, then Herman's clutching fingers relaxed, his chest heaved, and he was done. For a moment his lingering outline seemed to burn a hole through existence, seeming just nothingness, until it filled in with the floor of Sequoyah's cabin, and the pox went away.

"And now we are less one," Sequoyah said quietly.

Luke stuttered, taking a step back. "I don't even know what the hell just happened . . . He was fine a moment ago, now he's dead?!"

"Such is all our time, in the span of existence."

"Fuck that," Luke shouted, "I ain't rollin' over to take a gun blast for no reason."

"His reason will be apparent soon," Sequoyah said. "As will your own reasons."

"Your riddles, chief, they're gettin' even more baffling."

"Field Day, in one week. It's where we make our final stand. Use your time to prepare. I will work the Code, Pocahontas will rebuild. King, watch over Luke, and Luke, call upon your allies, spread your final tales."

"That it?"

Sequoyah nodded. "Isn't it always?"

SMITH MCCAIN, 1942

Most folks don't know this, but Smith McCain has a weakness.

It's an indulgence that causes addiction as much as any narcotic, a vulnerability to one's health, a detriment to concentration, logic, and even emotion. It's a vice not unknown to any child or romantically spurned lover, and a seduction so powerful and sweet it can influence even the most unyielding of men with its presence.

Chocolate.

That's right, get one bar or block of the cocoa in front of McCain, and *O!* watch his eyes alight with yearning. Smith McCain will lap like a dog or dance the jitterbug to get a taste of the confectioner's delight.

See, it was Tricky Willie who got him started. McCain came upon Willie one night while ridin' a flatbed, but Willie told McCain he couldn't be harmed, since chocolate is the fabled ambrosia of the gods, and Willie was eating it just then. Naturally McCain didn't believe it and cracked his knuckles in preparation to put that claim to the test. But Willie offered him some, and said he'd throw *himself* off the train if the taste of chocolate didn't make McCain feel glorious. Well, the taste *did* make McCain feel glorious, and while he was wrapped up in savoring that sugary treat, Willie threw himself off the train anyway, to escape McCain's wrath once the aftertaste had petered out.

Now it's come to be that Smith McCain's got an incurable craving, and he's just as easy to trick today as he was then. Spread the word: Any 'bo wants to get away, he just offers a bit of Hershey or Cadbury to pay his toll, which is a mite cheaper than normal train fare would be, but worth the cost to save a beating from that old bull.

And speaking of old, it's a sad thing when age catches up to a man. The long years have begun to wear McCain down, not to mention the sluggish health from his addiction to said chocolate. Last I heard, McCain tried chasing a 'bo from a railcar, but found himself gasping for breath at no more than three paces. And that 'bo he was after didn't even have legs, but was on one of those planks with wheels, and the wheels themselves were rusty and slow-creaking, and he was going uphill.

Poor Smith McCain, gettin' older and slower and fatter . . .

A pug-faced tramp interrupted Luke's story. "Say what? That ain't the way I remember hearing 'bout Smith McCain. McCain was the meanest cuss ever to set foot on a rail, big as a mountain and tough as the devil—"

"Shut your mouth," Luke said, narrowing his eyes to cold slits. "I ever hear you talk about McCain like that again, I'll slice out your tongue, real slow, and jam it up your ass 'til you taste your own turds."

That tramp never again repeated the stories he remembered of Smith McCain, and a few years later when he died, a bit more of McCain died with him.

LUKE AND BENJAMIN, 1942

The afternoon of July 13th was just as hot and muggy and bright and beautiful as every other day that past week in Boston.

The great stadium, Fenway Park, was already two-thirds full, and only the day's pre-activities had started. It would end as standing room only, that was for sure; Field Day, Luke was told, was an enormous event for Boston, a charity exhibition baseball game with entertainers like Orson Welles and Buster Keaton to warm up the crowd before the great national pastime began, all there to raise funds for under-privileged children and war bonds to support the troops overseas, and other kinds of charity endeavors to make man feel better about himself.

A singer Luke never heard of before, Frank Sinatra, belted out the national anthem, and soldiers on leave had tears running down their faces. After that, the bigwigs started talking.

All this, Luke watched from a distance.

It wasn't long after till Benjamin Franklin made his appearance, joining the city dignitaries on a wooden platform built at the base of stadium seating, about fifty feet from, and halfway along, first base line. Ben stood there, arms behind his back, gazing triumphantly at the crowds. Next to him, unknowing of Ben's presence, was Boston's mayor Maurice Tobin, and behind them were a dozen other movers and shakers sitting in double rows in their flush three-piece suits and straw hats. John Hancock and Sam Adams stood apart, looking odder than ever in coattails and powdered wigs, like they were stage actors.

Mayor Tobin was tall and lanky, with a stony face and big horse teeth, and he knew how to talk. He gesticulated and beamed and gave a mighty eloquent speech, and Ben Franklin took liberty to add his two cents' worth whenever the moment inspired him, so it sounded something like this:

Tobin: " . . . Some of baseball's greatest figures are brought here today—"

Ben cut in, "—by Benjamin Franklin and the Sons of Liberty!"

Tobin: "—for the benefit of the under-privileged, and for the benefit of—"

Ben: "—everyone who supports Benjamin Franklin and the Sons of Liberty!"

The eyes of the crowd seemed to bounce back and forth, like watching a tennis match between the living in Real World and the memories in the deadeye, each vying for their own slice of attention. More people kept coming into the stadium, packing it, and the roars of footsteps and small talk and food-chewing and seat-shuffling and rustling got louder and louder.

And that wasn't all that came . . . The pox started flickering in the air in great bursts of little red dots, like the face of the sky was growing voracious freckles.

Luke thought about where he was, that the Second World War was in full swing, that technology and the greatest weapons of mass destruction ever created were expanding, populations pushing the limits of sustainability, social consciousness getting overwhelmed with growth and change and all else, and who the hell would want to remember someone like himself or the other homeless of society?

His heart filled with lead: Today was gonna be a purge.

There was more activity on the field as ball players warmed up, and there was more activity in the stands as Ben's labor force began to appear: those sad barefoot people clothed all in white, whispering into the ears of the audience while the three slave-catcher "foremen" watched over—Lewis Robards, Anderson Jennings, and wicked Martha Cannon. The crowd might as well have been caught in a spell, between listening to Ben pontificate and hearing his subjugated workers whisper all manner of assertions into their ears.

Luke couldn't take any more. He felt himself sinking into oblivion, faster and faster, and this was his last push to free all the others sinking with him.

He made his entrance.

By now it seemed the easiest thing in the world for Luke to call a train in the deadeye. He thought it and it occurred; near as effortless as the thought going into lifting his hand to shake hello with a pal, did the engine pull up to his feet. Luke chose a Boston and Maine train, a big P-4 engine with the elephant ears-styled smokebox and metal shrouds and an air pump on her pilot's deck. She was majestic, enormous, intimidating, sterling silver and gold leaf lettering with a B&M herald gleaming under the sun. She came in pulling a half dozen passenger cars that nothing but the word "charming" might describe.

And that's what he rode in on, crashing through Fenway Park's service gate. Railroad tracks riveted and wended and leaped their way in front of him, and Luke made sure to hang on to that engine's whistle as they burst out onto the field. The ground trembled like an earthquake. Fencing and walls exploded. People screamed. Players dove out of the way by reflex, not knowing why. The stadium seemed to pull back from him in all directions.

Luke had all the attention he wanted now, and he'd never wanted much to begin with.

"Benjamin Franklin!" he roared, swinging himself out of the engine cab one-armed and dropping fast onto the turf. "You goddamned has-been! You liar, cheater, swindler! You killer, you bastard, you monster!"

Ben took the microphone entirely now, edging wide-eyed Tobin out of the way. He said easily, "And Luke Thacker. You . . . *nothing.*"

That hurt.

Ben went on. "You who come from nothing, you who have nothing, you appear here to relieve our nation of me, its greatest figurehead?"

"Oh, I've got *something*, all right," Luke said. "The means to make you go away."

The door of the first passenger car behind the engine opened, and King Shaw hopped out, landing awkwardly on his weak leg. His cap tumbled off, but he caught it, barely.

Ben said, "Another nobody. Oh, that's rich."

The door of the next passenger car flung open, and Pocahontas somersaulted out, a jeweled bow and quiver of bright arrows glinting beneath the sun.

Ben's voice dropped. "I see."

The door of the next passenger car casually opened, and there stood Sequoyah, holding a flat piece of slate board in one hand and a piece of chalk in the other.

Ben's face blanched. "My nemesis." He licked at his lips, a sight not unlike a snake's tongue testing what's on the wind. He went on, "Though to say I *wasn't* expecting you would not be true, for as the world knows, Benjamin Franklin *always* speaks the truth, and Benjamin Franklin is *always* prepared."

He snapped his fingers, and Wyatt, Morgan, and Virgil Earp walked onto the field, pistols dead-aimed straight at Luke and the others.

"Well, ain't you a one-trick pony," Luke called out.

"Then how's this for a new one?" Ben replied, showing his teeth.

There was a rustle from the home team dugout, a movement of something heavy, and a clacking sound. Luke had to squint, let his eyes adjust to see into those deep shadows.

When he saw it, he wished he hadn't. There was a Gatling gun mounted on big spoked wheels.

"Dr. Gatling, you see," Ben said, "was an inventor by heart, much like myself, and happens to be a friendly acquaintance of the Earp brothers."

The man behind the gun was lost in the gloom of the dugout, but Luke saw a hand crank turn, a gear spin.

Then came a second rustle, this one from beneath the very wood platform that Ben and the dignitaries stood upon. A red-white-and-blue banner fell to the earth, and the base of the platform parted to the side.

A twelve-pounder cannon pointed out, right at them.

Ben giggled like a child. "And here's Confederate Artillery General John C. Pemberton, who before his demise was honored for action in the Indian Wars against the Seminoles."

"I hate Injuns," General Pemberton said flatly to Sequoyah.

"Give up," Ben said to them, "and maybe you'll walk away. Otherwise, I'll erase you all from existence."

Luke was clearly outnumbered, outgunned, and he knew it. But he wasn't done yet . . .

Mayor Tobin was slack-jawed, backed up to the dozen movers and shakers sitting in their double rows of chairs onstage behind Ben. He, nor anyone else, noticed two of those men slowly rise from their seats, until they held Tommy machine guns pointed out.

The first one pulled away a pair of fake reading glasses and winked: John Dillinger. He said, "Howdy."

Next to him, Pretty Boy Floyd took off his straw hat and tossed it lazily into Ben's face, just as Ben turned around, gaping. The hat bumped him in the nose and fell away.

Ben's eyes watered from the sting, the insolence, the fury. The shock. He stared point-blank at the guns and muttered, "Hell and blazes."

Luke grinned. "Guess it's a stand-off."

Ben sighed. Put on his politician's smile. "Pray tell, what is it you hope to gain from this . . . confrontation?"

"I'm not as eloquent with the vocabulary as you, but basically to stop you from being an asshole and from ruining a lot of people's lives and *after*lives."

John Hancock shuffled nervously. John Adams fake-coughed into a hankie while he looked all around. Ben just snorted. Luke noticed that in the stadiums, the people in white were still moving about, whispering into the ears of the audience. The slave catchers grinned, gloating, watching only Luke, surely thinking of the plenitude of methods by which they were gonna string him up and fry him.

Ben snapped his fingers again. The nearest slave catcher, Lewis Robards—somewhere about the tenth row above first base line—gave the slightest of nods and sidestepped to a worker in white. He wrapped a long arm around the worker's neck and lifted up a large Bowie knife.

It took Luke only one double-take to see the worker Robards held was Daisy. Robards leered at him, long and hard.

"Now, in case I'm missing something," Ben said, "how exactly is it you plan to stop me? You know as well as I that if your gangster friends shoot me, I'll just come back again. Others—your lady friend, for example— won't be so fortunate."

The pox seemed to soar downward at that, a cloud descending upon them at its leisure, nearer and nearer.

"Let her go," Luke yelled. "She ain't part of this! You got no right to hold her!"

"I have every right to do what is best for the greater good. She works for me now."

"Against her will?"

Ben hooked a thumb under the sash of his pantaloons. "Her *will*? She's *dead*, boy. *Will* is not the same here, and you know it. Without purpose, you perish."

"She still has the will to be free of you, to do as she decides."

"I keep her in memory alongside me, longer than she could remain on her own. I take care of her, protect her."

"Like you would a *slave*?"

The power of a word. That was all it took for the crowd to gasp at Ben.

"You think you can paint me with that brush, boy?" Ben said. "I dedicated my life to freedom, to independence. I freed us *all* from the fetters of Her Majesty's royal subjugation."

Then the crowd was back on his side, nodding along. Someone yelled, "That's right, Benjamin Franklin!"

"Doing it while on the backs of another people don't make you much of an equalizer," Luke answered.

"And who are you to say otherwise, you *nobody*, that it wasn't I who single-handedly secured freedom all along, that it wasn't I who brought equality and harmony to the living, then *and* now?"

"Yeah, Benjamin Franklin can do no wrong!" another voice shouted. Murmurs of agreement came with it.

Ben's smile got bigger, his arrogance growing fast. "Everyone's learned I invented the lightning rod, I repealed the Stamp Act! Next they'll know it was I who discovered Neptune! I can declare myself the grand freer of slaves!"

A rattling thunk was heard as the next passenger car door on Luke's train opened, and there stood Harriet Tubman. She shook her head sternly. Her voice was harsh. "Don't you take credit for what others done, old man. You worked off the labor of slaves in your day, and you still do today."

The crowd let out a collective, "Oooh."

"I thought you were gone and buried," Ben said. "But no matter, for what you do in the shadows is of no consequence to what I achieve in the light."

"Maybe fifty years ago you could have still got away with that speech of superiority in some backwoods hovel, but not here, not *now*, not in this nation. So I come here to do what I always do, what I'm *known* to do. You let that slave girl go."

The crowd seemed to shift, raising distrustful eyebrows now, leaning forward, muttering. Ben tensed, realizing his error too late in front of all the twenty thousand or so sitting in the audience, not to mention those listening by radio all across the country. His eye twitched. "No, that girl is no such thing. She *works* for me, I take care of her, like I said. Like a laborer, a benefitted employee—"

"With a knife to her throat?" Luke asked. "Ordered by you, Benjamin Franklin?"

The scene was silent just long enough for Daisy to yell out as loud as she could, "Benjamin Franklin kidnapped me! He turned me into a slave! And he's impotent!"

Ben spluttered. "What—what, I'm not impo—!"

The crowd snickered. Ben tried to turn back the conversation, but it still went the wrong way. "All these present are my companions, or willing employees, fed and housed by me!"

Luke paused, and in that briefest of moments he heard the whispering from the crowd grow louder, a muttering that was a revolution of words. From the corner of his eye he glimpsed Sequoyah start drawing chalk symbols on his slate board.

Luke pointed one knobby finger at Ben. "You sure about that, *slaver?*"

Ben shouted, outrage darkening his features. "It's for the greater good, so all these people can be saved from the likes of you, from destitution and dallying!"

Sequoyah drew faster upon the slate board, and the Code made itself known. Over the great stadium scoreboard appeared the image of a fist rising up, shattering apart the links of an iron chain, all surrounded by zigzag lightning bolts.

The white-clothed people kept whispering into the ears of the audience faster and faster, louder and louder. Ben didn't get it yet, but Luke knew what it was they now spoke, what they'd been told to say today, till one of the audience finally stood and shouted it: "Benjamin Franklin's a goddamned slave holder!"

Others took up the cry. Out of left field came: "Franklin's a slaver, I always knew it!"

From center field: "History books lied, he never did none of those things he claimed!"

From right field: "Ben Franklin's a coward, a kidnapper of women, and he's *impotent!*"

Ben turned twelve shades of pale. "No, no, that's not true, you can't taint my legacy . . . " He suddenly changed tack, pointing at Lewis Robards. "I'm the good guy! It's him—that fellow's acting on his own, trying to besmirch my name by taking ladies hostage!"

Robards shoved Daisy away. "Why, you treacherous poltroon!"

Luke didn't know what a poltroon was, but it sounded righteous.

Sequoyah's plan had worked: the message Black Herman had lost his life to relay, the trigger for Ben's "labor force" to rise up. In the next moment, and with the greatest of roar, white-clothed people moved as one and swarmed the three foremen.

Anderson Jennings got off a thunderous salvo from his blunderbuss that tore two of the mutinous laborers to shreds, severing the nearest of them completely in half. Martha Cannon howled and rammed her pitchfork so hard into another of them that the metal tines went all the way through and out the man's back; but the pitchfork got stuck in him, and Martha was left unarmed of weapons, but for her claws. And Lewis Robards, he just lifted his big knife in Franklin's direction and screamed, with his bloodshot eyes turning even bloodier: "You deceiver! You fool! You bastard!"

Such were the last moments for all three of the slave-catcher foremen, as they were never seen again. Ben's labor force fell upon the trio and tore them apart with their bare hands, crushed their lifeless bodies under stomping feet, hurled bits and pieces of their hair and clothing to all directions, and then let the pox take care of the rest. The stands turned to chaos as the living went wild and bellowed, none of them knowing why; folks listening on the radio might have thought someone had slammed a home run.

Benjamin Franklin turned from the mayhem to find John Dillinger and Pretty Boy Floyd training guns on him.

"Uh-uh," John said. "Don't you move, sir."

Ben held out his hands in front of him slowly. "Wait, gentlemen, this has all just been a misun—"

Floyd pulled the trigger of his Tommy gun, riddling Ben with machine-gun fire. Ben shrieked, danced about a bit, then his smoking body collapsed. When Floyd's gun clicked empty, he said, "We told you not to move."

And everything else happened in a flash.

The entire crowd in the stadium took up a chant, repeating the new phrases whispered in their ears, and both the living and the white-clothed people echoed Lewis Robards' words: "Ben Franklin's a deceiver! Ben Franklin's a fool! Ben Franklin's a bastard!"

Gunfire erupted, and red pox shot through the air faster than the Earps' bullets, but none landed on Ben's lifeless body. Luke knew it'd take a helluva lot more to bring him down, but this, at least, was a start. Luke ducked down just in time as a cannonball roared past from General Pemberton, flames of hatred seeming to spew from it like a comet. The ball smashed into Harriet's boxcar, sending its top upward in smithereens. There was no sign of Harriet, except for her kerchief floating away on a cloud of smoke.

The Earps placed well-aimed shots, and Sequoyah took one in the foot and another in the hand, hobbling him and stopping his drawing signs. King Shaw rolled away, and a searing bullet parted his hair. He kept rolling like a half-assed wheel until he ended up at the home team dugout, looking into the eyes of Dr. Gatling and his namesake gun.

"Move aside, son," Dr. Gatling said in a voice that brooked no debate. "I was a Yankee man, and I don't back no slave holders. Fastest way to find oneself extinct these days."

King did as he was told, and Gatling pivoted his gun toward the wood platform where Pemberton's cannon nosed out.

"This is for the Union," Gatling said, and opened fire, and for half a minute nothing else could be heard but the storm of lead let loose. The platform's base turned to Swiss cheese, and Confederate General Pemberton vanished.

The pox dove here and there, looking who to take away next.

One of the figures in white let himself into the broadcast booth, and the voice that came out was amplified a hundredfold. "Ben Franklin's a deceiver! Ben Franklin's a fool! Ben Franklin's a bastard!" Luke recognized that voice straight away, even if it was quieter and less jubilant than it once had been, and he couldn't help but grin: Paul Revere had regained his own freedom.

Luke began his walk across the infield, feeling like a celebrity with everyone cheering him on, toward the wood platform where mighty Ben had fallen. Pocahontas walked in his shadow, her features, her scowl made darker. In one smooth motion, she notched an arrow into her bow and let it fly straight through the throat of Virgil Earp. He dropped without a sound.

"Goddamned Injun!" Morgan cried out. And he charged her, a six-shooter in each hand firing with bull's-eye accuracy where she stood; only by the time the bullets reached her, she'd already darted away, first to the side, then forward, straight at him. Her bone axe came to hand, flashing, and then it was buried in Morgan's face. He flipped up and down like a little pinwheel that circles itself, until he was out.

Wyatt wasn't so rash. He closed one eye, aimed at Luke, and shot.

Luke saw it coming, the puff of smoke, the flash of light, the bullet headed dead-center for his skull—

Pocahontas reached out in front of him and caught it tight between thumb and forefinger.

"Hog's puck," Wyatt said in quiet awe.

Pocahontas flicked the bullet back at Wyatt, as fast as he'd first shot it, and a bloom of red geysered from his chest. He fell. She looked around, seeming satisfied Luke could make the rest of the way on his own, and went back to Morgan's body to retrieve her axe. King had got up and put an arm around Sequoyah, helping him up from the field, and they followed after Luke.

By the time Luke reached the big wood platform, Benjamin Franklin was already coming to. He coughed; an elbow jittered. One mad eye rolled up. Beside him, John Hancock and Sam Adams stood frozen as statues under the withering glare of Pretty Boy and his gun.

Ben bled out from a hundred places, but he was recovering his strength fast enough. He sat up, saw Luke, and started to stand, until Dillinger's two-tone shoe rapped against his chest to shove him back down.

"This isn't over, *hobo*," Ben spat out. "One battle does not decide a war, and this war is mine only to win."

Luke nodded, shrugged, saw the audience watching him. Hell, everyone loved the victor, that was for sure. He'd never felt so confident before, so bolstered by support. He even caught sight of Daisy, beautiful, beautiful Daisy Rose, pushing her way through the crowds toward him. That did it. "I remember what you told me about Joseph Warren's spat with Poe."

"Whatever does that have to do with anything under the sun?" Ben growled.

"It's a new world, Alex."

"Alex? What are you dithering about?"

Sequoyah and King Shaw joined him on the platform. Mayor Tobin looked about ready to faint. Luke bent down to Ben's level. "I'm talking about you, Alexander James, when you and I were speaking of some things from the past. I think that almanac—what was it called? Oh yeah, *Poor Richard's Almanack*, named after its author, Richard Poor, not you, Alexander James, at all. And that electricity experiment, I think it was done by the Earl of Sandwich, who was looking for a way to heat his lunch."

Ben blanched. The color of his face paled, then flushed scarlet, then paled again. "That's outrageous, bloody preposterous. You can't undo my accomplishments."

Sequoyah lifted his chin to him. "But you did not really *accomplish* those accomplishments, did you? *Animate?*"

If Ben was pale before, he looked like a snowman now.

"See," Luke said, "it might be a lot harder to undo all you'd done if you'd actually done it. But since all the things you're known for are prefaced on a viper's nest of lies, I figure it's just like one of those loose threads that holds a cloth together; give it a few tugs and it comes unraveled."

"No . . . " Ben said.

"I been all over this nation," Luke went on, "and I never heard of anyone famous by the name Franklin, 'cept for a Benji Franklin who was a rapist and a slave holder. And that's you too, ain't it? Alexander James, the rapist and slave holder."

King nodded. "Uh-huh, same here. All my travels, only heard 'bout you, Alexander James, a slave holder who smells like old cheese."

Ben shook his head, and specks of blood flicked off his forehead. "It's not true . . . "

"You may not believe it," Luke said, "but the voice of us destitutes is a helluva lot stronger than you suppose. You claim credit for keeping Daisy around? Naw, that ain't you at all. None of your other slaves lasted much longer than a year or two, but here's this homeless girl with no family and fewer friends. No one at all to remember her 'cept me, and I've single-handedly kept her around just by telling others who she is."

Ben's glare could've burned wood.

Luke added, "All it takes is one whispered word, and with the right wind it'll spread like wildfire."

John Hancock polite-coughed. He was sweating through his waistcoat. "Ben, you tarry too long in this quibble."

Sam Adams nodded, whispering frantically, "Is it not yet time? You foresaw this, you prepared . . . "

Luke blinked, felt something change, like the world decided to spin the other way right under him. He opened his mouth to speak, but Ben beat him to it.

"Yes, it is time."

Around Luke, the air stilled. His flesh tingled. Daisy froze, still thirty feet away in the rows of stadium seats. Ben brushed John Dillinger's foot off his chest with a lazy swipe.

An explosion ripped through the side of the stadium. Bleachers crashed down, people shrieked and fell and burned in the flames. A nightmare-black train sped from the fiery wreckage onto the infield, its engine roaring like a demon, pulling a line of boxcars, each one worse-looking than the one before.

A few moments later, all the crushed, burnt people were restored to how they'd been, spellbound and smiling, but the black train was still there, parked on steel tracks that smoked like the floor of Hell. One boxcar door opened, and a great dark shadow unfurled, and there Smith McCain made himself known. He pointed a long, taloned finger at Luke. "Think you're the only one can call his own train, boy?"

LUKE AND SMITH, 1942

At the sight of McCain, King Shaw let out a scream so singularly shrill, Luke thought for sure the stadium lights would burst. Many of the white-clothed people added their own voices to the wailing, but none were loud as King, not even Daisy, who'd already been killed by the man, and all Luke could think was that the screams, the fear, were just making McCain stronger.

Ben knew it too. The color had come back to him, the bleeding already stopped. He smiled, and his lips moved so no sound came out, but Luke could read what he mouthed: *Fuck you, hobo.*

The engine of McCain's train trembled, seeming even to grow bigger, its boiler rumbling with a sound like the great flapping wings of a monstrous bird. That engine didn't look like nothing Luke had ever seen, either. Glistening metal that came to jagged points bolted piecemeal with no discernible pattern, just layer over layer of black steel, with three smokestacks belching smoke as thick as mud. The cars it drew were windowless, each with just a single cargo door that was wrapped in too many chains and shackles to make sense, and from each car came moans and cries and sounds of souls surely as damned as Lucifer himself . . . and there was McCain the railroad bull, with his bowler hat, his eyes yellow as a rail man's lantern, his stony bearded face, hangin' one-armed out a door.

"You rode in on a train," McCain said. "But where's your ticket?" He opened his mouth into something almost like a smile, and light glinted off long canine fangs.

A horrible sound began, drawn-out and screeching, that hurt Luke's ears, then a booming thud, and new tracks began to appear slowly, foot by foot from McCain's train leading up to Luke. The hell-train blew its whistle, and lightning crackled in the sky.

Pocahontas made her move, a motion so fleet Luke wouldn't have known what it was, except he was already familiar with how she could dart like a puff of smoke. She'd disarmed Blackbeard so easily, Luke remembered, and taken down the Earps so aptly, and he had hope now of her charging McCain like an attack dog: *Get him!*

She was still out on the field by Morgan's body, and then she wasn't. There was a flash and she was at the smoking black tracks, and her arm swung up, a stone axe hurtling at McCain's chest. But the giant bull slipped to one side as if a ripple of water and brought his own arm down in a quick hammering motion, like pounding a stake into the ground.

And Pocahontas howled like Luke had never heard, part pain, part fury, part disbelief. Her shoulder crushed in like a dented soda can, and her arm flopped useless, barely looking even connected. McCain took the stone axe from her hand as she collapsed, convulsing, to the earth.

McCain looked at the axe curiously, then he dropped it down his mouth and ate it.

From the podium, Pretty Boy Floyd reloaded his Tommy gun, and he and Dillinger opened fire. McCain ducked back inside the car he'd appeared from, closing the door behind him. Bullets pounded the train, ricocheting off in all directions to chew up bystanders in the audience. People shrieked in pain, blood geysering twenty feet high until it wasn't, and those same people were sitting there eating popcorn.

McCain's train breathed a big heave and kept chugging forward to Luke, taking all the time in the world, letting everyone watch, letting everyone grow afraid together.

Luke knew he couldn't stay. Too many others would be mauled, murdered by McCain, and everyone's fear was just feeding into the monster . . . the monster who'd aligned with Ben Franklin. Together, Ben and McCain were strengthening by the moment; but to retreat, run away? People would think he'd lost, and people don't follow cowards. People don't believe in cravens. People don't trust the words of deserters. Ben would rise to show them all he was still the champion, that no one could outsmart him. The crowd, they'd turn back to Ben easy, to what he offered . . .

Sequoyah questioned Luke with his eyes, opening a bloody hand to show what he held. The slate board was broken in half. There'd be no help there.

And still McCain's train grew nearer, indefatigable in its progress, the thump of each new rail shaking the earth as it appeared under those wheels, slowly, oh so slowly.

A voice drifted to him over the bullets pinging off metal, the screams, the thuds of tracks laying down, closing in: "I think you know, Luke Thacker, you've got to hightail it from here, and now."

Luke looked over. His B&M train was fifty feet away, parked at a diagonal, the earth chewed up under its own hasty rails and crossties. A face appeared from an open boxcar door near the back, matching the voice.

"Harriet?" he asked, squinting. "I thought—?"

"There's other ways to get on and off a train you don't know about, young man. I tell you, there's always a secret way, a passage in or out. But that don't matter now, does it?"

He turned to McCain's train, then back to his own. "No, but I can't run away. Not in front of all these people . . . I'll lose everything."

"It ain't losing if you're just moving to a new battleground."

Luke turned to face Daisy, still out of reach, but their eyes locked, and his heart broke. All he wanted was to touch her, to know she was there, to feel her warmth, to make it all better—

Harriet's voice went up. "C'mon, child. I'll let you back in."

Never mind that didn't make sense regarding his own train; Luke was convinced, more so since he had no other plan. He broke from Daisy's sight and took two nervous sidesteps toward his engine, as if everyone couldn't already tell where he was heading. McCain's train paused, daring him. Its boiler revved, the engine straining forward on a leash, ready to pounce.

Then he was off, sprinting full speed for that open boxcar that Harriet motioned from. And he didn't count on his feet alone to get him there in time, but coupled back with the train in his mind and drove it forward toward him, closing the distance by half.

McCain's train shot forward at the same time: whistles and screeches and screams and thuds and thunder, it came.

Luke's train charged one way, and McCain's the other, and Luke had to leap through the air, trusting his train to catch him at the last moment, otherwise he'd be crushed between the two behemoths. His trust paid off and he rolled into the boxcar, gasping and scrambling to get his bearings, and then they were off, blasting through the stadium and its bystanders and battle-fatigued memories.

Like jamming down a car's gas pedal, Luke slammed the train's Johnson bar forward as far as he could, and the world blurred. He had to imagine the tracks before him, creating them as the train ate them up, rocketing out of the city, out of the state. He was focusing ahead, so he couldn't look behind, but his confidence was brimming. He said, "It'll be a long spell 'fore McCain can catch up."

Harriet answered, "If by a long spell you mean right now, I'd say you got his measure."

Luke dared a glance back as they veered from the coastline, and saw McCain on his ass. "Is there nothing he can't do?"

"I can think of a thing or two," she said. "You first got to lead the devil out of hell, away from his strength, off his train."

"He'll follow me now," Luke promised. "Don't matter where I go, he'll be after."

"And you know where I want you to go, right?"

"I'm guessing, though I don't know why."

McCain's engine let out a horrible whistling squeal, like a cock having its namesake pulled off. It'd been right behind them before, but even closer now. The headlamp lit up Luke's train bright as the sun, and Luke could almost smell McCain's breath, rancid and hot.

"Faith, Luke," she said. "Faith and patience. That's two things the old hellion doesn't have. Two weapons you do."

Luke swerved his train to the left, sharp, and tracks kept flying into place, rising high into the air and deep into the ground like a Coney Island coaster, but McCain kept pace just fine. That nightmare train rammed hard into Luke's caboose and Luke felt the rear railing tear off, the slats of the car shattering. The whole train rocked, swerved. McCain smashed into him again, and the caboose crumpled.

"What if we don't make it there?" Luke asked.

Harriet bit her lip. "Faith, Luke, though maybe we can do away with that patience part."

"Hold on tight."

Luke slammed the brake cylinder, pulling hard to the right, and the tail cars swung out like snapping a towel. Sparks showered the air, and the valves groaned under pressure, but held. McCain shot past before trying to turn and brake too, but overcompensated; he flipped his train in wild corkscrews across the grassy plains of North Branford. Luke barked a laugh but didn't say anything. It was almost a jinx, thinking he could beat McCain that easy, like if he said anything celebratory, the bastard bull would be magically called back and right behind him again.

He sped forward anew, riding the hills and straightaways in equal measure, a rocket that cut through anything in its path. New York, New Jersey, Delaware, they went through each like footprints in the sand that one skips over, roaring south.

Then McCain was back, and his train looked even more fiendish, flying faster than anything in order to pull alongside Luke's. Mud and blood and rends of sharp metal stuck from all directions, and tears in the boxcar walls showed the damned souls of every 'bo McCain had killed and kept. McCain and Luke glared at each other from open doors, each standing fine as captains on their ships.

Luke flipped him the bird.

McCain drove his train against Luke's, sideswiping it, and both engines cried out and pulled away, metal cars rending, and ladders and pulleys tearing off.

McCain got control first, and drove his train again right into Luke's own, harder this time. There was a deafening explosion, a scream of steel; the boxcar directly behind Luke's exploded in a ball of smoke and debris, and it and all the cars behind it tangled and shattered up against McCain, pulling that nightmare train, at least, into their pulverization; McCain's train flipped again and there was a detonation, a flash, a shower of metal parts—wheels and bolts and couplings—and Luke didn't look back, just urged his train on, coaxing it like a horse, "Faster, c'mon, just a bit faster," even while it started wobbling out of balance, sliding as much as it sped onward. Maryland, Virginia, then the Carolinas, *just keep roaring south*, Luke pled.

"You can do it," Harriet urged, and somehow he knew he could.

Until Smith McCain returned. His train was shortened too—like Luke, he was now in the last boxcar in line, only he no longer rode within but on top, one leg impossibly over each side, like mounting the filthiest, most murderous steed ever. Even in daylight, the glow from his yellow eyes was unmistakable.

"I'm coming for you, boy, coming to furrow the earth with your squalid bones."

And he rammed his engine into Luke's train again, and this time Luke rammed him back, and they went on like this, charging up a mountain, jumping a crevice, skimming the tides and waterways and flying through the air. Harriet stopped talking and closed her eyes tight, her mouth drawn even tighter, and she was groaning like she was constipated, pulling onto whatever rivets afforded handholds on the floor.

There was a terrifying sound of rending metal, something giving way that probably should have done so long ago. Luke's train shuddered, and the burning of hot metal singed his nose, then came the smell of brimstone pouring in from McCain's train. Both their engines were on fire, both their trains were careening on tracks that had long ago lost control, like a mine cart plunging down the rails into a pit. There was a detonation, two pops, a roar of wind. Everything shook and clattered, the planks tearing themselves free from the floor Luke stood on, 'til he could see the ground beneath speeding by, and there was no stop on this ride, no polite "time out" to McCain. They were going to crash, and crash hard.

Luke turned to where Harriet had been crouching, pulling at the floor—

Only she wasn't there. Instead there was just a neat, open trapdoor that Luke stared at, dumbstruck, as his train headed for oblivion. Then her thin brown hand reached from the opening, scrabbling for something until it found Luke's ankle, and pulled.

The thunder of the crash was deafening, the heat blistering, the impact crushing. And Smith McCain welcomed it all, relished it, the fear he saw, the terror he'd caused, etched upon Lucas Thacker's face. He'd ridden into the middle of the explosion and drunk it like a fine wine.

The shit-sippin' hobo's greatest weapon had been taken away—his train—and Smith roared with delight for the first time in a century. Didn't matter he himself was weaponless too, the explosion was worth it. He hadn't blown anything up in a long, long time.

And what else could Lucas Thacker now be, but a charred filet o' 'bo?

He walked around the wreckage with the leisure of a dilettante, kicking over plates of burning steel, chunks of melted wheel, looking for sign of Lucas's corpse. They'd ended in a gulley that sliced through some forest. The last marker he'd seen said they were in Charleston. Not that it mattered, not that anything else mattered but that he was victorious again, or had at least completed his job, so to say.

Which meant he was still mighty, he was still goddamned monstrous, even if a part of him *had* somehow been feeling unusual of late . . . not slower or heavier or any weaker of mind—

—though he could hear the whispers, couldn't he, a rustle of voices like passing spirits saying exactly that: *Poor Smith McCain, gettin' older and slower and fatter . . .*

Smith's delight turned. He'd fix it, he'd fix them all goddamned good, and right goddamned now. *Lucas-shit sucker-Thacker . . .* the worst of the worst hobo defecates he'd ever had poach a ride off his trains, the worst of the worst to ever befoul his railroad lines. He'd find Lucas's skull, finger-fuck it for the world to see, and put an end to this whole mockery, no matter what.

Just at the thought of it, Smith's rage erupted in a howl that broke from his mouth like flames from a dragon, and he didn't hold back, and the very earth around him shuddered in terror.

Then something tender rose on the bridge of his nose, a tiny inflamed lump. He stopped howling, touched it. The lump felt swollen with pus, and a pimple or two felt to be cropping up on his forehead . . .

Acne? On him? What in pitch-fuck-hell?

Ahead, Smith saw something that made his blood froth even more. It was Lucas Thacker, standing in a grove of trees, watching him.

Smith could only freeze, watch him back . . . before he got ready to charge and pulverize that mangy head into rail-rider powder.

Around them, the burning train began to fade, and the tracks as well, eaten away by the pox.

Lucas Thacker held up something in his hand, and Smith grinned. Any weapon the 'bo had would just make Smith stronger. He fed on their fear, fed on their attacks, fed on their—

Chocolate? Was that a bar of chocolate Lucas Thacker held? Could it be the urchin was so bold, he'd thought to take break for some fucking dessert?

But no . . . the bastard hobo was pointing it at him like a gun or a knife.

Smith cracked his knuckles and bared his teeth before realization came: The bastard hobo wasn't pointing it like a weapon at all; he was holding it out like an . . . an offering. Lucas Thacker held it outstretched the way some bully child might tease a stray dog with a sausage link, with a little waggle, a finger wave.

Goddamned chocolate? Smith had never eaten chocolate in his life, never even thought about it, yet . . . he wanted it.

What the hell was happening? He couldn't understand, but there was some part of him that wanted what the 'bo held, and wanted it bad.

Chocolate?

Lucas Thacker waved a bar of sweet, sweet chocolate in the air, and Smith found himself longing for it, felt the dead lump of his heart tremble and crave with a yearning he could not explain.

Chocolate, chocolate, chocolate . . .

Smith started panting, his hands shaking like an opiate addict's. His eyes dilated, bouncing back and forth as Lucas waved the chocolate bar like a great red flag before Smith's turned horns. Even the veins seemed to be popping from his neck, trying to break free and reach for that sugary goodness.

The filthy 'bo started walking backward, deeper into the grove of trees, taking the chocolate with him . . .

No, no, no! Smith seethed, moving from the fading train wreckage, and a tiny voice in his head reminded him that the farther he got from the trains, the more his power waned. Smith told that voice to shut the hell up or he'd rip its bloody liver out.

He was going to catch Lucas Thacker, going to crush each bone of his body under his hands until Lucas was dead as dust, or maybe a pool of screaming flesh. And then he'd eat the soft bits and afterward enjoy a nice chocolate dessert.

But Lucas was walking away, trying to escape. Smith sped up. So did the 'bo.

The trees along this part of the line were grown so close together their branches formed a wall solid as brick, sort of like following the perimeter of a stone fortress, which was good, as the loathsome cocksucker couldn't break away.

And he was getting closer . . .

Out of nowhere Smith caught sight of an old colored woman; just a glimpse, really, a rag over her head, patchwork skirts, she taking Lucas by the arm. Another damned 'bo? How in Hades did the degenerates of the nation breed so many? Even he couldn't possibly catch them all, though he'd sure as hell try . . .

A distant gleam of blue electricity snapped, and the two shitheads passed under knobby oak boughs into a gloomy rift; if he hadn't seen the exact place they'd entered, he'd never have known to break through the trees right there. He followed them into the thicket, the sounds of the rail line, the woods, somehow growing muffled behind him.

There was Lucas again, now running on a narrow dirt trail, with no sign anymore of the old colored woman, if she'd even been there at all. That fucking craving for chocolate was fouling his faculties . . . Smith turned up his gait, powering those legs to speeds enough to overcome the soon-to-be-miseried Lucas Thacker. Closer, closer now, the 'bo and his chocolate, Smith opened his mouth to bellow in triumph . . .

Lucas Thacker rounded a bend, and when Smith rounded that same bend the long straightaway in front of him was entirely empty.

What in pitch-fuck-hell?

Smith's nerves flared at something unseen . . . a trap, but where? How? What was the snare? Lucas could only be hiding behind one of those thick black trunks or above in one of the long, tangled limbs, ready to spring out and attack as soon as Smith passed by.

Could the gutterpup be so cocksure of himself that he thought he could best Smith McCain? Didn't matter if Lucas Thacker came at him from on high or down low, from behind, armed, or begging for forgiveness, there wasn't a thing could be done to save him now.

"Bring it on, boy!" Smith roared to the night.

Nothing was brought. The yowls of muffled wildcats came from faraway, and he heard toads and crickets and owls that had no fear of him.

"Can't hide forever," Smith added, his voice fallen flat, a machine part of him taking over, driving him back and forth along the narrow path, soundless as a shade, listening for any noise to give Luke away. "Not forever . . . "

Some time passed before a distant part of Smith's spoiling brain began to wonder: *Where was he?* His legs churned like tireless pistons down that shrouded path, roving round and around, but how long had he been searching for Lucas Thacker? Hours? Days? Years?

It didn't matter how far he went, but every shape and shadow appeared like some pattern, repeating itself impossibly every few steps. And the sky never changed . . . it'd become midnight when he had entered these woods, his favorite time, but shouldn't the moon have shifted from its treetop vantage by now? Shouldn't the dawn have broken long ago? Had the fucking rail rider slipped past him, or was he even now cowering in the underbrush, pissing himself in fear and remorse as Smith prowled by?

He should smell Lucas Thacker by now; the reek of terror upon a man is strong as a whore's musk. He should sniff the putrid stink of desperation, the honeyed foulness of destitution, the brackish puddles of urine loosed from Lucas Thacker by Smith's sheer indomitability. These were all scents he'd become accustomed to by those caught stealing train rides, each as familiar and predictable as one's own bowels after eating a fine meal.

There was a sense of trickery amiss, of something occurring that he wasn't privy to, which was fine as two shits. A man could keep his own secrets, long as he didn't ride any rails on Smith's clock. But the sense was there nonetheless, and it bothered him even as he walked beneath the trees arched as woven steeples, even as he looked for Lucas Thacker, listened for Lucas Thacker, *smelled* for Lucas Thacker. The hobo couldn't hide from him forever. Not forever . . .

Hadn't he thought that exact conviction so long, long ago? *And where was he*, that distant part of Smith's spoiling brain again asked? The rail line he'd ridden here had been so fast, he hadn't paid attention, just following after Lucas Thacker, but there must be something nearby, something maybe on the other side of these trees that he could call to, and he tried, but there was no answer . . . and he couldn't break through the trees either, though he wouldn't, 'til he caught his goddamned quarry. He should never have wrecked his train like that, knew better'n to stray so far from the rails, but he'd make his way back . . .

He'd rip Lucas Thacker to so many ribbons it'd be like one of those ticker-tape parades, and Smith would ride past on his showboat car and shower the world with hobo confetti.

Not forever . . .

The night hadn't changed at all, so maybe his sense of time was just off-kilter . . . Smith rounded a familiar bend that became a familiar long straightaway in front of him that was entirely empty.

What in pitch-fuck-hell?

"Can't hide forever, boy!" he screamed with a voice suddenly less confident than ever he'd known. "Not forever . . . "

And he kept walking. Round and around and—*was this some tinge of weariness?*—his steps seemed to be slowing ever so slightly, his feet shrinking, the owl's knot on a pine a bit higher up than before.

And all he wanted was some chocolate.

Hours, days, years, of a night that didn't end? Or had he just gotten here? He felt another zit flare on his chin. Was that himself he smelled?

"Not forever, boy . . . " Smith McCain muttered.

LUKE THACKER, 1942

Daisy's head was on his shoulder, her hands in his lap. Luke had one arm around her and the other arm tucked up under her side, his hand rubbing her leg, feeling how warm she was, how *real* she was after so many years gone. They were squeezed together in an old chair; he didn't want to let her go, and she didn't want it either.

Daisy sneezed.

"Bless you," King Shaw said from next to them.

"The dust," she admitted.

Sequoyah smiled kindly. "It has helped me, but perhaps it's not for everyone."

He drew his finger through the dust that covered his table, making some symbols, and the cabin's room sorta shimmered and stretched and changed, and then they were all sitting inside a small train station depot. The floor was checkerboard brown and white, and the chairs were long smooth wood benches. Sequoyah sat behind the ticket counter, and deco-style chandelier lights gave warm light to it all.

Luke startled. "What, how?"

"Black Herman taught me some tricks."

"And all this time, we've been sittin' in filth and misery?"

"I slept in a hog's trough when I was a boy, *if* shelter were available," Sequoyah chided. "That old cabin, to me it was the palace of my older years."

King elbowed Luke in the ribs. "Don't get in on where *we've* slept some nights."

Luke grimaced. "Right."

"You can write the Code from wherever you like, Luke, but it must be a place you think of as home." Sequoyah lifted his arms around. "Here, for instance."

Luke's eyes sparkled. "Close, but this ain't quite it."

Sequoyah's smile turned knowing.

"So what happens now?" Luke asked.

"You will take over. Maker of the Code. It won't be today, but through a gradual transition, until you are ready. Until you *belong* here. Do you understand what that means?"

"When I die?"

Sequoyah nodded. "But you have some time yet. Say your goodbyes, do what needs to be done. Take care of things."

Luke squeezed Daisy tighter. "What about Ben Franklin? I know he's still around . . . He gonna come after us again?"

"I think we've reached an understanding with him."

"Say you have? You can't trust him for nothin', though."

"It's true. I wouldn't hold faith with the Great Fraud as far as I can spit, but we've got a little leverage held over him now."

"Really? What happened with him after I left with Harriet?" Luke asked.

"Pocahontas mended herself, and then she and your accomplice, Pretty Boy Floyd, took turns killing Franklin in increasingly inventive and competitive ways in front of all the crowd, until some agreements could be brokered. As I oft did with Pocahontas, at each of his deaths I rewrote the Code, changing Franklin bit by bit. He became a little grayer, a bit frailer, vulnerable, noted for less and less accomplishments, unweaving what he fabricated."

"He's a slippery one, you know, and gotta be still real powerful in all this shared consciousness."

"Yes, though if we kept at rekilling and rewriting him, perhaps within a couple years we might have gotten rid of him forever. The crowds, however, were by then beginning to thin, and Franklin begged for our mercy.

"So he's allowed to be remembered as a man of learning, sharing *legitimate* knowledge with those seeking it, but he's confined permanently within the Boston Library. His warden is Paul Revere, who was only too happy to take on such duty, and ready to sound any number of alarms—as he's known to do—should Franklin grow bold. His cronies have each been assigned as janitors to Boston museums. Pocahontas checks in on them, and she has a particular knack to instill sufficient terror for me to believe they'll be kept honest."

"All right," Luke said. "Sounds like things wrapped up real nicely on that end."

"Indeed," Sequoyah replied. "Now tell me of your other adversary, that railroad bull."

"McCain? He won't be comin' after anyone either."

Sequoyah raised an eyebrow.

Luke shrugged. "Harriet helped me. Let us into the Underground Railroad, this stretch of it that, well . . . like she told me once, 'You enter it and don't know the routes, you're liable to get lost inside for a long, long time.' I'm gonna let him roam there awhile, stir in his own juices."

"A caged animal?"

"Near enough, as the only good animal is a dead animal."

"What?" King blanched, and Sequoyah shook his head, *no.*

Daisy slapped Luke's chest. "What is it you've got against animals, anyway? How come you hate 'em so?"

"Well, it's a real story, ain't no crossbuck to it. I never told anyone before, but I suppose you should know . . . I was mauled once as a kid."

"I'm sorry that happened, and it must've been awful," Daisy said. "But you do realize, although some animals can be vicious, most are sweeter than candy?"

"Try telling that to a child who's just been mangled."

"What was it?" she asked. "A dog, a bear?"

"What's the most peaceful animal there is?"

Daisy thought a moment. "A dove, I suppose, since it's the actual symbol of peace. Why?"

"That's what done it."

"A dove mauled you?"

"Landed on my shoulder, and my momma said how precious and gentle it was. Only then the dove turned and pecked me hard in the eye, almost blinded me. And everyone else said, like you, that doves are the most peaceful animals in the world. So I got to thinking that if such a benevolent creature would flagrantly assault me for no good reason, it'd only be worse for every other critter out there. Machines, I know what to expect. Animals? Who knows what they're conspiring to do next."

King winced, clicked his tongue. Snickered a little.

"What's so funny?" Luke asked.

"All you've been through, all you *can* do. Ol' Crossbuck, here's a piece of advice: I'd rewrite that piece of legend, I was you."

The others agreed. Luke made a big show of rolling his eyes.

After that, they all left and went their separate ways, though each of those ways crossed each other down the road many times. The exception was Luke and Daisy's ways, of course, since they never separated again, and had a whole lot of cuddlin' and smoochin' and other romantic notions involved.

LUKE'S THREE LESSONS AFTERMATH, 1947

In 1940 the 'bo named Skipper went back to Colorado Springs, looking for his leg and for his love. He found one and not the other.

First thing Skipper came across in town was that "rich man's doctor" who'd treated him after his train accident. Turned out the doctor was John Salyer, and he'd become chief surgeon at Fitzsimons Army Hospital up in Aurora, where they needed volunteers to test artificial limbs for maimed veterans coming home from the Second World War. Skipper signed up on the spot.

He met soldiers more wounded and grieved than any men he'd met while riding the rails, and realized his lot in life wasn't half bad. Over the years Skipper even found himself counseling disabled vets against despondency, and in such a way became a sort of motivational speaker.

"You're going to get past this, you'll move on," Skipper told one weary-eyed soldier in a recovery ward.

"I can't hold a girl tight anymore," the soldier said. His right arm ended in a swaddle of bandages just below the elbow. "Can't even jack off."

"A man can handle himself with his left hand just as well as his right," Skipper answered sagely. "Ain't no crisis at all. And you'll find the right gal just as soon with one arm as with two. Your heart's not the part that's injured."

"How the hell you know anything?" the soldier shot back.

"I been there, friend," Skipper said, patting his leg. It made a clanging sound. "Look at this."

He pulled up a pant leg to show off his new prosthetic, made from steel and rubber that didn't crack in the winter or send splinters up his stump like his old wooden leg. "Used to be nothing but a length of oak."

The soldier grunted.

"More'n that," Skipper continued, "this new leg from Doc Salyer lets me run faster and jump higher than I ever could when I had the two naturals God gave me. You're in the best hands one could want."

Skipper winced at his poor choice of words when the soldier looked at his sad stump. Skipper changed the subject. "I never knew what happened to my cut-off leg, but I ended up with a real pretty gal from it. She seen me slip under the train the night it happened. I'd given up on her, given up on everything, but I met a man with as little as myself, and he convinced me not to roll over.

"See, the fella warned me, 'This is your only life, fight to make the most of it!' And ya know what, friend? I did, and it was worth the fight, and I pass that advice onto you."

The man grunted again.

Skipper continued. "Don't take much but some willpower to get over feelin' sorry for yourself and make a try for your dreams, ain't no one else gonna do it for you."

"I don't know, maybe you're right—"

"Hell I'm right! I done it, and the man before me done it. His name was Luke Thacker, and you can do it too."

And Luke's legend grew a bit more.

It was Fourth of July, and a young Army Air Corps pilot named Captain William Boy returned to his hometown of Knoxville, finding every resident and neighbor for twelve counties cheering his name.

"Blue! Blue! Blue!"

It was a nickname friends had begun calling him with the admiration one shows a religious relic that starts to glow and hum. Rumor was, he'd gotten the name "Blue" because enemy artillery could be looking up into the sky and see nothing but that color, when from nowhere William Boy came barreling down in his P-38 Lightning, guns roaring, bombs whistling, to blast 'em all to Kingdom Come.

"Blue! Blue! Blue!"

Parades filled the city, and he was hastened into a gold convertible sedan and driven down Main Street, where there were banners and blimps and flags and honor guards. After a couple hours of hollering thanks and greetings to all, his voice grew hoarse; it'd never recovered entirely from a screaming fit when he'd encountered a twister some years back.

Since then, William Boy had shot down twelve Japanese aircraft in the Pacific theatre, making him a genuine ace. And for gallant service, he'd also received the Silver Star, the Distinguished Service Cross, and lastly the Medal of Honor, of which President Truman had bemoaned there was nothing greater to laud onto William for his aid in winning the Battle of Leyte Gulf.

"Blue! Blue! Blue!"

The convertible sedan pulled up to Shields-Watkins Field, and William was escorted into its open-air stadium where a great stage awaited, covered in more banners and flags, and even posters of his face that towered forty feet high.

William sauntered up the stage steps, a languid motion many took to belie some brash ego, which he rightly deserved. Truth, though, couldn't have been further off, as it was just how he always walked, slow and at his own pace. Inside an aircraft, though, no one moved faster.

The mayor pumped William's skinny hand and awarded him a city key, and when the cheering subsided, said how proud everyone was.

"Thank you, sir," William replied.

"It's remarkable, just remarkable, all you've done. Why, you're a role model for every young patriot in the nation, an absolute bona fide American hero."

"Thank you, sir, it's an honor to be thought as such."

"Tell us, William, how'd it come to be that you are who you are?"

Blue Boy took the microphone, and he cleared his throat. He paused a long moment, weighing what to say, and then he shrugged and told all about the time he was saved from one beast of a tornado by a hobo named Luke Thacker who made trains soar.

"After that," Blue Boy concluded, "I never thought a thing impossible again, even me earning the Medal of Honor for flying fighter planes."

And Luke's legend grew a bit more.

Business was quiet one snowy evening at the Joint Track Griddle, which rail men named the best mash n' eggs east of the Potomac River. Ollie the counterman counted bills from a brass National register and Martha—known once as Po' Chili—leaned over the counter with spatula in hand, dishin' to a group of regulars, station agents from the Western Maryland depot.

"Can you believe," one of the agents said, "we caught a pack of bona fide hobos hiding on a fast train from Greenville?"

"What's strange with that?" Martha asked.

"This day? With the war being over, economy's flush, jobs and crops in every town, ain't no need to give up home, risk your neck on some wild train when a man's bounty is right in his backyard. The hobo is a dying breed."

Martha leaned in close. "Economy ain't gonna change the type of man who lusts to see more than what's in his own backyard. Some folks get a hankerin' to be whisked around this land, and nothing else will do."

Another agent snorted. "Ain't worth the trouble, hoppin' trains. Just get a ticket for Greyhound."

"Even bus tickets cost money," she said, "and economy or not, can't say everyone has the funds for fine passage to cross this country."

"Well, you're risking a lot more these days. Not just the 'bos that are fading, but the railroad dicks too. It's what you might say is irony; bulls begrudging rail riders' decline as the withering of their own livelihoods."

The first agent nodded. "Bulls that are still around just get meaner and meaner."

"Say, you ever hear about the Butcher of 'Bos? Some hired roustabout, goes by the name of Smith McCain—"

Martha's hiss was like a steaming kettle, and her hand tightened on the spatula. "We don't say that name around here."

The agent drew back. "Apologies, ma'am."

"It's Luke Thacker you oughta be wanting to talk about," she said.

The front door chimed open, and a gaunt man in derby hat and skinny tie entered, taking a counter seat beside the agents. He raised one finger for attention. "Coffee, please."

"Luke Thacker . . . " one of the station agents intoned. "I heard that name before, some rail rider."

Martha poured the newcomer a cup and nodded to the men. "Mm-hm, he was. He is."

"Yeah, I recall," another agent said. "He had some wild crossbucks, riding trains like you'd ride horses. Moving them around, slowing 'em down, calling 'em when he needed. Funny, right?"

There was silence a few moments. One agent coughed. Another clattered his fork on an empty plate.

An agent cleared his throat, finally spoke in a quiet voice like he was about to tell a campfire ghost tale. "Funny thing, I did see a 'bo like that once. Swear, looked to me like he was just standing there, watching the world go by, then this train comes outta nowhere as if the sky spat it out, and the 'bo, he jumps it easy as nothing, and he and the train shoot off so fast, I don't even see them go, and there weren't any tracks or nothing."

"That *is* funny, Jonesy," another agent said, his brow wrinkling. "I mean, it's funny 'cause I seen something like that too . . . "

"You guys are talkin' crazy," said the agent next to him.

"I know it, I said it's funny."

"No, I mean it's crazy since I seen that 'bo also . . . I never told anyone about it, thought I was seeing things."

The agents looked at each other.

The gaunt man in derby hat and tie set down his coffee. "Gentlemen, I was once a 'bo myself, rode the rails all the thirties, when honest labor was an extraordinary commodity."

"All right," the agents grumbled, unimpressed.

"It was not without its rewards, being in that army of bindle stiffs, though now my calling is as mere civil servant. My name is Nels Anderson, and I'm a sociologist in D.C., contracted with the government of our fine nation to pen a sequence of scholarly articles with nationwide syndication." Nels adjusted the spectacles perched low on his nose. "Please, tell me more about this brash young nomad, Luke Thacker. I'd like to enliven our readers with his tales."

One of the station agents whistled, low and long.

"Mix up a plate of mash fixins, hun," Martha called to her husband. "This is gonna take a spell."

And it did.

And Luke's legend grew a bit more.

LUKE THACKER, 1952

There were some who said Luke Thacker could land a ten-foot catfish from the river bottom just by baitin' his line with the word "please." Others said it wasn't a catfish at all, but a gator. And he didn't have to say "please," but just wish it hard enough, and the gator would surrender at his feet.

Crossbuck Luke could swim through a hurricane, walk through a twister, and jump over a volcano. *Had* done it, in fact, and more than once. Eyes closed, sick, naked, or asleep, it didn't matter.

Luke was tall as Paul Bunyan, and his blue ox was named the Union Pacific. Luke was a prince in exile, a comic book super hero, and the angel of mercy all in one, wearing a duster and riding goggles, hanging on a boxcar railing one-handed while showering the needy he passed with gold coins . . .

And even as he was these things, as he did these things, the real Luke Thacker couldn't help but notice the changing landscape of the nation, the fading away of things he'd feared, the fading away too of things he'd loved. Railroads consolidated and closed sympathetic lines, and diesel engines displaced steamers as the faster, more secure means to go a distance, with nary a handhold for any wayfaring man to catch a lift. But that was okay, as fewer families were starving, fewer men riding the rails, what with a wealth of permanent occupation to be found in postwar prosperity.

DOORWAYS TO THE DEADEYE

The papers said that homelessness was on the decline and soon to be stamped out entirely, and nothing finer could be heralded: Mining boomed with uranium discovery; manufacturing boomed with advents in technology; harvesting boomed so that crops filled every larder like paddocks of gold.

Prosperity, though, comes and goes, and the upswing in the nation's economy never did entirely take away the nomad proletariats who were still crawling in the cracks of America.

All around him, 'bos Luke knew died, and died again in the deadeye. A new generation of 'bos came forth, younger men and women who maybe weren't afforded the same opportunities as their friends and neighbors, and they became the homeless of their own generation. Sickness, circumstance, poor choice, whatever: they filled the rotted, sole-flapping shoes of their predecessors, and Luke knew where they were, and they knew him, and he appeared amongst them in the soup lines, in the wet basements of condemned buildings, in the fields and alleys where those who had little else could still gather together around a thin fire and swap tales, and every one of them had heard of the 'bo who could change his life, find his own track to love and happiness, and he gave hope to even the most despondent that even in life's privation, at least one among them was a champion.

And so his legend grew . . .

Some say to this day when Luke Thacker gambles, every card he pulls is an ace. When it rains, not a drop of water dampens his clothes or hair. If you look into a mirror at midnight and repeat his name three times, Luke Thacker will appear and grant an unselfish wish. Crossbuck Luke has tamed Bigfoot, ridden a mermaid, and allows his shadow leave to dance in the juke joints at night. And the hundred dollar bill . . . well, naturally that's said to soon replace Benjamin Franklin's portrait with his own.

And everyone knows those constellations way up high realigned themselves to make room for the likeness of Luke and Daisy together.

Crossbuck Luke can make trains appear from thin air and drive them where he wants.

Crossbuck Luke found a way to live forever.

Oh, and he loves all animals of the world, too.

SMITH MCCAIN, 1952

Fact is, there really was no Smith McCain.

The first railroad bull was a former well digger named Randy Paul. Smith McCain was just the name of Randy's goat that drowned in a cesspool one morning, causing a lamentable tragedy for all involved. For Randy it was tragic because he'd paid five dollars for that goat only a month prior and bemoaned his poor investment, and for Smith McCain it was tragic because it, of course, died. Tales of Smith McCain's depravity have since been greatly invented; unless you were a tasty piece of grass, the goat named Smith McCain was harmless as a soft wind.

The real story was Randy Paul. That bull could play checkers better than anyone alive, even frequently playing ten games simultaneously against ten other men, each of them others learned in the strategies and psychology of battle from military institutions like West Point or Annapolis. But their awards and degrees and accolades assisted those in the pursuit of victory no more than an extra can of beans would have helped General Custer facing the braves at Little Bighorn. Outmatched is simply outmatched. Randy Paul was a certifiable genius and should have taken the jobs of all those learned men and become general of the entire United States Army. But he didn't, on account he didn't care for yelling at people. Even being a bull and expected to verbally lambaste freeloaders, Randy would just ask them polite-like to come on out of the boxcar and play a game of checkers with him. Most often they'd comply, and drink a tall glass of lemonade together in the process . . .

LUKE THACKER, 1955, CONTINUED

"Been a long time, Johnny," Luke said.

"Even now, time is fleeting," the voice replied. There was a rustle, and something metal clicked. "But I still get around, and you wouldn't believe the things I hear. Everywhere I travel, tramps claim a Crossbuck Luke sighting, or they talk up one of your campfire hearsays. Some name you've built."

Luke smiled, aware of what that meant to him emotionally as well as consequentially.

A red glow materialized from the back shadows: the tip of a cigarette.

"I know what you're here for," the voice continued. "And I came to watch you kill Smith McCain."

Luke moved toward the rear of the boxcar, toward the deepest shadows, toward the man standing there smoking his Chesterfields that after all these years still smelled like burnt cat hair. "I appreciate it, my friend, but I'm declining your company today. This is personal, just me and him."

"Even after all we've been through, you're gonna close me out? I helped you beat Franklin."

"And you deserve a medal, but you know what McCain's cost me."

John Dillinger nodded. "What about Harriet? She'll be there to let you in?"

"Naw, I remember the entrance," Luke said. "She showed me around, same place as thirteen years ago. I won't get lost."

"Guess I'm just tits on a hog, then."

"Hog tits got nothin' on you, comes to glamorizing a life of crime and debauchery."

They shared a smile, and John took another drag off his cigarette. "Never thought the day would come, I'd get pity praise from a hobo."

"I know your vanity needs a little strokin' now and again."

"Speaking of, I've been mulling on a funny observation. Folks say I'm vain, but I haven't changed over the years. Now look at you, ain't the pimply-faced vagabond I once met. Seems you've grown half a foot, spine straight as a rod, face smooth as a movie star, even your hair's almost good as mine. You tellin' crossbucks about your charm and winsomeness too?"

Luke's high, round cheeks flushed darling pink as he mumbled, "Ain't nothin' but I've aged well."

John laughed, a mix of snicker and concession. "More than that, and you know it."

"Good looks never been my thing."

"They are now, way folks talk about you. Guess people like their heroes showing a bit more flash than flop. It's hard to idolize someone who smells like they shower in shit and call it perfume. I told you once, you've got to look like you own the city, and even riding the rails, you've got that covered now."

A shrug of indifference.

"And don't think I haven't seen Daisy changing with you. She's got this glow about her, like the morning after you lose virginity. Her scars are gone, she's filled out—" John held out his hands in front of his chest. "Am I right?"

Luke rose over him. "Wasn't I just saying how I'm declining your company today?"

John's snicker and concession made their way back. "Hint taken."

"This is where I'm gettin' off, anyway," Luke said, returning to the boxcar's open door. At its lip, he glanced back, and John's cigarette winked. "I never imagined you to ride the rails before."

John ran a finger across his pencil-thin mustache, and his oiled russet hair sorta shifted with a thought. "Just wanted to see what all the fuss is about."

Luke held up his hand in farewell, and he slowed the train, and he took a step normal as

any, from the car's door to the earth in bloom outside.

"See you around." John's voice grew distant and drowning under the roar of the train that bore him away. At the last, he flicked the butt of his cigarette out the door, a slow red arc turning through the air until it faded to nothing. Then it was quiet.

Luke walked the raised peak line of ballast fill, miles from the city main, where the ground was still soft enough to be called wetland. He felt good. The world felt good. It was warm and pretty all about. He heard soft thunks of a woodpecker, watched a muskrat waddle past. The air smelled of damp and bark and honeysuckle.

The rail line split off for a cove of clover, and Luke turned his feet the other way, toward thick forest. The elevation inclined and the earth firmed, and he came to a line of trees grown so close together their branches formed a wall solid as brick.

Luke licked his finger and traced along the spired boughs and woven limbs, and a faint blue spark of electricity twinkled where he touched. He made his way through the trees beneath knobby oak boughs, through a gloomy rift, past enormous thickets, and onto a narrow dirt trail.

Here, he began to search for Smith McCain, following the trail he'd once led the railroad bull.

He didn't search long.

McCain appeared before him at the path's first bend, eyes still glowing yellow as a rail man's lantern. He smiled a mouthful of long canine fangs. "There you are, boy. Said I'd get you, and bet I hold my oaths. No one hides from me forever." McCain moved toward Luke with raised hands, splayed fingers, nails like terrible talons. "You're fucking cream, and I'm the beast to lick it up."

Luke watched him, silent.

McCain neared. "I'm gonna hang your guts on every tree in this state."

Luke watched him more, until he got tired. He thought how Dillinger had taken him out of the moment he'd imagined this to be, with his absurd observations about good looks and winsomeness. Luke tapped his foot a few times, stretched and flexed long strong arms. Examined a rock with yellow flecks to see if it was gold, which it was not. Handsome rosebay blossomed nearby, and he picked a sprig to give Daisy.

McCain kept coming. "I'll fuck your eye sockets 'til trains fly to the moon, and then I'll find those friends of yours, the ones I already killed, and I'll skin 'em, I'll pull 'em apart bone by feculent bone."

Luke rubbed an itch. Blinked. He was gonna celebrate with Daisy tonight, they'd eat something real fine, make a fire, make out.

McCain squeaked something else, but his voice turned muffled as the round bowler hat—once looking so small upon his basin-sized head—shifted over his face, bouncing from side-to-side at his ears. The bull had to keep pushing it back to see where he was going. Finally he just let it fall away.

"I'm coming for you, filthy cocksucker. You're the fuckin' turd that won't flush, the one needs some plunging, some breaking up. I'll use you for manure, plant my garden of 'bo corpses with you as the fertilizer."

McCain had finally closed half the distance, each step bearing the ferocity of drying puddles. His shuffle had a curious motion that was more ooze than stride, and carried the vagaries of an overeager mastiff that remembers once being a puppy, while it's decrepit and gray and senile.

"You move any quicker to come get me?" Luke finally said. "I've a date tonight." He took a deep breath and exhaled hard, and the air whistled through McCain, and Luke knew he'd hollowed.

"No one rides the rails on my watch, bum. I get you, there won't be enough left for the crows to pick at, the maggots to roll in." McCain's beard had long fallen out, and his pale, skeletal chin was covered in pimples, as was the rest of him. "I'll pulverize your face, eat your heart."

Luke pulled out his pocket knife with a nicked, dull edge, the one he'd stabbed McCain with before, the one King had found and returned. It was powerful big now, gleaming bright as car-lot chrome.

"Ha!" McCain cheeped, his lantern-yellow eyes narrowing. He closed and opened his taloned fingers. "Knife ain't shit, and you know it. Nothing can save you, nothing, rail rider, but death itself, and that won't be quick in coming, I'm going to—"

"I can't take no more," Luke interrupted. "Even the pleasure of seeing you like this don't bring the happiness I expected. You're a nothing, McCain, a void to be filled, the question mark one wonders why it's so easy to steal a ride on any train, on any day."

"I'll rip off your cock and fly it from the boiler like a flag, barter your innards for chocolate—"

Luke sighed exasperated, impatient, and took three big strides to him. "This is for Zeke."

He plunged the knife into the monster bull's chest, and this time it did what it was supposed to.

McCain's fading wisp squealed long and shrill, and his legs softened and couldn't support him, and he fell back to pool in the earth, his mouth gaping open, his lantern-yellow eyes dimming.

"Noo . . . " A few of the bull's canine fangs fell out. "I'll get you yet . . . Lucas Thacker . . . "

The last thing Luke and Smith McCain saw together was the cycloning appearance of bright red pox that swirled down and set on the great railroad bull and ate him from memory.

VOICES, 2019

Over the years the Earp brothers had it out with John Dillinger, and at each occasion they recruited additional friends to their respective causes so it became a feud of generations.

The Earps were bolstered by a couple more family members, plus Doc Holliday, and even allied with Billy Clanton and the McLaury brothers, men they'd killed in real life at the O.K. Corral. But, as they'd learned, the enemy known was better than the enemy unknown. Others joined their banner too, Western nobility they'd never crossed while living, such as Billy the Kid, Tom Horn, John King Fisher, and Jesse James.

Though I wasn't always a lawman, I fought for what I believed in, and still do. Me and my brothers ruled the Old West with dash and verve. Don't call me a myth—I can shoot the shit out of a fly's butt even now.
My name is Wyatt Earp. Remember me.

It took a few years for Dillinger's ranks to swell, but by the 1950s, peers who'd outlived him met their inevitable fate, just to find themselves in a new rip-roaring gang. Against the gunfighters' horses drove Depression-era gangsters like Machine Gun Kelly, Bonnie and Clyde, Joseph Paul Cretzer, and Baby Face Nelson. There were others too, always others, men and women for whom it took years for their legends to gain traction.

I took the hard cards life dealt me and made my own straight flush. It's true I robbed from the undeserving, and that I killed men who tried to stop me. But I did it all with flair that's still admired today.
My name is John Dillinger. Remember me.

And though they fought as rivals for a greater share of notoriety, each side ultimately strengthened the other, so old hard feelings got pacified. The same can be said of other eternal foes, that by their conflict we remember them greatest: cops against robbers, cowboys against Indians, army against army, race against race. The fact is sometimes unfortunate, but such is nature that aside from notable talent or accomplishments, those who get memorialized are done so through the throes of violence. Folks just love bystanding a good conflict.

The papers said I murdered my father and stepmother with an axe, though the courts found me crimeless. I proclaimed innocence the rest of my life, so why does history think otherwise? We're not crazy, but the noises get so loud.
My name is Lizzie Borden. Remember me.

And there are many whose legends once were known but were

displaced by others with greater infamy, thus lost to the ages like forgotten books crumbling in sinking tombs. One could say that Father Time is the greatest sufferer of dementia, schizophrenia, Alzheimer's, psychosis, and every other mania that distorts the mind, causing loss or blurring in our collective reminiscence. Even now, what's known gets changed, and certainties are disproved while impossibilities wax to normalcy.

I travelled the world, won wars, brought peace and prosperity to your doorsteps as regular as postal mail delivery (of which, by the way, I was the nation's first Postmaster General). There's nothing I don't know, nothing I haven't done. Invention of origami? That was me. Invention of dynamite? Me. The space shuttle? You know who I am.

My name is Benjamin Franklin. Remember me.

A few souls may be revered as long as the world turns, though most who get spoken of are just as mortal in their post-ways as they were in actual life. Some are accepting of that, grateful for a bit more time to enjoy what they can, but there are those who get mean, fighting out of self-preservation to be remembered for any reason, and they do things to other folks they oughtn't.

It don't matter the era, don't matter the whereabouts, there's always someone downtrodden, someone exploited, someone forced low just to raise another high. I hope you'll stand with me when the time comes to cast aside oppressions, since that time is now. I'm no better than anyone else, but I'm gonna help those in need as long as I can.

My name is Harriet Tubman. Remember me.

And maybe we're all fighting for remembrance in our own way, in our own minds, yet is the fight worth it, when finality is the same sheer cliff we're all hurtlin' off, regardless how much longer it takes you to hit bottom than someone else? Life and death, memory and oblivion; what's the difference 'tween a kind word whispered today and the roar of cosmic muck ten billion years ago?

Maybe that answer is all the difference in existence. For we're born to a world of chance, and each with opportunities not for others, though we still follow the steps trod by forebears, and life rewards us and then breaks us in the end, until somebody braves otherwise.

I was born with nothin' and died with little else. But what of life is worth a nickel? I rode the rails as a king and learned secrets of eternity that those with wealth could never afford. I loved and lost and loved again, and gave it all to return Daisy Rose to my arms. And so is life like a great circular track, on which we're born at departure and die at arrival.

My name is Luke Thacker. Remember me.

And what stays true for us all is this: As we're molded in life by the perceptions of others, we're molded in death by their reminiscence. We become the dreams of sentience where all is laid bare, and who can say they've not a single regret in life, in love, in loss, in lore, so are those who came before and those who come after as voices on the wind . . . Can you hear them?

It's true cancer got me in '85, but only my shell was left behind. Enough saw to believe my dying breath was the whistle of an oncomin' steamer, and I might have been in an empty alley, but that track in the great sky wound down to me, and there were plenty of hands to lift me up. Listen close, 'cause I'm still around.

My name is King Shaw. Remember me.

LUKE AND KING, 1956

It was a night for the ages, more stars than King had ever seen, and each one twinkling rosy pink and white and the kind of sapphire blue that fairy tales chronicle as born from a godmother's magic wand.

King knew it was bad right then and there. Even with Luke walking to him, to tell him everything would be okay.

"Evening," Luke said.

"Evenin' yourself," King replied.

Luke wore a checked shirt with the sleeves rolled up long, lean arms, and crisp navy blue jeans held by suspenders that seemed to stretch the limits of elasticity over his barrel chest. On his head was a flat cap tilted in a way as to be utterly sportive, and on his feet were hand-tooled boots without a spot of grime on them.

"Lookin' dapper," King granted.

Luke shrugged in that off-kilter way of his that advised you took the good when you can, and get past the rest. "Some year, huh? You listening to that Elvis Presley fellow?"

"Sometimes. When it gets too quiet I turn the transistor on, when I think I hear voices whispering around me."

"Yeah, I'd say it'd get better, that the voices would fade, 'cept you're probably a little more attuned to them."

King shrugged in his own off-kilter way that suggested he'd been through a whole lot worse. "Ain't all bad. There's some voices I fancy to hear."

Luke nodded. King lit a stogie. In the pocket of his dungarees was another. "Want one?"

"Naw, but thank you. I'm on my way to see Daisy, and she ain't big on the smell."

"All right, tell her I said howdy."

"I will. I ain't coming back."

King raised one bushy eyebrow. "This it, then? Your duty, the new Code Maker?"

Luke cleared his throat, glanced down, took a step forward. "It is."

King turned cold, though he didn't know why. He looked around, saw no one else was there, not even a passerby or a groundskeeper.

They were at a crossroads of sort in Lebanon, Kansas, on an open field that was sometimes used as a parade ground, though at present was nothing but freshly-cut prairie grass for miles and miles, surrounding a big flagpole and bronze plaque celebrating the geographic center of the United States of America.

"You're not just sayin' goodbye for the sake of courtesy," King said. "So what's it mean to me?"

"I need to make my exit."

"You need my help?"

"When I say I ain't coming back, you know what that means?"

King looked him deep in the eyes. "Yeah."

"It's death. Only you and I both know it ain't the end of things."

"Go on."

"See, I, um . . . " Luke started shuffling his boots in the earth, toeing up little chunks of sod. "I kinda made something of myself, right?"

"If anyone did, it's you."

"I got a certain renown, trying to do the right thing. Helpin' others."

"Sure."

"Took a while to build it up," Luke said.

King grunted.

"It's a legacy of sorts, a folk hero's tale."

King blew out a puff of smoke. "You string this out anymore, I'm gonna beat the life outta you."

"That's what I'm gettin' at."

"Beating the life out of you?"

"Not that violent," Luke said, his voice lowering, "but I can't do it otherwise."

"What in jackshit you talkin' about?"

"I got to die while I'm on top, now. And I can't stay in Athanasia while I'm still alive, otherwise I'll fade. But suicide?"

King's stare into Luke's eyes returned.

"Suicide's a tragedy," Luke said. "It's a powerful end, to be sure, but it's sick with sadness. Folks feel sorry for the person who done it, think him or her were tormented all along, and whatever they'd accomplished is suddenly tainted. Their life remembered is bleak. Sure, Van Gogh painted lovely pictures, but he hated himself all the while. That ain't me, and I don't want to be remembered as such."

"I don't want to be remembered for what I think you're leading to."

"King, it's a mighty favor. Call it a ticket for your place by my side."

"As a murderer?"

"I'm gonna frame it as a friendship pact."

"You're serious . . . "

"My time here is done."

"What about me?"

"You keep things running on this side of life as long as you can. You're a storyteller, King. You got a voice, and people listen, even when you don't think so. You make us stronger here, and you find others to pass on the torch. Your day will come, my friend, and I'll be there with you. Hell, I'll be with you every day, whether you know it or not."

King shook his head.

Luke went on. "And King, you come visit us anytime you like. The door to Athanasia will always be open to you, literally. I'll write it so. You ever sick, feeling down, come say hi. I'll make you good. And some day, soon, you'll be visiting in finality, like me. But to make this work . . . well, a story's got to have a powerful ending. It's my way for 'happily ever after.'"

And King saw it then, that sign of a sideways eight for Athanasia sort of appearing in glimmer right over Luke's head, like he'd already become the doorway himself. "If I don't?"

"Times are changing, and I don't think it'd end well for any of us. Those who once were known strongly grow old and feeble in twilight years, unable to keep up with how they'd been remembered. I don't want to end up in a sickbed, shittin' in a bed pan no one will clean up. Like it or not, the fastest way to wreck youthful notoriety is age."

King's lip turned out. "I always meant to ask, that day back in '42, at Fenway Stadium—I don't even know why I was there. I didn't do much of anything, maybe bolstered the size of your group by one."

"I needed your support, needed people to see you with me."

"Luke, I hate to be contrary, but no one cared I was there."

"They will. Now. Friendship pact, see? You were with me at time of greatest need. Then *and* now."

"You had this planned all along?"

"Don't you think about these things?"

"I always thought the further out I could push those thoughts, the better."

"Yeah," Luke said, stepping closer to King, looking past him. "That's probably a blessing."

King stepped back. He heard a distant rumble like thunder rolling in. "What's that?" A shrill whistle came next, and that answered his question. "I ain't a killer, Luke."

"You're a man of honor, helping a friend."

A *chug-chug-chugging* sound grew, and a pair of distant lights appeared, like glowing eyes opening in the night.

"What's it matter?" King said. "There ain't no one around to see what happens, you do it yourself."

Luke smiled. "You know that's not true. There's a whole 'nother world watching us right now."

And there it came, rumbling toward them, not too fast, not too slow, just moving with purpose on tracks and ties that built themselves right before those steel wheels needed 'em. It was an older train, with a steamer aged from the '20s rather than the diesels that were taking over, and King even felt a pang of nostalgia upon looking at it. The locomotive had a jaunty red nose painted above its slatted plow, and the smokebox gleamed with polish. Behind it was the coal car, sleek and piled high with fuel that King somehow knew would never run out. After that came the rest of the train, which consisted of one single boxcar made of gold, and its loading door was wide open.

At that, King had two thoughts, one a vision and the other a memory.

He imagined his future, one marred by sadness and alcoholism, a life on the streets—a tragedy, to be sure—but he also saw overlaid above the face of that future his real story: his joys, his fulfillment, his adventures yet to come, both in Athanasia and in life. For there were ups and there were downs, but he was to conquer them all . . .

And too, King remembered the gypsy cards from long ago—the fortune he had dealt himself, that he would kill his dearest friend—and he knew the choice had already been made.

The train neared, and the tracks ran right behind Luke's feet.

King placed one hand on Luke's chest and gently pushed him backward.

The train struck, and after it'd passed there was nothing left of Crossbuck Luke Thacker but a legend.

DANIEL GREENBERG, 2019, FINAL

And it's all true, you know. It's true what I've written, because I believe it, I believe *in* it.

So I wonder, as I write these last few words, as the half-filled glass at my bedside begins to rock: Have I made good of my life, have I helped others, done my best, done my part? Will I be remembered fondly? Will my own stories persevere?

I hope so, for a certain darkness closes in, and the strength leaves my limbs, the cancer coming to its final grim close . . .

I hope so, for I hear a high, shrill whistle, and a steadfast *chug-a-lug* coming near . . .

I hope so, for the whole room trembles now, and it's a wonder the nurses don't rush in. There's a screech of brakes, a hiss of steam.

I hope so, for there's the sound of a metal car door sliding open, and a familiar voice asking, "Can you hear me still?"

This is where I end, both in tale and in life, with but a final parting thought: Though here I pass, I still go on, for of this crossbuck I've become, as have you, dear reader, for where else does a legend endure? Now go and make your own stories come true, and I hope, someday, we'll be on track to pick up you.

My name is Daniel Greenberg. Remember me.

ACKNOWLEDGMENTS

Most thanks, as always and with love, go to the support of my family—Jeannette, Julian, and Devin.

Great thanks also to Lisa Morton and Gene O'Neill, who first set me on the path to write this book, my first full-length novel. In 2013, Gene sold an idea to JournalStone Publishing to put out a series of novellas (half-length novels) modeled after the old Ace Doubles, in which two novellas are bound in the dos-à-dos binding method, each with its own cover art (creating two books-in-one, by flipping the work over to start at either the front or the back). The Double Down books paired an acclaimed author with a "gifted, new, cutting-edge author" selected by the eminent author. That eminent author was Lisa Morton, and she selected me as the newbie to write my first "long work," which would be published alongside hers.

For that project, I brainstormed two ideas. The first was about a gambler who bids in the hotel baggage auctions, made popular during the first half of the twentieth century. In the story, the character wins an old suitcase, which contains a haunted gramophone that speaks of frozen realms and the promises of Rasputin. That became the novella I wrote and published for the project, *Baggage of Eternal Night* (made a finalist in 2014's International Thriller Award for Best Short Story, which I'm still insanely proud of).

The second idea for the project, I loved more, but decided it would be way too long to be written as a novella, and had to do with a Depression-era hobo reading messages through the Hobo Code, which takes him to the land of our memories. It took a few years before I began writing it, but that eventually evolved into what you hold in hand (or view on-screen), *Doorways to the Deadeye*! It went through immense changes over the several years I wrote it, originally titled *Crossbuck 'Bo*, and coming in at an unpublishable 150,000+ words. Ultimately, the final trimmed version makes me very happy.

Which leads me next to thank JournalStone for publishing this book.

Specifically, thanks to JournalStone's helm Christopher Payne; acquisitions editor Jess Landry; and copy editor Scarlett R. Algee (who saved me from numerous instances of embarrassment by way of bad grammar, questionable context, or other literary flaws!).

Thanks also to the Horror Writers Association, who have been an immense resource of technical information, guidance, and insight over the years, especially my local friends in the Los Angeles chapter, who monthly vitalize me with awe and encouragement.

And, lastly, thank you, dear reader, for your time, and to all others who inspired or supported this book, or otherwise value dark, supernatural, and fantastic fiction! But for your interest and (hopefully!) enjoyment, this long journey has been worth the neurosis of indie writing.

ABOUT THE AUTHOR

Eric J. Guignard is a writer and editor of dark and speculative fiction, operating from the shadowy outskirts of Los Angeles, where he also runs the small press Dark Moon Books. He's twice won the Bram Stoker Award (the highest literary award of horror fiction), been a finalist for the International Thriller Writers Award, and a multi-nominee of the Pushcart Prize.

He has over one hundred stories and non-fiction works appearing in publications around the world and has recently released his debut short story collection *That Which Grows Wild: 16 Tales of Dark Fiction* (Cemetery Dance Publications). As editor, Eric's published multiple fiction anthologies, including his most recent, *Pop the Clutch: Thrilling Tales of Rockabilly, Monsters, and Hot Rod Horror*; and *A World of Horror*, a showcase of international horror short fiction.

He currently publishes the acclaimed series of author primers created to champion modern masters of the dark and macabre, *Exploring Dark Short Fiction*, and he also curates the new series, *The Horror Writers Association Presents: Haunted Library of Horror Classics* with co-editor Leslie S. Klinger.

Outside the glamorous and jet-setting world of indie fiction, Eric's a technical writer and college professor, and he stumbles home each day to a wife, children, cats, and a terrarium filled with mischievous beetles. Visit Eric at: www.ericjguignard.com, his blog: ericjguignard.blogspot.com, or Twitter: @ericjguignard.

CPSIA information can be obtained
at www.ICGtesting.com
Printed in the USA
LVHW021503090819
627129LV00002B/291/P

9 781947 654976